Rose Melikan was born  she has been a Fellow of St Catharine's College, Cambridge. She lives in Cambridge with her husband, Dr Quentin Stafford-Fraser.

THE MISTAKEN WIFE

Rose Melikan

sphere

SPHERE

First published in Great Britain in 2010 by Sphere
This paperback edition published in 2011 by Sphere
Reprinted 2012

A CIP catalogue record for this book
is available from the British Library.

ISBN 978-0-3513-2424-6

Typeset in Garamond by Palimpsest Book Production Limited
Falkirk, Stirlingshire
Printed and bound in Great Britain by
Clays Ltd, St Ives plc

Papers used by Sphere are natural, renewable and recyclable
products sourced from well-managed forests and certified
in accordance with the rules of the Forest Stewardship Council.

MIX
Paper from
responsible sources
FSC® C104740

Sphere
An imprint of
Little, Brown Book Group
100 Victoria Embankment
London EC4Y 0DY

An Hachette UK Company
www.hachette.co.uk

www.littlebrown.co.uk

For my parents

Acknowledgements

Without the help and understanding of friends, colleagues, and family this book would not have been possible. In particular I would like to thank Clare Alexander, John Baker, Eilís Ferran, Mark Elliott, Miranda Griffin, Zoe Gullen, Antonia Hodgson, Diane Mercuri, Quentin Stafford-Fraser, Jane Stevens, and Hans Van de Ven for their support, suggestions, and essential expertise.

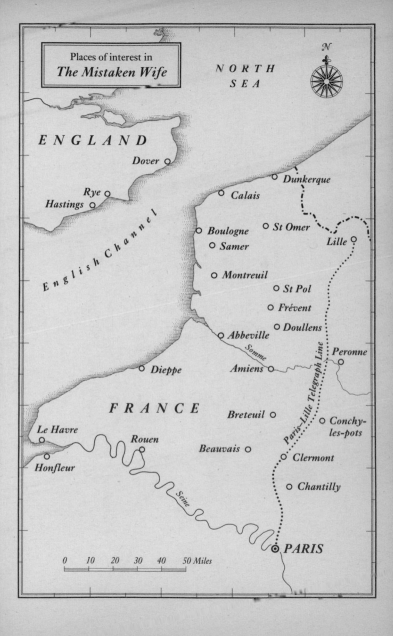

Places of interest in
The Mistaken Wife

N

NORTH
SEA

ENGLAND

Dover

Dunkerque

Rye
Hastings

Calais

Boulogne
Samer

St Omer

Lille

English Channel

Montreuil

St Pol

Frévent

Doullens

Abbeville

Somme

Peronne

Dieppe

Amiens

FRANCE

Breteuil

Conchy-
les-pots

Le Havre

Rouen

Beauvais

Paris-Lille Telegraph Line

Clermont

Honfleur

Seine

Chantilly

PARIS

0   10   20   30   40   50 Miles

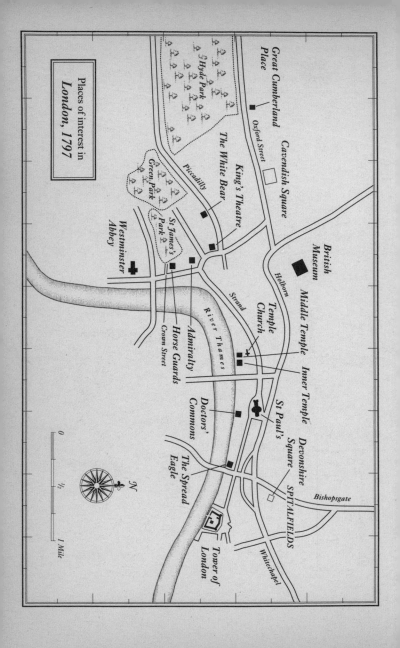

Places of interest in
London, 1797

Great Cumberland
Place

Hyde Park

Oxford Street

Cavendish Square

Piccadilly

The White Bear

King's Theatre

Green Park

St James's Park

Westminster
Abbey

Admiralty

Horse Guards

Crown Street

Holborn

Strand

Temple
Church

River Thames

British
Museum

Middle Temple

Inner Temple

Devonshire
Square

St Paul's

SPITALFIELDS

Bishopsgate

Doctors'
Commons

The Spread
Eagle

Tower of
London

Whitechapel

0

½

1 Mile

N

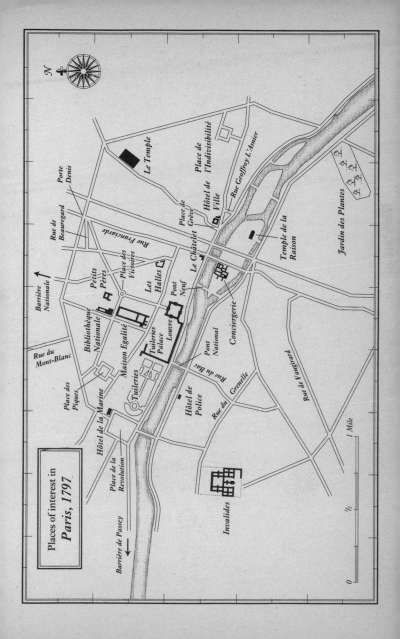

Places of interest in
Paris, 1797

N

Barrière de Passey

Place de la
Révolution

Rue du
Mont-Blanc

Barrière
Nationale

Porte
Denis

Rue de
Beauregard

Rue Francharde

Place des
Victoires

Petits
Pères

Bibliothèque
Nationale

Maison Egalité

Place des
Piques

Hôtel de la Marine

Tuileries

Tuileries
Palace

Louvre

Les
Halles

Pont
Neuf

Le Temple

Place de
l'Indivisibilité

Rue Geoffroy L'Asnier

Place de
Grève

Hôtel de
Ville

Le Châtelet

Temple de la
Raison

Jardin des Plantes

Conciergerie

Pont
National

Rue du Bac

Hôtel de
Police

Rue du Grenelle

Rue de Vaugirard

Invalides

0   ½   1 Mile

Prologue

As dawn broke from behind a bank of clouds and turned the sky above Calais pearl grey, the *Albatrossen* doused her night-lights and waited respectfully for permission to enter the harbour. She flew the Danish flag, indicating her country's neutrality in the war that had gripped Europe for the past four years, and she and her crew were well known in Calais. She waited, nevertheless, and even prepared to receive on board the agents from the *commissariat*, the local office of police. No one, whatever their nationality, was permitted to travel in France without the proper authorisation, and persons entering the country by sea were particularly subject to official scrutiny. The land war was going well for France in the autumn of 1797, but at sea the Royal Navy remained strong. Just over the horizon, moreover, stood England – implacable foe and architect of countless plots and stratagems against the French republic. Constant vigilance was necessary to guard against the importation of some new treachery, even in the innocent hold of the *Albatrossen*.

The fact that she had sailed from Copenhagen via Dover would only heighten the police agents' suspicions. The captain of the *Albatrossen* knew this, just as he knew that the French depended on neutral vessels to maintain something like their pre-war levels of trade. Only neutrals dared to brave the North Sea and the English Channel – 'La Manche', one ought perhaps to say

– nowadays, and even they were often harassed by privateers. It was a scandal, really, but what could be done about it? The French Navy did little to redress the balance; their ships were blockaded in Brest and Toulon, and their admirals showed scant interest in freeing the sea-lanes from British domination.

'Every war ends eventually,' sighed the captain as he prepared the ship's manifest for inspection. 'And so long as they do not crush the poor *Albatrossen* between them in the meantime, let them fight if it pleases them.'

He had already given orders for the passengers to present themselves on deck with their identification papers. Although fundamentally a cargo ship, the *Albatrossen* often carried passengers – merchants accompanying their wares to market, loyalists seeking repatriation, and neutral travellers determined to ignore the fighting. Of course, some might have other, nefarious aims, but that was not his affair. All of his passengers – thirteen on this crossing – had been cleared for travel by the British authorities and, so far as he could determine, bore no ill will towards France. Indeed, the majority were French – including a gaggle of women who had complained about the size of their cabins and the lack of towels, and the rest were neutrals. None of them had looked particularly menacing when they boarded in Dover, and that had been before an unusually long, rough crossing.

The thought of thirteen pale, sickly faces made him smile as he rose slowly to his feet and prepared to leave his cabin. He was not a cruel man, but he held landsmen (and women) in a kind of placid contempt and so felt little sympathy for their trifling complaints. The smile was still hovering about his lips when hurried footsteps halted in the passageway and knuckles rapped sharply on the cabin door. Before he could respond the door thrust inwards, and his first mate appeared in the opening, steadying himself against the jamb. His face was pale, but not with seasickness, and unnaturally bright patches coloured his unshaven cheeks.

'Captain!' he gasped. 'A terrible thing!'

'What is it, man? What has happened?'

2

The mate swallowed painfully. 'In the forward cabin! You must come quickly!'

The forward cabin was seldom used unless the *Albatrossen* was carrying a larger than usual number of passengers, for it was small, dark, and airless. Now, illuminated by lantern light, it presented a far more disturbing scene. To the right, a dead man lay huddled on the floor; one hand clasped a bloody knife while the other pressed ineffectually at a bullet wound in his belly. He had died suddenly, it seemed, and in great pain, for his features were creased in a maddened grimace. To the left, a second man was slumped in a chair before a small, disordered table, his arms stretched out in front of him. At first glance, he appeared to be sleeping, for his face was tranquil, but closer examination showed that blood from a wound in his thigh had stained his pale breeches and one of his stockings. A handkerchief tied to staunch the flow was almost unrecognisable.

The captain studied the two dead men and then turned his gaze to the jumble of playing cards and the half-empty bottle that rolled across the deck before coming to rest against an upended chair. Here and there, pieces of broken glass winked up at him, and a spray of silver shone where coins had been swept from the table.

'My God in heaven,' he muttered. 'Gambling and strong drink – and this is the result.' He frowned sternly before asking the men's names.

'The one in the chair is Johann Risse, and that one,' – the mate nodded in the direction of the other man, but without looking at him – 'is named Dunbar. Peter Dunbar.'

The captain found that he was still clutching the manifest, and he quickly located the names. 'Johann Risse of Königsberg and Peter Dunbar of New York. My God. They travel hundreds of miles to kill each other on my ship! Did they have friends on board?'

'No, captain, I don't think so. Risse went directly to the cabin when we left Dover, and Dunbar must have joined him.'

'They could not wait to begin their nasty game, I suppose,' said the captain, shaking his head. 'What a dreadful business –

just the sort of thing to give the ship a bad name. Say nothing to the other passengers, and then—' From overhead came the sounds of voices, and the thump of something against the hull. 'What was that?'

'I don't know, sir, but very likely the men from the *commissariat.*'

The captain groaned. 'Of course. We have a dead Prussian and a dead American on board, so naturally we must also have a visit from the French police. Well, they can take charge of the bodies – I am not carrying them back to England, not for any money. Ah, that reminds me, had both of them paid their fare? If not,' – he gestured vaguely at the coins – 'make sure that the *Albatrossen* does not lose by their folly.'

News of the deaths reached England nearly a week later. A fatal brawl between drunken foreigners would have been welcome copy to the English newspapers, but in fact the information travelled by means of a little-known, circuitous route that began at Dover and ended in a small set of private rooms in a London club. There it was read by a plump, middle-aged, thoroughly unremarkable-looking gentleman called Cuthbert Shy. On his instructions it was forwarded to the home secretary, together with some stinging observations about ham-fisted agents and a criminal lack of care by the Alien Office.

Such a rebuke, coming from a man who lacked both rank and official authority, might have seemed proof of eccentricity, but the home secretary certainly did not regard it in that way. On the contrary, he immediately set in train an investigation of how a known French agent could pass himself off as an American and sail, unhindered, from Dover. Deceiving the British authorities was bad enough, but in this case the agent had managed to frustrate an important intelligence operation. The action had cost him his life but that was slight consolation. 'Old Shy must be furious,' muttered the home secretary as he added a note to the file.

Mr Shy was, indeed, very angry. In particular, he condemned the loss of a valuable opportunity for prosecuting the war on French soil. Perhaps this want of personal sympathy was because

4

Risse had not been one of his own agents, not a member of the shadowy, highly confidential group that carried out his instructions and undertook his schemes. 'Shy's Men', they were called by those few officials who knew of Shy's existence, and who depended on him to protect British interests in situations when neither the government nor the military could do so. Perhaps, however, Shy merely disliked waste and incompetence, for he did not shrink from throwing his own men into danger when the situation warranted it, sometimes with fatal consequences.

He frowned and drummed his fingers impatiently against the arms of his chair. 'I would never have sent Risse in the first place. The fellow was a Prussian, after all! Excellent at following orders, no doubt, but wholly lacking in imagination. Of course he was in a tight spot with that Frenchman on board, but a clever fellow would have bluffed his way through.' He brooded. 'A *very* clever fellow would have turned the tables on Dunbar and denounced him as an émigré. *That* is the sort of thing one expects, not . . . a sanguinary quarrel that must end to nobody's satisfaction.'

Shy's secretary, a sober, grey man of indeterminate age, nodded distantly. His duty lay not in challenging his chief's views, but in setting into motion whatever plans might follow. He ventured a question. 'How much do you suppose that Dunbar knew?'

Shy raised his hands in frustration. 'No amount of fumbling among our friends in government would surprise me. Fortunately, Dunbar had not been among the first tier of French agents for some time – he was dismissed for drunkenness before the Revolution and had been prowling about for employment ever since – so I doubt whether he would have communicated any suspicions to Paris. He probably hoped to make this the grand coup that would reinstate him with his former masters, and he would not have wanted to give anything away prematurely.'

The secretary nodded again, but behind his placid, deferential façade three troublesome questions occurred to him. What would the government do now to rescue the situation? If they had possessed a better agent than Risse, would he not have been employed? And yet, the operation was an important one; surely the government would not abandon it?

'It *was* a government operation,' Shy corrected, as if his junior had spoken the words aloud. 'Now it is mine.'

'Indeed, sir.'

The words were spoken without inflection, but Shy smiled at the weight of knowledgeable scepticism that they conveyed. It was the first time that he had smiled since receiving the report. 'I will consider the possibilities,' he affirmed. 'Come back in one hour.'

The secretary doubted whether such a tangle could be unsnarled and a new solution sewn together within that time, but it was pointless to say so.

In exactly one hour he returned. Shy was drinking coffee, and the only indication that he had spent the last sixty minutes wrestling with a highly complex problem lay in the fact that he did not immediately acknowledge the other man's presence. Instead, he stared at the hearth, where a small, bluish flame ate slowly into a stack of paper.

The sheets burned, curled, and collapsed into black, feathery fragments, and the flame went out. Still Shy did not move. The secretary noticed two letters, folded but unsealed, lying on the desk. The addressees made him purse his lips, but he merely asked whether they should be recopied. Shy never sent anything in his own hand.

'Yes, copied and sent,' Shy affirmed, 'and quickly. The French post is damnably slow, and there is not a moment to lose.'

1

Crea-eek, crea-eek, crea-eek; a sharp, tuneless treble pierced the rumble of wheels and the steady clip-a-clop of horses' hooves. It was enough to try the patience of even the most well-disposed passenger, and that adjective did not apply to any of those travelling on the Ipswich to Cambridge coach on this particular afternoon. The weather was partly to blame – the elderly gentleman in a patched greatcoat and muffler remarked that a cold, drizzling rain was fatal to the strongest constitutions, on account of its tendency to chill the blood. A pair of garrulous spinsters, the Misses Hoope, identified a number of faults in the travelling arrangements, including the coachman's incivility, the unwholesome smell of the seats, and the extortionate price demanded for a cup of tea at the inns where they had stopped to change teams.

'And that *sound*, sister, has given me the worst headache I have endured this age.'

'Like a hot knife thrust into my forehead, sister.'

The fourth passenger, a young woman named Mary Finch, largely ignored these grievances and permitted the conversation, such as it was, to flow round her. Had she but known it, she was herself a topic of interest among her fellow travellers. The elderly gentleman appreciated a fair face and a slim figure, and he did not object to red hair when set off prettily by a black bonnet and green velvet bow. The younger Miss Hoope could have enlarged upon this matter of dress. She longed to point out the details of cut, colour, and fabric that rendered Miss Finch's ensemble wonderfully stylish while not at all *extravagant*. The elder Miss Hoope knew less about fashion, but she marvelled that such an obviously well-to-do young lady should choose to travel alone and by the common coach.

Mary's presence *was* rather surprising, for she need not have practised either form of economy. White Ladies, her Suffolk estate, boasted a considerable domestic staff, and since gaining her fortune she had acquired two companions and a self-appointed protector. She also owned an elegant, well-sprung carriage, and had travelled as far as London on the mail coach, which had the advantage of speed and catered to a more exclusive class of passenger. Money was not lacking, therefore, nor the willingness to spend it. And yet money provided the answer to the riddle, albeit obliquely.

Mary was greatly attached to Captain Robert Holland of the artillery regiment. Indeed, there was a sort of understanding between them that might have been considered an engagement, but for the fact that no one else knew of it, and Mary had been taught that secret engagements were wrong. Nevertheless, she and Holland had begun to make Plans, and almost immediately a problem had arisen. His income did not equal hers and probably never would. While acknowledging this state of affairs in principle, he struggled against it mightily in practice, with the result that they had been unable to agree upon a house in London. Holland thought that Mary must have a place in Town, at least while he was employed at the regimental headquarters in Woolwich. Fashionable London houses were far beyond his resources, however, and he baulked at her contributing the lion's share. Over the past two months Mary had communicated with a house agent in the fading hope of finding a suitable property, while her correspondence with Holland had become strained and unhappy.

Unable either to resolve the problem or to acknowledge it to her friends, Mary had begun to feel restless and out of sorts. She had even come to regard White Ladies as a place of confinement. When a letter had arrived from the Master of Catherine Hall,

8

therefore, she had read it with particular interest. A series of documents relating to the history of White Ladies had been found in the college archives. Although they could not be removed, the Master was pleased to invite Miss Finch to view them, if she should happen to find herself in Cambridge.

Mary had replied with alacrity and in the affirmative. A visit to Cambridge would provide exactly the fillip she required. She did not ask any of her friends to accompany her because she wanted to escape, for a time, from all the little annoyances that had contributed to her ill humour. She did not mind being alone, and had never accustomed herself to a private maid. And the common coach? That was a bit of whimsy that Mary scarcely acknowledged to herself. This journey to Cambridge was very nearly the mirror image of one she had taken two years ago. Then she had travelled from Cambridge to Ipswich, but the vehicle had been far from luxurious and her companions only a little less eccentric than the Misses Hoope. Yet that journey had set in motion the most surprising train of events – an Adventure of great import, which had utterly transformed her life. Had she not boarded that coach – the 'True Blue' had been its name, she remembered – *everything* would have been different. White Ladies, her second Adventure . . . why, she might never have met Captain Holland.

Small wonder that she had wished to relive that experience, and how tiresome to find that the reality did not match her expectations. As she gazed out of the grimy window ('never cleaned in the past six months, sister'), she found her thoughts turning to the captain, but they were not entirely happy ones. Their present disagreement, in fact, seemed to find echoes in his past conduct.

He always was the most stubborn man imaginable, she brooded, and sighed to herself. Not quite inaudibly, however.

'You see, sister,' cried the younger Miss Hoope. 'I declare that our poor fellow traveller is also tormented by that wretched squeaking. Has it given you the headache, Miss Finch?'

Mary smiled blandly. 'Yes, perhaps it has.'

★   ★   ★

9

The evening shadows were lengthening by the time the coach reached Cambridge, which rendered an immediate visit to the college impossible. Mary had no idea how the Master spent his evenings – feasting with his colleagues, perhaps, or engaging in deep intellectual meditations – but she doubted whether he would wish to entertain a stranger at such an hour. She proceeded to a respectable inn, therefore, where she consumed a modest supper and afterwards retired to her room. The Michaelmas term had only just begun, and even a respectable establishment – managed entirely by women, no less – might become noisy with undergraduates. On reflection, she thought that perhaps the very femininity of the place might even draw them in.

Undergraduates were certainly much in evidence the following morning as she made her way towards Catherine Hall. From her lofty vantage of twenty-two years, many of them seemed very young, mere children in their fluttering gowns. A laughing group pushed past her in the market and attempted to place an order for larks' tongues with a perplexed butcher. Dismissed with a word and a half-hearted cuff, they demanded snails from a fishmonger and ambrosia tarts at a baker's stall – all essential dishes for their Roman banquet, they claimed.

There were older men too, some in academic dress. Among them might be Dr Nichols, the only member of the university with whom Mary could claim an acquaintance. How odd it would be to see him again, and not quite pleasant, for he was a heavy, pompous man much given to imparting wisdom. She prepared to dart into a shop or eating-house if she spied his portly figure processing along King's Parade.

Fortunately she was spared both the encounter and the concealment, and at nine o'clock she presented herself at the college porters' lodge and asked to see Dr Yates. It was with some pleasure that she found herself expected. The head porter conducted her to the Master's lodge and thence to a small waiting-room.

Mary sat down and waited. That was what one did in a

waiting-room, after all. There were two doors – the one by which she had entered and another leading to the Master's study. Presently, however, she began to wonder. The porter had not *said* that Dr Yates would call for her – indeed, he had offered no guidance on the subject. Perhaps she ought to make herself known. How extremely mortifying to be discovered only when the Master emerged for his tea! But knocking would be terribly impolite if Dr Yates intended to admit her after he had completed the college's accounts or dashed off a letter in Greek. She tiptoed to the study door and listened for murmured conversation or the rustle of papers. Nothing.

Well, he is unlikely to eat me, she reasoned, and knocked twice.

'Enter,' called a muffled voice.

She opened the door and stepped into a larger, comfortably furnished chamber. A fire crackled in the grate, and bookcases lined the walls. Her attention, however, was immediately drawn to the plump, middle-aged, unremarkable man who rose from his chair behind a paper-strewn desk.

'Good Heavens!' cried Mary. 'Mr Shy!'

He bowed. 'I hope that your exclamation signifies no distress at our meeting, and the heavenly invocation merely a spontaneous effusion of delight?'

'N-no, sir,' she replied hurriedly. 'I mean, I beg your pardon.'

He gestured towards a chair by the fire and urged her to make herself comfortable. As she moved to comply, he might have added remarks about the weather and her journey from Suffolk, but her own thoughts were whirling and she did not attend. *Mr Shy – Cuthbert Shy!* Mary was aware of his confidential activities. Indeed, only a few months earlier she had performed a highly unusual service for the government at his request. What could he be doing in a Cambridge college?

'Where is Dr Yates?' she asked, as the possibility that the Master was in some way Shy's alias suddenly occurred to her.

'On holiday. The good doctor has been obliged to withdraw from the college for a time. His health is delicate, poor man, and it has been made worse by an unfortunate disagreement within the Fellowship. A quarrelsome brood, I fear, much given

11

to disputation and striving after trivialities. It is an unfortunate tendency among academics, *"which strain at a gnat, and swallow a camel"*.' Shy smiled thoughtfully.

'You prefer camels to gnats, sir?'

'Indeed. But I prefer to ride the first and swat the other.'

As Mary knew from experience, conversation with Mr Shy was no easy thing. Professional watchfulness or a quirk in his character prevented a simple give and take, and he seemed to take pleasure in wrong-footing even those whom he had taken into his confidence. But was she in his confidence? 'Perhaps I oughtn't to ask, sir, how you came to be here?' she remarked cautiously.

'It might be wisest not to,' Shy agreed, 'and yet you are clearly surprised by it. When you received my invitation, did you not suspect that it might presage something more *interesting* than estate papers, however venerable?' He gazed at her quizzically. 'No? Ah well, a pity.'

Mary felt as if she had been discovered in an act of particular foolishness. In truth, that Mr Shy should seek her out, so soon after the completion of her last . . . Adventure, had never occurred to her. 'I was, perhaps, distracted by other matters.'

'The varied delights of your bucolic retreat, no doubt. Still, you did not hover outside just now like an irresolute schoolboy in fear of the cane. That *would* have been extremely disappointing. Resolve is essential, do you not think? And firmness of purpose?'

'Ye-es, I suppose so,' Mary answered guardedly, but her heart had begun to beat with more than its usual energy. Mr Shy had summoned her, and this interview was a test. A test of what? Of her resolve, clearly, and her intelligence. *You have not made such a very brilliant start in that respect*, she informed herself, and felt instantly nettled. For Mr Shy's tests could mean but one thing. He had another task for her . . . if she was equal to it.

It seemed important to prove that she *was*. 'My bucolic retreat is not *so* delightful just at the moment,' she remarked. 'Not exclusively so, I mean.'

'Indeed? I am glad to hear it,' said Shy. He paused. 'Then you would not object – in principle – to a change of scene? A spot of travel? I speak hypothetically, of course.'

'No, sir, I would not object.' A slight niggling in the back of her mind prompted the caveat, 'If the object were an important one.'

'Oh, but it is – that is to say, it *would* be. It is not my habit to play ducks and drakes with the welfare of Britain, you know.'

Mary felt both the barb and the lure of that final sentence. 'No, sir, indeed not. I beg you will continue.'

'Well, well.' He paused again. 'What do you think of America?'

'Do you wish me to go to *America*?' Mary gasped. For some reason she had been thinking of Scotland. America sounded like the other side of the world – it *was* the other side of the world, practically. 'Why, I . . .' From another mental corner the word *Resolve!* sounded like a trumpet, and she continued aloud, 'I believe I would do it, sir.'

He smiled at her. 'Splendid. If we had a hundred ladies such as yourself, Miss Finch – nay, I would content myself with ten – the war would soon be won.'

'Has this to do with the war? But I was not aware—'

'That the Americans were in it? No, they are not . . . *yet*, but they might be very soon if we are not careful, and that is why I have it in mind to send you to France.'

To repeat her query with an amended destination would sound ridiculous, but Mary's expression gave ample proof of her perplexity – and her fear. 'But I cannot—' Again she held tight to her resolve and asked, 'If you could perhaps explain the matter more clearly?'

'Why certainly, my dear Miss Finch. I mean to do that very thing.' He poked the fire and then sat back more comfortably in his chair. 'You know very well the state of the war. The French carry all before them on land, but they are not very clever at sea.'

'Thank goodness.'

'Goodness is essential in these matters,' Shy agreed. 'Goodness and the Royal Navy. The latest peace negotiations have

13

failed – to no one's surprise – and soon we shall each attempt the throw that will determine all. The French will try to invade these islands, and we shall piece together a new coalition in Europe. Neither will be accomplished easily, however, and both sides look to shift the balance of power by less expensive means. The French will probably stir up trouble in Ireland. It is the surest way to baffle Britain with little cost to themselves. It is essential, therefore, that France be distracted in her turn. Fortunately, an opportunity has presented itself, if it can be seized.'

'And . . . would this be where America fits in?'

'It would indeed. The French and Americans were once firm friends, but recently they have suffered a grave falling-out on account of American neutrality. Relations are in such a critical state that American envoys have been sent to Paris in the hope of negotiating a friendly solution. More to *our* liking, of course, would be disagreement, confusion, and enmity.'

'Do you mean *war* between France and America?' Mary demanded.

'If it could be arranged. The Americans have no Navy to speak of, but I daresay they have men enough who would turn privateer if given the chance. But more importantly, a declaration of war would remove neutral American merchant ships from French ports and help to cripple French trade. In this war the control of trade may prove vital. It *is* vital while the French Army remains unchecked.'

'Would war result if these negotiations were to fail?'

'Nothing is certain in matters of diplomacy, but such is my hope. At the very least, we must keep America neutral and prevent a new Franco-American alliance from being formed. *That* would lead to a most dangerous state of affairs.'

'Yes, I see,' said Mary slowly. 'And our government—'

'Sees the matter as I do,' Shy affirmed. 'Unfortunately, it, ah . . . currently lacks the resources to act upon it. There *were* British agents in Paris, doing as they were told and reporting diligently to gentlemen in government whom we need not name. However, the most recent political turmoil in Paris has sent the poor fellows scurrying.'

14

'Have they no agent whom they may send?'

'None.' Shy raised his hands in a sort of mock dismay, although his tone was deadly serious and his expression grim. 'The cupboard is bare.'

Mary nodded. 'Do *you* have no one in Paris, sir?'

'Yes, I have, as it happens, an extremely valuable individual. I should be lost without him. Not suited to this task, however.' Shy shook his head. 'No, a new agent is wanted, and wanted very badly. If one cannot be found, this chance will be lost. Already it is slipping away, for the Americans reached Paris a fortnight ago. There is not a moment to lose.'

Mary nodded again but made no further reply. In her mind were nightmare images of France, images that had filled English prints and newspapers since the head of the French king had been held triumphantly aloft and war had been declared. Against these were the pictures painted by Cuthbert Shy – of England in peril, of French machinations, and no one to redress the balance. But France . . . Even the word provoked opposing currents of excitement and dread.

She took a deep breath. 'What would you have me do?' As she posed the question she knew that it was the first step towards acceding to his proposal, and that there might not be a second.

'Only that you strike up a friendly, sympathetic acquaintance with the envoys, one that would encourage their confidence. We have reason to believe that two of them have French prejudices and would actually favour an alliance with Britain.'

'An alliance?' cried Mary. 'You cannot mean that *I*—'

'No, no,' Shy urged, 'I do not suggest that you should carry proposals from the British government or anything of that kind, merely that you should appeal to the Americans' common sense in this matter. America has no natural affinity with France, while ties of kinship, language, history, and temperament bind her to us. The American Revolution sprang from an English sense of justice – it had no sequel in the bloody events we have seen in France.'

Even described in that way, the assignment sounded fantastic

15

to Mary and utterly beyond her powers. She felt suddenly that she was not so very different from the boys in the market, aping their elders' grand affairs and only making a nuisance of themselves. 'And you consider that *I* would be capable of striking up such an acquaintance with these American gentlemen and . . . reminding them of their natural interest?'

Shy did think so. While it was true that few men intentionally exchanged ideas with the opposite sex, many did so unintentionally. And women – clever, determined women – were the best possible agents. A woman was not readily suspected of intelligence in either sense of the word, and if she asked questions or went where she ought not, this was usually ascribed simply to inquisitiveness and a tendency to gossip, and not to some darker aim. As a consequence, men were less on their guard when conversing with a female agent and more susceptible to rational argument, while the danger to her was less than if she had been a man.

'Naturally, if you do not feel yourself capable of undertaking the commission, I would not wish to convince you otherwise. Confidence does not guarantee success, but irresolution leads to failure. I must tell you, however, that as soon as this affair came to my attention, I thought of you.'

Such an expression of belief could not but have an effect upon Mary, especially coming from Mr Shy, who was always so distant and guarded. The trumpet call to action – to heroic action – sounded more strongly in her head . . . and yet, one had to be practical. For her previous assignment she had merely visited a friend's estate in Kent. How would she ever manage a journey to France – to Paris?

'That is not so difficult as you might think,' said Shy, 'or at least, it need not be. But let us consider things in their proper order. I need not tell you that secrecy is absolutely essential.'

'Yes,' Mary agreed, 'but . . .' She could feel herself blushing. 'As regards my friend, Captain Holland, I must tell you that . . .'

Shy observed her carefully, not only the colour blooming across her cheeks but the way that she smoothed the folds of her gown, as if she were discussing a matter of scant importance when compared to the threat of wrinkled fabric. 'I see,' he said. 'Indeed. But that need not dismay us. What fond couple — what pair of friends — does not keep secrets? It is the way of things. Excessive revelation is death to a happy partnership.'

Mary looked at him. 'Oh, do you think so?'

'Certainly. It smacks of the confessional, the schoolroom. And if the information is important there are further concerns. Captain Holland has a confidential appointment in his regiment. Would *you* wish to know all of his professional secrets? The minutiae of mechanical calibration and calculation that distinguishes one weapon from another?'

'No, but—'

'No, indeed. It would be tedious in the extreme, and there would always be the chance that you might reveal some detail — harmless in itself, but when combined with other information acquired by our enemies, highly dangerous.'

'Yes, I see that.'

'Now, let us consider Captain Holland. An excellent fellow, undoubtedly, but of rather dogged, not to say fixed, views when it comes to the demands of espionage.'

'He has great resolve,' said Mary. Another word occurred to her, but it would have been disloyal to Holland to mention it.

'Precisely,' said Shy, 'but in this instance it would quite upset our plans. Were he to learn of your undertaking, he would either convince you to refuse it—'

Mary shook her head. 'No, sir, he would not convince me. Not to evade my duty.'

'I am pleased to accept your correction. The fact remains, however, that Captain Holland would object, and that would distress you, even distract you from the business at hand. Clear thinking on your part is our fundamental concern.'

'Yes.'

'Then you agree that Holland must not be informed or in any way alerted?' urged Shy. He could be ruthless when he chose. 'No assignment is possible unless we are clear on that point.'

Mary thought about Captain Holland's objections to Finsbury

Place, Devonshire Square, Clement's Lane, and several other perfectly acceptable addresses. The disturbance caused by an expensive London property would be as nothing when compared to the thunderbolt of Mr Shy's proposal. 'Yes,' she answered slowly. 'I agree.'

'Well done,' breathed Shy. It was the closest that he came to acknowledging that her decision had been difficult and might, possibly, have caused him some little uneasiness. He quickly recovered his self-possession, however, and smiling, he consulted his watch. 'I often have a little something at this time of the morning, and there is a bakeshop nearby that is terribly indulgent. Will you join me in a frosted bun or a slice of cake?'

Cake, thought Mary with a sinking feeling. *Was that not what the French queen recommended when the hungry people were demanding bread?* She dismissed the troubling thought, and said that yes, she would. 'And then I hope you will tell me how we shall manage such a complicated secret — both my going to France and my return.'

'Yes, that will be a most interesting challenge,' Shy affirmed. 'Let us put our heads together and see what we may contrive.'

2

Miss Sarah Marchmont was certainly no stranger to the principle of polite society that 'a lady's conduct ought not to be remarkable'. Indeed, she had repeatedly stressed it to her charges at Mrs Bunbury's school for young ladies, and since retiring from that establishment, discretion and respectability had been her watchwords. Nevertheless, on a brisk afternoon, this stout woman of a certain age set off for London, a journey of some ninety miles. In the absence of a suitable explanation, such conduct was not only remarkable but also distinctly odd.

In fact, there was an explanation, but it merely shifted the oddness. Miss Marchmont was going to London because her young friend, Mary Finch, had requested it. This was all very well, but Mary had already departed for the capital to pursue 'a matter of business'. Respectable young ladies simply did not conduct themselves thus — not if they wished to remain unremarkable. Those who understood that there *were* such things as matters of business left them to their husbands, brothers, guardians, or men of affairs. Mary was sufficiently wealthy to employ one of the latter, but she had nevertheless seen fit to grapple with this matter herself. And now she had sent for Miss Marchmont.

To refuse, of course, was out of the question. Miss Marchmont and Miss Trent, another survivor of Mrs Bunbury's school, lived with Mary at White Ladies, and they took their responsibilities as companions and sometime advisors very seriously. But what did the summons mean? Miss Marchmont said that Mary was simply being sensible, and doubtless that was the correct explanation. It was certainly the explanation with which she and Miss Trent reassured one another. When a young person was very clever and perhaps a trifle headstrong, she did not always stop to consider How Things Might Look, but dear Mary was really a very sensible girl.

'Now, Hetty,' urged Miss Marchmont from the carriage window, 'you mustn't stand about any longer in this chilly air. It is bad for your chest.'

'No, I shall go inside directly,' Miss Trent agreed. She was a thin, grey-haired woman, and for some time now she had been fluttering about like a nervous sparrow, endeavouring to be helpful but generally getting in the way. One of the footmen had almost knocked her down. 'Promise to write as soon as you arrive.'

'Of course.'

'I shan't be comfortable until I know . . . You are certain you will not have Mr Edwards' *History of the Work of Redemption* to read on the journey? I could fetch it in an instant.'

'But are you not reading that yourself?'

'Yes, but you may have need of it, and I could make do with Mr Doddridge.'

Miss Marchmont thought she could manage without the tomes of either gentleman, but she smiled fondly. 'No thank you, dear.'

'Well . . . I have wrapped up a parcel of Mary's painting things – it is there on the seat beside you.'

'My dear, Mary has gone to London on a matter of business, not to paint pictures!'

'I know, but she may be glad of a respite – something quiet. But she mustn't suspect that we have been concerned about her.'

'No indeed. Oh, we are moving. Steady, Rogers! Have a care for Miss Trent's toes! Goodbye, now – and do not worry!'

Miss Trent retreated to the safety of the front steps, waved at the departing carriage and, contrary to her promise, hovered distractedly. *Dear Mary . . . I do hope that all will be well.*

And dear White Ladies. How Miss Trent admired the walled courtyard with its beautifully squared flagstones, the rebuilt coach house and stately porch; and as for the large residence of weathered grey stone, could anything be more splendid? Fashionable persons frequently described properties of inde-terminate age as 'Gothic', but with White Ladies the adjective was deserved, for it had been built in medieval times to house a community of Cistercian nuns – the 'White Ladies' after whom the estate was named. Subsequent owners had made their own additions and subtractions, but these had not affected the essential temperament of the house, which was sober, serene, and detached from the world and its problems. *If only*, Miss Trent sighed.

Recalled by a gust of wind to her duties, she entered the house, shutting and bolting the door behind her. The effi-cient running of White Ladies now rested with her, and she mustn't let things become slack while the mistress was away. With this resolve, she summoned Merriman, the butler. After a brief and somewhat confused exchange, it became clear that no instructions were necessary, which was just as well, since she had not thought of any. In the end she requested a pot of motherwort tea and retired with her knitting and Mr Edwards' *History* to 'the schoolroom', the small sitting-room that she and Miss Marchmont had appropriated as their partic-ular domain.

Mary had given her friends a free hand in the furnishing of this room, which consequently bore the marks of middle-aged, spinsterish thrift. It suited Miss Trent, however, and she always found motherwort tea soothing. She was pouring a second cup and contemplating a muffin with jam when Merriman reported that Mrs Tipton had arrived.

Oh, no, thought Miss Trent, and only just managed, by a quick turn of the wrist, to avert a motherwort deluge. It was only after the door had closed behind the butler that she realised, blushingly, that she might have spoken those words aloud. Slipper, Mary's small, irascible dog, began barking and then hid under a chair.

The prospect of a visit from Mrs Tipton had inspired similar responses in more than one home in that part of Suffolk. In person she was small and elderly, and navigated with the assistance of two sticks, but in personality she dwarfed the heartiest gentlemen in the neighbourhood. She also called regularly at White Ladies, for she took a particular interest in Mary Finch and often sensed when something had happened that affected her favourite. Miss Trent dreaded the prospect of relating this latest . . . oddness to her.

Mrs Tipton initiated the conversation, as she generally did, with an account of the doings of their mutual acquaintances. These included an instance of public drunkenness, an unsuccessful dinner party (the two were not related), and Mrs Tipton's most recent visit to the rectory, where a great deal of advice had been dispensed to the incumbent, Mr Hunnable. 'Something simply had to be said about the man's surplice,' she concluded, 'and so I said it.'

'Oh, yes,' Miss Trent agreed, despite the fact that she secretly objected to all Anglican vestments as popish, and therefore considered that one was as good – or bad – as another. She purposely dropped and then recovered a stitch in her knitting so as to disguise her lack of candour on this point.

Mr Hunnable's surplice provided an easy, if dubious, transition to the fashions on display at Miss Cheadle's dress shop, but it gradually became clear that Miss Trent was not attending. Mrs Tipton tapped the floor smartly with one of her sticks. 'What is it?' she demanded. 'And where is Miss Marchmont?'

The possibility of concealment was fleetingly considered and rejected. Draining her cup, dregs and all, as Socrates might have done at the fatal moment, Miss Trent replied, 'She . . . she has gone to London.'

'To *London*?' Mrs Tipton's opinion of the capital was well known, and while this was no guarantee against it being repeated, on this occasion she merely asked, 'Indeed?' in a highly disapproving tone. 'I knew nothing of this.'

'No, I am afraid it was all arranged quite suddenly . . . since Mary has been away.'

'In*deed*,' Mrs Tipton repeated more sternly, and fixed her gaze on Miss Trent. 'And precisely what can have prompted this . . . reckless exploit?'

No one had ever associated Miss Trent with recklessness, even indirectly, and she experienced a little thrill. Nevertheless, she was obliged to put down her knitting before she could continue. 'Well,' she explained, 'you know that Mary went to Cambridge to investigate some papers having to do with the history of the estate? They had been located in one of the colleges, and the Master was kind enough to inform her—'

'Yes, yes.'

'—of their existence. So thoughtful of the dear Master, although perhaps one oughtn't to speak so familiarly of such an eminent person.'

Mrs Tipton managed to combine a wave of dismissal with a nod of encouragement. 'Proceed,' she added, for the sake of clarity.

'Yes, of course. I beg your pardon. Mary wrote to us straightaway to say that she had arrived safely and had secured a convenient accommodation not far from the college, which was a great comfort, but today we received a most surprising letter. She said that she was going to London and wanted Sarah to join her – indeed, I might have gone as well, only Sarah was worried about my cough, and someone had to look after White Ladies. She set out . . . oh, it must be nearly an hour ago. Sarah, I mean. I expect that dear Mary departed Cambridge the day before yesterday.'

'I see,' said Mrs Tipton, curtly. 'Have you the letter?'

Miss Trent produced it. The direction on the envelope said, *Miss Marchmont, White Ladies, near Lindham, Suffolk*, in Mary's dashing hand, but the message it contained was addressed to both her friends.

11th October 1797

My dear Miss Marchmont and Miss Trent,

I hope you are both well, and that all our friends in Lindham and Woodbridge continue to enjoy good health. You will be pleased to hear that my errand at Catherine Hall has been a success, and I have learned a great deal about one of my predecessors at White Ladies. I have also taken tea in the Master's lodge – imagine the honour!

Since my arrival a further matter of business has arisen, which requires my presence in London, and I have decided to go there straightaway. It will take some time to resolve, and as White Ladies may be rather dreary at this time of the year, why do you not join me? I daresay we shall find a great deal to amuse us, while my affairs are being sorted.

Pray do not tax yourselves with the cost of the journey, and come by the quickest and most comfortable means – even if it is the most expensive!

The address where I shall be staying is 12 Devonshire Square, which is not quite so fashionable as Cavendish Square, but is quiet and respectable and, I believe, will suit us very well.

Yours faithfully,

Mary Finch

P.S. Apologies for the quality of this pen (which I believe was plucked, inconsiderately, from one of the mascots of this establishment).

In the short space of time it took for Mrs Tipton to adjust her spectacles and read those words, the atmosphere of the room changed. Miss Trent felt it, and she tried to ignore the prickling fear of looming calamity, urging, 'You see, it is all quite clear,' in a determinedly hopeful voice. 'She has business in London, and Sarah has—'

'Nonsense!' proclaimed Mrs Tipton, lowering the paper.

'—followed her . . . Oh dear.'

24

'*Business in London,*' repeated Mrs Tipton, scornfully. 'What business? Why does she not explain herself? And *if* she must go to London, why does she not return first to White Ladies and then make the journey properly, instead of rushing off in this mad way? I tell you plainly that the affair is entirely too insubstantial for my liking, and this tone of levity is intended to distract us from something far more serious.'

'Do you . . . do you think so?' asked Miss Trent.

'Certainly.' Mrs Marchmont eyed her shrewdly. 'And so do you.'

Miss Trent bit her lip, wavered, and then capitulated. 'Yes,' she admitted. 'Sarah said we ought not to worry but—'

Mrs Tipton dismissed that lady's interpretation with an airy gesture. 'What do you suspect?'

'I am so afraid that these old documents may prove that there has been some dreadful mistake,' Miss Trent confided, wringing her hands. 'That Mary is not the rightful owner of White Ladies after all, or the boundaries of the estate have shifted over the centuries.' She glanced about nervously, as if a bailiff might appear at any moment, brandishing a notice to quit. 'I would not mind for myself, of course, but if dear Mary should lose her home . . .!'

Mrs Tipton did not reply immediately. Little as she liked to admit it, since it had not previously occurred to her, this sugges-tion was not impossible. *And that Miss Trent should have conceived it . . . extraordinary.*

Then she frowned and returned to the real world, in which good-hearted but essentially simple persons like Miss Trent did not resolve mysteries. 'There *may* be something in what you say, but I fear the matter is even more grave. Do you wish to hear my reading of the situation?' she asked, in a tone that effectively eliminated the mark of interrogation from the sentence. 'It is that Mary has embarked upon an elopement.'

When her listener had recovered from the shock of the final, terrible word, she added, 'With *that man.*'

That man was Captain Robert Holland. Mary had met him under highly unusual circumstances, and Mrs Tipton considered

25

the resulting friendship between them most unsuitable. He might, it was true, have certain professional merits (although even there she had her suspicions), but he clearly lacked the financial and social qualifications to aspire to Mary's hand (and of this aspiration she was in no doubt).

Miss Marchmont and Miss Trent were not quite so adamantly opposed to the captain's suit, for they were not immune to the charms of romance, and both secretly thought him rather splendid. An elopement, however, was another matter entirely. If true it meant scandal and very possibly social ruin.

But was it true? 'Do you believe that . . . Captain Holland has followed Mary to Cambridge?' cried Miss Trent. 'And . . . proposed marriage while she was studying the ancient documents? Surely the Master of Catherine Hall would not have allowed such an impropriety. But perhaps the captain won his confidence by professing an interest in scholarship?'

So described it did sound rather silly, and Mrs Tipton replied hurriedly. 'Something of that nature might have occurred, perhaps. But very likely the entire story of the documents was a ruse, designed to separate Mary from her friends and place her in that man's power. You know, I protested against her going to Cambridge alone.'

Miss Trent did know. 'Yes,' she acknowledged, humbly, 'but Mary said—'

'Yes, yes. Naturally, she convinced the two of you that it was quite all right, an easy journey, and she knew Cambridge very well.'

Miss Trent nodded. 'And she does know it, from our time at Mrs Bunbury's.'

Mrs Tipton disliked all references to Mary's former life as a schoolteacher – such an unfortunate, *lowering* epoch – and she passed over this one with a lofty frown. 'It is the time that man spent here in July that is important,' she complained. 'A most regrettable business. You may depend upon it, *that* is when the damage was done.'

'Mary has been rather . . . distracted these last weeks,' Miss

Trent admitted, 'not quite herself . . . and you know that she has always been a very good-humoured girl.'

'Do they correspond?'

'I do not . . .' Miss Trent wilted under Mrs Tipton's eye. 'There may possibly have been a letter from Woolwich.'

'Yes, I thought so, and doubtless more than one. Pray, did you not wonder how Mary managed to secure London premises so readily? This letter was posted in Cambridge, yet she seems already to have leased a house in Devonshire Square. No doubt that was *his* work. She admits the address is not fashionable, and *he* has scarcely tuppence to his name.'

'Oh dear,' mewed Miss Trent. The immediate prospect of Mary in some miserable London garret was far worse than the eventual loss of White Ladies. 'Whatever shall we do?'

Mrs Tipton considered. 'Under the circumstances, it is probably fortunate that Miss Marchmont set out immediately – although she might have waited to receive instructions. The scene she encounters in London may overwhelm her. I shall write and tell her what to do.' She enumerated the important points on her fingers. 'If they are actually married—'

'*Can* one be married in London nowadays?' asked Miss Trent. 'I mean, without the banns being read?'

'I expect it is possible to do most things irregularly there. However, I believe it would require the archbishop's licence, and Captain Holland cannot *possibly* know Dr Moore. Very likely, therefore, they are *not* married. In which case, Miss Marchmont must bring Mary home immediately.' Mrs Tipton hesitated. 'So long as, ahem, no harm has been done.'

Miss Trent gasped at the possibility that harm *might* have been done. Mrs Tipton continued fiercely, 'In *that* case, a prompt wedding is the only course. Prompt, quiet, and accompanied by a three-fold curse upon the scoundrel who has brought us to such a pass!'

Mrs Tipton clutched her stick – she almost brandished it – and if Captain Holland had entered the room at that moment, his friends would have trembled for his safety. The sight of Miss Trent's pale face, however, caused the avenger to relent, and she added, 'But until we know the worst, let us hope for a more fortunate outcome. Mary did send for Miss Marchmont, after all. Perhaps that means she has realised her folly – whatever this Holland fellow may have promised. Let us hope that Miss Marchmont may confound him and perform a timely rescue.'

'Oh, yes, a rescue!' cried Miss Trent. 'Let us pray for it. And . . . it may end happily, you know, somehow.'

That evening, Miss Marchmont ate a solitary meal at the Great White Horse Hotel, Ipswich, prior to boarding the mail coach for London. She was a robust, practical sort of person, who did not readily indulge in the sort of speculation favoured either by Miss Trent or Mrs Tipton. Nevertheless, on this occasion all of their thoughts tended in the same direction: Mary's attachment to Captain Holland had resulted in an unfortunate escapade, from which it might just be possible to extricate her, or at least protect her from a worse catastrophe than becoming Mrs Robert Holland.

It was not Mary's letter that had convinced Miss Marchmont, however, but the confidential postscript, which comprised a separate sheet. In the privacy of the nearly deserted parlour, she re-read that missive, which seemed to admit but a single interpretation.

My dear Miss M,

Please come with all haste and, if possible, prevail upon Miss Trent to remain at White Ladies. I mean to lay a charge upon you, which I hope you will accept, but which I fear might trouble her.

Seen through the prism of fond friendship, the decision I have taken may seem misguided, but I trust you will think differently when I explain the circumstances. Indeed, I shall rely upon you to help make matters well with our friends afterwards.

I cannot explain further, but will do so when we meet.

Your very grateful friend,

Mary Finch

3

Devonshire Square was a quiet and, in its way, highly favoured enclave on the eastern edge of the City of London. True, the houses were sober rather than beautiful, and the warehouses rising to the south, east, and west of the square made for gloomy neighbours. But there was much to be said for sobriety, and if the men who had made their fortunes in distant bazaars and counting houses chose to live near the fruits of their labours, who could blame them? While not precisely built upon commerce, Devonshire Square had been sustained by it for many years, and the result was an address that denoted enterprise, fortitude, and success. From here, London merchants and financiers communicated not only with ministers and the Bank of England, but also with their factors and suppliers on the other side of the world.

Miss Marchmont had made tactful enquiries of her fellow passengers on the London mail. The talkative driver of a hackney carriage had provided further information while her baggage was being loaded for the short drive from Gracechurch Street. She therefore possessed a certain image of Devonshire Square, and, as her vehicle entered from Devonshire Street, she was pleasantly relieved to find it accurate.

How difficult to imagine anything *untoward* happening in such a quiet, respectable-looking place! Indeed, if one were bent upon . . . improper conduct, this was hardly the location one would choose. Then, too, there was the financial aspect.

While not the equal of fashionable Mayfair or St James, houses in Devonshire Square must be expensive – certainly beyond Captain Holland's modest stipend. Could they have been mistaken about Mary's actions? Might she have, in fact, come to London to pursue a matter of business in which the captain played no part?

While Miss Marchmont was considering that pleasing thought, the door to Number Twelve opened and a man appeared on the threshold. Short, stocky, with a round, swarthy face and luxuriant white moustaches, he peered at her suspiciously before breaking into a sunny smile.

'Good morning, lady!' he boomed, descending hurriedly and bowing at the carriage door. He wrenched it open and bowed again. 'You are friend of Mary *djan*? Yes! Welcome, welcome to our house!'

This was not at all the sort of greeting that Miss Marchmont had expected, but before she could do other than register her surprise, the diminutive figure was handing her out and advising her to care for nothing, he would arrange all. At close quarters, he cut something of a comic figure, with his highly correct suit of grey broadcloth strangely augmented by an embroidered skullcap and slippers with turned-up toes. But the grip of his hand was like iron, and he moved strongly even when encumbered by her baggage.

'You go inside, lady,' he called, gesturing with his chin. 'I pay this fellow all right. From Spread Eagle *bahntog*? Yes, yes, I know him – very good place!'

Thus prompted, and with her enthusiastic retainer urging her on, she mounted the steps to Number Twelve and walked into a narrow passageway. There, a rather more conventional maidservant took her hat and pelisse, and conducted her into the parlour. Comfortably furnished, it had the carefully maintained look of a room that had not been used recently, and some of the decorations were unusual – the large brass globe, for example, engraved with strange figures and symbols, the illuminated book written in a foreign language, and the silver incense burner (at least, that was what it appeared to be).

Of course, thought Miss Marchmont, determined not to be surprised if she could help it, *Mary would have taken a furnished house*. Turning purposefully to the maid, she asked, 'Where is your mistress?'

'Mary *djan* not here,' announced the voice from the passage He set down the last of Miss Marchmont's baggage and appeared in the parlour doorway, mopping his bald head with a large white handkerchief before replacing his skullcap. 'She is going out every day, shopping and conducting the affairs of her business. Buying presents for you, maybe.' His eyes twinkled. 'She will be so happy to know you are here. All the time she speaks of Miss Marksman, and when she is coming.'

'March*mont*,' that lady corrected.

'Marksman,' he repeated, nodding. 'I am Vartan Nazarian, *varich* of this house and also for Mr Hyde. Anything you want I get it for you, only you have to ask. But now you must rest yourself after journey and wait for Mary *djan*. You want tea? *Good* tea?'

'Yes, please. That would be lovely.'

'Of course. Here we have best tea in London – in England – if only that woman makes it right.' The assertion ended in a grumble and, turning to the maid, he commanded, 'You heard. Miss Marksman is hungry. Right away bring her *chay* and a plate of cakes.'

'We've only English cakes, Mr Nazarene,' warned the maid. 'Cook says she hasn't had time for—'

'Eh? What is that? Oh!' He growled like an elderly lion. 'Bring English cakes, then, and quickly! Guest does not go hungry in this house!'

'Yes, sir.'

Nazarian shook his fist at the retreating figure and then smiled sheepishly at Miss Marchmont. 'English servants always complaining. In Aleppo they would be beaten – or they would marry, and their husbands would have no peace. Here they are not beaten or married, and I have no peace. Everywhere Vartan Nazarian speaks and is obeyed, but in this house he hears only complaints! These women, they make me crazy.'

Miss Marchmont could think of no fitting reply, nor was she

31

quite sure that she ought to encourage the man's conversation. What was a *varich*, anyway? She inclined her head in a manner that she hoped conveyed a dignified benevolence. 'I am certain that the cakes will be delightful.'

'Maybe,' he agreed, 'but English cakes are dry – like dust.' He coughed to illustrate this. 'You will need the *chay* – that is very good. Tomorrow you will have proper cakes, if I must watch that woman so that she has time for baking and not only for talking! But now I take the baggage to your room. The most beautiful room in the house, after the room of Mary *djan*.'

The cakes were eaten and the *chay* – a surprising potion with more spices and less milk than any tea Miss Marchmont had ever known – drunk. It was a refreshing meal, so much so that she felt equal to the task of unpacking, and she proceeded to the second most beautiful room in the house to deal with her own trunk and the several parcels that Miss Trent had considered indispensable. When all was put to rights, she drew one of the chairs up to the window and sat down with a book. This room overlooked the square, and she could keep watch for Mary's return as she read. What she would say when they met, she had not decided.

Even *chay* could not undo the effect of nine hours on a mail coach, and she was dozing comfortably when a commotion downstairs roused her from sleep. This was followed by the very unladylike sound of feet pounding up two flights, and the door burst open with scarcely a pause after the knock.

Miss Marchmont caught her book just before it slid onto the floor. 'Mary!' she scolded. 'How many times must I remind you about stairs? I thought it must be a team of horses.'

In fact, it was a slim young woman, dressed in a plain but well-cut gown of coffee-coloured linen and a striped Parisian cloak. She was still wearing her bonnet and veil, but the latter had been tossed back to reveal a countenance marked by both beauty and character.

'Yes, I am sorry,' Mary laughed, dropping companionably upon the bed. The bonnet followed, and what had been a neat coiffure collapsed into a torrent of auburn curls on one side. 'Oh, bother,' she muttered, searching vainly for a hairpin and then pushing the worst offenders behind her ear. 'Only, everything has been so much at the gallop since I arrived that it is difficult to pull up.'

'Hmm.' Miss Marchmont removed her spectacles – she only used them for *very* small print; she could see quite well without – and considered her young friend. A dash upstairs did not account for those flushed cheeks and sparkling eyes. *High spirits*, she mused, *and if I am not mistaken, mischief or a rare scrape.* Aloud she said, in answer to a query about the journey from Suffolk, 'Oh, quite tolerable. The road to Ipswich was much encumbered by flocks of geese on a similar errand to my own, but being wise birds they prefer a stately pace. *I* would not choose to come tearing down to London, of course, but—'

'No, and you were a dear to do it, particularly as I have been so mysterious. But I mean to put that right.' One of Mary's eccentricities was her habit of carrying a gentleman's pocket-watch, and now she extracted it from her reticule. 'I must go out again, I am afraid. I did not expect you so quickly, and I have another appointment at two o'clock.' She turned to her friend. 'But I shan't keep you in suspense. You see, matters did not proceed quite as we had expected them to in Cambridge. I never met the Master of Catherine Hall, and I did not actually look at letters or anything else to do with White Ladies.'

'Ah. But a meeting did take place.'

'Yes, and I made an important decision on the strength of it – a sort of promise, really, and that is what has brought me to London.' Mary paused, and then the words came quickly, not quite 'at the gallop', but baldly, and without any attempt at circumlocution or justification. Very likely she had considered beforehand what she would say. Certainly her explanation had the air of a hurried recital.

When it was over, Miss Marchmont did not reply immediately, and her hand gripped the arm of her chair as if she required a steady support.

'Well?' prompted Mary. Her chin had risen defiantly over the course of her speech, and now it sank a little.

Miss Marchmont stared back at her. 'I am astonished.'

'But . . . you do not think that I have done wrong?'

From a slow start, Miss Marchmont began to gather speed. '*Wrong*? My dear Mary! I think you have taken leave of your senses, and right and wrong scarcely come into it! How did you . . . What can have possessed you to agree?'

'It does *sound* reckless,' Mary allowed, 'but—'

'Going for a drive with Mr George Nesbit after a festive supper would be reckless,' corrected Miss Marchmont. 'This proposal of yours is . . . I hardly know *what* to call it.'

'—I have considered the matter quite carefully.'

Miss Marchmont countered tartly that thought, care, and common sense had been conspicuous by their absence, but her heart sank. She recognised the too straight back and the steady, unflinching gaze of the girl opposite. There was no reasoning with Mary in this humour, and no way of shifting her from the course she had chosen, short of locking her in her room – and then there were always windows. 'I suppose you are resolved,' she grumbled, 'whatever I might say?'

Mary nodded, but her smile was hopeful. 'Yes, I am afraid so . . . but I would like to think that I have your good opinion.'

'Ha! *My* opinion—'

'And your support. Have you forgotten what I wrote in my second letter? I do not say that you *must* help me, but it would make matters so much easier if you would.'

'I do not see quite how everything may be . . . *hidden*.' Miss Marchmont frowned distractedly. A confidential undertaking . . . Americans . . . discomfiting the French . . . It was difficult to take it all in. She felt as if she had been buffeted or shaken violently, and her brain had not quite recovered from the trauma. In her confusion, she even found herself wishing that Mrs Tipton were present. *She* would not tolerate this nonsense. 'Let it be understood that I do not in the least approve of all this. In fact, I quite *disapprove*.'

'I understand.'

'But I suppose . . .' She sighed. 'It *would* be best if the others were prevented from worrying.'

'That is precisely what I thought.'

With the distinct feeling that she was being managed, Miss Marchmont asked, grudgingly, 'When do you mean to set out?'

Mary rose and glanced out of the window, perhaps to hide the triumphant gleam in her eye. 'In three days' time, if everything can be arranged. There is not a moment to lose.'

Miss Marchmont threw up her hands, which uninspiring gesture won her a fond hug and a kiss on the cheek. 'And now I must fly,' said Mary. 'The carriage is waiting for me downstairs. But we can discuss matters further this evening – including your part in the affair. Goodbye!' She snatched up her bonnet and was gone.

Miss Marchmont smiled wanly. 'Ah, yes – *my* part.'

They dined that night in splendour, Nazarian having produced the silver dinner service and a superfluity of engraved glasses 'for the honour of the house'. A competition of sorts between him and the cook, Mrs Jakes, had also resulted in a curious and extravagant menu, whereby domestic and exotic dishes jostled for space on the crowded table. Nazarian did his best to influence the diners in favour of the latter, grumbling, 'Ha, English,' when the maid, Annie, brought in a poached haddock or a sirloin of beef, but greeting his own creations with a cry of 'Good food!'

'You will not mind staying on here while I am in France?' asked Mary, during a lull. 'It is quite a pleasant house, I think, and Nazarian will do anything to please you.'

'So he informed me on my arrival.' Miss Marchmont was still feeling out of sorts, but seemed resigned to her fate as Mary's confederate.

'He *will* call me "Mary dear", which I suppose he oughtn't, but I haven't the heart to check him, and really he is quite fatherly – even *grand*fatherly. Do you know that he is almost eighty years old?' Mary nodded persuasively in response to Miss Marchmont's look of disbelief. 'It is true. He was a factor for one of the Levant trading houses, and he came to London when his principal, Mr Hyde, wound up the business forty years ago. Mr Hyde retired to the country, but this house – and Nazarian – remained in the family.'

Nazarian appeared with dessert offerings that he described as, 'Try-full: English, not so good' and '*Bourma*: very nice, with special sauce – ladies must try.' When they had duly pronounced the sweet, flaky, nutty confection far superior to its domestic rival (Mary was obliged to eat a second roll, dipped in syrup, and never mind fingers), they managed to gain from him a promise not to produce any further courses, nor to return until summoned. They would take tea upstairs presently.

'And Devonshire Square,' Mary added as the door closed behind him, 'is precisely the sort of address for my purposes. It sounds well enough to those who do not know London—'

'Like Mrs Tipton.'

'Very much like Mrs Tipton, but it is out-of-the-way for those in Town who might know *me*.'

'You intend to keep your presence here a secret from all but our friends in Suffolk?'

'Mm,' said Mary. 'This is really quite delicious but I mustn't eat another, or I shall be obliged to ask Madame Clothilde to let out my new gowns.' She slid the tempting plate out of reach. 'I have been quite careful to avoid the best dressmakers and jewellers, and I believe I may creep away without anyone the wiser.'

Creeping away. That was the aspect of the business that Miss Marchmont did not like. Or rather, it was the aspect that she most disliked, and without it the entire scheme would dissolve. '*Must* you go to France?' she asked, not for the first time. 'Something could easily go wrong, and then where will you be? At the mercy of those cutthroats – I am frightened even thinking about it! Perhaps I ought to come with you.'

'Oh no, that would never do,' said Mary, smiling at more than the incongruity of her friend's final remark, 'but you are a dear to suggest it. Everything depends on your being here, you know, providing sturdy evidence to Miss Trent and Mrs Tipton that all is well.'

'If only everything *were* well,' complained Miss Marchmont. She was one of those people who eat when they are unhappy, and now she took another helping of trifle.

Her 'sturdy evidence' would take the form of regular letters to their friends in Suffolk, in which Mary's business affairs would be described and other details of their stay in London chronicled. Miss Trent's conjecture about the Cambridge documents would serve for the former – she would be informed that an old parish map had been discovered that threw one of the boundaries of White Ladies into question, and Mary had been obliged to make further enquiries. (These would prove important, tedious, and – most importantly – not at all frightening.)

'Do you think that you can produce convincing accounts of visits to Oxford Street and Drury Lane from the prospect of 12 Devonshire Square?'

'*That* oughtn't to tax me,' chuckled Miss Marchmont. 'I visited shops enough on our previous visit to London to last a lifetime, and the newspapers will provide details of the operas and concerts that I – or rather *we* – might have attended.'

'Ah yes, of course. But if your imagination should flag, I suggest that you consult Nazarian. He does know London, and I expect he would be a bountiful source of information.' The *varich* had, of necessity, been informed of certain details related to Mary's undertaking – but not the reason for them. 'Fortunately he is not the least curious to know anything more. If only others of our acquaintance were the same.'

The next two days passed quickly. Mary had a busy schedule, and Miss Marchmont accompanied her faithfully to shoemakers, hosiers, hatters, and leather-workers, even to the haughty Madame Clothilde, who received them with grave condescension at a tiny shop in Montague Street.

That Spitalfields address was the least eligible, but none of the neighbourhoods they visited could have been described as fashionable, and Miss Marchmont wondered at Mary's habit of paying for her purchases on the spot and taking them away with her. There were such things as robbers and pickpockets, and very likely they thrived in precisely those gloomy regions of the capital. But when the expressions 'payment on account' and 'the convenience of delivery' were mentioned, just in a casual way, Mary was unmoved. 'Oh no,' she chided. 'We haven't time for that sort of thing.'

Usually Miss Marchmont played a conspicuous part in the shop or warehouse. She had to be certain that her young friend was spending her money wisely, after all, and she prided herself on being able to detect sharp practice. Her role was less prominent with respect to Mary's other appointments. She neither knew nor wished to know what took place in the discreet government office in Crown Street, and as for the affair at the Temple, she declined to dignify it with her presence. Great Cumberland Place, where the American minister lived, was the first decent address Miss Marchmont had heard since coming to London, but she waited in the carriage and made such conversation as was possible with Nazarian. He had insisted that the ladies must not venture out alone after dark. 'Many bad men about.'

On returning from that final appointment, Mary set about packing. This proof, if more were needed, that she intended to go through with her plan only deepened Miss Marchmont's sense of gloom. Having grudgingly complimented Mary's midnight blue spencer and embroidered Norwich shawl, she rounded on the new gowns, calling them far too insubstantial for polite wear – for polite *public* wear. 'And when I think what you paid for those flimsy things,' she sniffed.

'Fashion begins in Paris,' said Mary, 'and Madame Clothilde understands the latest styles *exactement*. Her father was a count, you know.'

Miss Marchmont was not convinced either by the lady in question's taste or her parentage. 'Judging by the number of so-called aristocrats who have landed in England since the war began, complaining of their troubles and expecting us to feel sorry for them, I am surprised there were any left in France to be executed. And you must promise never to wear that turquoise muslin without a buffon neckerchief . . . a very substantial buffon neckerchief.'

Mary promised and produced just such an item from her trunk, together with a sufficiency of winter undergarments, all of which had then to be refolded to Miss Marchmont's satisfaction. She was not quite such a stickler in these matters as Miss Trent, but she had her standards.

The luggage was eventually packed, and early on the following morning, the two women set out. An overnight freak of autumnal weather had resulted in a pale, drifting fog that lightened the pre-dawn square, but in no very pleasant way. The bare trees appeared all the more black and skeletal, while the street lamps and the houses opposite, which ought to have lent a sense of wholesome security to the scene, were obscured. Miss Marchmont was too sensible a woman even to consider the adjective 'ghostly', but she shivered as she stood on the front steps, and wrapped her cloak and shawl more securely against the damp. It was certainly not a morning in which one's heart was lifted by the prospect of travel.

'You needn't come with me, you know,' said Mary, as the faithful Nazarian returned with a hackney carriage.

'Oh, I must see you properly on your way,' Miss Marchmont retorted fussily. 'You went to Cambridge on your own, and see what has happened!'

This was not quite fair and both of them knew it, but Mary only smiled and told Nazarian to expect Miss Marchmont's return to Devonshire Square on the following evening.

'Of course,' he agreed, and after instructing the driver to take the ladies to 'White Bear Inn, Piccadilly, driving very careful', he kissed his hand to Mary – perhaps to both passengers – and urged, 'we see you again very soon.'

The Dover coach was crowded all the way to Rochester, which made the journey less comfortable than it might have been, but also limited the opportunities for private conversation. This was fortunate because if she and Mary had been alone Miss Marchmont might have asked about forgotten items or dismal eventualities, and neither was a very cheerful subject. Instead, she kept these and other troubling thoughts to herself, and concentrated upon the miles rolling away beneath them and the stops that remained until they must part. Chatham, Rainham, Newington, Sittingbourne; she promised herself that she would not become anxious until they reached Canterbury.

Darkness had fallen by the time they arrived in Dover, so they had no view of the castle. 'Oh, what a pity,' Mary lamented, peering ineffectually into the gloom. 'I should have liked to see it.'

'Perhaps another time,' said Miss Marchmont, in what she hoped was a confident voice. There was nothing to be gained by being morbid, after all, and she could not bear to part from Mary on a discordant note. 'Another time we shall make a proper tour.'

The coach stopped at an inn called the City of London, and on inspection it seemed a suitable place for Miss Marchmont to spend the night. The morning coach for London, they discovered, departed at six o'clock, and they booked her seat. These tasks accomplished, Miss Marchmont thought that Mary ought to eat something – the Lord knew when she would next have a proper meal – but Mary was adamant. As the hour of departure neared, her excitement grew. Only when she was certain of her arrangements could she contemplate something as mundane as supper.

War had sharply reduced the maritime traffic in and out of Dover, and the Custom House was nearly empty when Mary stepped cautiously across its threshold. Nearly empty but not quite, and she smiled when she recognised the tall, fair-haired man seated on his trunk in the corner of the ante-room, reading a newspaper. They greeted each other cautiously, but not like persons of only slight acquaintance. Anyone observing them would have said that it was the occasion that made them shy.

'I've spoken to the controller,' he began.

'Ah, have you?'

'Yes, a very decent fellow. He did not seem to think that there would be any difficulty, but he wanted to examine both of our papers together. I hope to goodness they are in order.'

The controller *was* a decent fellow, neither examining their baggage very closely nor showing immediate surprise when they handed over the documents signifying who they were and what they were doing. On closer observation, however, he frowned. He was used to seeing passports from neutral states; French émigrés wishing to slip back into France often claimed to be Danish or Swedish, latterly even Prussian, and American travellers were certainly not unknown. All of them had their different trimmings and flourishes — there was nothing like a bit of paper got up by foreigners for trimmings. This gentleman's papers seemed genuine enough; he had registered upon arrival at Harwich ten days ago, and there was his passport to travel to London and thence to Dover. The lady's papers were more surprising, with their collection of signatures, and the archbishop's seal . . .

He glanced at her. She was blushing, but that was hardly unexpected. *Well, well,* he thought, *it goes against the grain, what with there being a war on, but they do say that love conquers all.*

'Your name please, sir?' he asked, in an official voice. He could easily copy it from the documents, but he liked to do things properly.

'Samuel Vangenzen.'

'Place of birth?'

'Newark township, New Jersey.'

'And your allegiance?'

'I am an American citizen, sir.'

'And your name, ma'am?'

Mary's blush did not fade, but she answered strongly. 'Mrs Vangenzen.'

4

A little after three o'clock in the morning, the Swedish brig *Freya* cast off her moorings and slipped out of Dover harbour. When the inevitable tumult associated with departure had ceased, the first mate advised the passengers that they might safely leave their cabins. The night was fine but brisk, he said, and there were a great many stars to be seen. It would be a pity to sleep, despite the lateness of the hour, and with this beautiful, steady wind, their crossing was likely to be a short one. Dawn would surely find them in Calais.

He spoke reasonably good French, and almost all of his observations were understood the first time. Of the four men and three women who heard them, however, only Mary decided to venture on deck, wrapped in a heavy woollen cloak. This was her first ocean voyage, if a mere Channel crossing could be so described, and she did not mean to miss a moment of it.

A raw, wintry wind stung her face and searched out the gap at her throat where a button had been left undone. 'Fine', she decided, was something of an exaggeration. But the stars were beautiful, like diamonds scattered across an expanse of black velvet, and in their midst the crescent moon shone like silver. The moving deck felt strange at first, but Mary quickly found her balance, swaying with the rise and fall. As soon as she did so the motion became thrilling; together with the rush of water against the hull and wind against the sails it inspired a sense of power – as if she were in control of a vast creature racing, even flying through the darkness. She lifted her face to the night sky and breathed in the cold, salty air, marvelling that anyone could prefer a stuffy cabin. Mr Vangenzen, for instance.

Whatever the potential advantages, there were practical difficulties in employing a female agent. Initially Mary had baulked at Mr Shy's proposal for surmounting them, but she was no fool and had bowed to their necessity. How else could a young Englishwoman expect to enter France, unless transformed into a harmless neutral? And how could she achieve that transformation except by marriage? The answer to both questions was clear, and so she had become Mrs Samuel Vangenzen, with a ring, a licence, and a husband to prove it.

Mary was very conscious of the first of these, an unfamiliar weight on her finger, and she twisted it absently. It was a silver gimmel ring, a style said to be popular among Americans. Again, Shy's words returned to her. *They are generally a prickly lot, Americans, especially where their national honour is concerned. "Don't tread on me" and so forth – one would imagine they had been a nation for centuries. But you will not object to Mr Vangenzen, I think. Quite an agreeable young fellow, and not at all prickly.'*

In so far as she could judge from three brief meetings, Mary had found this assessment accurate. It was difficult to imagine a more amiable colleague, and when she had been in London, Vangenzen's friendliness had been highly reassuring. Now, however, poised on the doorstep of France, she felt vaguely uneasy about him. Her reasons for undertaking the assignment were clear enough, but what of his? Was he not troubled by the prospect of a British agent spying on his nation's envoys?

I would be, she brooded.

The sound of approaching footsteps caused her to turn, and she recognised the man himself. He coughed slightly, by way of greeting, and joined her at the rail. The mate of the watch tipped his hat to them, and they nodded in reply. Presently they moved further forward, so that their conversation would be out of earshot.

'I oughtn't to have abandoned you,' Vangenzen murmured.

43

'For the look of the thing, I mean. I daresay you are perfectly capable of amusing yourself without my help.'

Mary responded with the sort of polite, illogical observations that often characterise conversations between near strangers. She enjoyed solitude – he mustn't reproach himself – but of course his presence was most welcome – was it not a lovely sky?

He studied it thoughtfully. 'Mm. Smalt, Ivory Black, and Prussian Blue. That is the combination I should choose for a painting. In France they call it "Parisian Blue", which I always find amusing. That reminds me, ought we still to be speaking English?'

Mary's command of the French language was very good, but she was a little shy of parading it before Vangenzen. He spoke English with what she supposed was a colonial accent, but hearing him speak oddly was much less daunting than the prospect of doing so herself. Without revealing either of these views, she suggested that it would be most polite to converse in French when they were in company. In private, however, why should they not speak English if they wished? *We are not pretending to be French, after all*, she added to herself.

'We always speak English in the *appartement*,' Vangenzen confided. 'Er, in my lodgings, I should say.'

'Are there many Americans living in Paris at the present?'

'Oh, no, not so many. I mean, the Maison des Chevrons, where I live, is very quiet.' He frowned and toyed with the fastening of his cloak. 'What I meant to say when I spoke of having abandoned you was that I usually try to sleep during a night crossing. If you arrive half awake, the Customs procedures and the arrangements for travel can be rather fuddling. At least, I have found them so.'

'I am sure you are right,' Mary agreed, 'but I could not possibly sleep now. This is my first time at sea.'

Vangenzen said that he quite understood; on the voyage from America he had spent so many hours on deck that the captain had asked whether he wished to have his name entered as a member of the crew. 'Not a very effective one, I regret to say.'

'*Were* you allowed to help?' asked Mary. 'That must have

44

been marvellous. But I suppose you were rather sad to leave America.'

'Oh, no.' He shook his head. 'I believe I was never so happy as when we bade farewell to Boston – we could not risk passage on a Newark vessel, you see – and I counted the days until we reached Portsmouth. Thirty-three days! A famous crossing for the old *Dolphin*, for she was certainly no flyer.'

Although this information meant little to Mary, she agreed with it, and when Vangenzen expressed his fondness for England she thought that she began to understand him. An established loyalty would explain many things. She knew that Vangenzen's grandfather, a man of some enterprise, had left Amsterdam to study the common law and had lived in London for many years. His son, it seemed, had gone to America, but it was well known that not all Americans had supported the rebellion there.

'Was your father a Loyalist during the last war?' she asked. 'Loyal to England, I mean.'

'Goodness, no,' laughed Vangenzen. 'My grandfather sent him to New Jersey on family business at the time of the Stamp Act crisis. Father sided with those who objected to the principle of the tax, and from there it was a short step to independence and the republic. A short step for him, anyway. My father is a man who believes in making up his mind quickly and moving on to other matters.'

Mary nodded and murmured, 'Ah.' She was also familiar with persons of that temperament, but it might have been rude to develop the point.

Vangenzen, apparently, was untroubled by that prospect. 'I do not say that my father was wrong about American independence, but patriotism is . . .'

'"The last refuge of a scoundrel?"'

'No, no. Certainly there have been many great patriots who were worthy men. What I meant is that patriotism is an ideal, and ideals are dangerous. I—' He hesitated again. 'You do not want to hear my philosophy.'

'Indeed, I would like that very much,' Mary protested. She was rather surprised that he *had* a philosophy – he did not look particularly philosophical, with his broad, open features and cautious smile – but he was also an artist, and therefore might be unusual in all sorts of ways.

'Well . . .' He glanced at her dubiously, but her face was hidden in the hood of her cloak. 'I believe that ideals and principles are too absolute . . . too easy to fall back upon. It sounds terrible to say, but ideals stop you from making up your own mind.'

'The wrong sort of ideals, perhaps.'

'*Any* sort.' Vangenzen looked round, and then explained, 'I believed in ideals when I came to France. The Revolution was fought to break down the rotten old principles of government and replace them with wonderful ones like Freedom, and Equality, and the Rights of Man. I thought the French would manage things better than we had done in America, but instead there has been the Terror and this dreadful war. Other nations have contributed to the war, of course, but—'

'Mr Burke says that a revolution is dangerous *because* it sweeps away the old ideals and ways of doing things, and people do not know how to conduct themselves,' said Mary. 'If they have no safe guide, they will naturally make a mess of things. And besides,' she added, with a hint of defiance, 'I do not think that a person can live *without* ideals. They give you something . . . a goal beyond your own happiness.'

'What is wrong with seeking your own happiness?'

'Well, it is rather selfish – or it might be.'

Vangenzen was silent for a time, and then acknowledged that Mary's view might be correct, for the English, anyway. 'But for myself, I place little faith in ideals – except in art, where they cannot do much harm . . . and perhaps the ideal of friendship. That is an exception to my philosophy.'

Mary thought of the only friend of his that she knew. 'You are thinking of *Mr Shy*?' She whispered the name.

'Yes. He has always been a good friend to me. He bought several of my paintings at a very welcome time. My father had stopped my allowance, you see, when I left home . . . and I don't believe that the paintings were very good, either.'

46

'I expect the artist is an unreliable judge of his own work.'

Vangenzen protested, laughingly, and their conversation shifted to art, which was clearly his passion as well as his profession. He was pleased to discover that Mary had brought sketching materials and made her promise to show him her drawings, and when she revealed that she had actually taught the subject, he gazed at her with genuine admiration. That her pupils had, for the most part, been chattering girls who cared more for the figure *they* would cut than any that might be produced on paper, made no difference.

'If I had an atelier full of students — whatever their talent — I should be perfectly happy,' said Vangenzen with a smile. 'Paying students, of course.'

The first mate's prediction proved correct; dawn found them at Calais, but the crossing did not end as smoothly as it had begun. The beautiful, steady wind faded to a capricious breeze as they made their landfall, and then they were not permitted to continue, but must receive on board two men from the *commissariat* to examine passports. This process proved a lengthy one and by the time it had been completed, the tide was such that natural, rather than national, law kept the *Freya* where she lay. Not until mid-morning did she finally creep into the harbour.

Mary was glad to disembark; the last two hours, with the ship bobbing and rolling on the swell, had been very unpleasant. But she was apprehensive too. Why had such a careful study been made of their documents? Was it usual for one agent to remain on board while his colleague submitted his report? What if her status were to be questioned? It was all very well to say that the French government would respect her marriage to an American *in London*. The Calais officials might not be so accommodating.

The pier was crowded with people: curious onlookers, servants crying up the merits of rival inns, ragged porters who tried to seize the luggage as it was unloaded, and women hawking buns and national cockades. Scruffy children, some without shoes, screeched and chased each other; for them, any commotion among their elders was an occasion for mischief.

47

This, at least, did not increase Mary's anxiety, for Vangenzen had predicted just such a tumult. She calmly surveyed the crowd from the rail as she waited her turn to board the boat that would take the passengers ashore. Then she stiffened. One of the police agents was returning, shouldering his way through the crowd, and behind him were two soldiers. Someone touched her on the shoulder; it was the other agent. 'You are next for the boat, citizeness,' he urged.

She glanced at Vangenzen, who was already descending. He looked calm enough, but perhaps he had not seen the soldiers. *This may be perfectly usual*, she reminded herself, *you mustn't panic. Or, if it is not usual, why should it have anything to do with us? One sees a great many soldiers in London nowadays, and I expect it is the same in Calais.*

These thoughts distracted her, so that she climbed down to the boat with hardly a care for that awkward manoeuvre, and took her place on an empty bench. The remaining passengers followed, and then they were moving steadily across the final stretch of water that separated them from France. The air was cold and damp and smelled of fish, but Mary scarcely noticed. She watched the rowers' oars dip and thrust through the grey-green water. It was already too late to go back – whatever was going to happen would do so in a very few minutes – but she nevertheless felt that her freedom was slipping away. It would end when she touched French soil, and every stroke was bringing her closer, closer.

Not quite French soil, for they were waiting for her on the pier. The soldiers looked bored, but the police agent, a short, heavy man with a tricolour scarf wound loosely about his thick neck, pronounced his instructions with relish. 'Citizeness Vangenzen must present herself before the Committee of Public Safety – yes, and Citizen Vangenzen too. And the luggage, certainly. Oh, so much! The citizen is a rich man, it seems. Let him have the use of that barrow. The Committee will answer your questions, citizen, and ask some of their own, I have no doubt. This way.'

Under the curious gaze of the locals, the little party made

its way, first along the pier, and then across a cobbled square. Vangenzen's barrow, alternately rumbling and squeaking, provided an ominous accompaniment to the soldiers' heavy tread. *Like the tumbrels*, thought Mary, grimly, *on their way to the place of execution.* They halted before a squat, stone building that might have been the *hôtel de ville* – the town hall. That it had served a municipal function before the Revolution was evident from the defaced royal emblem above the door. In its place, someone had daubed the phrase *'Liberté, Égalité, Fraternité, ou Mort'* in black paint.

The final assertion seemed to shriek at Mary as one of the soldiers thrust open a complaining door and motioned for her to enter. *They cannot possibly know anything to your discredit,* she told herself. *Show them that you are unafraid, and all will be well.* Even as one part of her mind uttered those bracing words, however, another part quailed. There had not been time to discuss with Vangenzen how they ought to behave before the Committee, yet it was essential that they gauge the situation properly. *What if he begins explaining his views on ideals of government?*

The Committee consisted of three men seated behind a long table, and nothing about them was reassuring. The youngest sprawled in his chair, toying first with a penknife and then with a bit of string that he knotted aimlessly. His face had a petulant expression, as if he not only held in contempt those who came before him, but also considered the task of reviewing their cases and signing their documents a tedious chore. At the other end of the table was an older man, busily writing in a ledger. Tufts of grey hair on either side of his dark head stood up like ears. Indeed, his features generally were wolfish: yellow eyes, a long nose, and a lean, bristly jaw. Between them sat a large, florid man in a dirty shirt; a round hat with feathers was on his head, and this seemed to indicate his chairmanship. He breathed heavily and, although the room was chilly, he was sweating.

The wolfish man continued to write for some minutes, and the other two were equally absorbed in their own business; the string was knotted and re-knotted. Mary tried hard not to be unnerved by the deliberate disregard, and instead studied her surroundings. The floor had once been a fine one, but now it was scuffed and dusty. At least two of the windows were cracked; perhaps that accounted for the cold breeze that blew through the room and made the candles smoke and gutter.

Someone ought to trim the wicks, she thought. *Young sullen-face could make himself useful with his penknife.* Out of the corner of her eye she could see one of the soldiers yawn and scratch himself. *It is all the same to him whether we are condemned or set free — I daresay he would prefer the former, as it would provide an afternoon's entertainment. Do they execute people in the afternoon or only at dawn?*

She started when the man in the hat commanded, 'Approach, citizen.' The wolfish man had laid down his pen, and now all three were studying Vangenzen as he stepped towards their table. 'You are Samuel Vangenzen?'

'Yes, citizen.'

'Give an account of yourself in a clear, audible voice.'

Vangenzen explained that he was an American, but had lived in Paris for the last seven years. He was an artist, a portrait-painter—

'Huh, an artist,' interrupted the young man. 'Could you paint me?' He turned his head to present a not very inspiring profile.

'I could,' said Vangenzen, thoughtfully, 'but it would take some time, and I would not choose this light. The shadows in this room would also be quite difficult.'

'Hush! Do not distract him, Marot,' the wolfish man complained. 'Never mind shadows, citizen. Proceed with your account. You went to England . . .'

'Yes, as you see from my papers.' Vangenzen nevertheless explained his itinerary. From Dover he had gone to London by the usual route and had remained there for nine days. He had lodged at Froome's Hotel, Covent Garden.

'What were you doing in London for nine days?'

'Buying colours, mostly.'

'Colours? You mean for painting? Why was it necessary to

50

go to London for these colours? French artists do not need English colours.'

'Indeed they do,' Vangenzen countered, and his tone made Mary wince. Surely he ought to be more conciliatory? The artist, however, continued sturdily. 'Everyone knows that there is not a colour-man in Paris to rival Norgrove & Langley of Oxford Street, or Mr Reeve, if you prefer watercolours. Even if you wish to mix your own oils, the English pigments are quite different and greatly valued. You need only glance at my list—'

'What list?'

Oh dear, thought Mary. *He makes lists! What else has he written down?*

Vangenzen produced a notebook. 'This list of artists' wants. For Bismuth, for Carmine – Red Lead, of course, comes from Wales . . . and only in London can you obtain the true Indian Yellow.'

The heavy man gestured for the notebook. Muttering the names 'Girodet . . . Isabey . . . Guerin', he stopped partway down the page and stared at Vangenzen. 'You are acquainted with Citizen David?'

'I am acquainted with them all. We are colleagues, and, when I go to England, they place their orders with me.'

The heavy man blinked slowly. 'Very well. You seem an energetic young fellow, and you understand these . . . pigments and where to obtain them. Why did you require nine days to complete your purchases?'

Vangenzen replied that he had also seen clients during that time – men who had purchased his work in the past and might do so again. 'And . . . citizen, my . . . wife was also living in London.'

'Ah, yes. Your wife – this woman. How long have you known her, citizen?'

'Oh . . . some time.'

Even to Mary it sounded weak – as if she had been less important than the acquisition of a good supply of Brunswick Green.

The wolfish man leaned forward. 'When you requested permission to depart the Republic, you stated that you wished to conduct business in England,' he snapped. 'You said nothing of contracting a marriage to this woman. Why did you keep this matter a secret?'

Vangenzen's confidence was ebbing away. He opened his mouth to reply, but no words came. Instead, a crimson flush spread across his cheeks, and he gestured vaguely. 'I . . . I did not—'

Mary cut him off. 'Pardon me . . . citizen, but the matter is clear, only my husband is too good to mention it. Too modest, I mean.' Her throat had gone dry and she was blushing in her turn, but she continued somehow. Thank Heaven the French words came easily. 'It lies with a woman's prerogative. A man may know that he will ask, but he cannot be certain of the woman's answer.'

The wolfish man grunted, but the others grinned. The young man shifted in his chair and eyed Mary appraisingly. 'Huh. Have you painted *her* yet, citizen?'

'Silence!' snapped the heavy man and handed back the notebook. Then he jerked his head in Mary's direction; she was to step forward. 'Where are her papers?' he demanded peevishly, and there was a delay while the wolfish man passed them across.

In London it had been debated whether to produce such an array of documents. French officials were sticklers for form, it had been argued, particularly under the current regime, and even a trivial omission might be sufficient to block her entry. Too strict an attention to detail might arouse suspicion, however, as if she had *expected* her status to be challenged. Did the innocent traveller really carry quite so many proofs? Now, as the seals and signatures were scrutinised, Mary felt the force of that question. She stared at the tabletop where the veneer had cracked.

Again the heavy man startled her. 'What is this "Temple"?' he demanded, tapping her marriage licence with his thick, stubby finger. 'Are you Jews?'

'No, no.' She tried to answer calmly, but a flood of fearful thoughts swirled up, confusing her. Was this a particularly dangerous accusation? Ought she to appear indignant? Christianity had been restored in France — it was tolerated — she *believed* it was at least tolerated — but perhaps one ought not to appear too devout? A not-very-devout Anglican? How did one say that in French? And how to tackle his first question? The church of the Templars. An ancient order of chivalrous monks was unlikely to find favour with a Republican tribunal . . .

She was tempted to invent a simple, uncontroversial explanation — that it was a church for foreigners . . . for Americans, even. *He will never know the difference.* The heavy man did not raise his eyes, but something in his posture stopped her. *No, do not risk a lie*, and with barely a pause she replied that the Temple was an area in London where many lawyers kept their offices, and which also contained a church — an Anglican church.

'A church for lawyers? Perhaps they have need of it. We also have our Temple in Paris, from the old times. Did you know that?'

'No, sir— citizen.'

'It is now a prison.'

The heavy man turned to his wolfish colleague, and they exchanged remarks in low, confidential voices. Mary was asked about her knowledge of French and where she had been taught, and as she explained, the two men continued to communicate in whispers and shrugs.

'And what do you think about politics, citizeness? Are you an admirer of Mr Pitt?'

The danger of saying too much or too little hovered momentarily as Mary framed her reply. 'I do not claim to understand English politics,' she admitted, 'but I think it is a terrible thing that there should be a war. Especially between England and France.'

'I doubt it lasts much longer,' remarked the wolfish man. 'When England is invaded, there will be a need for our officers to speak the language. When they visit Froome's Hotel, yes? Perhaps you could perform this service for the Republic and become a teacher of English?'

She nodded. 'Perhaps, citizen.'

'How do you like the sound of that, eh?' demanded the young man with a smirk. 'The invasion of England.'

'I dislike fighting anywhere, citizen, but you forget that since my marriage I see things as an American.'

'But—'

The heavy man shook his head and muttered, 'Enough.' Then he gestured in Mary's direction. 'It is enough,' he repeated more loudly. 'Your passports will be ready this afternoon.'

And so they were dismissed. Mary did not permit herself even to breathe until she and Vangenzen were outside but when she did so, an immense weight of anxiety and trepidation also seemed to slip away. She had done it! She was actually in France and ready to begin her work. How she would do this, she did not yet know, but that was a worry for tomorrow. Today she had passed the first test.

The scrutiny of their luggage at the Custom House was an altogether less burdensome affair, but it took time. When they emerged at last, Vangenzen wondered whether they would have difficulty arranging transportation to Paris. Calais was not London, after all, and the war had naturally disturbed some of the old establishments.

'Not Dessein's, I hope?' asked Mary, venturing a smile. 'I was wondering . . .'

'Whether it exists? I did the same on my first visit to Calais,' he laughed. 'Yes, there is indeed a Lion d'Argent, and it is just as Mr Sterne described it in his book. Shall we try our luck there?'

'Yes, please!'

As they walked, he praised her coolness before the Committee, her *sang-froid*. 'I find that sort of thing so daunting,' he acknowl-edged, 'I become confused and generally say the wrong thing. But you did very well.'

Mary thought likewise but aloud she discounted both the praise and the censure. She hoped, however, that Vangenzen's artist friends would not suffer in any way for having been included in the affair.

The suggestion surprised him. 'Oh no,' he assured her. 'Why should they?'

'I do not know . . .' Mary shrugged and lowered her voice to a whisper. 'That their names were found on a list might be considered . . .'

'Suspicious? When it was for the purchase of artists' colours? How could that possibly constitute a threat to the Republic?'

It did sound ridiculous, and she smiled at herself. She was more distrustful than the members of the Committee! 'Why did he ask you about Monsieur – I mean, Citizen – David, particularly? Who is he?'

Vangenzen's frown disappeared. 'Ah, he is a marvellous fellow, and the most accomplished painter in France – perhaps in Europe. I am honoured to have had his support and tutelage. When he was released last year—'

'Released?' hissed Mary. 'He was imprisoned?'

'Yes, but that was a mistake – he is a fervent Republican. I don't quite understand how he got himself into trouble, but it was during the Terror, when a great many people were arrested. However, he was released and has had no further trouble from the authorities. His work is very popular, and he has a number of students.'

This endorsement failed to quell Mary's fears, but she did not pursue the matter further. And perhaps Vangenzen was right. Certainly no one could take *him* for other than a dedicated artist. The contents of his trunk had surprised the Customs officers, but his concern for the several jars, boxes, and packets, and his plea that they not prod or in any way disturb the various paint bladders could not have been manufactured. That his conduct would be reported to the Committee she had no doubt, but that gave her confidence, for it would further establish his *bona fides* . . . and hers.

55

5

The Lion d'Argent marked the culmination of Mary's journey that morning, and as she entered the famous inn she experienced a mixture of sensations. The first was relief. The survival of Dessein's proved that France was not a wholly dangerous and threatening place, and that the more attractive image created in Mr Sterne's novel had some foundation in reality. Relief, however, was tempered by exhaustion. She had been travelling for almost twenty-eight hours, much of it at an unusual pitch of excitement, and this had taken its toll. She smiled, therefore, at the thought that *here* was the courtyard where Mr Yorick had hidden in the *désobligeant*, and *there* the door before which he had clasped the hand of the beautiful Madame de L—, but tiredness dulled her appreciation of these literary landmarks.

Seated at a small, corner table in the parlour, with a cup of coffee and a basket of rolls before her, she felt like a clock that had utterly, completely wound down, its gears stripped, and its hands broken. A contented clock, if that were possible, not particularly troubled by its decrepit condition, but from which no great effort must be demanded.

The coffee – hot and very strong – revived her briefly, and she enjoyed the crisp rolls and delicately flavoured jam that accompanied them. *Confiture d'oranges*, it was called, and was apparently part of a hidden cache of treasures from the time when English visitors had been common at Dessein's establishment. It was like no marmalade that Mary had ever tasted, but she was grateful for the sentiment that had inspired it. Frenchmen, clearly, were not all bad.

Not all bad, although the members of that horrid Committee would have been better for a spoonful of this confiture. Le Comité de la Douleur Publique. She smiled bemusedly. *Now, I shall finish this roll, and then we really ought to be going. I feel much better . . . Really quite comfortable . . . I do hope that Mr Vangenzen will be ready to . . .*

A touch on her arm caused her to open her eyes, and she phrased her observation. Blinking, she repeated it in French.

'*I* am ready,' replied Vangenzen with a smile.

Mary frowned confusedly. 'What is it? Has something happened?'

'I am afraid so. You have had a sleep, our papers have been handed over, and our transportation is booked and prepared to depart. Would you care to step outside and see it?'

'A carriage? You have organised it already? I mean, well done – yes.' She intended to rise quickly, but the muscles in her back and legs protested against such inconsiderate treatment, and the result was more like a stagger than a spring. 'Oh,' she gasped, 'I feel as if— No, no, I am quite well.' She waved away Vangenzen's helping hand, although she was still slightly dazed. 'Have I really been asleep? I do beg your pardon.'

'Not to worry. I expect you needed it.'

He led the way to the door, with Mary risking a backwards glance over her shoulder. 'Yes, but . . . and in a public room! I hope that no one saw me.'

'Very likely not,' Vangenzen assured her. 'It was only a few minutes.'

In fact, nearly an hour had passed since they had entered Dessein's, as Mary's watch proclaimed. During that time, the industrious Vangenzen had hired a vehicle, collected their papers, changed some English money, and paid the bill for their refreshment. He had done everything, while she had been no help at all.

You are little more than an extra piece of English baggage, Mary lamented to herself, *easily left in a corner until you are collected and carried to the next stop.* As she trailed after Vangenzen, she wanted very much to re-establish herself as a bold, active person who was not at all *trunkish*, except perhaps in being hardy.

The latter resolution was immediately put to the test as they crossed the courtyard to view their *chaise de poste*. It was, Vangenzen said, the ordinary French travelling carriage, but perhaps not quite what she was used to. He was correct on both points. The vehicle was smaller than Mary had expected and possessed only two wheels — rather like a gig, but with a partially enclosed body. It looked light and manoeuvrable, but how would it fare over a long distance? And, more importantly, how would those fare who were riding inside it?

The *chaise* would be pulled by two horses, and the pair standing between the shafts seemed undersized, even for a journey of one or two posts. Mary recognised the postilion from the crowd at the pier; a small, unshaven, rather melancholic-looking fellow. Dressed now for the road, he wore a cocked hat and patched woollen jacket, while his thighs were encased in bundles of straw and his feet in enormous jackboots. He smoked a pipe with the air of one who did not expect that the mere act of driving would interfere with this practice, and he carried a large whip.

When she saw it, Mary was torn between her desire to proceed to Paris with all haste, and her wish to preserve the horses' scrawny backs from harm. She only nodded, however, when informed that the postilion's name was Lagroix, and that they could depart as soon as their trunks were secured on board. If Vangenzen did not shrink from this strange mode of travel, then neither would she.

Lagroix went forward to make a final adjustment to the harness, and Vangenzen muttered to Mary from behind his hand, 'We shall aim to reach Samer tonight and Amiens tomorrow. It is not so common in France to travel overnight — not so common as in England. I hope you will not mind that?'

'Oh, no,' Mary replied, with a conscious air of intrepidity. She was certainly not going to quail before a mere inconvenience, and they might welcome reprieves from the *chaise*. 'I should prefer whatever is most *usual*.'

Once she had taken her place in the vehicle, she began to feel more confident. It was helpfully arranged for two passengers, and the open front afforded an excellent view of the countryside. Lagroix proved almost all bark when it came to his whip, although he wielded it energetically and with many flourishes. Indeed, even without that instrument he communicated a great deal with his team, alternately praising and threatening them with muttered injunctions. 'Onward, sluggards!' 'Ah, my beauties, my children, such a pretty piece of road lies ahead!' 'Quickly now, or I shall tell them not to feed you when we reach the inn.'

And so they bade farewell to Calais. At first Mary's attention was absorbed by the scenes around her – the hills and fields, and the cottages set in gardens that reminded her of Kent. Springtime in Artois would be quite pretty, she decided, with the flowers blooming and the corn rising in the fields. Presently, however, such idle reflections were interrupted by more practical concerns. The road was in a very poor condition, and as they bumped, dipped, and swayed, sometimes slithering along a mass of stones and at others jolting violently into and out of deep ruts, Mary began to wonder whether any vehicle could long survive – and theirs in particular.

When she mentioned this to Vangenzen, he agreed rather too readily for her liking. Accidents and breakdowns were very common in France, he said. Fortunately, because the speed of travel was not very great, few serious injuries occurred.

'Do you not consider this a very great speed?' asked Mary, as a lurching bump caused her to rise bodily from her seat. 'Goodness!'

'Oh no,' said Vangenzen, bracing himself. 'I believe you will find that we do not exceed the usual speed of an English post coach – probably we do not equal it – only the jolting makes it feel faster.' He compared it with his experiences in America, where the roads were of varying quality, but the coachmen rendered them perilous by their tendency to race each other, often while in a state of intoxication. In his youth, Vangenzen had frequently been obliged to direct his pony into a ditch to avoid a collision, and on one occasion he and his fellow passengers had chosen to leap from a violently swaying vehicle as the lesser danger.

'Was anyone hurt?' asked Mary, astonished both by the incident and Vangenzen's matter-of-fact reference to it.

'One old fellow broke his leg, but he counted it a fair exchange, and fortunately there were enough of us unscathed to carry him home.'

'*Carry*— Do you mean that the coachman abandoned you?'

'No,' said Vangenzen, slowly, 'I expect he did not quite realise that *we* had abandoned *him*. He must have been surprised when he finally pulled up and found none of us aboard! In any case, it was only a matter of walking a mile or so, and much smoother for the old fellow with the leg than if he had been rattling along in a coach, even soberly driven.'

Mary pondered a witticism linking Jehu to New Jersey, but she could not make it come out satisfactorily. Instead, she asked to hear more about America. The request was only partly contrived, for she had a genuine interest in foreign places. Vangenzen's stories, moreover, would help to illuminate his character. In the weeks to come, his might be the only friendly face she would see. Certainly she would rely upon him a great deal, and that would be difficult if he were a stranger.

His account was an intriguing one, not so much in what he said as in how he said it. When he spoke of public matters such as the landscape, the seasons, even the people that one met on the indifferent roads, it was with great fondness and sympathy. He described scenes with an artist's eye, but the image was softened by a desire to paint an appealing picture, rather than one that was merely accurate. When he touched on more personal matters, however, his tone became reserved. He spoke blandly of Newark, the town where he had been born and raised, and of his family, who lived there still. The Vangenzens had considerable shipping interests, and his brother-in-law would very likely succeed the elder Vangenzen in due course.

As she listened, Mary wondered whether this was not the

key to Vangenzen's departure from America. *He was probably a disappointment to his father and went abroad to pursue his artistic career.* Vangenzen's next remarks seemed to confirm this interpretation. When she asked whether artists were much demanded in New Jersey, he laughed and said the clamour had never reached *his* door. It was different in Boston and New York, but there one competed with men of the first rank – those who had studied in Europe.

'I attended Princeton University for a term or so, but what I wanted more than anything was to study with a professional artist. I thought of going to Mr Stuart, perhaps, or—'

'There is quite a famous American painter in London,' said Mary. 'Mr West.'

'Indeed yes! I have visited his atelier. He is very generous with his time, and I could have wished . . .' Vangenzen's expression changed rapidly from delight to resignation. 'But I did not stay long in London, and I have had wonderful opportunities since coming to Paris.'

Painting and Mr West kept them occupied for more than a mile, but gradually conversation faded along with the afternoon sunshine. The air grew colder, and it seemed to Mary that the autumnal landscape looked less hopeful. She struggled to envisage the bare trees clothed in new green leaves, or animals grazing amid the clods of heavy earth, or the top of the brick wall repaired. Her gaze passed through a larger gap in the wall, and fastened upon a darkened edifice set well back from the road. As they drew nearer, the building's proportions began to make sense to her. Part of the roof was gone, so that one side of the structure looked squat and lumpish, while the other retained at least a suggestion of grandeur. That it was a façade became clear when she considered the broken windows, and the broad front door, hanging crazily upon its hinges as if struck by a giant fist.

The postilion chirruped his horses and the ruined château passed swiftly out of view, but as they drew nearer to Boulogne, further scenes of desolation greeted them. On both sides of the road and at different distances stood the ruins of a gate-house; a charred grove of trees surrounding an equally battered folly; the remains of another wall with gaping openings like black, staring eyes; a large heap of rubble. Near the last, it was possible to discern the remains of a graveyard – had a church been ransacked and destroyed? Such allegations were commonly made in England, but seeing the evidence with one's own eyes was shocking, nevertheless.

Mary was grateful for the concealing gloom; surely it would be worse to survey the burned, mangled, and broken structures in full daylight. But she could not help imagining them as they had once been. What forces of oppression or jealousy, right-eousness or wickedness could have precipitated such violence? And what of the people who had lived in this château, managed that estate, and prayed in such a convent? Surely the destruc-tion had not been limited to stone and glass, nor was it likely that, in their rage, the rioters had distinguished the guilty from the innocent. Mary had seen angry children turn on each other and drunkenness inspire a crowd to noisy violence – but these could scarcely be compared to the forces unleashed across this landscape. She could almost hear the cries of anguish and fury.

When they reached Boulogne, they were made to stop and produce their papers, and Mary found the process sinister. Such had been her introduction to the town that she half-expected it to be populated still by wild-eyed Republicans intoxicated by their orgy of destruction, and she was very much on her guard. The gloomy, down-at-heel officer and his shuffling constable did not look very fanatical, but that might be a ruse. She was glad that Lagroix could honestly report that they were travelling on to Samer, which was the next post town.

The officer shrugged. He did not think much of the accom-modation in Samer, but he did not think much of foreigners either, and if they wanted lumpy beds and breakfasts fit for a pig then they were welcome to Samer. They were welcome to each other.

Something of this was conveyed in his remarks to Lagroix, whom he appeared to know, but Mary was paying more atten-tion to her travel documents, which rose and fell in his grasp as he gestured. Although none was more than a week old, they constituted her identity and – she hoped – protection. How worryingly flimsy they seemed. A gust of wind, a moment of carelessness, and they would be lost. Against her will, she imagined the officer tearing them asunder in a fit of pique.

The constable raised his lantern, and Mary flinched at the sudden light. Then her passport was thrust into her hand, and they were free to proceed. She sat back in her seat and smiled weakly at Vangenzen. Perhaps the only danger had been in her imagination, but she was glad to be moving again.

'Huh, a pig's breakfast,' muttered Lagroix, when they were out of earshot.

They covered the eight or so miles to Samer in good time and disembarked at the posting house. It was, as the officer had predicted, a small, poor place, scarcely an inn at all, as Mary understood the term. She was not surprised to discover that she and Vangenzen were the only guests. The landlord conducted her to a draughty bedchamber that was sparsely furnished with a table, chairs, and what promised to be a lumpy bed. The hearth was cold; indeed, it looked as though it had not contained a fire for many years, and the room had a damp, faintly musty smell.

'Might I have some hot water?' asked Mary hopefully.

'When I bring the supper,' the landlord replied.

Come, that is something. At least there is going to be supper.

Left alone, she sat down wearily. Not only had the day's travel been physically taxing, but also her brain felt numb from having spoken and thought so much in French. Had she made many mistakes? She did not think so, but she also doubted whether Vangenzen would have pointed them out. *He really is a very good fellow*, she thought, and pressed her lips together against a yawn.

The landlord returned, bearing a jug of water, a basin, and a not very clean towel. His wife followed with a tray. Together, they set the table for supper, which consisted of brown bread, milk, a sliver of cheese, and coffee. Neither the size nor the paucity of the meal surprised Mary, but the fact of its appearing in her bedchamber did. She had not understood the landlord's words as having a literal application.

'Apparently one eats in one's bedchamber in Samer,' she informed Vangenzen when he appeared.

'Oh, that is generally the French way. It would be unusual to dine – or sup – at a common table.' He surveyed the room uneasily. 'But I am sorry that . . . I mean, of course they would not think it at all strange . . . And we are newly married, after all.'

He turned bright red as he spoke those words, and Mary could likewise feel herself flushing. Newly married! She had almost forgotten it – or rather, she had forgotten to think about it as something between the two of them, for she had answered to 'Mrs Vangenzen', 'Madame Vangenzen', and 'Citoyenne Vangenzen' readily enough.

She thought about it now, and twisted the wedding ring upon her finger. *Heavens! This is not my bedchamber, but ours!* It was the first time that she had felt really awkward with her new husband, and she was uncertain how best to proceed. After a short while, she managed, 'Yes,' in a less than confident tone of voice.

They stood motionless on either side of the table in an attitude of intense, mutual embarrassment. Fortunately, the hot water broke the spell. Vangenzen noticed the steam rising lazily from the spout, and Mary invited him to wash his hands. From there, the conversation limped forward to the supper (both had eaten bread and milk as children), and slowly gained speed as they reflected on the day's events (Mary wished she had thought to purchase some of the *confiture* from Dessein's, if only to sweeten the coffee).

'Oh, don't you like French coffee?' asked Vangenzen.

Mary made a face and shook her head. After they had compared the merits of coffee and tea, she asked about the ruins they had passed. 'Of course, in England one hears of such things, but they are so much more terrible in real life. I suppose that French people are used to them now – but surely they cannot still be proud of that awful time?'

Vangenzen said that the matter was too complicated to bear a simple answer. 'The Terror has subsided, thank goodness, but the . . . upheaval is still too recent for people to know quite what they think about it all. As you travel through France, you will still see red caps and Trees of Liberty, but you may also hear those who complain that the aristocrats and the monasteries provided employment for those who could work and charity for those who could not. The crops failed badly a few years ago, and that made some people long for the old days, however bad they might have been.'

'But it would not be safe to express an opinion on such matters,' Mary suggested. 'I did not like to say anything today.'

'That was exactly right. Of course, you can be perfectly frank with *me*, but in general you must be very careful of what you say, or even of what you notice, until you are certain of your audience.'

After supper, Vangenzen went downstairs to confer with their hosts on arrangements for the morning. Amiens was a distance of sixty-five miles, and they wished to make an early start. While he was gone Mary's thoughts were free to wander, and they drifted uncomfortably back to their earlier exchange. She and Vangenzen were newly married after all . . . and what came 'after all' but sleep?

When Mr Shy had proposed that Mary go to France, he had assured her that she need have no fear of any *impropriety* arising from her enforced relationship with Samuel Vangenzen. She might safely regard him in a wholly fraternal light, for he would have no interest in anything resembling an *intrigue*, nor would he embarrass her by a *dishonourable proposition*. These unequivocal endorsements had carried great weight with her, and they still did. Standing before the dusty mantelpiece, she did not actually believe that Vangenzen would misbehave, but surely they would have to discuss the matter of sleeping, and how was *that* to be accomplished in a wholly fraternal light? If only the chamber were larger, it might have been possible to pretend that they were in separate rooms. But the chamber was small, and there was only one bed and . . . how would she manage it?

A cracked mirror hung on the wall above the mantelpiece, and she studied herself in it. The reflection looked tired but reassuringly serious, like the sort of person who could think her way out of difficult situations. She frowned in an effort to do away with the tiredness. *Of course, there are many instances in literature of ladies and gentlemen living quite familiarly with each other, but without the least suggestion of anything wrong. Perhaps I might mention some of these to Mr Vangenzen, as a way of raising the topic.*

She thought there was some merit in this idea, until she considered the likely examples. Had not the unchaperoned ladies in Shakespeare's plays generally disguised their state by masculine attire? And Maid Marian had always enjoyed the protection of Friar Tuck. Lately, Mary had become familiar with the Indian story of Rama, in which Hanuman behaved very gallantly towards the lady Sita. But was he not a monkey? Or at least a god in the shape of a monkey? It was hard to be certain on this point. *Perhaps I oughtn't to mention him, and in any case, Hanuman may not be so well known in New Jersey.* Finally, she remembered Una and the knight of the red cross.

There was a tap at the door and Vangenzen entered. He was carrying an extra blanket under his arm, but Mary did not notice it. She turned towards him confidently. 'I was thinking just now,' she began, with an air of unconcern, 'of *The Faerie Queen*.'

Vangenzen answered briskly. 'Ah, indeed. Now, I propose to lie just here, before the hearth – subject to your approval, of course. The chairs are a bit short for my height, and I am tired of sitting. How does that sound to you?'

'Lady Una— I mean, oh yes, certainly.'

'Our hosts would become suspicious if I slept elsewhere, you know, in the stables, or—'

'Slept in the . . . Oh, no – you mustn't *think* of that,' said Mary hurriedly. 'The . . . floor is exactly right . . . If you do not think it will be too uncomfortable.' She strove to adopt an interested expression, as if the contrast between floor and chair had been at the forefront of her mind, and slid the toe of her boot against a broken floor peg in a quest for splinters.

'Not at all,' said Vangenzen, 'and I am no stranger to this sort of thing – sleeping on hard ground, I mean, not . . . Ahem. I am very sorry that there is only the single room, but we may hope for better tomorrow. Amiens should offer a wider choice of accommodation.'

Mary agreed politely and continued to study the floor. Ought she to say that she did not mind? Or perhaps try again with Lady Una?

She hesitated over these questionable alternatives, which was just as well, for in the interval Vangenzen continued, 'I ought to explain something to you. It may make the present situation somewhat less . . . and in any case, you will have to know eventually.'

If he had tried, he could not have begun in a more intriguing manner. The floor lost its attraction, and Mary stared at him. 'What is it?' she asked.

He smiled at her cautious tone. 'Nothing to alarm you, I promise. It is only that I am married.'

'*Married?*' She sat down on the bed, all thoughts of propriety forgotten. 'But how?'

His smile broadened. 'Oh, in quite the usual way.'

'Of course, but Mr Shy . . . I mean, what of my work? How can *I* pretend to be Mrs Vangenzen if you—' Then she glanced up at him hopefully. 'You are married in America, you mean. Your wife is waiting for you in New Jersey.'

Vangenzen shook his head. 'No, I'm afraid she is waiting for me in Paris. You needn't worry, however — but let me explain.'

Her name was Aminata — although Vangenzen called her Minta — and she had been born in the west of Africa, where the trade in slaves had long existed. Minta and her mother had come to America in chains, and their situation had been rendered more pitiable by the fact that Minta's father was Portuguese, the captain of one of the ships that plied between Cape Verde and New York. No one knew whether he had actually condemned mother and child to a life of servitude, but he had done little to protect them from that fate.

In America they had been more fortunate, for they had neither been separated nor sold to a brutal master. On the contrary, Mr Bacon was a scholarly, if somewhat unusual man, with an interest in the habits and customs of savages. He had purchased Minta's mother, therefore, both to keep house and to teach him the Wolof language. On discovering that Minta was a clever girl, he had arranged to have her schooled in accounting, bookbinding, and the classical languages, so that she could manage his bookshop while he collected the songs and stories of an exiled people.

The shop was located in Princeton, and it was there that Minta had met Vangenzen, during his abortive career at the university. They had fallen in love and had wished to marry, but had lacked the resources to secure Minta's freedom – Mr Bacon having proven not so eccentric as to misjudge her value. The elder Vangenzen had been applied to, but he had declined either to give or to lend the necessary funds. In desperation, the star-crossed pair had fled, first to England and then to France. There they had settled, but concealing their true circumstances. Having married in secret, they lived, officially, as bachelor and housekeeper.

'Only you and Cuthbert Shy know the truth. I had meant to tell you on the ship, but the moment never seemed quite right.'

Mary did not reply and Vangenzen, who had been standing in front of her, turned towards the hearth. He raised his eyes to the mirror and studied her reflection. 'I am afraid you are astonished.'

'Indeed, I am,' Mary acknowledged, and then added, 'and I am terribly sorry for you, and for . . . Minta.'

'Thank you,' muttered Vangenzen. He turned again to face her. 'It *has* been rather difficult – not that I ever doubted that we were right to do as we did.'

It was clear from his tone of voice – a mixture of truculence and relief – that Mary's view of the matter was important to him. She perceived this and marvelled at it. *But it is not so very strange, I suppose. They have had only each other's reassurance these last seven years.* 'No,' she agreed firmly, 'I am certain that you *were* right.' Presently she asked, 'Is your father a great supporter of slavery?'

'No, but he liked it well enough when it suited his purpose. He said that as *he* had no use for a slave, he would not purchase one in circumstances that would undermine the institution.'

'By granting her freedom? That does not sound very logical to me. In fact—'

'Oh, I am probably not explaining it properly,' Vangenzen

allowed, 'but in any case he plumped more for morality than for logic. "Jesus threw the money-lenders out of the Temple", he said, "but not the slave-owners". "In Heaven there shall be neither slave nor free, but on earth we are called to follow the laws of Caesar." And Caesar's law – by which he meant the law of New Jersey – places a stern barrier between the European and African races, which must not be overcome lest we incur everlasting damnation. That too is in the Bible, or so my father would say.'

'My friend Miss Trent would have a good deal to say about that! About the Bible, I mean. The Queen of Sheba was an African, was she not? And a very worthy person.'

'As I daresay King David would have thought, so long as Solomon did not marry her!'

'Of course,' Mary acknowledged, 'that was the root of the problem. Marriage is really a terrible business.'

'Indeed!' laughed Vangenzen, 'I have not found it so.'

'But people have such different ideas of whom one ought to marry, and it is so easy to make a mistake. A dear friend of mine was guided by her mother, but her husband turned out to be perfectly dreadful! And another friend—' Suddenly a very different thought occurred to Mary. 'But what of Minta? Does she . . . know about *me*?'

The act of laughing had expelled much of the remaining tension from Vangenzen's posture and expression, but now he appeared uneasy again. 'N-no, not precisely.'

'Not *precisely*?'

'Well, she knows about my going to England, of course, and that it was for Mr Shy's sake. But everything happened so quickly, and he could hardly set down his plans in a letter!'

Mary stared at him. His explanation was eminently reasonable, but it surprised her nevertheless, and it made her think. 'Then . . . you also knew nothing about my assignment when you left France?'

'No, but I did not like to disappoint Mr Shy, and I knew that my journey would be useful even if I could not be of any help to him.'

'How so?'

'I had my colours to buy.'

'Er, yes, the colours,' said Mary, trying to keep the impatience out of her voice. 'But when you saw Mr Shy, he convinced you that it was important that I . . . meet the American envoys?' Without quite knowing why, at the last moment she amended the sentence.

'Well, diplomacy is hardly my business,' said Vangenzen, 'but it seemed clear that, in the present state of things, there oughtn't to be an alliance between America and France.'

And what if they should go to war with each other? Did Mr Shy mention that possibility? Or that he hoped for it? She wavered on the brink of saying more, and then retreated to the safety of omission. 'American neutrality would be the safest for everyone,' she agreed.

Even as she spoke the words, Mary felt uneasy, conscious of her duplicity. The sensation was far worse, in fact, than her earlier embarrassment about the single room. Vangenzen was her colleague, and she was deceiving him. And he was such an open, ingenuous sort of fellow. *'I had my colours to buy', for goodness sake!*

She told herself it was better that he not worry about such things – after all, she had yet to meet the envoys – and at the same time listened to what Vangenzen was saying. He had no notion, it seemed, that anything was being kept from him.

'And as for Minta, I daresay she will see things exactly as you and I have. There did not seem to be another way for you to come safely to France, other than as my wife.'

'Yes, the marriage,' said Mary. 'Indeed, if there *had* been another way, we should have taken it.'

'Exactly,' Vangenzen agreed. 'And Minta is very fond of me. She will understand.'

Mary nodded, but she doubted very much whether the second statement necessarily followed from the first.

6

Mary and Vangenzen set off at half past six the following morning – later than they would have liked, but Lagroix had proven to be neither a prompt nor a very cheerful riser. Mary had not slept very soundly either, for Vangenzen's presence had helped to keep thoughts of him and of her assignment turning uneasily inside her head. She had dozed, finally, and was too disciplined to lie long abed, but the hours of rest had brought scant refreshment.

They breakfasted at Montreuil, and over more brown bread and coffee Mary tried to remember why the town seemed familiar to her. Did it feature in a poem or a play that she had read? Perhaps some important event in history had occurred in Montreuil. *Your knowledge of French history is woeful*, she scolded herself, *except when it is really English history in disguise, like the battle of Crécy or the mise of Amiens*.

Vangenzen could say nothing on the possible historical or literary significance of Montreuil, and there the matter seemed likely to end. When they returned to their *chaise*, however, Mary noticed a sign affixed to the principal door of the church.

THE PEOPLE OF FRANCE RECOGNISE THE EXISTENCE OF A SUPREME IMMORTAL BEING.

She did not consider herself a superstitious person, and with the reasoning part of her mind she knew that the sign could have nothing to do with her. Moreover, while history proved that God generally did favour the English side in wars, one oughtn't to rely upon divine intervention in any particular case. The message was surely a very strange one, however, and quite out of keeping with the desolate condition of many of the religious buildings they had encountered since leaving Calais. She took it as a good omen, therefore, and her opinion of Montreuil improved as a result.

When dawn broke in London that morning, Major the Honourable Francis 'Dick' Whittington was still in bed. He would not have dreamed of rising at such an early hour, even for an omen. As a gentleman of fashion as well as an officer of the 1st Regiment of Foot Guards, he was far more likely to have *retired* at dawn. It was not until Mary and Vangenzen were well on their way to Abbeville, therefore, that Whittington undertook his morning's task – a visit to the Woolwich Warren.

The Warren was rather a curious place. In addition to being a depot for men and machines of the Royal Artillery, it housed the regiment's laboratory, where experimental work of various kinds was carried out. Whittington knew little of exploding shell cases or mortar-boring machines, but he did have a professional interest in secret information. Behind his smart uniform and nonchalant manner lay a career in Army intelligence, and secret information of a technical nature could often be obtained at the Warren.

On this occasion he came specifically to see Robert Holland. Holland and Whittington were unalike in almost every particular – appearance, wealth, family, and professional circumstances – but they were friends of long standing nevertheless. Recently their friendship had suffered a severe strain, almost a dislocation, but the injury had healed; certainly Whittington believed that it had. The reason for his visit, moreover, could not fail to intrigue even the most guarded gunner. He announced himself at the main gate with the air of confidence that rarely failed him.

It did not fail him on this occasion, even while Gunner Drake, Holland's officious and frequently exasperated soldier-servant, escorted him to the officers' quarters. Drake considered Whittington a bad egg and someone 'Captain Haitch shouldn't oughter get mixed up with', and he made his feelings known by a series of grunts, shrugs, and short answers to the major's attempts at friendly conversation. Even the clump of his feet on the stairs signalled disapproval, and he announced the visitor with a curt knock and a grim, 'Major Whittington 'ere to see you, sir.'

Holland looked up from his desk – a stained deal table across which were spread a dismantled pistol, paper and inkpot, and a range of small tools. A quill pen joined the rest, and he greeted his friend with a tired smile. 'Morning, Dick.' He straightened, and then rubbed the back of his neck before rising. 'To what do I owe the pleasure?'

'Oh, I happened to be in the vicinity, you know,' breezed Whittington, 'and I thought I would look you up on my way back to Town.'

The two men shook hands. Holland was nearly as tall as Whittington, but a critic might have said that in those few inches lay the grace, style, and elegance that characterised the major. Certainly Holland was a much less polished specimen, and with his shirtsleeves rolled up and his dark hair barely contained in a haphazard queue, the physical contrast was marked. Even the partial Drake pursed his lips. He fought a never-ending battle to keep his officer looking smart, and that Holland should appear like a scarecrow beside a prince, however disreputable, was deeply frustrating.

'Well, it's good to see you,' said Holland, apparently oblivious to his subordinate's chagrin. He motioned Whittington towards the room's two 'comfortable' seats, a pair of sagging armchairs that appeared to have prostrated themselves before the hearth.

Whittington let himself be guided. 'You look very busy, as usual. When Drake said you hadn't been to bed, I thought perhaps you were turning over a new and more interesting leaf. What is that mess?'

'Oh, nothing.' Holland replied with the habitual caution of a man long engaged in confidential work before admitting, 'It's an idea I have for a revolving pistol – an improved mechanism. I ought to be in the laboratory, I suppose.' He frowned thoughtfully and then tucked in his shirt-tail before sitting down opposite his guest. 'What's the time?'

'Nearly a quarter past ten,' said Drake in an aggrieved tone.

Whittington promised that he would not long delay the great work, but he made himself as comfortable as the armchair permitted, and expressed a desire for a spot of something – perhaps a pot of coffee, in deference to the early hour. 'And I would not object to a splash of brandy,' he added to Drake. 'I prefer it to cream, you know.'

Drake received this information in silence, but when he retired to the pantry he expressed himself amid a clatter of crockery. 'Prefers brandy to cream 'e says. Well, and don't I hope 'e won't be too put out that we ain't got any. As if pots o' coffee grew on trees, fer Gawd's sake. It'll be bloody cocoa next, with a drop o' maraschino. "I prefer it, you know".' He returned with two cups of coffee – one black and the other ostentatiously white – and deposited the dented pot on the sideboard.

When they were alone again, Holland demanded to know what had really brought his friend to Woolwich, for he placed little faith in the story of a casual meeting. Instead, his thoughts slipped back to the matter that had brought them together in the spring – a case of treason and sabotage that had put both their careers in jeopardy. 'Not in any sort of . . . trouble, are you?'

Whittington frowned loftily. 'Hardly. I have been diligently ploughing my lonely furrow, and my employment today is wholly virtuous. Say, do you suppose that Drake is listening at the door?'

'Probably, but you can trust him, you know.'

'Indeed, I *do* know,' and in a louder voice he remarked, 'this milk has gone off.'

'Well then, what do you mean about your "employment"?' persisted Holland. 'Nothing like the last time, is it?'

The wariness in Holland's voice made Whittington smile as he set down his cup. 'No, this is something quite different.' He observed Holland thoughtfully. 'What is your opinion of sea monsters?'

'Sea—? Hell, Dick.' Holland was used to Whittington's banter, but that did not prevent it from being annoying. The work on the new trigger mechanism, moreover, had been interrupted at an interesting juncture. '*I* don't—'

'You are sceptical, naturally, but I really think you ought to keep an open mind. Think of the precedents – Proteus, Scylla . . . I am certain there is something extremely edifying in the Bible about Leviathan and a hook, and my old nurse, a dour Scotswoman, used to terrify me with stories of kelpies and other devilish creatures that drowned and ate their victims, apart from their livers. I too would leave a Scotsman's liver well alone, but—'

'Yes, all right, very amusing. And you've come to Woolwich – to ask me about sea monsters?'

'Well, not precisely, although that is what the French are calling it – *le monstre de mer*. Mysterious occurrences that admit of no other explanation. Strange booming sounds at the dead of night, boats thrown up on shore with wounds from giant teeth, even an unnatural shape seen in the water, moving against wind and tide.'

'What a load of . . . I suppose the French newspapers are saying that this monster sank the Dutch ships at Camperdown?'

'*Batavian* ships,' Whittington corrected gravely, 'of the Batavian Republic. Thus far, the creatures of the deep have not appeared in the pages of *Le Moniteur*.'

'Then where did the sea monsters come from? The stories, I mean.'

'Local fishermen.'

'Ah, they're highly reliable, then.'

'We also have our own men – or rather, the Navy does –

operating confidentially off the French coast, and they have seen and heard enough to be interested. And seriously, Bob, might there be something in it? Some kind of secret . . . machine or other that the French are building?'

Holland shrugged. 'Of course there could be *something*, a mine or—'

'A mine that works under water? Why have I never heard of these devices before?'

'Well, *you* were probably too busy reading about Scylla and Proteus. But don't run away with the idea that the French – or anyone else – use naval mines. They're marvels in theory but tricky in practice. You need a reliable timing mechanism, for one thing, and a waterproof shell. And then the mine has to be placed close to the target, which can be damned awkward. Also, navies generally consider them immoral.'

'And so they are! One likes to be able to see one's enemy before the engagement begins. This other hardly seems fair.'

'Armies mine fortifications on land, which isn't so very different.' Holland shrugged. 'And I'm surprised to hear you complaining about any kind of secret warfare.'

'Oh, my view is distinctly flexible,' Whittington retorted, 'according to whether we have the upper hand in it. And espionage is not without its rules, you know. But let us not be distracted by such legal niceties. I suppose that these mines would only be used against ships in port. No device could be brought close enough to harm those at sea.'

'Probably not.' Holland replied slowly and then fell silent, his fingers drumming on the arm of his chair. He was thinking of something . . . something that he had read . . . but he could not quite remember it. Whittington watched him, smiling faintly, and waited for his friend to voice his question. At last it came. 'But what does all of this have to do with you? Isn't it an Admiralty matter?'

'Yes, but our paths cross on occasion, and we like to help the sailors when we can. In fact, this particular affair does not concern my office, and I am employed simply as a friendly intermediary. A colleague in the Admiralty asked me to have a quiet word. You are the one they want – you and your understanding of diabolical machines. I am not privy to the details, but I have warned them that you do not speak a word of French and are sick as a dog in anything that floats—'

'Thank you very much for passing that on.'

'A pleasure. I daresay they may recruit someone else for whatever they have in mind, but they want to know whether you would be prepared to lend a hand, if necessary.'

Holland said that he was more than willing to give such assistance as he could. Indeed, quite apart from any sense of duty, he was curious about the technological advance – if one had actually been made. It was a very interesting subject, after all, involving a range of chemical, physical, and mechanical problems.

Whittington had expected such a response, and he even made an effort to listen as his friend launched into a soliloquy on the subject of waterproof carcasses and the competing advantages of rigid and pliable materials when it came to strength and survival in salt water. At a fortunate pause, Whittington pronounced the subject fascinating and suggested that the Admiralty would proceed in the usual way if anything came of their investigation.

'It might not, you know. There is nothing so changeable as the military mind – and if the civilians become involved they confuse things utterly.'

Holland swallowed the last of his coffee. 'Most interesting projects in the service come to nothing, and the daft ones are taken forward. But I'll read what I can on the subject. I think that there was something in the last war.' *What was the fellow's name?*

'Ah yes, excellent,' pronounced Whittington, beaming pleasantly.

The matter of Holland's tentative recruitment resolved, Whittington took his leave. At least, he rose and moved towards the door, but at the makeshift desk he paused. 'What do you hear from Miss Finch?'

Holland's expression altered from faint distraction to particular dislike. Mary Finch was not a subject he cared to discuss with Whittington. 'Why do you ask?'

'Merely a friendly interest in your welfare – although, funnily enough, I thought I saw her in Town the other day. She hopped into a carriage in Hare Court – that's rather good, don't you think? She would not have come up to Town without informing you, I suppose? Some matter of business?' He glanced speculatively at his friend.

Holland felt it and tried to divert the conversation. It oughtn't to be too difficult, as Dick enjoyed the sound of his own voice on most subjects. 'Where is Hare Court?'

'The Temple – Middle, or Inner, or Outermost – however the several precincts are designated. I was visiting the family solicitor, of all people. There is to be a rearrangement of my sister's finances on account of her marriage, which necessitated a grand congress of the Whittingtons. I glanced out of the window during a particularly tedious stage in the proceedings, and there was Miss Finch – or so I imagined.' Whittington idly straightened a pen and penknife before continuing. 'If she is not hopping about in Hare Court, I presume she is presently in Suffolk, content in all things apart from your absence?'

'No – I mean, she's content, I suppose, but she's gone to Wiltshire.'

'Oh yes? For what purpose?'

'I think she's visiting someone – I mean, she *is* . . . visiting someone,' said Holland. He could feel his face becoming hot. *Damn!* He wished that Drake would come in again. His palpable disapproval would be the perfect diversion, and might even succeed in moving Whittington away from the desk.

'Hmm, I see.' Whittington set his gloves down on the only clear space, an action that provoked another silent curse. 'Matters romantic have been settled between you, I trust?'

Holland said that of course they had been, nearly, and Whittington uttered a second, more pronounced, 'Hmm'. The efficiency of Holland's pursuit of Mary Finch was a subject on which they did not tend to agree. 'If you want to hear my opinion—'

'I don't, but that has never stopped you before.'

'Far be it from me to interfere, but I really do think— Ah, what is this?' Whittington extracted a sheet of paper from the clutter. He had the decency not to examine it closely, but it was unmistakably a letter, written in a woman's hand. 'Well, well.'

'All right,' muttered Holland, and now his blush was obvious.

'Not at all,' said Whittington encouragingly. 'I congratulate you. Indeed, I—' Whatever else he might have said was over-taken by a burst of laughter, for having turned the letter over, he revealed a scrawl of notes and calculations, even a sketch of some kind of mechanism.

'Trust you to find that,' Holland grumbled.

'In my line of work one is obliged to be highly observant – but good Lord, Bob,' Whittington chuckled, 'is this how you treasure the lady's missives?'

'No, it was the only bit of paper I had to hand. I mean, I'd written on it before I realised what it was. I didn't want to forget the idea – it might be important.'

Whittington regarded him dubiously. 'I see now why you are not yet married. The work of the artillery regiment is intensely fascinating, but a woman likes to believe that she is not competing for your attention with a . . . a revolving pistol.'

'Well, I don't intend to show her these notes.'

'Certainly not! But why not show her a bit more attention instead? The poor girl is languishing in Wiltshire, pining for the sight of you . . .'

'I'm not going down there, if that's what you're suggesting,' Holland warned.

'What a splendid idea!'

'I thought I was supposed to stand by for the sea monsters. And besides,' Holland added defensively, 'she has gone there to . . . Go on, you might as well read it.'

Whittington hesitated and then turned the paper over a second time.

11th October 1797

My dearest friend,

You will be surprised to read from the address of this letter that I am in Wiltshire! I hasten to explain that this is not the result of a whimsical desire for a change of scene, but of a determination to serve my dear friend, Miss Trent. Her mother, a resident of this place, is unfortunately suffering from a serious illness. (Indeed, in view of her age, I fear it may be her last.) Miss Trent, who is not so very robust herself, determined to go to her, and as it was a journey of some distance, I could not allow her to undertake it alone. Now that I am here, I am determined to remain for as long as my presence may in any way alleviate the suffering of either lady.

Yours most faithfully,

Mary Finch

P.S. Miss Trent begs to send her respectful compliments.

'The three of them in a country cottage,' Holland complained. 'I don't think I could face it.'

Whittington frowned in sympathy. 'No, perhaps not, but one makes these sacrifices for love, you know. Think of Leander. He swam the Hellespont on a nightly basis for the lovely Hero's sake – the least you could do would be to brave a pair of elderly females in . . . Ogbourne St Andrew. I daresay it is a charming place. The perfect rural retreat.'

'Charming,' said Holland.

'They might even like to hear about the improved mechanism. You could discuss it with them along with recipes for barley gruel and jam roly-poly.'

Holland folded his arms, and Whittington recognised that the matter was closed. Bob could be very stubborn sometimes – frequently, in fact – and when the arms were folded, the mule emerged. 'Well now, I really must be pushing along,' he affirmed, moving at last towards the door. 'Remember me to Miss Finch, when next you are in communication.'

'I will.'

'And let us have dinner when you come to Town . . . when you have been to the Admiralty.'

'So that I can tell you everything?'

Whittington smiled. 'You are damned suspicious. I expect the tars will discover that there *is* a sea monster – old Charybdis, and not a mine at all.'

'Hold on – I remember,' cried Holland, his expression easing at last. 'When you speak to your friend at the Admiralty, ask him to find out what he can about the *Cerberus*. It may be—'

'No, no,' said Whittington, 'wrong sort of creature entirely. Cerberus was the three-headed dog that guarded the entrance to hell. Undoubtedly fearsome, but prone to falling asleep at crucial moments, as I recall.'

'His Majesty's Ship *Cerberus*, you blockhead. It may be useful to know if any of the officers who served in her during the American war are alive and at hand.'

Whittington paused on the threshold. 'Useful as regards our present business? You speak in riddles, my friend.'

'Yes, I do, sometimes. Would you like Drake to see you to the main gate?'

Miss Trent would have been surprised, embarrassed, and secretly delighted to find herself the centre of so much epistolary attention, for even as the two gentlemen were reflecting upon Mary's letter, Miss Marchmont was penning one of her own to her friend at White Ladies. Unfortunately, its account of life at 12 Devonshire Square was almost as false as Mary's tale of a Wiltshire sojourn had been, but that could not be helped.

I am in the most impossible position, Miss Marchmont lamented as she wrote the salutation. *Having pledged myself to deceit, I am bound to disappoint someone.*

Like sentiments accompanied the rest of her efforts, for it was really a very difficult letter. Although she had written once

81

to Miss Trent since departing Suffolk, it had been a simple confirmation of her own safe arrival and of Mary's good health and unmarried status. Misleading, perhaps, in what it had *not* said, but not unduly troubling to one's conscience. Now, however, the situation was quite different. An edifice of lies, omissions, and half-truths must be created to hoodwink poor Miss Trent, and she, Miss Marchmont, must be its principal architect. Miss Trent, on the other hand, would be spending her days guilt-lessly, performing good works and reading devotional litera-ture. It was really most unfair.

Then she remembered that she was also misleading Mrs Tipton, and this somehow raised her spirits. Mrs Tipton would undoubtedly stir up some difficulty if she knew the true state of affairs, and *that* must be avoided at all costs. Why, it might even put Mary's safety at risk! Miss Marchmont hardened her heart. Very well, as it was in a good cause, she would deceive with the best of them. Indeed, it was her duty to do so.

There was also the comforting thought that no one was likely to know about it. So long as Mary returned safely to England – and Miss Marchmont would not allow herself to imagine otherwise – this little ruse would remain hidden. Quite without warning the description of *'Hypocrisy, the only evil that walks invisible, except to God alone'* occurred to her, but she forced it aside. She was *not* being hypocritical, and she had never really cared for Milton. She clasped her pen with renewed vigour.

Vigour, however, only got one so far. The parlour clock chimed the half hour, and Miss Marchmont sighed as she stared at the few bald lines she had managed to draft. *I really must do better than this.* Perhaps she ought to include as many true things as possible; they would help to leaven the untruths. She wrote, *'Mary and I have discussed making a visit to Dover to see the castle. Not a very pleasant journey at this time of year, but perhaps the three of us might consider it in the spring'* and contemplated a reference to Canterbury. Would it appeal to Miss Trent's general theological bent or expose her Dissenting bias? Dear Hetty had no truck with saints, certainly, at least not as regards their miraculous manifestations. 'But my dear,' she would ask, 'why would a sensible person *wish* to walk about with his head under his arm?'

The memory made Miss Marchmont smile, but presently she became aware of a confrontation of some kind taking place in the front passage. Voices were raised, or rather one voice. Vartan Nazarian was quarrelling with someone, but only his side of the argument was audible.

'Best of its kind, maybe, but we don't want . . . That is all, now. Go away, or I bring dog. *Hungry* dog . . . *Arjuk! Arjuk!* Here is very bad man!'

The front door slammed, and the bolt shot firmly into place. After a short pause, during which Miss Marchmont's pen hovered above the inkpot, the truculent *varich* strode triumphantly into the parlour, not unlike a cockerel that has disposed of his adversary in the pit. Then he caught a glimpse of something through the window and dashed the curtain aside, shaking his fist fiercely and mouthing imprecations.

'Good gracious, what is the matter?' asked Miss Marchmont.

'Ha!' growled Nazarian, straightening his skullcap. 'I see him off. I put the fly in his ears.'

'But who was it?'

'Only *mooratsgan* – beggar. In London there is too much beggaring and not enough working. In Aleppo it would not be allowed. The man's right hand would be cut off if he did not work. Then we would see.' He made a firm, chopping gesture with his left hand against his right.

Miss Marchmont forbore to comment on the efficacy of the practice and instead asked, 'Are you certain the fellow was not trying to sell something?'

'Oh yes, selling. That is what they say – but really, they are beggars. This one want to sell me candles. I tell him, we have plenty candles in this house.' If possible, his chest swelled more broadly.

'Well, he ought to have come to the tradesmen's entrance,' Miss Marchmont allowed. *And then Mrs Jakes could have dealt with him, without all of this rumpus.*

'Ought not to come at all. Every day they are coming here

– "buy soap", "buy string", "buy broom". *I* buy broom and sweep them all away.'

'It does sound like a nuisance,' said Miss Marchmont, 'people knocking at the door all day. But what did you mean about a dog?'

'That is secret,' admitted Nazarian craftily. 'That is what I tell them. But maybe we should have a real dog to frighten beggars and also criminals, if they come. I will find one, maybe.'

The image of Slipper appeared fleetingly to Miss Marchmont. Such a bad-tempered, snappy little dog, rather like Nazarian, in fact. They even had the same white moustaches. 'Mm, perhaps,' she agreed cautiously, and when she was alone again, she wrote, *'Nazarian, our butler, is thinking of buying a dog to discourage peddlers. One wonders whether the sound of barking would be more or less irksome than their patter. I do hope that Slipper has been behaving himself and is not causing you any anxiety.'*

7

Travellers who broke their journey at the posting inn at Chantilly, particularly those fortunate enough to secure a table near the window, were afforded a view across the park of the old château. And the park, travellers were informed, had not been much harmed 'during the bad times'; its beauties remained.

Mary had this good fortune, but the view held little interest for her. Perhaps the park did not show of its best that morning, for the sky was grey, and drops of rain spattered, now against the glass, now onto the stone sill, and now in the puddles on the road. The dismal weather, however, merely echoed Mary's present disposition, for she was thinking of the incorrigible Lagroix. How much longer would they be delayed?

The door rattled behind her, and a jolly, masculine voice greeted the landlady. Mary did not look up, even when footsteps moved in her direction.

'Good morning, miss — madam, I should say.' He chuckled. 'That is the best of the new forms of address, don't you think? With "citizeness", one is always correct.'

'Yes, certainly,' Mary agreed, and now she faced the speaker.

Politeness and the man's friendly tone caused her expression to soften. She was becoming accustomed to seeing French soldiers, and he did not look so very formidable — chubby and curly-haired, with soft brown eyes that crinkled at the corners, as if he might need spectacles. The absence of a substantial pair of moustaches also stood in his favour.

He introduced himself as Sergeant Fondard, but expressed surprise at her reply. 'Vangenzen?' he repeated, cocking his head like a dog that had received an unfamiliar command. 'But you are not a Dutchwoman, I think. Perhaps you are from England?'

She admitted as much, and explained that she was the wife of an American.

'Ah, perhaps I saw your husband outside. There looked to be some trouble with your machine.' As he was speaking the landlady cleared away the remains of Mary's breakfast and set down a cup of coffee at the place opposite. 'May I join you, Citizeness Vangenzen?'

What answer could she give? And there did not seem to be any harm in him. 'Yes, if you please.'

Fondard moved with that lightness characteristic of some heavy men, and his speech was similarly mild-mannered. Having laughingly described his military career as essentially literary (he carried his superiors' letters between Paris and the Chantilly depot), he apologised for not offering to assist with the *chaise*. 'Unfortunately, I do not comprehend machines of any kind – nor horses, apart from my dear Jacou. I would be of little help.'

'Indeed, I doubt whether my husband does much good either, but he hopes by his presence to encourage our postilion.'

'Oh ho, that one. You think he has the . . . *"lazy bones"*, as the English say?'

'I certainly do,' said Mary, 'although at present his trouble seems to arise chiefly from the calendar. Or rather, the *calendars*,' she added, reading the question in Fondard's eyes. 'Yesterday, as you know, was the thirtieth day of Vendémiaire according to the new calendar – one of the three rest days of the month.'

'Yes.'

'Being a good citizen of the Republic, our postilion said he did not like to work on a day of rest. We managed to overcome his objections, but only at the price of much grumbling and hard looks – and we travelled a mere fifty miles.'

'Well,' Fondard allowed, 'it is an unfortunate situation for you, who are in a hurry, but—' He shrugged his shoulders. 'A man must have his rest.'

'Indeed he must, but today is the twenty-second of October according to the old calendar, and Lagroix says that, being also a good Catholic, he cannot possibly work any more enthusiastically on a Sunday!'

Never had Mary seen an expression change so quickly from resignation to merriment, and to a smile in which twinkling was so much in evidence. 'He invokes the rest day *and* the sabbath? Oh, the scoundrel!'

'Of course, he may well be a good Catholic, and there are many people in England who would not wish to travel on a Sunday, but I cannot help thinking—'

'You think very rightly, I am sure of it,' said Fondard, laughing and scowling at the same time. 'I think this fellow wears both his patriotism and his religion too lightly.'

'And now I fear that our repairs will prove so complicated that we cannot continue today – and that tomorrow will prove to be the national holiday for coachmen!'

'Indeed it would, if your postilion had the naming of the days,' chuckled Fondard. He rose and straightened his coat, assuming as he did so a more serious mien. 'For the honour of France, I think perhaps that I will add my encouragement to that of your husband.'

Possibly by coincidence, Lagroix located the trouble with the *chaise* shortly after the sergeant made his appearance and stood, arms folded, beside Vangenzen. The repair followed, and all were ready to depart in less than an hour. *All* in this case included Fondard himself. He had business in Paris, he said, and if they did not mind his company, he might be of assistance in the event of 'further difficulties'. Travel, after all, was unpredictable at the best of times. Lagroix made an inarticulate, grumbling noise at this observation, but both Mary and Vangenzen expressed pleasure at the prospect of the sergeant's presence for the final stages of the journey.

'Is this Jacou?' asked Mary, as a stable boy led out a large, rough-coated animal, grey in colour, and more like a carthorse than a charger. The rain had stopped, and she stood in the road, stroking the horse's nose while Fondard tied two large leather satchels behind his saddle – the first containing his letters and the second a substantial meal prepared for him by the land-lady.

'Yes, this is Jacou. A good fellow, ugh—' Fondard grunted as he swung himself into the saddle '—who never complains.'

So they set off towards Paris, with Fondard sometimes approaching to converse about the weather or the condition of the road, but more often keeping to himself. As the day wore on, he sang snatches of Republican songs in a mellow baritone, and while Mary would have preferred to hear less about the sound of the cannons, aristocrats being hanged from lampposts, and the inevitability of French victory, she knew that she mustn't be squeamish about such things. The sergeant was merely being patriotic, after all, and 'Heart of Oak' and 'Britons Strike Home' would undoubtedly sound equally unpleasant to anyone in England who was loyal to France. *Although I hope there are not very many of those*, she added thoughtfully.

She and Vangenzen had little conversation. For her part, Mary was thinking about Paris. Like everyone in England who could read a newspaper or understand a cartoon, she knew the dreadful stories of what had taken place in the French capital since the fall of the monarchy. The massacres, the executions, the lust for blood so powerful that a machine had been devised in order to despatch victims more quickly. Surely a city where such evil had taken place would not be unmarked by the experience. Some memory of that time must survive in its people. Its very streets and buildings must have absorbed the Terror. And that was where she was going, not as a prisoner but willingly.

Receipt of a fresh team at Ecoun invigorated Lagroix – that and a warning from Fondard that the neighbourhood north of Paris was not always safe at night. Consequently, they reached Montmartre in the late afternoon, when there was just enough light for Mary to see the windmills and appreciate the wide, tree-lined road that led to the capital. Fondard explained that there were immense gypsum quarries on – or rather, *beneath* – Montmartre, and it was from these quarries that Paris had been built. 'As we say, there is more of Montmartre in Paris than there is of Paris in Montmartre, ha ha!'

At last they reached the city wall and halted before a pair of stout, firmly closed gates. Paris, it seemed, had no welcome for them. The evening sky looked cheerless, while a brisk wind blew wisps of cloud above their heads and rattled the leather covering of their *chaise*. Mary shivered, and for a moment she experienced a perverse wish that they would be denied entry, that she would be turned away and sent back – where?

To England, of course. Then she smiled at herself. *Do not be absurd. If they stopped you, it would mean that you were suspected of being a desperate person, and then there would be no returning to England! Indeed, they would probably insist that you remained – to be imprisoned, and tried, and . . .*

A member of the National Guard approached and demanded their passports. He glanced briefly at the documents with the air of a person not wholly comfortable with the printed word, and, after an injunction against moving, returned to one of the wooden booths that flanked the gates. Mary shot Vangenzen an uneasy look and then flinched at the sound of a voice on her other side. Sergeant Fondard had dismounted and was leaning against the wheel of the *chaise*.

'These fellows – they know their duty, but sometimes they are not so helpful,' he acknowledged. 'But do not worry, my friends. I will explain the situation.'

'Oh, would you?' asked Mary, turning towards him. 'We would be so grateful.'

'But of course.' Fondard blinked and smiled. 'For the honour of France!'

As she watched him approach the booth, humming the tune of *La Carmagnole*, Mary was conscious of his bulk; it made him seem both trustworthy and ineffectual. Would such an essentially soft, good-natured fellow have much influence with the National Guard of Paris? Its members, she knew, were Jacobins of the worst kind.

Vangenzen offered an account of the history of the wall and its magnificent toll barriers – but she listened vaguely. 'A system of tolls paid to farmers? I am not surprised that it has been done away with.'

'No, no, the General Farm collected taxes on behalf of the king. The Farmers were not agriculturalists, but enormously rich administrators – tyrants and blood-suckers, some said.'

'I see. And they built a wall around the city to prevent people entering – to prevent them paying—'

'To prevent certain persons from entering *unless* they had paid the tax. It was actually on goods rather than people, and was very unpopular.'

'Yes, of course. It would have been. Unpopular, I mean.'

Time passed. A second guard emerged from the twilight and peered at them. Mary shifted in her seat, and Vangenzen was considering a second foray into French administrative history when she remarked, as if their conversation had not flagged, 'In America, one either pays the tax or flings the goods into the sea. Is that not so?'

Vangenzen smiled at her. 'Something like that.'

Mary smiled back, but her assurance wobbled when the first guardsman returned, accompanied by Sergeant Fondard. The sergeant bore a shaded lantern, but it was impossible to judge either man's expression in the dim light.

Vangenzen's passport was handed over, and he was asked to confirm his address. 'The Maison de Chevrons, in the Rue Beauregard.'

'Which section?'

'Bonne Nouvelle.'

'There, you see?' urged Fondard. He opened the lantern and held it aloft, as if it were the light of truth.

'You have registered with the minister of police?' demanded the guardsman blandly.

'Yes, citizen. When I first arrived in Paris and again when I moved to my current lodgings.'

The guardsman nodded and returned Vangenzen's papers. 'Very well. Your wife must also register. Tomorrow morning will be soon enough. You must both go and explain your circumstances.'

He then stared at Mary for what felt like a very long time. It was important, she reminded herself, not to *look* guilty. Did that mean that she ought to smile? Appear surprised at the delay? *No*, she decided, *they might imagine that I was not taking their procedures seriously.* She composed her features into what she hoped was an expression of deferential alertness. Her papers were also returned.

There was a further exchange about Lagroix – was he Citizen Vangenzen's servant, or did he mean to return to Calais, or where was he going? *His* papers were not in a very satisfactory condition; one could scarcely understand what they said! Lagroix took exception to that remark, although in truth his passport looked very greasy, even by lantern light. His reply was sharp and combative. He would sleep at the Cheval Blanc in the Rue Mazet – as he had done these many years when he came to Paris with no objections from anyone – and depart for Calais in the morning, if that was not too much trouble.

The guardsman received this information with a slight pursing of the lips. 'Indeed. See that you depart by this gate. I will leave a note that you are expected, Citizen Lagroix.' He turned away before the postilion could signal either his gratitude or some other emotion, and stumped towards the gates, calling for his assistant to stir himself.

Fondard had remained beside the *chaise*, and now he asked softly, 'There, not so bad, eh? Like a fairytale. You pass through the gate – with the ogre – and enter the magic city.'

Mary inclined her head. 'Thank you for your assistance, sergeant.'

He grinned up at her. 'Not at all. It is good to have friends sometimes, and even better to help them.'

Lagroix grunted, either at the sentiment or to rouse his tired horses. This team had done the final two stages, and now they stood with heads bowed, as if they too were worried about their eligibility to tread the streets of Paris. The gates slid open with a grating sound, as the edge of one of the bars extended a semi-circular gouge in the pavement. The assistant was instructed to lift – had he not been told three times to lift that very day? Did he have wax in his ears or a marrow for brains? The horses advanced, were frightened by the noise and halted, shaking their heads distractedly. But they stepped through the open portal at the second time of asking and increased their pace to a shambling trot. Mary leaned out of the *chaise* to wave goodbye to Fondard, and he raised his hand in reply.

Vangenzen exhaled like one who had been holding his breath and clasped Mary's hand companionably. 'Here we are at last.'

Mary agreed, but her first impressions of the magic city were not particularly optimistic. Night had fallen while they were at the gate, and the streets were not so well lit as those of London. The *chaise* advanced slowly along what appeared to be a broad avenue, and then turned right into a narrow way that led uphill. Buildings, more felt than seen, stood closely on either side, and she tried not to acknowledge the feeling of oppression, of being overlooked by gloomy, unfriendly eyes. An empty bell tower looked like a gaping hole in the sky.

They halted before a row of buildings and unloaded their baggage. Then came the parting with Lagroix, which was performed with little ceremony. On receiving the final instalment of his fee, he merely shrugged and fingered the coins before placing them in his pocket. A tip had been included, but not a very large one.

'Farewell, Lagroix, and good luck,' said Vangenzen, to which the other grumpily replied, 'Good luck, citizens.' Then he flicked his whip in advance of the horses, and they trudged forward. In a few paces he had disappeared into the darkness.

Just as quickly, Mary dismissed him from her thoughts. Lagroix belonged to the journey, but now the journey was over. They had reached the Maison des Chevrons, and somewhere behind those darkened shutters was Minta Vangenzen, who knew nothing of her husband's new wife. *Good luck indeed*, Mary repeated to herself; *I hope I shall have it.*

Vangenzen opened a pair of heavy wooden doors that gave way to a small lobby, and Mary stepped inside. An oil lamp revealed the first steps of a plain stone staircase and wooden balustrade, both curving upwards into darkness. 'If you will light the way,' he suggested, handing her a lighted candle, 'I will follow you.'

Mary cupped her hand to preserve the flame, as Vangenzen heaved the largest trunk to waist height. Up they climbed, the feeble light throwing flickering shadows on the plastered walls and the central stone pillar. No sounds issued from the doors they passed, nor did their own footfalls provoke a response. Only the building seemed to change; the treads and risers becoming steeper and narrower, and the space between floors decreasing. The first floor landing was large and spacious, the second seemed smaller, and the third was positively dwarfish, with a low ceiling and mean, narrow entrance.

Vangenzen edged past her – there was only just sufficient room when he had set down the trunk – and unlocked the door. It was dark within.

'Minta seems not to be at home,' he said, 'but I daresay she will return directly. She sometimes visits a neighbour of ours in the evenings – a bookseller.'

From relief that their meeting had been postponed, Mary quickly decided that Minta's absence had rendered the situation more difficult. For now she would return and find Mary ensconced in *her* home, and under such strange circumstances.

Vangenzen ran down the stairs and returned, puffing, with the rest of their baggage. Then he conducted Mary along a narrow, inner passage and into the sitting-room. The furnishings were haphazard, with unmatched chairs, a heavy oak settle piled with cushions, and a round table of a lighter, finer design, but everything was clean and well tended. The addition of small items of decoration, moreover, imparted a sense of style to the room that Mary found reassuring.

But what did you expect, she scolded herself, *a room full of Jacobins, sharpening their knives in the dark? Undoubtedly, this is the home of an artist.*

The artist in question was on his knees beside a corner alcove, busily investigating the internal compartment of what appeared to be a ceramic tree – its roots formed squat legs and its trunk disappeared into the ceiling.

'Is it a stove?' asked Mary, wonderingly. 'I have never seen such a thing.'

'We used to have an open fire,' Vangenzen explained, 'but it smoked terribly and was a nuisance to tend. I bought this with the proceeds of a portrait I painted two years ago and had it specially fitted.'

'Whoever designed it must have had a sense of humour – a tree that burns wood.'

'That is what first appealed to me about it. Fortunately, it also heats the *appartement* wonderfully well, and even keeps the chill from my studio.'

With the heat from the stove steadily warming the room, Vangenzen announced his intention of leaving her for a short while, in order to purchase some supper from the café at the end of the street. 'Their food is quite good, but they always seem to dawdle when one is particularly hungry. I shan't be long,' he added, somewhat illogically, 'and do please make yourself at home.'

That was precisely what Mary did not intend to do, but to prove to herself that she was not at all nervous she moved to examine the bookcase that stood, or rather leaned, beside a painted door at the far end of the room. The books were mainly an assortment of prose and poetry – works by Racine, a complete set of Shakespeare's plays, an illustrated copy of John Gay's *Fables*, and *La Gerusaleme Liberata*. There was also a well-thumbed French grammar, several volumes on plants and human anatomy, and pamphlets by Thomas Paine.

An expensive-looking copy of *Les Quatre Fils d'Aymon* had an inscription on the frontispiece that read: *'For Guillaume, with sincere admiration, T'*. Before she had time to query this message, the sound of voices in the passageway caused her to close the book and return it swiftly to its place. She was on her feet when Vangenzen swept into the room. His face was flushed, but not, it seemed, simply as a result of the climb.

'Our supper!' he cried, setting down his burdens on the round table. 'And see who I found on the stairs. Minta?' He waited until a woman, still wearing her cloak and bonnet, slipped in after him. 'Minta, this is . . . I suppose she is Mrs Vangenzen.' He paused. 'And Mary' – it was the first time he had so addressed her – 'this is my wife.'

Minta inclined her head solemnly. 'Good evening.' At first she kept her eyes lowered, then she glanced cautiously at the visitor.

Mary scarcely knew how to reply. Vangenzen must have said *something*, but what kind of explanation could he possibly have given on the stairs, or in the street? And then there was Minta herself. Mary had never actually spoken with an African before, nor seen one close to. Until that moment, her nearest contact had been the pamphlets of the anti-slavery society, of whose efforts Miss Trent was a fervent supporter. 'I am so grateful to you,' she said at last. 'And I am terribly sorry to . . . intrude upon you in this way.'

Minta's gaze flickered in her husband's direction. 'You are welcome in our house,' she said, her voice low and faintly musical, 'and I daresay you are tired from your long trip and wanting supper. Will you excuse me for a moment?'

She retreated, murmuring something to Vangenzen, and then disappeared through the still open door. He moved to the side-board and extracted plates, bowls, cutlery, and glasses, which he carried to the table.

'May I help?' asked Mary, as he arranged the places.

'Oh no,' he assured her. 'I am under strict orders to allow no such thing. Tonight you are the guest.'

'But—' Drawing nearer, she mouthed the words, 'Is it all right? What did you say?'

'Eh?' He hesitated, glasses in either hand, and then affirmed, 'Of course it is all right. I told you that it would be.'

Just then Minta returned, having cast off her outdoor things. Dressed now in a plain woollen gown and apron, with neat leather shoes replacing the heavy sabots, her beauty was apparent. Her skin was the colour of *café au lait*, and above a high, rounded forehead, her black hair was gathered in glossy ringlets. 'Are we ready?' she asked.

'More than ready,' Vangenzen replied. 'And I for one am perfectly ravenous.'

'Than shall we give thanks? First for Samuel's safe return and then for Mary's' – she hesitated only for a moment – 'safe arrival.'

While supper was being eaten at the Maison de Chevrons, Sergeant Fondard was pursuing the business that had brought him to Paris. He had described himself to Mary as a military postman, and in a way this was true. He did bear letters having to do with the security of the nation, and what soldier was not concerned with the same? He also wore the uniform of the Army of the Revolution, such as it was, for in those days soldiers of France could be found dressed in the white coats of the old royal army, the blue coats of the volunteers, and even civilian dress augmented by the cockade and the Phrygian cap. Perhaps he adopted a rather humble military character to suit his convenience rather than to satisfy any lawful obligation, but such deceptions are not unknown in wartime, and Fondard served his country as enthusiastically as any combatant.

That it was a deception was evident from his welcome at the several addresses he visited across the city. His letters were received with great deference, and if he stopped to read those given in return he was generally favoured with a private office, which might have been surprising for a mere sergeant. At the Conciergerie, the infamous seat of Revolutionary justice, he sent out for a meal, and again no one questioned the order or suggested that he might be satisfied with the fare provided to the soldiers guarding the prisoners. The patient Jacou was also well treated, and when his master decided to travel to his final assignation by carriage, it was accepted that Jacou would be housed comfortably until called for.

Fondard arrived at the Temple prison at ten o'clock, just about the time that Mary was being shown to her bedchamber. Fondard too wanted his bed, much more so than a meeting with Augier, the deputy governor. He had no great liking for the man, and so had left the Temple until last so as to discommode Augier, but that was scant consolation when he was himself nodding in his carriage.

On arrival, he went directly to Augier's office, a set of rooms in what had formerly been the grand prior's palace. Its incumbent was a small, thin man, as unlike Fondard in temperament as he was in physiognomy. Augier disliked these interviews, and never more so than when Fondard chose to play the bluff comrade. It was on those occasions that he was most dangerous – like a great, shuffling bear, whose blows were no less deadly for being random.

'Oh Lord,' he muttered, as the melody of *La Carmagnole* drifted down the passage. Footsteps followed, and then a peremptory knock. 'Enter.'

Fondard loped into the room, his tunic unbuttoned at the throat. 'Well, Augier, old stick, what have you for me today?'

'*Tonight*, you mean,' grumbled Augier. The candles on his desk flickered in the draught. 'And close the door, won't you?'

'Hmm?' Fondard gazed about him, as if he had been unaware of the time. 'Yes, I suppose you are used to more fashionable hours, but the work of the Republic, you know, does not sleep.' Almost as an afterthought, he closed the door.

With a terse nod, Augier indicated a slim file of papers on the corner of his desk. 'Here it is.'

'Indeed, only one? What is it?'

'A Royalist spy – or rather, a courier.' Augier shrugged dismissively. 'Captured in Arles. He presented himself at a rendezvous, but his accomplice had already been apprehended. He was not, therefore, carrying anything of substance, only a token that established his character with his friends – and us.'

'You have questioned him?'

'Naturally.'

Fondard opened the file and scanned the first page. Then he hoisted himself onto Augier's desk, his substantial buttocks upsetting a separate stack of the deputy governor's correspondence. One ought to get some enjoyment out of this tiresome business, after all, and how better than by baiting old Augier?

Augier endured this insolence – as he judged it – for almost three minutes, at which point he pushed back his chair with a huff of exasperation. Neither that nor the complaint of the chair legs against the stone floor had any effect upon Fondard, who continued to read placidly.

At last he closed the file. 'Very well. A Royalist courier – a minnow, who ought never to have been brought to Paris. You recommend execution?'

Augier shrugged again. 'According to the law the sentence is clear.'

'I agree,' said Fondard. 'I had better see him, however.'

'As you wish. He is in the small tower.'

Augier led the way outside, across the courtyard and past the former church, and into the heart of the old fortress, where state prisoners were housed until the state had no further need of them. All the while he silently reviewed the measures that would be taken to speed this particular prisoner to his appointed end. It was a considerable procedure but Augier did not mind; indeed, he enjoyed the orderly arrangement of business by report, return, docket, and release. In that way, he was very suited to prison life, which must be well ordered to succeed. One could not lose prisoners, after all, and hope to continue in one's place! It had been difficult, during the Terror, to maintain the proper routine, but they had managed it at the Temple and were proud of their achievement.

'He can be transported first thing in the morning,' Augier noted, even taking some pleasure explaining things to Fondard. Whatever the fellow's bluster and bad manners, he had to conform to the Temple's schedule. Why, without Augier's good word, Fondard might whistle for an interview with a prisoner. 'The usual arrangement of guard and carriage will be sufficient, I think. I doubt if he gives any trouble in that way.'

'You mean to send him to the Conciergerie?'

'Well, a formal condemnation by the court is required,' said Augier. 'It is unlikely that the justices will wish to see him, but it is as well to be prepared for that eventuality. And then it is also more convenient for the Place de Grève. Getting him there will not be our responsibility, but I always instruct our men to stand by until the business is completed, for safety's sake. And we must have the proper release, of course.'

'The Place de Grève,' Fondard repeated. 'Does it occur to you, Citizen Augier, that the public execution of such a fellow is not in the best interest of the Republic?'

'Perhaps not.' Augier stopped to unlock a door. 'But since the, er, instrument is no longer generally in use in the Place de la Revolution, there are no special facilities for state prisoners, unfortunately. We have no choice but to bundle them in with the usual murderers and highwaymen.'

They began to climb a steep, curling stair. Every ten stairs or so lighted lanterns were set into niches in the wall, so that they moved between darkness and light.

'The people should be content with the ordinary criminals,' Fondard grumbled. 'Surely they provide entertainment enough. And this fellow is pale and tragic-looking, I suppose. Royalists generally are – the ones who are caught.'

'As to that, you must judge for yourself,' sniffed Augier. 'However, he *has* made a bit of a nuisance of himself by demanding to be shot. If he were to be condemned to death, I mean. He says that a firing squad befits his rank.'

'What rank? He is a child.'

'He claims to hold a commission from the king.'

'Bah!' Fondard waved a dismissive hand. 'What was good enough for his master is good enough for him.' He began to sing under his breath, *'Despotism will fade away / Liberty shall win the day / Ah, ça ira, ça ira, ça ira . . .'*

'Well, he has a rather romantic sensibility. A Catholic, of course, which is another difficulty, for Father Marcel is ill – or he was yesterday. A problem with his bowels, I understand.'

Augier stopped on the landing and indicated a heavy wooden door, blackened with age and ornamented by iron studs. 'Here it is.' He opened the judas and peered through it to the cell beyond. 'Do you wish me to announce you?' he whispered to Fondard.

Fondard shook his head and indicated that the door should be unlocked. 'And friend Augier . . .'

'Yes?'

'The man is a prisoner. You needn't whisper.'

Augier opened the door and then stepped back. Whatever interview Fondard intended, he could conduct it alone. Why was a further conversation with the prisoner necessary? Everything had been made perfectly clear in the report. *I suppose he considers it his responsibility, although I have never found him so punctilious before. Now, has anything been forgotten? Will they have a priest at the Conciergerie? I expect so. That would save time tomorrow morning, if we were not obliged to wait for Father Marcel. I sometimes wonder—*

Suddenly a shot rang out. Augier started and dropped his keys. 'Holy Mother of God!' he cried without thinking, or perhaps his mind was still on Father Marcel.

He sprang towards the door and almost into the arms of Fondard, who slipped out of the cell at that moment. He could move lightly when he chose. Behind him the smoke was still visible, and the tang of gunpowder followed him into the passage.

'What happened?' Augier demanded. 'What have you done?'

Fondard raised his pistol and then slipped it into his pocket. He was smiling. 'Oh, merely tidied things up. Political executions can be messy affairs, you know – much better this way. And I have given our little Royalist what he wanted. I expect he was grateful.'

'But . . .' Augier could not answer; he could scarcely appreciate what had occurred. Prisoners simply were not shot in the cells of the Temple! 'What of my records?' he wailed at last. 'What account shall I give of this affair in my report?'

'Say that he was shot trying to escape,' laughed Fondard. 'Or that he was a nuisance. *Ah, ça ira, ça ira, ça ira . . .*'

8

The Maison des Chevrons had originally belonged to a man named Antoine Chœur, one of Cardinal Richelieu's messengers in the last century. Built on the top of a low hill, it had afforded a view of the cardinal's palace, such that when a certain flag there was raised, Chœur could set off discreetly and without loss of time. Presumably, he had maintained a regular watch as well as a stable of horses, for it would not have done to disappoint the great cardinal, in whose hands the government of France had rested during the reign of Louis XIII.

Vangenzen explained the story over breakfast the following morning. 'Sometimes I have my doubts about Monsieur Chœur,' he acknowledged. '"Chœur" means choir, you know, which seems a very convenient name for a person who conveyed instructions. The cardinal's escutcheon exists above the door, however – the three chevrons were his symbol – so perhaps there is something in the tale.'

Mary nodded politely and even acknowledged that she hoped the story was true, but she was giving Vangenzen only half of her attention. With the other half she watched Minta, serenely pouring out the coffee and handing round the fresh rolls and butter. Mary had seldom seen anyone so calm, so apparently unmoved by the strange situation that had suddenly befallen her. It gave Minta a kind of strength; certainly she appeared far more dignified than her jovial husband. And yet it also made Mary uneasy. She would have preferred anger, surprise – certainly she had expected questions – but there had been nothing like that. Not a harsh word had passed Minta's lips, not even a curious glance after their first meeting, only a strange, detached civility. *As if my coming means nothing to her*, thought Mary. *And yet, how can it not?*

After breakfast the three of them went upstairs to view Vangenzen's studio. This consisted of a single room and occupied the top floor of the building. It could scarcely be called furnished, for the floor was bare, and the unadorned walls were painted chalky white. In one corner stood a cupboard filled with brushes, pencils, pots, and jars, and in another, canvases and rolls of paper were piled against the wall. Between them, a cloth-shrouded easel and three-legged stool had pride of place. The glory of this attic, however, and what made it an artist's workplace, was the windows: four large dormers admitting light from all directions.

They also admitted the cold, autumnal air, as Mary discovered when she stood before one of them, surveying the pattern of streets and rooftops. Minta briefly explained the immediate geography. Below was the Rue Beauregard, and the wide, tree-lined street was the Boulevard Bonne Nouvelle. 'And just there,' she added, pointing down the hill towards the Rue Franciade, 'that is where a man attempted to rescue the king as he was being conducted to his execution.'

'Really?' asked Mary, standing on tiptoes and craning her neck as if evidence of the deed might remain. 'What happened? Did you see it?'

Minta admitted that she had not. 'We lived in the Rue Perdu in those days, close to the river. I remember the day of the king's death, however. Most of our neighbours behaved as though it were a festival, a great event that would bring an end to all their misery. There was singing and dancing . . . and the execution of the queen caused even greater excitement, for she had long been unpopular.' She gazed down at the church where Louis's would-be rescuers had sought sanctuary after having failed to secure their prize. 'I suppose that some people mourned them, but not in the Rue Perdu.'

'I think you will find the view is better from this side,' called Vangenzen.

Mary joined him, and now she could see the heart of the city – lofty towers, gothic steeples, the upper storeys of grand townhouses, and here and there gardens like islands of green in a sea of tiles, slates, and thatch. 'Oh, yes,' she agreed. 'I expect this is where Monsieur Chœur watched for the flag. Can you see the cardinal's palace from here? Does it still exist?'

'Yes, it exists, although it has a different name now, like most things in Paris. I have never been able to identify the roof, however, nor the flag pole.'

Mary turned regretfully back into the room. 'It must be a wonderful place to paint,' she acknowledged, 'but with such views and such history on every side, I think I should find a great many distractions.'

'Ah, that reminds me,' said Vangenzen, cautiously. He darted a look at Minta. 'I, er, had some unfortunate news when I was in London. Citizen Barthélemy has been deported to Guiana.'

The change in Minta was immediate, her poise slipping as clearly as a dancer's who had missed her step. 'Oh, my dear!' she cried. 'Your lovely portrait!'

'Yes, I doubt he wants it now.'

Vangenzen removed the canvas from the easel and revealed a half-finished painting. It depicted the head and shoulders of an older man in a plain coat and neck cloth. The features were incomplete, but the eyes conveyed an interesting mixture of compassion and calculation.

'Citizen Barthélemy was a diplomat and member of the Directory,' he informed Mary. 'Unfortunately, he was on the losing side in the most recent political troubles. I suppose he was lucky not to have been executed, but the "dry guillotine" is certainly no pardon. They say the fevers in the Guiana jungles are so terrible that few who are sent there survive for long.'

Mary nodded. 'In England too it is considered a death sentence. But with the other sort of guillotine as the alternative, I would take my chances with the jungle. In fact—'

'Dead or exiled, I doubt whether Citizen Barthélemy will

have much need of a portrait,' Minta complained, 'or will pay for the work that has already been done.'

'If only I had managed to complete it before he got himself into trouble,' said Vangenzen. 'Ah well. "If wishes were horses . . ." It was good practice, and I can always show it as proof of my ability if I am asked to paint another portrait.'

Mary glanced from wife to husband – one downcast and the other determined to make the best of things – and tried to redirect the conversation. 'How does one obtain artistic commissions?' She nodded at the painting. 'Had you known him beforehand?'

Vangenzen shook his head. 'I cannot remember quite how it came about – very likely someone knew someone, and I did not charge a very high fee. That is the usual way, until one becomes very famous, and then the clients seek you out. I wish that David would put in a good word for me. He is offered many more commissions than he can accept, and sometimes he recommends another artist to the client.'

'Well, if he has any clients to spare, please tell him not another politician,' urged Minta. 'Find someone nice and steady to paint, like a banker or his wife.'

'Shall I tell him that?' asked Vangenzen with a twinkling smile. 'Or perhaps I should ask about General Bonaparte – would he suit? If I were to paint a flattering likeness of him it would make our fortune.'

After stiffening, Minta surrendered to laughter and shook her head. 'No, thank you. A nice, steady banker who pays his bill would be fortune enough for me.'

Minta's laugh made a difference to Mary – that and the close clasp of her hand as Mary buttoned up her cloak in preparation for her interview at the Ministry of Police. Vangenzen had turned aside to find his gloves and did not see the wordless exchange between the two women. On one side, an entreaty to be careful, especially for Vangenzen's sake, and on the other, an assurance that she would do all she could not to expose him to danger. At least, that was how Mary interpreted it.

Receiving this mark of trust made her feel more confident, and as she and Vangenzen descended the hill towards the Rue Franciade, some of her natural curiosity returned. She observed everything about her with great interest, from the café that had provided their supper to the old man pushing a handcart filled with bolts of fabric. The wooden sabots worn by men and women of the poorer sort made an odd, clopping sound, but they were exactly the right footwear for streets without footpaths. Streets, moreover, that sloped towards 'the kennel', a noisome central ditch. The unwary pedestrian could easily find himself forced by slippery conditions and the press of traffic to pursue an insecure and insalubrious route, and without proper footwear – disaster!

By keeping a close hold on Vangenzen's arm, however, Mary could maintain her balance and also gaze about in relative safety. She stared into all of the shop windows – a milliner's, a notary's office, the bookseller's where Minta helped the proprietor, the widow Girard. Then they were at the bottom of the hill, and a monumental structure loomed up in front of them. Massive and beautiful with a vast arch mounted upon two smaller ones, the creamy stone was decorated with sculptures depicting the military triumphs of Louis XIV. Formerly, kings and queens wishing to make a ceremonial entrance to Paris had processed through the Porte St Denis and then driven south along the Rue St Denis, perhaps to the cathedral of Notre Dame. The arch and street remained, but they had lost their saintly associations, while the cathedral now paid homage to Reason rather than to God.

'Ho, there!' called Vangenzen, gesturing towards a line of cabriolets – trim, two-wheeled vehicles, rather like hackney carriages. 'Oh, bother – that one is engaged. Let's see about that one – ho!' and he hurried Mary forward.

This time they were successful, and Vangenzen handed her into the cabriolet before settling beside her on the seat. The attendant passed him the reins. 'Do you know the way, citizen?' He nodded at Vangenzen's affirmative reply and climbed up behind.

'Is it usual to drive oneself?' asked Mary, as they set off.

'I cannot imagine attempting such a thing in London – or a coachman who would allow it.'

'Well, London is bigger and busier than Paris,' said Vangenzen, who appeared reassuringly capable as he manoeuvred their vehicle into the stream of traffic. 'But I believe that the aristocrats drove – or were driven – quite furiously before the Revolution, and the streets are becoming very crowded again.'

They followed a rather unusual route towards the river, in order to avoid the worst congestion. Along the way Vangenzen explained the basic geography of Paris. On the right bank were the markets, the former royal palaces, and many of the old convents and townhouses, while the university and the hospitals stood on the left bank. 'The Bastille was also on the right bank, and while the eastern part of the city used to be the more fashionable, at least on this side of the river, now the cream of society is moving west towards the Champs Élysées.'

Mary listened attentively. She liked to be able to orient herself, and this knowledge might prove important in the future. 'What I do not understand,' she acknowledged, 'is why one speaks of the Seine as having a left and right bank. Surely a north and south bank would be more correct. In London we speak of "the Surrey side" of the Thames, but Surrey does not move about, according to which way one is facing. Do people not find this business of "left" and "right" very confusing?'

'No, I don't think that they do,' said Vangenzen. 'I suppose . . . well, to be honest, I have never thought of it before.'

Mary nodded, but continued to turn the matter over privately. She wondered if perhaps an important event had taken place sometime in the history of Paris, when everyone was facing in the same direction. *An event when everyone was facing in the same direction? Do be sensible! Churches generally face east, but that would make the south bank 'right' and the north bank 'left', so that cannot be right – correct, I mean.*

Their cabriolet rumbled across the Pont Neuf, and as they proceeded along the Rue du Colombier she remembered that Julius Caesar had very likely arrived in Paris from the east – perhaps *he* had determined how left and right ought to be understood according to his first orientation. It seemed like the sort of thing he would have done. Perhaps she should suggest this to Vangenzen. She turned to him.

'Here we are,' he announced.

'Where?'

'The Hôtel de Police, of course.' He nodded at a forbidding stone structure, formerly a bishop's townhouse.

The Ministry – already! Oh why had she wasted time with Caesar when she ought to have been thinking about the Ministry of Police, and steeling herself for another ghastly interview?

She did not voice her fear, but some hint of it must have been communicated to her companion. Or perhaps the dour stone façade and the knowledge of what lay behind it were also making him nervous.

'We have had no trouble thus far,' he reminded her. 'I see no reason why this should be any different.'

'You said that you have done this before?'

'Oh yes,' he replied, with an affected lightness. 'It was all quite straightforward.'

And so, to their great relief, it proved on this occasion. They joined a long queue, and when they reached the front, their case was not handled by the minister, but by minor functionaries who viewed the range of seals and signatures adorning Mary's several documents with professional pleasure. It was the sort of thing they appreciated and saw too little of nowadays, with everybody in a hurry and no one taking pride in his work. ('Say what you like about them, citizen, but the English gener- ally produce good documents.' 'I never said anything about them, but this seal is very fine. Tell me, citizen, is the arch- bishop of Canterbury a *real* archbishop?' 'Real like the bishop of Autun, eh? Ha ha! No, their archbishop is a heretic like the rest of the English – but his seal is good.')

The whole process took over an hour, but when at last they retraced their steps across the courtyard, Mary was the proud possessor of a valid *carte de residence*. This document, she had been sternly informed, must be produced in the event of a food shortage, or a disturbance on the street, or trouble. The open-ended nature of the last word gave her pause, but she resolved not to let it worry her.

A stout figure at one of the first-floor windows watched them depart. Had they chosen to look back they would have seen him, for his blue coat stood out starkly against the cream of the draperies, but they were absorbed by their conversation and did not turn.

Mary's hand touched Vangenzen's arm, and the man in the window frowned, his lower lip protruding. He remained in this pose until disturbed by footsteps in the passage behind him. Turning, he beckoned to one of the clerks, who halted cautiously in the doorway. 'Those English documents – you are certain they were genuine?'

The clerk flinched. He *had* been certain until that moment, but he was not so resolute in character that he could lightly endure questioning from Citizen Fondard (for no one addressed him as 'sergeant' in the former Hôtel de Juigné). His reply came cautiously. 'Er, yes.'

'You are familiar with their forms?'

'Yes, citizen – from the old days.' The clerk paused, glancing first at Fondard and then at the other occupant of the room before adding, 'If there had been some suspicion – I mean – if it had been mentioned to us . . .'

Fondard shook his head. 'No, I have no suspicion, and it is better that you considered the papers in the usual way, without prejudice.' He smiled at the clerk. 'Had there been an irregularity, it would have revealed itself to you without any prompting from me, eh?'

The clerk smiled nervously. One did not bow, nowadays, but he bobbed his head, and his arms seem to spread of their own volition. 'I trust it would have been so, citizen.'

'Very well then, that is all. Ah, wait a moment. You are off to Anton's? Bring me a cup as well, will you? There's a good fellow. And perhaps a slice of his chestnut tart.'

Fondard returned to his desk and sat down, but his smile faded as he stared across a pile of papers to the small, unshaven man perched on the edge of a wooden chair, a cocked hat clutched between his gnarled fingers. 'Well?' he growled. 'A mistake has been made, it seems.'

Lagroix shrugged irritably. 'Not by me. *I* never said there was anything wrong. The Committee had some suspicions, not me. They told me only to watch and listen, and if possible to turn them over to you.' The postilion's voice assumed an aggrieved tone, but he did not dare to raise his eyes. 'I have done what was asked of me, exact to the last detail. Why should I be made to suffer an interrogation . . . like a common criminal?'

Fondard studied him dispassionately. 'Patience, my dear Lagroix, I am nearly finished. And this is not an interrogation, merely a friendly chat. So, you watched and you listened, and learned nothing of interest about these two young travellers?'

'No. In my presence they spoke only of America . . . and art.'

'And when they were alone? As a diligent servant of the Committee, I am certain that you seized every chance to listen to their private conversations?'

Lagroix shrugged again and shifted uncomfortably in his chair. The skin across his knuckles whitened. 'I tried to, but it was not always possible – there were servants about. And when they were alone they spoke English.' He hesitated, and then finished in a hurried bluster. 'I did as I was told. If things went wrong, the blame lies with the Committee.'

'Oh, I quite agree that the Committee are a set of prize fools,' Fondard agreed, 'and the plainest evidence is the fact that they imagined you could perform such a simple task as listening at a door.' In front of him was a paper with a long list of names. He made a notation next to 'Vangenzen, Citizen Samuel' and 'Vangenzen, Citizeness Mary' and observed, 'No harm has been done, fortunately, other than to waste my time, but in that you are not alone. Very well, that is all.' He laid down his pen.

'I can go?' asked Lagroix suspiciously.

'Of course.' Fondard frowned with impatience when the other man did not move. 'Hurry up, I said that you could go! I haven't all day, you know. Go, and tell the next person in line outside to come in.'

★　★　★

109

Vangenzen had paid off their cabriolet upon arriving at the Ministry, so he and Mary crossed the Pont National on foot, in search of another vehicle. As they walked they agreed that their next task must be to visit Mr Shy's agent in Paris – the man whom Shy could not do without.

His name was Tobias Jens, and he could be found at an establishment known as Vrillac's, which sold artists' supplies. It was frequented by students and artists alike, the former dreaming of the day when they might place an order for crow quills and English rubbers, and the latter aware that 'old Jens' would have hog-bristle brushes and prime linseed oil when no one else did. It was also a print shop, dealing with copies of well-known paintings, illustrations, maps, and scientific drawings. On first arriving in Paris, Vangenzen had found essential employment colouring prints for Vrillac's, and he still enjoyed browsing there. This was fortunate, for it meant that his visits, even when not of a strictly professional nature, were unlikely to attract attention.

'Who is Vrillac?' asked Mary. 'Do you know him?'

'He was *"M. de Vrillac, fournisseur de Beaux-Arts"* according to the card in the shop window,' Vangenzen explained, 'but that is all I know. I imagine he is long dead, for the card is very faded, and no one uses *"monsieur"* any more – I believe it has been proscribed. Perhaps there never was such a person, and Jens created him to make the place seem more French. He is Swiss, you know. Ah, here is a cabriolet.'

They did not re-cross the river, but drove eastward along the quays, where stallholders had set out their wares. Mary was surprised at the variety of goods on offer – everything from bedsteads to footstools and from hairpins to greatcoats – and the assumption that customers would purchase them in such a venue. Pointing at an elaborate picture frame, she asked whether Parisians were really likely to visit the Quai de l'Ecole to find a frame that would set off their latest painting by Vangenzen?

The artist demurred with his usual modesty, but he affirmed that the stalls generally did a brisk trade. 'After '93, it became

110

possible to buy a great many things here – and often for very good prices.'

Although casually spoken, his words were chilling. *After '93?* thought Mary. *My goodness, he means during the Terror* . . . She pictured the odd assortment of furniture in the Vangenzen *appartement*. Were some of those pieces plundered from a château or a prosperous townhouse? And what had become of 'Guillaume', the erstwhile owner of the copy of *Les Quatre Fils d'Aymon* that she been perusing only the previous evening? Had he been executed? Or had he perhaps escaped and been declared an émigré? Both fates would have led to the seizure of his property – either by the agents of the Republic or by private persons with an eye to the main chance.

Vangenzen coughed and made a slight gesture to remind her of the servant perched behind them. Of course she would say nothing, but her spirits were dampened. It seemed that everywhere one turned in Paris there was evidence of violence and death, and the more one saw of smashed windows, of gates torn from their hinges, or of finery displayed like a pirate's hoard, the more difficult it was to believe that the time of looting and killing had ended, and might not begin again – perhaps without warning.

This feeling was sensibly increased when the mighty stone towers of the Conciergerie came into view, for who in England had not heard of the awful Revolutionary court where the queen had been condemned and hundreds more imprisoned and tried? Even at a safe distance she felt dwarfed by such a display of power, for this was no ruin, no testament to medieval barbarity. Its horrors belonged to the present age.

So too the Châtelet, a fortress built to guard the entrance to the Pont du Change, but for many years a prison for the most dangerous criminals. Only five years ago, a mob had entered and butchered its prisoners – part of the orgy of bloodletting that had convulsed the capital and dashed all hopes of moderate political reform.

They left their cabriolet in the Place de Grève and walked along the Rue de la Mortellerie. From somewhere came the sound of a clock tolling the noon hour, and it occurred to Mary that Paris, with its many churches and convents, must once have been a city of bells. Now most were silent or had been melted down to fulfil some other purpose 'for the good of the Republic'. *And the men who used to ring the bells – what has become of them?*

The fourth turning on the left was the Rue Geoffroy l'Asnier, and a little way down it, they could see the sign for Vrillac's. That the street had once been fashionable was clear from the few stately doorways, a beautiful entrance gate, and an ornamented balcony – but in general it was dark and melancholy, and rather malodorous. There were a few signs of life. Women gathered outside a bakery, and someone had hung washing in the overgrown courtyard of a once fine townhouse. And there was Vrillac's, of course, a small shop with a bow window, its frame painted green. Even here, however, the gloom of the street was such that lights were burning inside, despite the early hour.

The front of the shop was crammed with artists' supplies – shelves stacked with different grades of paper; glass cabinets displaying pencils, pens, and crayons; and pyramids of boxes containing an assortment of bottles and jars. Everything was neatly and precisely arranged, but such was the volume and variety that the untried visitor was loathe to move for fear of treading upon something or upsetting something else.

Mary, hovering nervously beside Vangenzen, perceived a man at the back of the shop, where a row of wooden cabinets with shallow drawers lined the wall. Several of the drawers were open, and he appeared to be organising their contents. She recognised him from Vangenzen's description: a small, colourless fellow, with an odd temper. The last was not immediately apparent, but it became so soon enough.

He turned, peering at them in no very friendly way. When it was screwed up in a frown, his pale little face gave him the look of a troubled ferret. 'Well?'

The terse greeting had no effect on Vangenzen. He stepped into the light and replied, 'Good afternoon, Jens,' in a cheery voice.

'Ah, Vangenzen,' allowed the other, somewhat pacified, 'I was wondering when you would turn up, and it is a good thing that you have. The Genoa paper that you ordered has arrived, and I have had the devil of a time keeping a hold of it. Everyone wants Genoa paper, it seems. You had better take it with you.'

'Yes, I shall,' said Vangenzen, 'but I have come on another matter. I would like to introduce you to my wife.' He motioned Mary forward. 'She has lately arrived from England.'

'From England?' The three of them were alone in the shop, but the little man looked about him furtively. Then he continued in a cautious voice, 'I have been wondering about *that* too. Why, only yesterday I wondered . . . but, well, it appears I needn't have done, for here you are.' The realisation of this truth appeared to bring him little pleasure, for he added, apprehensively, 'My goodness, here in my shop! Why did you bring her *here*, Vangenzen?'

'Well, I hardly knew where else to—'

'No, of course not. But *really*, you know . . .' He sighed and a shiver of distaste passed through him as he acknowledged Mary. 'Oh my. It cannot be helped now, and unless you want to go away again, I suppose that you had better come upstairs, Citizeness Vangenzen, for we certainly cannot speak *here*.'

He set down his stock of prints and indicated a small door to his left. 'This way, if you please – and you must forgive the disorder, for I was not expecting you.'

'Thank you,' said Mary, but she did not move in accordance with his sign. 'Shall you come too?' she asked Vangenzen.

'Come too?' cried Jens. 'Vangenzen come too? What an idea! He must mind the shop. Surely you see that, citizeness? It is my shop, after all, and there are my customers to consider.' He gestured as if crowds of artists, bereft of essential supplies, were poised to descend upon Vrillac's.

Mary thought that the shop might safely be closed for half an hour without inconvenience to anyone. The pressure of Vangenzen's hand upon her arm, however, prompted a different reply. 'Certainly – he must mind the shop. Please excuse me.'

'Yes, well,' sniffed Jens, 'then do come along, please, before something else happens.'

113

Mary made her way gingerly to the rear of the shop and stepped through the opened door. Inside was a narrow staircase with a second door at the top. The passage was dark, but Jens handed her a lighted candle and then waved her forward, as one might shoo a goose.

'Go, go,' he urged. 'And you must forgive the disorder.'

The upstairs room was smaller than the shop and far less crowded. A window overlooked the street, and tall bookcases lined the side and rear walls. There was a further stack of books on the floor, and this might have constituted the disorder of which she had been warned. Also, the chairs surrounding a small table were not perfectly aligned, and the table itself bore a stack of prints.

Jens straightened the chairs and then urged Mary to sit down by means of further goose-herding gestures. 'I suppose that you *are* the one who was mentioned – who was *referred to*?' He sat down opposite and squinted at her, first leaning forward and then back, as if her physiognomy might change as he altered his perspective. He did not offer to speak English.

'Yes, if you mean . . . yes.'

He sighed the heavy exhalation of a man preparing himself for a great task. 'Very well. You wish to have it confirmed to *a certain gentleman* that you have arrived in Paris, I suppose?'

'Yes,' said Mary, 'and I thought that we might say—' She halted as the rest of her sentence was swept aside by a grimace and a slow shake of the head.

'*You* thought? *You* would deliver an opinion on the matter of my communication? Quite out of the question. This is my profession, you know.' He gazed at her sternly. 'Are you aware of the proper mode of communication between persons in my profession? Do you generally converse on commercial matters of an artistic nature?'

'No.'

'No indeed. I thought not. This affair is irregular enough without such a deviation from proper procedure. The composition, therefore, rests entirely with myself. *You* may read it,' he

114

added like a magnifico who had bestowed a particular privilege upon one of his less-deserving followers.

'Thank you.'

Jens selected paper, pen, and ink, and began to write in a slow, deliberate fashion. Having completed the names and addresses of the parties, he set down his pen and leafed through the pile of prints, sliding one of them across the table. 'What do you think of that?' he asked without looking at her.

It was an illustration of a small, brightly coloured bird in the branch of a tree. 'I believe it is a goldfinch,' she replied.

'*Carduelis carduelis*, to be precise. And does it have any associations for you?'

'Only that my name – my unmarried name – is Finch.'

'Ah,' pronounced Jens, nodding approvingly. 'That is excellent and highly satisfactory. I am pleased to discover that not *all* standards have been cast aside.' He resumed writing, and in a little while handed over the result. 'One is obliged to write in English, of course, if one wishes to be understood in London,' he complained in the tone of one who bore many burdens.

Chez Vrillac: Fournisseur de Beaux-Arts
Rue Geoffroy l'Asnier
Paris

2ⁿᵈ Brumaire Year VI

Citizen Henry Carrington Bowles
Bowles & Carver, printers
69 St Paul's Churchyard
London

Citizen,

I write to inform you that your consignment of fifty water-coloured scientific prints, including the Sciurus vulgaris, *the* Carduelis carduelis *and related songbirds, and several of the* Lutra lutra, *has arrived safely and is in a generally satisfactory condition. I would question the colouration of the* Mustela nivalis, *as it seems to me that the coat should properly be a gingery red rather than brown,*

115

but I do not find the colouration so controversial as to render the print unacceptable. Doubtless the gentlemen knowledgeable in such matters will indicate, by their willingness or otherwise to purchase, whether it is a reasonable likeness of the least weasel.

As the market for such work is limited, even in Paris, perhaps you will refrain from sending me future consignments of a like nature until I am in a position to report on the popularity of these.

I remain, your most respectful colleague,
Tobias Jens

Mary smiled as she read. 'It is not so very different from the way that I communicated with Mr Shy on a previous occasion. Although,' she quickly added, 'I could not have produced such an elegant letter, nor one so appropriate to this particular situation.'

Jens placed a hand upon his breast and nodded graciously. 'We speak of my profession, you know.'

'It is fortunate that my name is something straightforward like "Finch". How did you manage to find a print that would signify "Vangenzen"?'

'I made no attempt to do so. Citizen Vangenzen is an artist and may travel openly to England for artistic purposes. In your case, naturally, it was otherwise, and a contrivance was necessary.'

'Yes, I see. And do the . . . letters and prints travel directly between France and England?' she asked.

'Who can say? *I* know nothing of such matters. Letters come and letters go. The process by which they do so is a mystery to a professional man such as myself. So,' he continued, folding the letter and placing it to one side, 'our business is concluded, I think. Shall we go downstairs? I hope that Vangenzen has not jumbled my anatomical drawings.'

'Er, yes,' said Mary, 'I mean, I trust that he has not.' Jens had risen, and she gazed up at him. 'I beg your pardon, but . . . I thought that you might be able to advise me on how best to proceed.'

'Advise you?' Jens was indignant. He had short, grey hair that stuck up all over his head, and now it was fairly bristling.

'Certainly not. *That* is not a professional matter – how could I possibly advise you?'

'But you are aware of my assignment here?'

'I might be. But what you ask is impossible. What do I know of Americans and their negotiations?' He shot her a sharp glance. 'Vangenzen is the only American of my acquaintance, and *he* is practically a Dutchman.'

It occurred to Mary, pointedly, that *she* knew nothing of Americans and their negotiations either, or very little, and yet *she* was willing to carry on. 'I thought that, perhaps, Mr Shy might have asked you to . . . ' She shrugged. 'Stand by.'

'Stand by for what purpose? How could my standing here, there, or anywhere be of any use if the . . . matter is not within my knowledge or competence?'

Stated in that way, it certainly sounded impractical, although she suspected that Jens had chosen his words deliberately. She swallowed her irritation, however. 'Of course, you are correct. And I am grateful to you for writing the letter.'

He bowed and indicated that she should precede him to the stairs. When she had reached the top step, he added, casually, 'I have heard it said that the gentlemen of interest to you are residing in the Rue de Grenelle.'

She paused, her hand upon the railing. 'The Rue de Grenelle.'

'So it is said. And, if you were so minded, you might choose to present yourself to them as newly married to one of their countrymen resident in this city.' He shrugged. 'Tomorrow morning might be a suitable opportunity. Who can tell whether it would be useful, but such a presentation would not be wholly irregular. As for any other matters, of course, I can say nothing.'

'No, indeed,' Mary agreed. He had not smiled, and neither had she.

9

'Mortars for the Navy, my arse.'

Those were the words of Gunner Drake as he watched his officer depart for London on a grey morning that was spitting with rain. Drake knew very well that Captain Holland had been summoned to the Admiralty for confidential discussions – he had seen the order – and he knew that Holland's story of improved mortar fixings for use on board Navy bomb vessels was just that – a story. He also suspected that the summons had something to do with the visit of Major Whittington. But that was the extent of his knowledge, and he felt the restriction keenly.

Drake was aware that Holland's work in the regiment was of a confidential nature, and that sometimes he was drawn into strange and even dangerous matters. Why, only that spring there had been the business at the Purfleet gunpowder magazine, in which Drake himself had played a not inconsiderable hand. Yet now he was in the dark, or at best a murky twilight. Drake did not expect Holland always to confide in him; that would not have been the captain's style. Rather, he expected to get round whatever official barriers had been erected to maintain secrecy – not for any perfidious reason, but because a fellow ought to know things, especially when they concerned his officer.

On this occasion, however, Holland had been particularly

tight-lipped, and very few other opportunities for obtaining information had presented themselves. An ill-timed query had prevented Drake from discovering the purpose of Whittington's visit, and the communication from the Admiralty had given precious little away.

> *Captain Robert Holland of the Royal Regiment of Artillery is hereby required and directed to wait upon the Right Honourable Lords Commissioners of the Admiralty or some of them, and to inform and otherwise offer them the benefit of his expertise in various matters of a technical and scientific nature, at ten o'clock in the morning on the twenty-fourth day of October, 1797.*

The order had come directly from Evan Nepean, Esq., first secretary to the Admiralty. To Drake's mind, this lent a further air of mystery to the business. If the meeting in prospect were a straightforward one, an anonymous Admiralty clerk would have composed the document in the name of their lordships, and the signature would have been that of Earl Spencer, the first lord. *Why should this Evan Nepean, esquire, be interested in Captain Haitch?*

Drake had no answer, but he resolved to keep his eyes and ears open. In the meantime, he took comfort from the fact that, if he did not know exactly what the captain was up to, he knew more than just about anyone else.

As Drake had suspected, Holland's business that morning was with the first secretary, and it was in his office that the meeting took place. The room was comfortably furnished but wholly businesslike in its atmosphere, and Mr Nepean fitted his surroundings very well. His gaze was shrewd, but his round face suggested that the management of Admiralty affairs did not oblige him to miss his dinner very frequently. He was expensively dressed, but not ostentatiously so.

The other man present was a Navy captain named Martel. He was the eldest of the three, if a lined face and thinning brown hair were reliable evidence of age – of hard usage, perhaps. Captain Martel was one of a handful of men who conducted secret operations up and down the coast of France. Commanding small, inconspicuous vessels manned by French-speaking crews, they accomplished by stealth what the might of the Royal Navy could not. Sometimes they collected information on enemy troop movements, sometimes they communicated with French Royalists, and occasionally they discovered other interesting phenomena.

Drake's second guess was also correct – their lordships had no particular interest in mortars at present, although that explanation had been given as the object of the meeting. Artillery officers were not often seen at the Admiralty, and even within those walls absolute security could not always be relied upon. It was advisable, therefore, to take precautions when solemn and confidential matters were being discussed. The matters under discussion on this occasion were certainly solemn; their confidentiality would depend on the conclusions that were reached.

'What we must consider, gentlemen, is whether such a thing is possible,' said Nepean. 'Or indeed, *likely.*'

'We know that the Americans experimented with naval mines in the last war, sir,' Holland replied.

'Yes, I took up your suggestion about *Cerberus*, and while I was unable to locate any of the men who served in her in '77, I did manage to find Captain Symond's report of the attack launched against her in August of that year. Apparently, the device was designed to float with wind and current towards its target and become entangled with the ship's mooring line. This would very likely bring it into contact with the hull, and the motion would also trip the detonators. As regards *Cerberus* herself, the attack proper failed, but the damned thing exploded when it was brought on board another vessel for examination.'

The account made Nepean frown, but his next words were measured. 'Unfortunately, the report does not end there. The fellow who tried to destroy *Cerberus* seems also to have been experimenting with an underwater vessel. According to Governor Tryon's informants, David Bushnell built a ship called the *Turtle* in his workshop in' – Nepean consulted his notes – 'Saybrook,

Connecticut, in order to attack our warships. As far as I can tell, nothing came of the scheme – perhaps the *Turtle* was never actually built – but *might* it have been?'

Holland did not answer straightaway, and then his opinion came cautiously. 'Well, sir, there have been *stories* about such vessels for at least . . . well, since early in the last century. Cornelius Drebbel certainly claimed to have built a boat that could be propelled under water – there is even an old Ordnance warrant to build more of them.'

'When you say "claimed",' began Nepean.

'I don't believe that he produced any plans – at least, none that have survived. But Drebbel wasn't the only one. A Frenchman named Papin also designed underwater boats. They might be feasible.'

'You have seen *his* plans?'

'Yes, sir. In the *Gentleman's Magazine*. I did a bit of digging after I spoke with Major Whittington.' Holland paused. 'If vessels carrying naval mines could be propelled under water, they would present a danger to ships at anchor and perhaps even in the open sea. Certainly to docks and bridges. And even without the mines, an underwater boat would have a tremendous advantage for espionage or for attacking and boarding enemy ships. But I would have to see the plans to be certain – the plans or the vessel.'

'Indeed,' said Nepean, nodding. 'Perhaps Captain Martel can help us with regard to those points.'

Martel cleared his throat and then began in a low, diffident voice. A Guernsey man, he spoke English well, but with a strong accent. 'Myself, I have seen neither, but I have conversed with the men of Honfleur – that is on the coast of Normandy, Captain Holland. They say that an Englishman named Boyle has come to Honfleur with a peculiar machine for sailing under the sea. Also, that he has something that they described as a *piqûre de feu* – a fiery sting – which I believe to be a weapon of some sort.'

'Has any of *them* seen these things – the boat and the, er, sting?'

121

'Yes, but their descriptions are various. One says the boat is like the *coquille* – the shell of the sea – and another like the ram's horn. But they also speak of the Bible.' Martel shrugged, adding, 'They are not engineers. Nor am I.'

'But are they reliable?' asked Holland.

'I think so. They say that Boyle is very friendly, but his French is not so good, and they cannot always understand him. One fellow I spoke with – one of the younger men – says that he has helped Boyle take the machine into the sea, but that Boyle always conducts the experiments himself.'

'If he has actually sailed the thing and not been drowned, that in itself is important,' said Holland. 'I wish we knew more about Boyle.'

Nepean consulted a paper. 'Fortunately, we do. Mr Samson Boyle, aged about sixty years and an Irishman. Not a Patriot, however, nor a Friend of Liberty or whatever the gentlemen over the way are calling themselves at present. Indeed, he does not seem to have expressed any clear political views while in Ireland – apart from peace on earth, of course.'

'Why "of course"?'

'Only a soldier would ask that question,' replied Nepean, smiling. 'Is not a longing for peace universal? The natural aspiration for mankind? One would hope so. But in this particular instance, the inclination is also a professional one – the gentleman is a clergyman.'

'*Mon Dieu*, and he invents underwater machines?' Martel demanded.

'He is a Protestant priest with a country parish in County Wexford. I expect he does not have a great deal else to occupy him.'

'He has picked up radical ideas from somewhere,' Holland complained, 'or he wouldn't have decided to make a gift of this boat to the French.'

'Hmm, yes,' said Nepean. 'He corresponded with Dr Priestley before the good doctor removed to America – possibly on scientific matters – and also with Mr James Watt. Mr Watt speaks of Boyle's "dogged, enquiring mind", which I suppose is meant to be a compliment.' He looked across at Holland and Martel. 'I suggest that we reserve judgment for the present. Prior to this meeting, I had determined that the wisest course would probably be for Captain Martel to apprehend Mr Boyle and bring him to London. Snap him up, as it were, before he could do any mischief. Hearing Captain Holland's views on the possibility of an undersea vessel has confirmed my judgment. But I would like to know what you think of such an undertaking.'

Martel was worrying a darned patch on the knee of his breeches, and he spoke without raising his eyes. 'This snapping up is not so difficult for myself and the crew of the *Lizette*. I know Honfleur very well, and even if we are seen, no French ship can catch us.'

'I think we've got to have him, sir,' said Holland. 'And the sooner the better.'

'Then we are agreed.' Nepean sat back in his chair and re-arranged some of the papers set out in front of him. It was difficult to tell whether he was considering what he might say or merely inserting a pause before saying what he had already decided. The exercise completed, he leaned forward again, and this time rested his elbows on the desk. 'Captain Holland,' he continued, 'I would like you to join the expedition, if you would. As Captain Martel has acknowledged, he is not an engineer, nor has he experience of machines of this sort. It would be a damned shame if something were to go amiss for the lack of an expert close at hand.'

'I'm no expert, sir,' Holland cautioned, 'but I'm happy to go along if I could be any help.' Of course he would go – who wouldn't jump at the chance of a little excitement, of getting away from Woolwich and its tedium, even for a day or two? Very likely he would also be sick for the duration of any Channel crossing, but it would be worth it – especially if Boyle really had managed to build an underwater vessel.

'Excellent,' pronounced Nepean, 'then let us make it so. Captain Martel, I believe I can leave the practical details to you?'

'Of course.'

'And Captain Holland, I will complete the necessary formalities to secure your services for an additional period – for you will naturally wish to join the formal study of the device once Mr Boyle has been secured.'

'Yes, sir, thank you very much.'

'Thank you, gentlemen,' Nepean confirmed with a nod.

It was the signal for departure, and the two officers rose and took their leave. Martel suggested that they dine together; he was devilishly hungry, and they could discuss matters while they ate. Holland assented, and their fading conversation compared the merits of Slaughter's and Fladong's, two of the London establishments popular with gentlemen of their respective services.

Alone in his office Nepean made some further notes, but before he had completed them a second interruption occurred. A modest, inconspicuous door opened, and a middle-aged man of a similar description slipped through. He had not, it was clear, come along the common passageway, for the door led to a second private room.

'Well?' asked the first secretary, setting down his pen. 'That was all very satisfactory, I believe. Thank you for the information about Boyle – he sounds an interesting fellow.'

Cuthbert Shy nodded graciously. 'One always likes to assist one's colleagues in the services when possible.' He sat down on the chair vacated by Captain Martel. It was the more comfortable of the two available seats, but it also enabled him to consider, as it were, the shade of Captain Holland.

That he seemed to do so, or at least to be not wholly at his ease, prompted Nepean to rephrase his initial remarks. 'You have reservations?'

'Yes, since you ask. I am strongly opposed to Captain Holland participating in any French project. Two years ago, their intelligence service made a concerted effort to capture him, you know, for the sake of his knowledge of armaments.'

'But that plan failed, with fatal consequences for its authors.'

'Just so,' Shy agreed. 'All those responsible have either been executed or exiled to Guiana – which fortunately amounts to

124

the same thing. Files, however, have a habit of surviving, and I expect that Holland has quite a sizeable one.'

'I see that would be a concern if this were an actual deployment, but it is not,' Nepean argued. 'And the requirements of this Boyle business are highly unusual. We must have a knowledgeable man on the spot.'

'Indeed, I agree wholeheartedly – only *not* Holland. But this is your affair, not mine, and Holland is not my agent. You are confident that the landing and retrieval can be accomplished with a minimum of risk?'

'As much as one can be. Philippe Martel is very experienced in capers of this sort.' Nepean selected one of his papers and studied it before handing it across. 'Share and share alike.'

Shy pursed his lips as he scanned the single sheet. 'Yes, I see what you mean. *"Impatient, highly confident, something of a braggart, but also clever and extremely competent."* The last frequently pays for all, in our line of work.'

'Indeed it does. You might have questioned them, you know,' said Nepean. 'I would not have objected in the least.'

'You are very good, but I did not like to intrude. Such bad form, you know. I believe it is important to keep the proper distance between our different spheres. As well as that . . .'

'Yes?'

Shy shook his head, but then explained, 'I was thinking of Captain Holland. Seeing me at this juncture might distract him, turn his thoughts from the business at hand. And that would do none of us any good.'

'I see,' replied Nepean. He did not quite, but he sensed that no further illumination was likely.

'I knew you would understand. And if you would be so kind as to let me know your opinion of Mr Boyle when you have made his acquaintance, I would be most obliged. He certainly does sound interesting.'

What Shy did not say had partly to do with Robert Holland and partly to do with Mary Finch. As he made an inconspicuous departure from the Admiralty by way of a private door

125

he was thinking wholly of Mary and her likely progress. He did not expect to hear anything from her for some time yet, but the Boyle affair had brought her particularly to mind.

In fact, that morning Mary and Vangenzen called upon the American envoys in the Rue de Grenelle. They were duly received, and Mary was welcomed as a compatriot by a group of boisterous men also waiting for an interview. French privateers, it transpired, had recently captured their ships, and they had grievances against the privateers, the French courts, and the American government as a result of these acts of unacknowledged war.

They freely expressed themselves in loud, truculent voices, and after enduring this for a while Mary felt obliged to withdraw. She began a less volatile conversation with an Englishman named Hubbard – the junior partner in the Dutch firm that acted as the American government's European bank. Before they could exchange more than a few pleasantries, however, the young secretary called for the new arrivals. Possibly he felt that the shipowners' language was inappropriate for a lady's ears, and possibly he guessed that the Vangenzen interview would be uncontroversial and wished to ease his chief into the day's business.

The interview *was* uncontroversial as well as brief, consisting of little more than introductions, explanations, and mutual expressions of esteem. The gentleman who spoke to them, Mr Marshall, was pleased to make the acquaintance of Mr and Mrs Vangenzen and even expressed the hope of meeting them again, but without indicating how this might be accomplished. The nadir of the conversation was his remark that they needn't have come in the first place – although it was always pleasant to meet fellow Americans. Having made this dampening observation, he summoned the secretary.

Conscious that they were about to be dismissed, Mary seized upon the first topic that occurred to her. Ought she to remove her savings from Coutts Bank now that she had severed her ties with England? The sum concerned was not very large, but she and Mr Vangenzen valued it. Might they do better entrusting it to Van Staphorst & Hubbard? What was Mr Marshall's opinion of continental banks?

'Do you have some acquaintance with the firm in question, ma'am?'

Mary admitted that she had none, apart from her conversation with Mr Hubbard, and this provoked a decided frown. 'Good Lord, is he here again?' Marshall demanded.

'I am afraid so, sir,' replied the secretary, 'and most anxious to see you.'

'That will be impossible today. The plundered American ships are my first concern, and I am fully engaged with their representatives.'

'Yes, sir, I have tried to make that clear to him. Perhaps if I could pass on a more specific message?'

'Very well, you may tell him – with my compliments – that we have met the gentleman he mentioned and no further action on Mr Hubbard's part is necessary or desirable.'

When he turned again to Mary, Marshall had recovered his good humour – if indeed he had ever lost it. He regretted being unable to advise her, and when she apologised for troubling him on a personal matter, he demurred most politely. It was simply that, in his experience, bankers tended to be rather busy, intrusive fellows. If her present arrangements at Coutts were satisfactory, perhaps it would be wise to continue them.

He then nodded to the secretary, and the Vangenzens had no alternative but to follow the young man out. All too soon they were on the pavement again, fastening up their coats.

Mary was disappointed with the interview and with herself. Why had she not asked about the privateers? They were bound to have been a more promising topic of conversation. 'We shall have to try harder the next time,' she resolved.

'The next time?' asked Vangenzen, startled.

'Oh yes, certainly. Matters cannot be allowed to remain as they are, you know. I must conjure a reason for another meeting with Mr Marshall.'

Conjuring, however, was easier said than done. A chance encounter was extremely awkward to plan when the person

127

one wished to meet was practically a stranger. Mary could not simply place herself in Marshall's path, for she did not know his schedule or habits, nor could she appear a second time at the Rue de Grenelle without a reason.

She was considering the matter as she and Minta returned from shopping on the following morning. Relations between the two of them were not yet what Mary would have described as friendly, but she thought they were tending that way. When Minta slipped behind to let another woman pass and did not resume her place, therefore, Mary asked, 'What is the matter? Is that too heavy? Shall we exchange?'

Their baskets *were* heavy and full of unusual delicacies, for Mary had insisted on contributing to the Vangenzen coffers. ('Consider it some of Mr Pitt's gold,' she had said, in reply to the protestations of her hosts. 'One reads so much about it in *Le Moniteur*, it would be sad to think that it did not exist.')

Minta shook her head. 'No, I am well – and yours is heavier.'

'Then why do you not walk beside me?'

Minta did not answer, so Mary slipped her arm through the other woman's. After a few paces Minta gently freed herself and, while not straying from Mary's side, walked with her head slightly bowed.

Mary affected not to notice. Presently she asked, 'Would you say that American ladies are particularly *advanced*? In their manner,' she added, as Minta looked at her questioningly. 'A lady I know in England would use the term "brazen".'

'Well, I hardly know,' Minta replied. 'They do not generally curse or chew tobacco.' She frowned in an effort to think of other examples of brazen conduct. 'I once heard of a New Haven woman who shot squirrels from the upstairs window of her house. I believe that she shot at her husband once, when he had been drinking and came home late.'

Mary laughed and then continued in a low voice, 'Would an American lady *write* to a gentleman whom she did not know well? And if she did, would he be shocked and consider it a great liberty? I must find a way of . . . pushing things along, you see, even if it involves a bit of a risk.'

Minta stared at her. 'A risk? But Samuel said . . . You will not—'

A cart darting across their path interrupted her entreaty. The vehicle rolled through a puddle, and the women were obliged to retreat peremptorily. Minta slipped on the cobbles, and mud oozed over Mary's boots as she struggled to find a secure foothold. 'Oh!' cried Minta. 'My word!' Mary gasped, and for a moment they clung to each other.

Then the danger passed, and Minta urged, 'A letter to – no, do not tell me his name – would not be wise. I am afraid he would think you very odd indeed, and . . . would *wonder* about you.'

'Well, if his wondering caused him to write back—'

'But he would not do so! Not if he were a gentleman and he imagined you to be . . . a bad woman.'

'Perhaps you are right,' Mary conceded, 'but I must think of something.' Grasping her basket in both hands, she sprang across the kennel, causing a group of approaching women to screech and move hastily out of her way.

Minta chose the more sedate route, but the muddy channel was not the only obstacle. The street was becoming more crowded as shops unfastened their shutters and clerks hurried to their offices. Carts and wagons competed with pedestrians, and hawkers stood in doorways, crying their wares. It was no easy thing to maintain a conversation, and Minta seemed to have little interest in pursuing theirs. Instead she walked stolidly, sometimes at Mary's elbow and sometimes a further step behind, as the press of traffic demanded. There was disapproval even in the set of her shoulders.

When they returned to the Maison des Chevrons it was time to undertake the next activity of the morning – baking bread. This took place in the large, common kitchen on the ground floor of the building. Like other former townhouses, this one had been built as a single residence, and now its several *appartements* lacked separate cooking facilities. The kitchen was usually crowded when dinner and supper were being prepared. At this time of the morning, however, all was quiet, for the other women bought their bread from the bakery at the bottom of the hill. Only Minta rose early on baking days, started a batch before setting off for the market, and finished it on her return.

Mary's admission to the Vangenzen household had made little impact on this routine. Having admitted her ignorance of baking, she was not trusted with any of the skilled aspects of the process. She stood to one side, therefore, watching Minta knead dough and fashion it into loaves; under direction, she floured the table. This trivial action, and the inability to set her own affairs in order, turned her thoughts in a different direction.

'I was wondering . . . I expect it is terribly rude and prying, but . . . why have you kept your marriage a secret? You cannot have *liked* . . . I mean, is such a thing necessary in France?'

Minta pursed her lips. 'What is necessary and what is wise are not always the same.'

'No, but—'

'You keep secrets,' Minta continued. 'You must know that there is only one way to test the wisdom of revelation – and then it is too late.'

'In America, perhaps, the risk *would* have been too great. But have you not considered that your situation might be different in France? The law regarding slavery—'

'The *law*. What does the law matter? The trouble lies in people's hearts. Good, decent people who nevertheless do cruel, terrible things. I have been in the power of such people for most of my life – why should I run the risk of being so again?'

'But . . . if you remain afraid to show yourself as a free woman, are you not still in their power?' asked Mary. 'And consider what you have lost . . .'

'I have lost very little. The world outside is nothing to me. I care only for the world inside, and there I know I am secure. And I am not a fool. I know that the outsiders may cause me great pain, so I make myself invisible to them. In that way I avoid the harm that the world may inflict, and I endure no hardship, for I merely do without that upon which I place no value.'

Minta kneaded in silence, firmly pressing the dough against

the table with the heels of her hands, and then turning, folding, and pressing again until she had produced a smooth, taut ball. The flour turned her hands pale, and the effort of the task was transmitted up her slim arms, across her shoulders, and to the slight frown upon her brow. A dark ringlet tumbled from her prim coiffure, and she swept it back with her forearm, leaving a smudge of flour.

'Yet you are frightened of something,' said Mary, watching her.

Minta raised her eyes. 'I am frightened for Samuel – of what this venture of yours may cost him. I do not blame you,' she added, before Mary could speak, 'but rather that man, Shy. Why could he not leave us alone? And you, too? Why must he send you here while England is at war? For you are in danger as long as you remain in France – terrible danger.'

She turned abruptly away and stood, hands clenched, her words slowly evaporating into the air. Presently she resumed her work, shaping the dough into a loaf, placing it on a long-handled baker's peel, and sliding it into the oven. Perhaps she did not expect an answer to either of her questions; certainly she did not look as if she intended to speak further.

Mary, however, could not remain silent. She did not know how to answer Minta's first demand, but to the second she replied softly, 'I agreed to take my chance against the danger, as . . . Mr Vangenzen did, so neither of us has a right to complain of it. But I will be as careful as I can.'

'But you will also take risks! You have said so! That is what happens when one ventures into the world outside. In an instant one may lose all that one holds dear – and for what?'

'For friendship, I suppose,' said Mary, 'and to preserve other things more important than ourselves.'

10

Late on the evening of the twenty-sixth of October, with rain and low clouds masking her departure, the *Lizette* slipped out of a quiet cove near Rye and set a course for the Normandy coast. She was a two-masted Bermuda sloop, the favoured rig for smuggling, privateering, and other activities that required utmost speed and manoeuvrability, and in the hands of a man who knew her well, she was very fast indeed. Philippe Martel was just such a man, and he had made similar crossings many times. Nevertheless, by four bells in the middle watch, things were not going according to plan.

Martel was cautious when it came to the *Lizette*, and he had not brought her right in close to the land, but had stood off and on, studying the coast and the occasional shore lights, and watching for unfriendly ships. His caution had been rewarded, for they had fallen in with a night-fishing vessel. Its captain, the cousin of one of the men known to Martel, had come across for a drink and to exchange such pleasantries as were appropriate to the occasion. From him had come the disturbing news: Boyle was no longer in Honfleur.

'You understood what he said?' Martel asked Holland when they were alone again.

'I think so – the gist of it, anyway. Boyle left for Paris a week ago.'

'Yes, he is gone. Eight days ago, strictly – soon after our last

132

visit to Honfleur.' Martel paused. 'At that time there was no hint that he would make such a decision, of course.'

'No,' Holland agreed. In the swaying lantern-light his face looked pale and unhealthy. As well as feeling ill for most of the crossing, the last half hour in the airless cabin had made his head ache. 'Boyle kept his own counsel when it came to his experiments, it seems. If he had been close to an important advance, he wouldn't have said anything about it.'

'You think that likely? Damn the fellow!' Without waiting for an answer Martel announced his intention of following the inventor to Paris.

'Bundling him across the Channel is one thing, carrying him halfway across France is another,' warned Holland. 'Especially if he does not wish to come.'

'Well, I shall go. The task is dangerous' – Martel shrugged – 'but that does not frighten me. And if this machine has been perfected, any chance is worth taking to recover it.'

'Yes,' said Holland, 'and I had better go with you.' To Martel's look of surprise he added, '"Experimental machines", remember? If we can obtain the plans, we might not need Boyle. The French would hardly invest in a speculative, unproven device if they knew we were aware of it and also able to build it ourselves.'

'There is another way to be certain about Mr Boyle,' growled Martel, drawing his index finger across his throat. 'I wish now that I had done it straightaway, when I first learned of his damned boats and stings.'

'It may still come to that, but it is also possible that the vessel does not work. Having the plans would make that clear.'

Martel nodded, and observed Holland thoughtfully. 'You are not as I expected. When they said "an expert in military science", I imagined a man of books, a dreamer, impractical, but you are not like that, I think. And Mr Nepean says that you have a good record – in India and also in England.' He smiled. 'Not so good a sailor, perhaps.'

'No, I'll be happy to be on dry land again,' Holland admitted. 'The *Lizette* can put us ashore, I suppose. How do we get back to England?'

133

'I will arrange a rendezvous with my lieutenant, Jean-Achille – a series of meetings and signals to commence one week from our landing and to last for seven nights. If we cannot manage to return in a fortnight, I doubt whether we shall have need of transport.'

'Agreed. And papers? We won't have any, if we're stopped.'

Martel thought they could manage without. His plan, in so far as he had one, was to travel across country, avoiding the *gendarmerie* and Republican sympathisers rather than trying to fool them with disguises. It was far better to be unseen than to explain oneself. Martel could fade easily enough into the *milieu*, and Holland . . .

'I'll never pass for a local. I can read French, especially on subjects having to do with my own line of work, and I can understand, sometimes, if the person speaks slowly, but—'

Martel shook his head dismissively. 'No, no. For you a French manner would be impossible. If you are obliged to speak, let it be in English. You may even speak French – but like a foreigner: *"bone swar, monsure; ou vaunday-vous le pudding de beefsteak?"* Then we will say that you are an Irishman or an American.'

'Yes, but,' began Holland, smiling at the other's performance, 'I certainly don't speak English like an Irishman! I haven't met many Americans, but—'

'But in France, no one will know the difference. You must not reveal any sympathy for Britain, of course, but instead espouse the cause of Liberty. And if we encounter any Irish or Americans, we shall not attempt our charade with them – although Americans, in my experience, have every sort of speech. Some clipped, and everything through the nose, and some long and slow, like honey. I expect that you could deceive them, if necessary.'

'Well, perhaps,' Holland acknowledged, 'but I think my best chance will be to keep quiet. You know your way around Paris, I suppose?'

'Of course. Three times I have been before the Revolution' – he smiled – 'and twice since.'

*   *   *

Mary did write to the American envoy, and she received a favourable reply. Yet even as she congratulated herself on having devised an excuse for paying Mr Marshall a visit, the prospect of doing so troubled her. Was she risking more than she ought? Perhaps, but the alternative – inaction – was not to be thought of. She did not cry off the appointment, therefore, but when she presented herself in Marshall's study, she bound that gentleman by ties of honour and upright dealing, and also withheld certain pertinent details affecting those most closely concerned in the matter.

If Marshall was concerned by the former or suspicious of the latter, he gave no sign. It was quite usual for persons seeking confidential legal advice to retain a lawyer formally for that purpose, he said. He was happy to conform to that practice if it suited Mrs Vangenzen.

'Thank you, sir. It does suit me.'

'Well then, I must tell you straight off that I am nearly as ignorant of French law as I am of the French language. I understood a little of how they managed their affairs before the Revolution, but I wouldn't like to say, definitely, how things stand today. So, having warned you not to depend on what I know' – he smiled – 'let me tell you what I *think*, which is all a lawyer can do anyway, when asked about a hypothetical matter.

'It is my understanding that, in the old days, slavery in France was not recognised by the courts, although it was lawful in French colonies. Men who had made their fortunes abroad got themselves into difficulties when they came home again and tried to bring their slaves with them. The courts would not allow it.'

Mary nodded. 'That is also the position of the English courts, I believe.'

'Ah, you refer to *Somersett's Case*,' said Marshall, his long, rawboned face beaming with pleasure. 'I did not know that you were a lawyer yourself, ma'am, although I suppose I ought to have done, from your questions about confidentiality.'

'I am interested, of course, but my understanding is really very modest,' Mary protested, and for once she did not regret the warm flush that she could feel stealing over her cheeks. 'I have some familiarity with Blackstone's *Commentaries*.'

'You could not have chosen a better foundation for your studies. Well, well,' said Marshall, shaking his head, 'I have never met a lady with an interest in legal science. But it is a great object, and I honour you for it. Of course, the precedent of *Somersett's Case* is not so clear as one would wish.'

'Indeed,' Mary agreed, wishing that she had read the anti-slavery pamphlets more closely. She ventured a guess. 'But the general principle . . . No one would argue that slavery is lawful in England, whatever may hold in the West Indies. And many people are trying to bring an end to the trade.'

Marshall acquiesced, and when he returned to the situation of French slaves, Mary thought she noted a change in his tone. While previously he had been friendly, even slightly indulgent of a lady's whim, now he sounded interested – perhaps in the topic and perhaps in her.

'It was one thing to hold that slavery could not exist in France, for the economic situation of the country did not depend upon the labour of slaves and never had. In the colonies, however, it was different. I expect the planters have a strong voice in French politics, just as they do in the States, and they kept their slaves right through the Revolution – right up until there was a slave rebellion in Santa Domingo. That was contrary to the war effort, so the French government decided to abolish slavery once and for all. It brought the rebellion to an end and the former slaves onto the French side.'

'That would mean that any slave who came to France would certainly be considered free *now* by French law,' concluded Mary. 'Even if it were argued that the Revolution had swept away the old laws and judgments, the government's decision to end slavery in all French territories would fill any void.'

'So I believe, ma'am.'

'And this would be the case even if the slave's owner were not a Frenchman?'

Marshall nodded. 'I see that you've thought of all the exceptions. And if the French government had any little qualms about causing bad relations with another nation – if the owner concerned were British or American, let us say – well, I surely doubt that such considerations would weigh heavily with the French courts.'

'That would hold for a British slave-owner,' Mary agreed, 'but are not France and America allies? Forgive me,' she added, lowering her eyes, 'but I thought that was so.'

'We are allies, ma'am, at the present moment of speaking, and I hope we shall remain so. But since this trouble began, I have started to have my doubts.'

Mary sat back in her chair. 'Trouble?' she cried, and then, as if she had only tumbled to the cause, 'Oh, you mean the French privateers. When my husband and I called upon you the other day, we spoke to several American ship-owners. They were most eloquent on the dreadful losses they had suffered.'

'Yes, I expect they were.'

'How difficult it must be, listening to your countrymen's sad stories and knowing that there is very little – for I suppose that is the case – that you may do to ease their suffering.' She regarded him sympathetically.

'You are exactly right, ma'am. It is very hard indeed.'

'Are there not steps – I do not know the proper diplomatic term – that the American government might take?' She smiled. 'But I suppose that you and your colleagues constitute the American government in France at the moment.'

'Yes, we have that honour,' Marshall acknowledged. 'But precisely what steps we ought to take is not clear to me. The French, as you may guess, take a different view of the privateers, and of other matters.' He smiled grimly. 'We Americans speak and act plainly – too plainly, perhaps – but we kick against all of the etiquette and protocol required before anything can be done in Europe. It seems to us— Ah, I beg your pardon.'

Mary assured him that she took no offence at his words, except perhaps in the assumption that England and Europe were alike. 'For England is quite different – quite different from France, at least. Indeed, I have found Americans to be quite similar to Englishmen.'

'I take that as a compliment, ma'am,' said Marshall, his smile softening, 'and I beg your pardon again for my misjudgement.'

Mary smiled in return. She wanted to encourage him but shrank from a direct question that might put him on his guard. 'I wonder whether Americans—'

At that moment the door opened partway, and an older, round-faced man appeared in the gap. He apologised immediately for the intrusion, but Marshall said that it did not matter – he and Mrs Vangenzen had completed their business. 'May I present my colleague, ma'am, Colonel Pinckney? He had the good fortune to study at Oxford.'

'Ah, indeed.' Mary wondered fleetingly about extending the interview by a comparison of Cambridge and Oxford. Before she could attempt it, however, Pinckney asked whether he might solicit Marshall's opinion on a particular matter. 'I have received another request from Hottinguer,' he added.

'Ah, yes, certainly.'

Mary concealed her chagrin as best she could. She even shook hands with Pinckney and thanked Marshall for having spared her so much of his time. Both men offered polite, largely meaningless remarks, and she smiled as she received them.

When the study door closed, however, her smile faded, until she perceived that here was an unlooked for chance. Her sudden dismissal meant that there was no secretary to escort her down the passage. She could remain by the door and listen – if she dared – to whatever was being discussed within. It was a terrible risk for a questionable gain, but she was curious. Who was Hottinguer, after all? She hesitated, and then leaned close to the door.

From the other side of the panel came the sound of voices, but it was difficult to make out all the words. She heard the name 'Hottinguer' again, and the assertion that he had someone's confidence. *Hau— or could it have been 'Hubbard'? Perhaps. Fifty thousand pounds. 'He' says that fifty thousand pounds will see us right. But who is 'he' and whom does Colonel Pinckney mean by 'us'? The men whose ships have been plundered? The American government? Goodness, the colonel is not very pleased, but I wish he would swear less and explain more. Mr Marshall says . . . something.*

138

Do please speak up! 'Hottinguer assures us that when one is in France one must learn to . . .' To drink a pot–de–vin? What can that mean? What does the drinking of wine have to do with the Americans?

In his little office at the end of the corridor, the young American secretary looked up from his desk. The waiting-room next door was empty that afternoon, and his face had lost its harassed expression. A friendly smile from Mrs Vangenzen also lifted his spirits. She looked remarkably pretty as she adjusted her hat, and seemed neither disappointed nor irritated. He particularly noticed these details, for it had not been usual, since the envoys had taken up residence, for meetings in the Rue de Grenelle to end so satisfactorily as hers must have done.

In fact, Mary was far from satisfied. She was intrigued by what she had heard, and determined to understand what it meant. Fifty thousand pounds, after all, was not a trivial sum, *and 'fifty thousand pounds will see us right'*. But how? Might it have something to do with Mr Hubbard, the English banker? And how could she manufacture another opportunity for learning more?

An opportunity presented itself shortly thereafter. Vangenzen's friend, the eminent painter Jacques-Louis David, announced that he would receive guests at his studio in the national museum at two o'clock on the tenth of Brumaire. Vangenzen and his new bride were invited, and Mary pressed for the inclusion of a third person: Mr John Marshall. No doubt he had a keen interest in art, and even if he did not . . . it would be a shame to visit Paris and not meet Citizen David.

Vangenzen, unsurprisingly, raised no objection to Marshall. On the contrary, he said that there would be others present who scarcely knew one end of a paintbrush from the other, and Marshall had seemed a sensible enough fellow. Minta was much less keen. David's reference to the likely presence of 'several persons eager to commission portraits' had thrilled her, and she was adamant that nothing should impair Vangenzen's chances in this regard. But she submitted to persuasion. It was only a reception, after all, and Mary must be allowed do her work if she could.

The invitation was issued, therefore, and promptly accepted, and on the appointed afternoon they greeted Marshall outside the Pavillion de l'Horloge, the magnificent central section of the museum's west side. As this was the first visit for two members of the party, Vangenzen conducted a brief tour of the precinct. Being an artist and, more importantly, one who was known to the attendants, he could come and go even when the museum was not generally open to the public.

The museum had previously been a royal château, but for many years the kings and queens of France had seldom lived there – preferring instead their vast residence at Versailles. This explained the different conditions that were to be seen, for some rooms or galleries were beautiful, even excessively grand, while elsewhere roofs leaked or looked to have been unfinished at the time of the Revolution. As well as royal neglect, the Louvre had suffered from undue private attention. Various royal societies had established their offices there, while artists, students, and royal pensioners had taken up lodging. Against the walls of the château and amid the rubble of the half-finished sections, moreover, shops and stalls had flourished like mushrooms. Most of the latter had recently been cleared away, and Mary did not like to think what had happened to the royal pensioners. The artists remained, however, and they had transformed some of the rooms and galleries into workshops and living quarters, with scant regard to the effect of their labours upon ancient walls or floors.

Despite these vicissitudes, there were great jewels to be seen, such as the Salle des Cariatides, where Molière had performed, the Galerie d'Apollon with its ornate ceiling, and the Renaissance stairway of Henri II. Most impressive of all was the Grande Galerie, an immensely long and richly decorated passage that linked the Louvre with the Tuileries palace. This, Vangenzen explained, would become the repository for the most important paintings and sculptures seized from private owners or captured from foreign enemies since the Revolution. 'Claimed for the nation' was his diplomatic phrase.

They ventured only a short way along the Galerie, however,

for David's atelier was in the opposite corner of the museum, and they did not want to be late.

'Even so, I doubt we are able to see many of his paintings,' Vangenzen warned them. 'He does not often open his studio nowadays, and when he does, there is always a crowd. Be prepared to use your elbows.'

The warning was certainly apt. The atelier proved to be a large room, rather dark, and filled with people. On entering, it was possible to catch a glimpse of two of the artist's most famous compositions, the 'Brutus' and the 'Oath of the Horatii', but thereafter the conflicting currents of the human tide determined what one saw and how one moved. Two students recognised Vangenzen and drew him into a professional conclave. Mary was parted from Marshall when a servant bearing what looked to be an antique bronze tripod darted between them. She was pressed instead against a woman with gaudy make-up and dressed in an extreme version of the Grecian style – sleeveless, and very nearly sheer. Its effect as an article of clothing was purely notional.

'Oh my,' said Mary, who was still wearing her outdoor cloak and hat. 'I beg your pardon.'

As she backed away, she noticed other strange details of dress. One woman's fashionable gown contrasted with a spotted kerchief reminiscent of a washerwoman; another had tied a red ribbon around her neck, as if her severed head had been restored with no other ill effects. Quite a few had forgotten their chemises. The men, in their different ways, were no better. Several wore their hair in long, bedraggled curls, except at the back, where it was plaited, turned up, and secured with a comb. Some looked more like courtiers than Republicans, while others affected the style of the *sansculotte*. Mary supposed that the young fellows in long, square-cut coats with enormous lapels and printed cravats were a species of dandy, but what could explain the beards and linen tunics of another group? Were they waiting upon Citizen David or John the Baptist?

Gradually she moved to the periphery of this oddly assorted crowd. Their manner, as well as their mode of dress, was so *foreign*, so different from what she had experienced in London drawing-rooms, that she found it off-putting and even vaguely wrong. English men and women might posture or argue, but their way of doing so was familiar to her. In London one knew when one was being made game of and how to respond to it – in David's studio it was difficult to be certain of either.

Marshall's height allowed Mary to pick him out; he was attempting to converse with one of the apostolic figures on the other side of the room. As the American did not speak French, his efforts were unlikely to succeed, but the prospect gave Mary a thrill of satisfaction. She would offer to translate.

As she made her way towards him, however, she was distracted by another sight: an elderly woman, who appeared to be in some distress. She looked uneasy, even flustered, and she moved unsteadily in heeled slippers with pointed toes. 'May I help you, ma'am? Citizeness, I mean?' asked Mary.

'Help me? Oh yes, you are very kind,' replied the other distractedly. She had a light ebony cane, but clung instead to Mary. '"Madame", did you call me? How lovely.'

She had a robust figure, and when she clung, the force was considerable. *Oh my*, thought Mary, *we shall both be down presently*.

The crowd surged around them, chattering noisily and apparently oblivious to their plight. Mary looked for Vangenzen, but could not find him. Then she spied an odd-looking wooden chair standing against the wall, and guided her charge slowly in its direction. *I expect this will prove to be an important national treasure and in no circumstances to be sat upon,* she brooded. *Well, it cannot be helped.* 'Here we are, ma'am.'

'Ah.' The old woman descended with a gasping sigh and thanked Mary again. 'Oh my, I can barely breathe! And I must look a sight – not that anyone would notice.' She began fussing with her hat and adjusting the copious folds of a long, embroidered pelisse, which was draped round her. Beneath this she wore a pale pink gown, also voluminous, and a quantity of gold jewellery. 'Thank you so much, my dear.'

'Not at all,' Mary assured her. 'The crush is very difficult. A person with experience of these affairs recommended the use of one's elbows.' She caught a glimpse of Marshall. Was he still endeavouring to communicate with the artist? (Mary felt certain that he *was* an artist, somehow.) Yes, and none too successfully, judging by the latter's expression.

'Do not let me keep you from your friends,' said the old woman, who had followed her glance. 'I am quite comfortable now.'

Mary turned to her with a polite smile. She was pondering a suitable reply, one that would enable her to withdraw gracefully, when she had an uncomfortable thought. Here was an elderly lady, apparently friendless, and in strange surroundings. It would be very rude simply to walk away, whatever the competing attraction. She would not behave so in England. 'Indeed, my friends seem to be amply engaged at present,' she replied, 'and my elbows are tired.' Her smile became warmer. 'Are you an admirer of Citizen David's work?'

'To speak truthfully, I have never seen it, but I am told that he is a great talent. I had hoped to interest him in a commission, but that seems unlikely. He is too busy to care about an old woman like me.' She nodded at the crowd. 'As are they all.'

'A commission – for a portrait?' Straightaway Mary's thoughts turned in another direction. If she could not advance her own interests that afternoon, she would endeavour to aid her friends. 'As it happens, my husband is also an artist. Not such a famous one as Citizen David, but I can assure you that he is a very skilful painter of portraits. His name is Vangenzen.'

The old woman frowned. 'Van *what*? He sounds like a foreigner. Not an Austrian, is he?'

'No, ma'am, he is an American.'

Just then Marshall edged through the crowd and appeared on Mary's other side.

'Is this him?' demanded the old woman. 'He does not look like an artist.'

'Is everything all right?' Marshall asked in a low voice. 'I saw you helping this lady. I hope she has not had an accident.'

Mary assured him that all was well. 'This is Madame . . .'

'Thierry. I am Marie-George Thierry. My husband is the noted advocate, Philippe Thierry. I daresay you have heard of him.'

143

'And this Mr Marshall,' said Mary, translating back and forth between them. 'He is a representative of the American government.'

Madame Thierry gave Marshall her hand, and he duly bowed over it. 'You have very pretty manners for a foreigner,' she said. 'But what are all of you doing in Paris? Is the city not crowded enough without you?'

'Indeed, ma'am, sometimes I wonder that very thing myself.'

On the following day Mary went to the Jardin National des Plantes at the hour when Jens would be taking his walk. In deference to Minta's feelings, she did not ask Vangenzen to accompany her. It was perfectly proper for a young matron to walk unaccompanied in the botanical garden, and if she met a friend – an older, highly respectable friend – what could be the harm in that? It was hardly likely to attract untoward attention.

She met Jens on the avenue leading to the Ménagerie, which now housed the collection of exotic animals that had formerly belonged to the king. They walked together for a short while, amusing themselves with conversation about the national museum and the eccentric behaviour of artists. When it had been established that they were both sufficiently warm to risk sitting on one of the benches in the herb garden, however, they turned to the more difficult matter of the American envoys.

Mary was conscious that her information was rather thin and not entirely logical, but she was keen to present it. 'I am convinced that something interesting is afoot,' she urged, 'interesting and important.'

Neither word, not even in close proximity, had much of an effect on Jens. He paused at the mention of *'pot-de-vin'*, acknowledging that it corresponded to 'inducement' or even 'bribe' in English, but he dismissed Mary's triumphant 'Ah ha!' with a frown. Yes, fifty thousand pounds was indeed a handsome sum, but who had asked for it? And what was to be offered in exchange? The envoys undoubtedly came into contact with a great many men, most of them wanting something and some of them rascals. It was the way of things.

Mary tried again, wondering whether the banker, Hubbard,

might be involved. He was English, after all, and would naturally think in pounds rather than a foreign currency – and Mr Marshall had not liked him.

Jens neither agreed nor disagreed; a proper judgment was impossible unless more could be discovered. As for 'Hottinguer', he knew of no one by that name.

They concluded, regretfully on Mary's part, that the information gained did not merit a communication with London. Jens counselled patience and due attention to her instructions, but Mary found both his words and the tone in which they were delivered hard to endure. Was there no other way to learn about the negotiations than through the envoys?

'The foreign minister, Citizen Talleyrand-Périgord must be conducting the negotiations on the French side. Perhaps I ought—'

'No, no!' Jens cried, and his look of self-righteousness vanished in a flash. 'Do not even consider going to see Talleyrand! Why, if you smiled at him he would have the teeth out of your mouth before you closed your lips!'

'Oh, come now, indeed,' said Mary. 'Mr Marshall and Colonel Pinckney have met him and survived the experience. I daresay I could—'

'You could *what*? Charm him? Deceive him? Bah, you agents are all alike,' Jens stormed. 'You think you are immortal, that nothing can go wrong. That is what that fellow Risse thought.'

'Risse?'

'The first one. *He* was full of confidence, and what happened? Killed during the crossing – he never even reached France.' Jens sat back on the bench and folded his arms, his sentence ending on a note of surly triumph.

Mary stared at him. 'Do you mean . . . another agent had already been sent to meet with the Americans? And I was only given the job when he failed? But Mr Shy said . . .'

Even before she spoke, Jens realised that he had made a mistake, but rather than attempting to retreat he advanced more forcefully. 'Shy says a great many things. Of course there was another agent and a sensible plan, not some wild scheme, thrown

145

together on a whim. Johann Risse and the American, Pinckney, were acquaintances. They knew each other from the military college at Caen. Risse had a chance of succeeding.'

From the turmoil of her dismay, that assertion struck Mary like a blow. 'So do I.'

Jens humphed into his neckcloth. 'Perhaps.' Then, stealing a glance at her from the corner of his eye, he relented slightly. The sight of her pale, young profile might have touched his cold heart, or perhaps he secretly admired the firmness of her response. 'We shall see. And now I think you should go. Speak again with your friendly American, and stay away from Talleyrand.'

'Very well. You have not . . . received any further messages from Mr Shy, I suppose?'

'From Shy? No.' A shake of the head strengthened the negative. 'Messages will come from us, not from him. When you learn anything more, come and see me at the shop. It is too cold to meet here again.'

They parted, and Jens made his way leisurely towards Vrillac's. When he arrived he did not open the shop, as was his usual custom, but instead went upstairs to his private room. There he poured himself a small glass of brandy to drive away the chill, and re-read the letter that had arrived the previous day.

Bowles & Carver, printers
69 St Paul's Churchyard
London

28th October 1797

Mr Tobias Jens
Chez Vrillac: Fournisseur de Beaux-Arts
Rue Geoffroy l'Asnier
Paris

Sir,
I trust that our previous consignment, despatched from this estab-lishment on the 18th of October, has reached you in a satisfactory

146

condition. If you have sent a note of confirmation, kindly disregard this further reference on the subject; the disordered state of the mail in this country has thrown our regular communications with customers into some disarray.

I must also beg your indulgence on another matter. It has come to my attention that a second consignment was mistakenly despatched to you two days ago. Contained therein are prints by the rising engraver and colourist, Andrew Ogbourne, whose Dutch landscapes have already sparked considerable interest among collectors. As well as the Ogbournes are a set of anonymous historical prints. These came to us unexpectedly, and Bowles & Carver have been unable to identify the artist. The prints chronicle important events in the lives of ancient French worthies, including Philip Augustus and Charles Martel, and evidence considerable artistic skill.

Knowing that you take an interest in works of this kind and are likely to come into contact with customers of a like mind, I trust that the prints will not remain long within your premises.

If you obtain commissions and wish to fulfil them through the agencies of Bowles & Carver, we shall be pleased to accommodate you, but due to the special circumstances under which these particular prints have been despatched, I must inform you that we cannot offer the same terms as for our previous consignment. Indeed, you would oblige me by considering them as quite separate and distinct.

I remain, sir, your most respectful servant,
Henry Carrington Bowles

11

When Mary recovered from the shock of Jens' revelation, her first conscious emotion was anger at having been deceived – lied to by Cuthbert Shy. How could he have done such a thing? How dared he be dishonest with her? She understood now why her assignment had been thrown together so quickly, even why she had been chosen. Not because Shy thought her particularly suited to the task, but because an earlier, better plan and a more skilful agent had already failed!

But hers was not a naturally choleric temperament, and she soon began to judge the matter more evenly. *She* after all, could hardly be exonerated from a charge of deception, for she had misled Miss Trent and Mrs Tipton, been less than candid with Vangenzen, and had positively lied to Captain Holland. (The last admission came with a particularly uncomfortable pang.) Very likely, Mr Shy's actions had been well intended and possibly even justified. Perhaps she would have declined his proposal if she had known of her predecessor's failure, or she might have wavered, and there had simply not been time for that.

The consciousness of having been managed, and of not being so near the centre of things as she had imagined, continued to rankle, but she told herself that this was mere vanity. *If you had stopped to think, you would have appreciated that Mr Shy must know a great many secrets, and that you have no special claim on*

his confidence. Having chosen to place yourself under his authority,
you must either accept the consequences or withdraw.

Withdrawal did not tempt her. She had meant what she said
to Jens, and his indiscretion reinforced her belief in the importance of her task. *And after all*, she told herself, *I have already
achieved more than Mr Risse.* As she lay in bed that night, however,
the question of what one knew and what one said returned
to her in a different guise. It had begun innocently enough.
After supper, Minta had wanted to clear the table, but Vangenzen
had demanded a more important service – rendering her opinion
on some sketches. Would any of them suit a series of small, still
life paintings he had in contemplation? Straightaway the dirty
plates and cutlery had been pushed aside, and Minta had not
merely listened to his explanations, she had also offered
thoughtful criticism. For nearly half an hour the two of them
had been absorbed by the exercise, exchanging ideas and
squinting at the sketches. Vangenzen had even taken up a piece
of charcoal to make the suggested alterations.

Mary thought how happy they were, how contented. They had
suffered for their happiness, and did not deserve to have it upset
by 'snares and stratagems'. She reminded herself that Vangenzen
had also thrown in his lot with Shy, but could not feel that the
parallel was the same. He knew so much less than she did, and
Minta was relying on Mary alone to keep them safe. It was a
weighty burden, and the deeper she delved into the affairs of the
envoys, the more she learned of her assignment, the heavier it
would become. But what was the alternative?

*I cannot do other than continue as I have begun, as carefully as I
can*, she resolved, but it was not a resolution that encouraged
untroubled sleep.

A chance to put her words into action came in the form of
an invitation from Mr Marshall and Colonel Pinckney to visit
the Hôtel des Invalides. The prospect of meeting both the
Americans did away with any squeamishness Mary felt about
visiting an asylum for maimed and wounded soldiers. The two
men might be tempted to converse about their own affairs,

little suspecting that she was paying the closest attention. It would, she felt, be an excellent opportunity.

In the event, the Hôtel itself was not so distressing as she had imagined. The sight of so many disabled men was sobering, even if they belonged to the enemy, but the grounds were ample, the wards spacious and convenient, and everything relating to the care of the inmates seemed to be conducted with the greatest order and regularity. As an occasion for advancing her particular interests, the visit was less successful. A garrulous old soldier accompanied them on their tour, and while informative, his anecdotes left little time for private speech.

She did learn two interesting pieces of information, however. Colonel Pinckney revealed that he was a Federalist – one of those American politicians who favoured closer ties with Britain – and Mr Marshall spoke of his deep enjoyment of Citizen David's reception and of artistic occasions generally.

'Oh, then I hope that you will be our guest at the opera, sir,' said Mary, 'and perhaps take supper with us afterwards at Beauvilliers? I am told that the Paris opera has no equal for . . . artistry, and I wish very much to see for myself whether the French singers are better than those I have heard in London.'

'Indeed, ma'am, I would be delighted.'

'And Colonel Pinckney – I hope that you will also join us?'

The colonel's expression of delight was perhaps not quite so genuine, but Mary was more than satisfied. *If only we may be lucky with the opera*, she mused. *Either a brilliant or a woeful performance will inspire conversation, and who can avoid chatting over a good meal?*

The following evening the Vangenzens and the two Americans sat through a dreary performance of *Iphigenie*. Mary looked handsome in her new turquoise gown, which she daringly wore without a buffon neckerchief, but she scarcely heard the compliments. Instead she was straining to find something in the opera that she might turn, skilfully, to the advantage of Britain. It seemed a hopeless task. How could one, in all conscience, argue that war was sometimes necessary, and that nations with a common sensibility should unite, when faced with a tale of bickering Greeks and a father who would kill his daughter in order to pursue a dubious martial aim? The soprano's voice *was* weak and tremulous, but that hardly justified her execution.

Mary placed her hopes on the ballet, *L'Offrande à la Liberté*, which sounded far more promising, and she was not disappointed. A series of patriotic tableaux punctuated by the singing of the *Marseillaise* hymn, it culminated in the appearance on stage of uniformed soldiers (all in excellent health), brandishing their sabres and crying, 'To arms, citizens!' and 'War against the English!' The audience expressed its enthusiastic support, and Mary shuddered with every indication of dismay.

Over dinner she broached the matter cautiously. 'Naturally, I consider myself an American,' she said, nodding affectionately at Vangenzen, 'but I confess that I found this evening's performance very alarming. Ought I to tremble for my friends in England?'

The colonel promptly reassured her, even patting her hand. (Although he disliked opera in all its manifestations, his spirits had risen remarkably with the arrival of soup and the first bottle of wine.) The Royal Navy stood guard between France and Britain, he explained, whatever people might claim about French military might. 'And you know the old saying, ma'am, "Brag is a good dog—" '

'"But Holdfast is a better"?'

'Exactly.' He toasted her and emptied his glass. 'I believe you may put your trust in the Royal Navy and Mr Pitt's gold.'

Mary had been smiling, but now she produced an expression of innocent curiosity. 'I am happy to do the first, sir, but the second sounds very odd indeed. What do you mean by "Mr Pitt's gold"?' A sudden thought stuck her like a thunderbolt. *Mr Pitt's gold — fifty thousand pounds! But surely Mr Shy would have told me if our government was attempting to . . . pay the American envoys? Surely he would have spoken . . .* Struggling to control her voice, she asked, 'Do you mean the money that the British government spends on the Navy?'

Marshall and Pinckney smiled at her efforts to grasp the complexities of international relations, and Pinckney endeavoured to explain. The British government would naturally wish to build a new coalition – a new partnership with another European state – which would no doubt involve loans and subsidies to support the armies in the field. That was what *he* meant by 'Mr Pitt's gold'. The French and their cowardly supporters in America, however, frequently employed the phrase insultingly.

'The implication being,' added Marshall, 'that the aid is more in the nature of a bribe. I am afraid that such underhand exchanges are not unknown in the affairs of nations. I make no accusation against Mr Pitt, of course.'

'Oh no,' Mary agreed. 'I have always understood Mr Pitt to be strictly honest. That is his reputation in Parliament, I believe.'

'And well deserved, I am sure,' said Pinckney. 'English pounds, however, seem to have a particular attraction on this side of the Channel. Citizen Talleyrand, for instance, prefers them to French francs and *assignats* these days.' He threw his colleague an arch look.

Mary saw it – and the quick frown that it provoked – and her heart began to beat faster. *Talleyrand . . . English pounds . . . Could the bribe – the* 'pot-de-vin' *come from the French government? From Citizen Talleyrand himself?* She risked a cautious glance at the tables nearest them. The colonel's remark seemed to have been lost in the general hubbub; she could detect no one who appeared to be interested in their conversation. Still, she wished they were in a less public place. *Why did I suggest such a popular restaurant as Beauvilliers?*

Did she dare risk another question? It mustn't sound other than part of a polite exchange. 'I wonder what sort of man Citizen Talleyrand is,' she mused. 'He is very wise, they say.'

'He . . . keeps his own counsel,' said Marshall.

Pinckney was drinking wine and almost choked. Recovering, he said that it was indeed a wise man who knew when to speak, and turning to Mary, asked, 'What would you say, ma'am, of a fellow who wanted fifty thousand pounds before he would open his lips?'

'Well, I . . . I hardly know.' She forced herself to answer playfully, as if she knew that a joke had been told, but did not comprehend its meaning. 'Only, I suppose, I would hope that, when he did speak, he had something very interesting to say.'

While Mary was learning about wisdom from the Americans, Jens' attention remained focused on the arrival of Mr Shy's mistaken agents. His first thought, upon learning that the men had been despatched under less than ideal circumstances, had been to prepare false papers for them – papers of identification and papers authorising them to travel to Paris. Almost immediately, however, his project had been halted for lack of information. Were the agents desirous of appearing as harmless neutrals? As rebellious Irishmen? Did they wish to claim any particular qualifications? He supposed that one of them might safely be designated Mr Andrew Ogbourne, but what of the other?

The documents would have to be put aside until he had met the gentlemen and confirmed their requirements. That was the correct procedure for matters of business, and it applied equally where espionage was concerned. Then he had a more worrying thought. What if they did not know about Vrillac's? Could the 'mistake' extend even to a lack of that vital piece of information? Jens decided it very well could. The English were hardly methodical at the best of times, and when an undertaking was thrown together haphazardly, chaos on several fronts could be expected. *What a nuisance these people are*, he complained to himself.

After failing to receive a visit from Mr Ogbourne or Mr French Worthies (as Jens privately designated him), he decided upon a different course. Before they had taken flight, the British agents working for Mr Wickham of the Alien Office had frequently conducted assignations at the Bibliothèque Nationale, and Jens was familiar with their routine. If the two newcomers also knew of it, they would probably present themselves at the library in the hope of gaining such support as might be provided by their compatriots. (Always assuming that they managed to reach Paris in the first place, of course, for Jens was not confident that anything could be relied upon in this strange affair.)

The library was open to the public on particular days of each month, from ten o'clock until two. Jens duly visited the Galerie des Médailles on the morning of the thirteenth of Brumaire and again on the sixteenth. A very tedious exercise, but what could one do? As he was gazing at a large silver plate said to have belonged to Hannibal, a tall, lean man appeared beside him. Jens studied him covertly. The fellow was suffi- ciently scruffy either to be a noted scholar or to have made his way secretly across France. Well, he would wait to see what happened. The English invariably revealed themselves as soon as they opened their mouths.

He was quite surprised, therefore, when the lean man observed rapturously, and in an accent that betrayed no hint of an English schoolroom, 'Ah, here we have a treasure most exceptional, I think, and most ancient. The great general dined from this very plate, perhaps! One likes to think so.'

'Indeed,' said Jens, covering his surprise with a cough. Of course, the reference to the Carthaginian was hardly surprising, anyone might manage it. He would try the fellow with Cato. 'But what remains now of Hannibal or his city?' he asked. 'Only that plate. Cato said *"Delenda est Carthago"*, and so it was destroyed.'

'Because he had the honour to command the Roman army,' replied the lean man. 'As it was said in those days, "The voice of Cato is the voice of Rome".'

'And "The voice of Rome is the consent of Heaven",' agreed Jens, completing the quotation with a satisfied nod. Even the most eccentric French scholar was unlikely to quote the English dramatist Ben Jonson in such circumstances. He guided Martel, for it was he, into the largely deserted manuscripts gallery, where they could speak more freely.

A short while later, Martel had left the library and was making his way cautiously towards Les Halles, a bustling, but less respectable neighbourhood in the centre of Paris. In one of the alleys near to the teeming market he and Holland had found accommodation of a sort – an attic room above a wine shop and brothel. They could not take rooms at a respectable inn or boarding house, for they lacked identity papers. Nor dared they risk descending too deeply among the criminal fraternity of Paris, whose members might deliver strangers to the police for the price of a glass of brandy. Yet Sophie, the woman who managed the wine shop (it would have been impolite to query her other commercial interests), had taken pity on them. So long as they paid in advance and made no trouble for the house, she was content. Also, 'the quiet one' must remain out of sight. He was a handsome enough fellow, but dangerous. Dangerous how? A Gallic shrug. She did not wish to find out.

It was sensible advice. Holland and Martel had entered the capital surreptitiously, but travel within the city remained dangerous, particularly for Holland. He required an identity that would both defuse any suspicion of his foreignness and provide him with a plausible introduction to the Reverend Boyle. Until such an identity was established, he would be wise to avoid the streets of Paris. Therefore, while Martel foraged for information, Holland remained in the draughty attic, plotting out likely exchanges with the inventor on the backs of receipts from the wine shop, which Sophie had provided for his entertainment along with a pen and cheap bottle of ink.

He looked up from his work when his colleague appeared, bearing rolls and a jug of coffee, and looking pleased with himself.

'Success,' Martel announced, setting down his burdens on the little table just inside the door. He poured each of them a cup before adding, 'In a manner of speaking.'

Holland did not ask unnecessary questions, so the qualification hung, mysteriously. After a suitable pause, Martel continued, 'The proper British agents — all of those whom *I* knew — have been withdrawn. Paris has become too hot for them. Now there is only an odd little fellow called Jens who works for an Englishman. This Englishman seems to conduct espionage as if it were his private affair. While his authority is not certain—'

'It's Cuthbert bloody Shy!' complained Holland, and he threw down his pen with a frown. 'I might have guessed he would stick his oar in, somehow or other.'

'Ah, yes,' Martel admitted, and he also frowned. His revelation had fallen rather flat, and instead of explaining how he intended to deal with Jens, he asked grudgingly, 'You know this man, Shy?'

'Unfortunately.'

'You do not sound as if you approve of him. Is he untrustworthy?'

'I suppose he is honest enough,' Holland admitted. 'He has some kind of arrangement with the government. Ministers don't admit to it, but I think that they keep Shy informed of most things having to do with spies and secret plots.'

'That is what must have happened on this occasion,' said Martel with greater confidence. 'Jean-Achille reported our situation to Mr Nepean, and he passed the information on to Shy. His man, Jens, knew that we were coming to Paris.'

'Well,' Holland acknowledged with a sigh, 'I would rather we had more reserves than one odd duck working for Shy, but I suppose he is better than nothing. Is he able to help us?'

'He said he could provide papers that would withstand ordinary scrutiny. We can collect them tomorrow at his shop in the Rue Geoffroy l'Asnier.'

'Thank God for that.' Holland looked quizzical. 'Why tomorrow?'

Martel shrugged and sipped his coffee. 'The papers take time to prepare, or perhaps he must make other arrangements. He complained bitterly about the demands of his work.'

'Can he compose the letter of introduction?'

'Yes, and I told him of our plan of battle – you an American traveller, and me your faithful French valet. Everything will be done as you specified.'

'Good. Then we can proceed with Boyle.'

'I think so. One detail occurred to me as surprising when I made the arrangements with Jens. My name, Philippe Martel, he was content to use, but for you he had a suggestion. It sounded like a strange name, but perhaps it is a common one in England.'

156

'It wouldn't be safe to use my own, and as long as the other is common in America, I don't mind. What is it?'

'Andrew Ogbourne. It is odd-sounding, no?'

Mary completed the day's shopping before setting off to see Jens. While keen to report her findings as soon as possible, she did not want to alarm Minta. So she delayed her departure until the early afternoon, and said only that she wished to discuss a few matters with Jens. Nothing particularly important, but she liked to keep him informed even of small details.

'Well, be careful,' said Minta absently.

'I shall,' Mary assured her.

She decided to walk at least part of the way to Vrillac's, in order to rehearse her explanation of what she had learned. It was simple, really, yet quite extraordinary. *The negotiations between the French and American governments have not begun – that is why Mr Marshall is unhappy and the American ship-owners clamour outside his door.*

It seemed to be the hour for taking one's dog for a walk. Mary passed an elegant woman accompanied by a small, mincing creature whose tail curled rakishly over his back; a man was towed by two large animals, more like young bulls with square heads and broad, powerful chests. Another dog, smooth-haired and nervous, and with no apparent owner, sniffed Mary enquiringly and then dashed away. *But the envoys have been in Paris for several weeks – what accounts for the delay? Quite simply, the foreign minister will not see them. Is he too busy? No, but he demands payment – a* pot-de-vin *– from the Americans before he will speak.*

The collision of a cabriolet and a private carriage caused Mary to turn into one of the small streets that crossed the Rue Franciade and continue south on the Rue Martin. She had no wish to be caught up in an argument about who had obstructed whom and whose horses had misbehaved. Her experience was that few people remembered accidents in the same way, but most knew precisely what had happened. *Unless Citizen Talleyrand receives the sum of fifty thousand pounds, Mr Marshall*

157

and his colleagues can either go back to America or remain in Paris, amusing themselves at the theatre, and Invalides, and artists' studios.

A little farther along the Rue Martin, Mary hailed a cabriolet that she hoped would be driven carefully. 'The Rue Geoffroy l'Asnier, citizen, if you please.'

As she opened the door to Vrillac's, she felt that something out of the ordinary ought to happen, in recognition of her astonishing news. And Jens *would* be astonished – for all that he would try to conceal it with an account of an order for turpentine that had gone astray. She smiled to herself.

Unbeknownst to Mary, there was a private room at the rear of the shop, and at the sound of the bell, Jens' head appeared from around a corner (rather like a small animal emerging from its den, if one were being unkind). He frowned peevishly at the disturbance, but that was hardly surprising. As there appeared to be no other customers, she greeted him in a marked tone and followed it with a significant glance, but he seemed to take both of these in the wrong way. Far from provoking interest or even surprise, her actions only strengthened his annoyance.

'*Pardonnez-moi, Citoyenne Vangenzen, mais ce n'est pas le moment bon pour une visite,*' he complained, shaking his head and even employing one of his goose-herding gestures to encourage her withdrawal.

'*Mais*—' She tried to explain herself, but before she could do, an unfamiliar voice repeated, '*Citoyenne Vangenzen?*' and a very familiar one, demanded, 'Damn him, I knew it!'

Then everything happened very quickly. A tall, lean man loomed up behind Jens; Mary perceived the open door; something fell over; and Robert Holland, looking dishevelled and furious, pushed past both men to glare at her in no very friendly way. He had cut his hair, she noticed, and he always looked unfamiliar to her when he was dressed in civilian clothes.

'Oh my,' she said, retreating a step. 'I mean, good afternoon . . . citizen.'

'Good afternoon,' he replied, folding his arms across his chest. 'You did not care for the cottage in Wiltshire after all, I see.'

Mary shook her head. She could feel the colour rising to

her cheeks. *How is this possible? How has he managed . . . ? And in front of Jens, too!*

'I hope Miss Trent is feeling better now?'

'What?' She shot Holland a startled glance, but his expression was difficult to read. He could not possibly be making game of her, could he? 'She is—'

'She did not feel the need to accompany you to France, I mean? To lift her spirits?'

Abominable man! 'It was *Mrs* Trent who was ill,' Mary retorted, and with a defiant lift of her chin she added that both ladies were presently enjoying excellent health, so far as she was aware.

Holland rubbed the bridge of his nose and answered from behind his hand. 'I am glad to hear it.'

'*Qui est Mlle Trent?*' Jens demanded, looking more like an angry ferret than usual. '*De quoi parlent-ils?*'

Martel, to whom Holland had reluctantly provided a bald explanation of certain facts, smiled complacently. He replied, '*Les amoureux anglais. C'est comme ça qu'ils se saluent.*'

'*Mais non!*' groaned Jens. '*Quand les amoureux se rencontrent, la raison part.*'

It was impossible to explain everything or to ask all of her own questions, not with Martel grinning and pretending to study a catalogue of prints, and Jens not pretending at all but looking extremely vexed. Mary made do with a brief description of the task that Mr Shy had set her. Everything else, she decided, could wait for a less . . . turbulent occasion. Holland's account immediately made her regret that decision, but when her marvelling query, 'A boat that sails underwater?' met with an exasperated clucking from Jens, she gave way.

It was scant consolation. Jens hated disorder and valued discretion, yet he had been exposed to the first and denied the second – and all in a very short space of time. What did this fellow Ogbourne mean by coming to Vrillac's in advance of his appointment and demanding to know what Jens knew about Mary Finch? And what did Citizeness Vangenzen (it was so very unprofessional to mention any names not relevant to the matter

159

at hand) mean by appearing without warning, making mysterious gestures, and speaking of unknown Englishwomen? What did either of them mean? The Frenchman Martel was also provoking with his airs and opinions about how things ought to be arranged. Did he imagine that responsibility for the conduct of affairs in Paris had somehow devolved upon him? It was outrageous.

They all deserved to be sent away, but Jens was long-suffering. Sighing deeply, he instructed Martel to mind the shop and then ushered Mary and Holland into the private room. Small, close, and musty-smelling, it was where he did all of his particularly confidential work, such as the preparation of false papers. There was not sufficient space for all of them to sit comfortably, so while Jens resumed his place at an undersized desk and Mary perched on a crate, Holland was obliged to stand, bending awkwardly to accommodate the slanting walls and low-pitched ceiling. In this rather deferential posture, he received Jens' ill-humoured observations while the other hunched over his work.

Martel's French papers had been simple enough – for the professional – but an American passport required much greater attention. It could not be thrown together so quickly. 'You must come back tomorrow, as I requested, at which time I shall have a decent set of documents for you, Mr Ogbourne.'

'*As you requested?*' Mary repeated incredulously. 'Do you mean that you *knew* Captain Holland was in Paris?' She turned from one to the other. 'And Andrew Ogbourne . . . you spoke of the Admiralty, but this is something to do with Mr Shy, is it not? And yet he said—'

'It's an Admiralty job all right,' said Holland, 'but I wouldn't be surprised if Shy knew all about it.'

'Quiet, both of you!' snapped Jens. 'If you were not told it was doubtless to prevent such scenes as this one! Agents treading on each other's toes – Vrillac's in a mad confusion! How can I be expected to work in such chaos?'

Mary bit back a sharp retort of her own. 'And how can *I*— No, I beg your pardon. Please continue.'

'Well then. *If* I am not interrupted again, I shall have your documents tomorrow.' Jens looked baleful, but then relented and produced two *cartes de residence* with the names 'Philippe Martel, servant' and 'Andrew Ogbourne, traveller' carefully inscribed, as well as their lodgings near Les Halles.

Holland nodded and murmured his thanks. 'I was hoping to pay a visit to Mr Boyle tomorrow,' he observed tentatively. 'Martel believes he has found him out.'

'Mr Martel is laudably efficient, of course,' quipped Jens. 'Nothing escapes him.' He paused. 'Well?'

'The letter of introduction from Mr Watt?'

'Ah, yes.' Jens had actually forgotten all about Holland's request, but he concealed this by complaining about the heavy labours that had been imposed upon him. There was never a moment's peace. 'I suppose I *might* be able to manage it now.' He selected a sheet of paper and chose a likely date for Mr Watt's composition.

'How do you know— I mean, can one be certain that the gentleman writes so neatly?' asked Mary in what she hoped was a suitably deferential tone.

'A Scot *and* an engineer, and you expect extravagant penmanship? Believe me, he has a small, neat hand – very much like this. Now, what is his address? A testimonial of this kind requires a due formality.'

Holland considered. 'I know that Boulton & Watt have recently built a foundry at Smethwick in Staffordshire – you had better use that.' He watched as Jens wrote. 'You've forgotten the "w".'

'What?'

'In Smethwick.' He spelled out the last four letters.

'Smeth*ick* with a "w"? Only in English could there be such foolishness!' Jens grumbled. With a heavy sigh at this profligate consumption of Vrillac's best writing paper, he selected a fresh sheet and began again.

When the letter was completed, he set down his pen and folded his hands. Having frowned first at Mary and then at Holland, he issued a stern lecture on the subject of their future relations while in Paris. Although somewhat disadvantaged by the necessity of speaking English, his gist was clear – today's unfortunate encounter ought not to be repeated. There was nothing more dangerous than the promiscuous mingling of unrelated activities, particularly when those activities were of a confidential nature.

Holland attempted to intervene, but Jens bore him down. He could be surprisingly forceful for one so small. 'I detest all reckless, romantic, ill-conceived schemes,' he affirmed, and waited until the other flushed before continuing. 'We are agreed? There will be no nonsense? Good. Then I believe our business is concluded for the moment, Mr Ogbourne.'

Jens rose and gestured uncompromisingly towards the door. 'I shall just accompany you . . . it will be necessary to close the shop briefly. Such a nuisance for my customers at this time of day, but *they* are never considered by persons with confidential business and romantic entanglements.'

'After we have met with Boyle,' said Holland, hesitating, 'either Martel or I shall contact you.'

'Yes, yes. Good day to you.'

'Here – at the shop.'

'Where else? Goodbye!'

Holland could manage little more than a meaningful glance in Mary's direction before the presence of Jens, standing so close as to be almost under his chin, obliged him to retreat into the body of the shop. Mary called 'Goodbye!' but the door closed on the second syllable, and she was left alone in the dusty little room.

When Jens returned, he looked so superior and pleased with himself that Mary felt obliged to apologise for her part in the 'unfortunate encounter'. 'You see, I never imagined that . . . Mr Ogbourne—'

'Pooh,' said Jens with a wave, 'let us leave Mr Ogbourne to his aquatic concerns for the present. Tell me instead what you have learned from the Americans. For it was that, I presume, which drew you to Vrillac's this afternoon?'

162

12

Holland and Martel set off promptly the following morning, for what they hoped would be a meeting with the Reverend Samson Boyle. 'Where is he staying?' asked Holland, as they walked westward along the Rue de la Ferone.

'This way,' Martel replied, gesturing vaguely; he disliked explanations. 'Let us spare our legs, however, and take a cabriolet.'

Holland was the better driver, but Martel was familiar with the streets of Paris. Rather than argue the point, they tacitly agreed that the attendant should sit beside Holland and hold the reins, while Martel climbed up behind, as befit a servant. The attendant proved a talkative individual, and when he perceived that Holland was new to Paris and had come from America besides, he felt obliged to offer a commentary. There were a great many scenes to delight and astonish the foreign visitor.

With Martel translating, the attendant held forth on the most notable sight upon their route: the Place des Victoires-Nationaux. On reaching it, he insisted on circling the noble space, so that Holland might admire it from all angles. The central statue – of Louis XIV crowned by Fame and surrounded by his dejected opponents – he described at great length. This was just as well, for it had been melted down for military purposes some years earlier. A somewhat less inspiring wooden pyramid now stood in its place.

'We have melted Louis to make cannons for more victories, eh, citizen?'

'Yes, very likely.'

'And against the same dogs we defeated that other time, I expect – the Austrians, the Spaniards, the Prussians, and . . . I forget the fourth.'

'I believe it was the Dutch,' said Holland, who knew something of the Treaty of Nijmegen.

'Ah, yes, those silly butter boxes. But they are all our allies now – after we thumped them, ha ha! Soon we will make the English our allies too, eh? After General Bonaparte gives them a good thumping.'

Holland expressed a proper enthusiasm for this eventuality, even venturing a few remarks on how the Americans had shown the way as regards thumping the British Army – with French assistance, of course.

After a few more exchanges about thumping and glorious French victories, Holland and Martel descended, intending to travel the rest of the way by foot. 'It is not much farther,' Martel confided, 'but it is better that we are not watched. That chattering fellow may have a better memory for faces than he does for battles.'

Their destination was the former convent of the *Augustins déchaussés*, familiarly known as the Little Fathers. The convent church had recently been converted into a stock exchange, but other buildings remained at the government's disposal, and in one of these Mr Boyle had taken up residence.

The convent proper had a street entrance, so they chose it rather than venturing farther into the grounds. At least they would appear like regular visitors, although it was not clear what sort of welcome they would receive. The door looked ill tended, with dead leaves clustered on the step and a faded handbill clinging to one of the panels. Someone had scrawled the customary *'Liberté, Égalité'* on the stonework and then seemingly grown tired of the exercise.

Holland rang what appeared to be an iron bell pull; rusting flakes came off on his hand. After a pause, he thought he could hear a dull clanging from somewhere behind the dark stone walls.

The sound faded. Holland rang a second time, and was glancing interrogatively at his companion when the bolt shot, a key turned in the lock, and the door swung open. The draught blew the leaves against the shoes of a small, round-shouldered man, dressed in a plain black suit, leather apron, and what appeared to be a dressing-gown. Grey hair peeped from beneath a nightcap. Had they interrupted his work or his slumber?

He blinked myopically behind a pair of spectacles and then removed them. Two further pairs and a single lens hung from separate chains around his neck, and he selected the last of these. Placing it before his left eye he surveyed Martel and then Holland before venturing a cautious, *'Oui?'*

Martel pushed forward, bowing and gesturing in a babble of French. He seemed to carry a number of characters ready formed inside his head, and he could assume any one of them as circumstances required – the illiterate farmer, the sober tradesman, the layabout, the drunkard or, as now, the officious, fawning servant. His tone of voice, even his posture changed to suit the particular role.

The transformations had surprised Holland at first, but he had quickly learned to accept them and play along as well as he could. He did so now. As the diminutive figure in the doorway retreated a pace, urging, 'Slowly, please, my good fellow,' Holland advanced, smiling earnestly. 'Ah, you speak English, sir, thank goodness – that is enough now, Martel, er, *suffisamment*. I will speak with the gentleman. Sir, have I the pleasure of addressing the Reverend Samson Boyle?'

'Indeed you do, sir,' replied the other, peering more inquisitively through his lens. 'And who—'

'Andrew Ogbourne of Connecticut, at your service.' Holland held out his hand.

Boyle accepted it. His own clasp was gentle, a mild squeeze of soft, thin fingers. 'Ah, most happy, sir, most happy. Ought I to know you? I mean, forgive me, but I do not recognise the name. "Ogbourne", did you say?'

Holland assured him that there was nothing to forgive and launched into his piece. He was a student of machinery, and he had come to Europe in order to improve his education on that fascinating subject. Various gentlemen in England had been most helpful, but the French had a particular genius in mechanics that he particularly wished to observe. And having heard that Reverend Boyle had lately come to this country, 'I naturally hoped to make your acquaintance.'

'To Europe,' Boyle repeated slowly. 'Do I understand you, sir, to be an American?'

'Yes, sir,' said Holland, hoping that Boyle had never heard one speak. *Surely a few of them still sound like Englishmen?*

'All the way from America we have come,' echoed Martel. 'Such a long voyage, and the *mal de mere*' – he placed his hand delicately upon his stomach – 'dreadful!'

'Oh my.' Boyle nodded distractedly at Martel before returning to Holland. 'And you are interested in machines, you say? Mechanical devices? How marvellous, splendid. I myself have some small interest in the subject.'

'Yes, sir, I know that you do. Indeed, when I said that I would be travelling to France, *Mr Watt* particularly mentioned your name.'

The reference to the illustrious engineer provoked a momentary confusion, as Boyle imagined that Watt had either said something or sent something related to Boyle's canal project. 'And that would be tiresome, because, you see, I have been obliged to put that project to one side, and I should not like to disappoint Mr Watt or seem ungrateful.' Then he had to be convinced that *Holland's* interest was not primarily in canals. 'For I have been obliged . . . I would not say that I have abandoned the idea completely – indeed, I hope not – but I have put it to one side for the present, along with my rope-making machine.'

'No, sir, I have no particular preference,' Holland assured him, 'and both of those schemes sound very interesting. What I meant to say is that Mr Watt has been good enough to provide me with a letter of introduction.'

'Ah, a letter? To me? How charming. Mr Watt is a most agreeable fellow, to be sure.' Boyle received the document and started to fumble with his assortment of ocular aids, which had become entangled in the buttons of his waistcoat. 'Oh, but you must come inside,' he urged. 'A *letter*, after all. You will come in, won't you, and have a cup of tea?'

Holland accepted the invitation. He would like nothing better than to drink tea and, he hoped, hear about Mr Boyle's ideas and experiments. 'And perhaps, if you could spare the time, you might comment upon some ideas of my own.'

'Hmm? Ideas? Oh yes, certainly. An excellent suggestion.'

After affirming that the door was locked and bolted behind them – 'boys, you know, ring the bell sometimes, and try to make mischief' – Boyle conducted his visitors down an empty passage, at the end of which was a small room. It was decorated with odd pieces of furniture, most very plain, and some broken or knocked about. The centrepiece was a large wooden armchair set behind a table littered with diagrams, tools, scribbled notes, pens, a set of scales, and metal gears of various sizes.

'This is where the abbot used to preside,' Boyle explained. 'Rather impertinent to take it for my study, but none of the other rooms has a working stove, and it has grown very chilly of late, particularly in the evenings.'

'Not at all,' Holland murmured, removing a sheaf of papers from a less magisterial chair. He sat down, holding the papers on his lap, and glanced at the uppermost: '*A New System of Small-Gauge Canals, which, if it be adopted, will produce the most considerable part of the public revenue.*' Silently damning the system of small-gauge canals, he assumed an attitude of patience, while Boyle continued to speak, half aloud, and then to read his letter.

'I was in Normandy before coming to Paris, and I found it much warmer. Funny, that. Winter is drawing in, of course . . .'

Holland agreed that it was and asked whether Martel could make himself useful by brewing the tea.

'Who? Ah, and Martel is . . .? Oh yes, you did say – why, certainly, if he would be so kind.'

Boyle turned to the purported servant and voiced his request in that species of French peculiar to the Anglo-Saxon race. Holland had to look away, so nearly did it mirror the tone, volume, and style imitated by Martel, but that individual received it without a trace of a smile.

'*Le thé?* But of course, *monsieur. Immédiatement* I bring him.'

'Excellent,' said Boyle, clearly pleased with this testament to his linguistic prowess. He then launched into a series of instructions relating either to tea-making or to the location of the kitchen. Apparently satisfied with whatever he had been told, Martel bowed and made his exit. 'Splendid fellow,' Boyle concluded as the door closed.

'I couldn't do without him on this trip,' Holland acknowledged. 'I'm afraid that I don't have your command of the French language, sir.'

Boyle nodded benevolently. 'Much easier if we all spoke English, I daresay. The world is a veritable Tower of Babel, nowadays. And that reminds me of an exceedingly odd experience I had in this very room. A fellow from the Ministry paid me a call, full of questions as usual. Imagine the scene. There he was, rattling away twenty to the dozen, but instead of asking him to pull up, as I generally do after missing more than a sentence, I found that I could understand him quite perfectly – apart from the accent. How do you account for it? He was sitting just about where you are now – in that very chair.'

Holland dutifully surveyed his immediate surroundings, as if the alignment of chair and desk might provide an answer to the riddle, and then eyed the distance between himself and his interlocutor. 'I hardly know, sir.'

'Ho, ho, it's clear as day,' laughed Boyle. 'He was speaking English, of course! I had taken it for granted that he would speak French – they generally do, you know – and had listened as hard as I could, trying to understand him, but never noticing that he was actually speaking English all the while! Silly old fool.' He chuckled again at the memory.

Holland smiled in sympathy and asked cautiously, 'He was . . . from the Ministry?'

'Yes, yes – er, no, what am I saying? I mean the Directory.' Boyle waved his letter, as if dismissing the chief political officers of the Republic. 'Some clerk of the basin or second assistant to the first secretary of tea towels – you know the sort of person. The other is wishful thinking on my part, for I have not yet had the opportunity of speaking with anyone in authority at the Ministry of Marine. However, that is beside the point. Ahem. Mr Watt says here that you are quite a polymath. "Mr Ogbourne has a lively curiosity and a keen interest in all scientific progress of a practical kind." That is what he writes.'

'Yes, sir, I hope that I am – interested, I mean.'

'And your own background is primarily in . . . let me see . . . my goodness – in *armaments*. Can that be right?' Boyle retrieved his single lens (he had been reading with the aid of one of his pairs of spectacles), and peered doubtfully at Holland through it.

'Well, sir, my family has a foundry business in *Saybrook*, and during the last war my, er, father was naturally engaged in the weapons trade. Gun-making, mostly. But now our work is more varied. We do both heavy casting and fine work, and we have quite a reputation for quality in our part of the world.' Holland tried to speak confidently; Americans were known for their self-assurance, or so he had been told.

'I am glad to hear it,' said Boyle, lowering his lens. 'But it proves my point, you know: the utter wastefulness of war.'

'Indeed, sir?'

'Both wasteful and unproductive. As I am sure you know, every society depends upon its productive members – but war creates a great mass of *un*producers. Soldiers, who are supported by the productive work of others, and armament-makers, who are distracted from their proper work by the ghastly requirements of the killing trade.'

'Yes, sir, it is unfortunate, but sometimes wars are necessary,' Holland suggested.

'So we have been told by the men of blood – and free trade, the guarantor of peace and prosperity, has been choked in consequence.' Boyle shook his head. 'There are three cardinal

169

principles that a healthy society must avow: education, improvements to the domestic condition, and the free circulation of producers and the fruits of their productive capacity.'

Boyle seemed to be rehearsing a familiar argument for the comfort of hearing it rather than for the benefit it might confer upon his audience, but Holland felt compelled to respond. 'You are a philosopher, sir, as well as an inventor.'

'Eh? Yes, perhaps I am. Each man has an obligation, you know, to leave the world a better place than he found it, and to do that, he must reflect upon what is wrong and how it may be corrected. My canal project, for example – but I doubt very much whether that will interest anyone while this terrible war continues.'

'No, sir,' Holland agreed. 'But sometimes,' he hesitated, 'even war may throw up interesting challenges to a man of vision and scientific understanding. Interesting . . . opportunities.'

'Mm. One ought to leave the world a better place.' Boyle's own thoughts were clearly at least as interesting to him as Holland's words, but something had attracted the old inventor's attention. 'From where did you say that you come, sir, in America?'

'*Saybrook*, sir, in the state of Connecticut.' Holland tried to emphasise the word without seeming to do so.

'My goodness – Saybrook, Connecticut,' echoed Boyle, beaming. 'But this is most astonishing. You are sure that – but of course you could not be mistaken about such a thing, and it must be the very place . . . Astonishing. Do you happen to know a very ingenious gentleman named Bushnell? David Bushnell?'

Relying more upon his own wit than Boyle's instructions, Martel found the room that had once served as larder and kitchen for the Little Fathers. Now it conveyed a dismal air. The bread oven had been destroyed, and the open hearth was cold and empty. Apart from a large sack, torn open and emptied of its contents, the shelves were bare. Someone, probably Boyle, had swept the floor and placed the pieces of a broken chair in one

170

corner, but occasional shards of crockery remained, to be crunched beneath the visitor's boots. A few stores had been placed upon a large, wooden table.

The tea-making things were easily discovered: a canister, spoons, chipped mugs, even a silver teapot with a spout like a bird's beak. No milk, however. Martel shrugged. Only Englishmen would regret the loss. There was also an odd-looking device that appeared to be some kind of charcoal burner. *Very well*, thought Martel; his task would be simple enough.

Leaving the pantry, he set out to explore the rest of the convent. It consisted of four buildings in addition to the church, together with a walled garden, now sadly neglected. The building where Boyle worked was the largest. An L-shaped stone structure of two storeys, it would have been the centre of the Fathers' domestic life, comprising dormitory, chapter house, refectory, and offices. The remaining buildings were smaller and made largely of wood. Standing in a row, they huddled against the stone structure like poor relations and comprised a second, smaller 'wing'. Perhaps they dated from the consecration of the church, or perhaps they represented the more recent needs of the community. Not being a student of architecture, Martel could not judge; all of it had a dilapidated appearance to him.

The convent was not wholly desolate, however. While some of the upper rooms in the main building stood empty, their windows smashed and doors ajar, others contained the spoils of the war that France had been conducting against its own past: lead sheeting from a church roof, furniture and carpets from despoiled châteaux, statues, stained glass windows, and religious ornaments. Some of these might find an eventual home in the national museum or grace the refurbished dwelling of a wealthy merchant or politician; others would be melted down to make armaments to defend France against her remaining foes.

Martel investigated thoroughly, peering through grills and keyholes when thwarted by doors. The exercise might have troubled some searchers, for there was evidence that the convent had not met its end peacefully. Even if the inhabitants had escaped with their lives, the fabric of the place had suffered. A willing mind, moreover, would have shuddered at the charred psalters among the remnants of a bonfire, at the stairway defaced by shot holes, and at what might have been smears of blood on a door jamb, just where a man of Martel's height would have placed his hand.

Such sights did not trouble Martel, however. While not unfeeling, he had a great fixity of purpose and an ability to dismiss everything that might distract or prevent him from obtaining his goal. Certainly he had put aside his own Catholicism easily enough to obtain a commission in the Royal Navy. Slipping on the scattered beads of a rosary, therefore, merely caused him to curse under his breath and move them out of his way with the toe of his boot.

When he had learned all that he could, and not forgetting his ostensible task, he returned to the pantry and duly coaxed a fire in the charcoal burner. There was an empty water jug on the table, and he went out to the garden, hoping to find either a fountain or a well. He found both, and the latter was unspoiled. As he was filling the jug, he noticed several leather buckets lying outside one of the wooden buildings. He examined them; they were damp inside. From the dew, perhaps, or something else?

With its locked door and shuttered windows, this building had withstood his initial survey, and that very security now piqued his suspicion. *Someone has carried water in those buckets not long ago, perhaps yesterday. If not to this building, where? And for what purpose?*

An answer came to him, but it did not make sense. Mr Boyle's vessel was intended to sail under the water; therefore, he must use water to test it. *But how?* Martel had discovered no pond or pool, certainly nothing that could accommodate a boat. *A model, perhaps? Yes, or he may wish to test particular parts of the mechanism, and for that he would need only a large basin.*

Not wishing to leave evidence of his presence, Martel had avoided damaging the shutters, but now he reconsidered. Might it be worth trying to force one open? As he was deliberating,

172

he heard something behind him, footsteps on the flagged path. *Damn!* He turned quickly as a man's shape emerged from the gloom of an overgrown shrubbery – well dressed, seemingly, beneath an expensive cloak and round hat. The man flinched when he noticed Martel, and his hand slid unconsciously to his side. Was he reaching for a pistol?

No, his purse, concluded Martel. He was immediately conscious of being too near the suspicious building for his supposed errand. There was the jug, however, which he had filled, and his knife was in his pocket. One man, unarmed, would not present a serious threat, but how much had he seen, and what might he guess? Gathering and sifting all of these details, Martel resumed his servile demeanour and advanced tentatively. 'Your pardon, sir – citizen, I mean. You startled me. Did you see him?'

'See whom?' demanded the other. His tone was suspicious, but he glanced about him. 'Who are you? What are you doing here?'

'A dark man – I thought I saw him creeping here in the gardens.' Martel was midway between the building and the well.

'A beggar, most likely, or a cutpurse.' The newcomer drew back. 'Your confederate perhaps!'

'No, no, sir.' Martel halted and bowed. 'Philippe Martel, if you please. I was preparing refreshments for the gentlemen, and I thought I saw—'

'Eh? What gentlemen?'

'In the house of the Fathers,' Martel explained, gesturing. 'Mr Boyle – Citizen Boyle, I mean. My mas— my employer confers with him. They are both men of science.'

'Hmm, perhaps, if one cares for that sort of thing. I know him quite well, of course, old Doyle. He often confers with me.'

The man spoke loftily, and Martel was encouraged. The greater the reticence, the greater the danger, in his experience. He drew nearer. 'Sir is also a man of affairs?'

'You might say that. I am one of the managers of the stock exchange.'

Martel was suitably impressed. He was now quite close to

the other man and could smell his perfume. 'Have you also been inside the convent, sir?' he asked, and then continued in a whisper. 'It is a terrible place. Everywhere, I see eyes and feel them watching me. I think maybe the holy Fathers . . . maybe I have seen a ghost here in the garden.'

'A ghost? Nonsense.'

'Sir does not have experience of such matters in the stock market,' Martel allowed, 'but the thing I saw . . . it was exactly like the phantasmagoria. The tableau they called "the ghostly killer". Even the knife I saw, maybe.'

'But those are mere entertainments,' the stockbroker protested, 'they do not depict actual gho-*oh*!'

His sentence finished in a cry as Martel grasped his arm. 'Ah! What was that?'

'I heard nothing. There are no ghosts in France, you fool. Unhand me this instant.'

Martel begged his pardon and attempted to repair the affront by brushing the other's arm. 'I thought I heard something – a step on the path, or a twig snapping . . .'

'Then it was not a ghost! I take my exercise in this garden every evening, and I have never seen – or heard – anything untoward. Very likely it was only a beggar, as I said, or . . .'

'Yes, sir?'

'Never mind.' The stockbroker adjusted his cape and glanced about him again, with the conscious air of unconcern. 'But perhaps one ought not to walk here alone. A respectable citizen was stabbed in the Rue Vivienne just the other day, and the light is uncertain this morning. I shall return to my office. You will accompany me.'

'*Me*, sir? But what of my gentlemen?'

'They can certainly spare you, and this will not take a moment. Come along.'

'Ah, the tea!' cried Boyle. 'Just what was needed.'

'*Voila, monsieur,*' Martel replied, bowing over his laden tray. 'Please accept my regrets – my apologies – for the delay.'

'No, no, we have been deep in our discussions. Was it that

174

dratted burner? I am certain it was. Gave you no end of trouble, I expect.'

Martel shrugged helplessly and, having deposited the tray upon the only clear space on the desk, performed various gestures intended to signify his struggles with the device. Only by a flickering glance did he convey a different message to Holland.

Turning to his guest, Boyle explained, 'I expect it was my own fault. The charcoal burner works according to various adjustments – improvements, really, that I hit upon some time ago. It works well enough for *me*, but others have found it rather temperamental. I really ought to have told you the secret,' he added to Martel, regretfully, as if he had accidentally made things difficult for a child or faithful pet.

'Secrets are a bad thing in the kitchen,' Martel agreed, 'and between friends – impossible. Myself, I have no secrets, only sorrowful news.' He paused, hand over his heart, and then raised an empty jug. 'No milk!'

13

The kitchen of the Maison des Chevrons backed onto a small courtyard. It might once have been the haunt of Monsieur Chœur's horses, but the stables had long since tumbled down, and now smaller creatures patrolled the branches of a stunted chestnut tree and fluttered upon the cracked flagstones. Mary stood in the doorway, watching as sparrows and a determined robin hopped among the morsels of bread, pecking fitfully at their breakfast. When a squirrel caused the sparrows to retreat, the robin held his ground – even puffing out his chest to demonstrate his ferocity.

The scene inevitably recalled White Ladies and Miss Trent's faithful distribution of alms each morning to the birds of the vicinity. One blackbird regarded all of the paved area outside their breakfast room as his particular domain. He appeared each morning and chirped his demands, but he also felt obliged to hide when Miss Trent emerged, as if she were not wholly trustworthy. Miss Trent, for her part, tempted him with bits of fruit and periodically announced that 'Blackie' was becoming quite tame. 'Such a dear little fellow.'

Mary smiled at the memory, and experienced a sudden desire to communicate with her friends and hear more about the simple, ordinary world. She mustn't do so, of course. Even at 12 Devonshire Square, a foreign letter might create all sorts of complications. And what could she possibly write? No, she was committed to secrecy and deception, at least for the present, and there was nothing to be done about it.

In fact, a letter arrived that very morning. Not foreign, but causing an even greater disturbance. Miss Marchmont was reading the newspaper and enjoying her second cup of tea when the blow fell. Vartan Nazarian was its bearer. He cast a disapproving eye upon the remains of her wholly English breakfast and announced, 'Another letter for "Miss Finch". Silly people. You know this one – Tipton? When you see him, tell him that Mary *djan* is married lady.'

'Hmm? Yes, certainly,' replied Miss Marchmont distractedly. Of course she had no intention of doing anything of the kind, but a month under the supervision of the irrepressible *varich* had taught her that it was far better to agree than to argue with him. Indeed, in a moment of comic inspiration, she had privately decided that his title derived from a 'far-reaching' sense of authority. (Miss Marchmont's comic sensibilities were not perhaps of the very highest order.)

She glanced at the letter, thinking that even Mrs Tipton's decrees need not interrupt *The Times*' account of Mr Pitt's speech, when she received her first warning of danger. The instruction was not in Mrs Tipton's thin, spidery hand, and when she turned the letter over, she found a Norfolk return address. *Oh dear*, she fretted, *Storey's Court*.

Storey's Court was the Norfolk home of the Armitage family, lately consisting of Lady Armitage and her daughters, Susannah and Charlotte. That the relentlessly proper Lady Armitage should write to Mary was not impossible, but Miss Marchmont suspected a far more awkward correspondent, who would not be satisfied with an account of the progress of Mary's estate business.

'Oh dear, *Charlotte*,' she murmured, and a premonition of commotion, confusion, and sore feet was confirmed when she broke the seal.

10th November 1797

My dear Mary,

I hope you are well. I have learned from Miss Trent that you are in London, which is the most tremendous luck, for can you guess? We are also coming up to Town!

The official reason for our visit is to attend my uncle Stephenson, who has a palsy in his leg. Susannah and I have been informed that his condition is most pitiable, but I overheard Mama saying that it is all the fault of his frivolous character and having no one to look after him, which I do not believe she regards in a pitiable light. We do not yet know whether the palsy may be cured — Mama speaks of bringing him back to Storey's Court where he may benefit from a more healthful and sober regime. I hope this does not happen, for we are already quite sober enough.

Although I am coming in order to be useful, Mama is unlikely to need my help in putting Uncle to rights. He is her brother, after all, and I daresay he is used to it. Therefore I have it in mind to attend all of the really thrilling amusements and entertainments — and now we can do so together! How fortunate that this is not our first visit to Town, for we have already seen the important sights that no one really likes, so we needn't bother with those.

Miss Trent says that you are conducting important business that cannot be disturbed, but I expect it is very dreary, and you will be grateful for the chance to enjoy yourself. I am longing to see you and shall visit as soon as we arrive.

Yours faithfully,

Charlotte Armitage

P.S. We are setting off on the thirteenth. Hooray!

Nazarian returned as Miss Marchmont was reading the letter for the second time. He did not approve of protracted breakfasts, and employed the technique of discreet harassment to discourage lingerers. On this occasion his adjustment of the curtains so that the morning sun shone directly in her eyes broke the train of thought that the letter had inspired, and she sighed. After observing him unnecessarily rearrange some items on the sideboard, she asked, 'What is the word in your language for "storm" or "great tumult"?'

He considered for a moment. *'Portoreeg.'*

'Well then, please inform Cook and Sally that a *portoreeg* is coming to London shortly, and will doubtless descend upon us with full force.'

Written by anyone else of her acquaintance, a promise to visit 'as soon as we arrive' would have been a friendly exaggeration. The writer would call after he was comfortably settled, having sent a note announcing his arrival. Or he might not come at all; the assertion was merely an expression of hope – and hope was often dashed. Miss Marchmont knew that with Charlotte, however, there was no such variety of meaning, and as a further decline in Mr Stephenson's health could not be relied upon, she resigned herself to a visit on the fourteenth. Indeed, she began preparing for it immediately after breakfast on the day in question.

The *portoreeg* duly arrived at two o'clock, bubbling with news about her journey and the state of the Armitage townhouse, and overflowing with questions. Why had Mary decided to live in this part of Town? It seemed rather dark – much darker than Cavendish Square; how could that be? Did the important business keep Mary busy *every* day, and when would it be finished? That queer old fellow at the door was the most tremendous butler she had ever seen. Where *was* Mary?

Miss Marchmont offered a vague reply to the last of these. 'Mrs Crosby-Nash did not accompany you?'

'No. Susannah never really cared much about London, you know, and now I believe she positively dislikes it, which is a great shame. She has remained at Storey's Court, and is making preparations in case we must return with the invalid.'

That information put paid to the possibility, never very seriously entertained, that the elder, more responsible Susannah might be prevailed upon to distract Charlotte, and even keep her away from Devonshire Square. Little as she liked it, therefore, Miss Marchmont knew that she must take the more dangerous step of recruiting Charlotte to preserve Mary's secret. Even the prospect made her shudder. Before she could begin, however, Charlotte had charged ahead with her own remarks.

'I do hope that we shall see Major Whittington while we are here – and Bobs, of course. I wrote to him from Norfolk, but did not receive a reply.'

'Both gentlemen are doubtless very busy,' said Miss Marchmont, paling at the thought of Captain Holland making an appearance in Devonshire Square and demanding to see his cousin *and* Mary.

'Perhaps Bobs is busy, but not Major Whittington. He is in a fashionable regiment, so he is not obliged to do so much work.'

'Well, fashionable or not, you really must not meet Major Whittington – certainly there must be no public acknowledgement.'

'Because of the duel, you mean?' Both Charlotte and Miss Marchmont were under the erroneous impression that Colonel Crosby-Nash and Major Whittington had fought a duel, with fatal consequences for the former. It is but fair to say that Whittington would have encouraged this belief, while Mary and Holland, who also knew the truth, had actually done so. 'But I am certain that Major Whittington fought fairly, and if one *must* be killed, I think that being shot in a duel is much the best way.'

'*Much the best way?*' sputtered Miss Marchmont. Her teacup was halfway to her lips, and she returned it hurriedly to its saucer.

'Yes,' Charlotte assured her. 'Much better than being carried off by a palsy in your leg – although I do not believe my uncle is in any danger that way. And it is not as if any of us *liked* Colonel Crosby-Nash, you know. He was such a miserable old stick – I am certain that Susannah did not really mind losing him.'

'Charlotte, *really*!'

'Well, she is not cast down or mournful – she never sighs – and those are the marks of true love and a broken heart. She is only rather quiet, but so she has always been. However, I expect that Mama will take your point of view – about Major Whittington, I mean. Still, we shall have Bobs, and I daresay that will please Mary. Have you seen much of him since coming to Town?'

'Er, no.'

'*No?* What is the matter? Have they had a row?'

After hovering irresolutely for the time it took to place cup and saucer on the side table, out of harm's way, Miss Marchmont took the plunge. 'No, only . . . Mary has had to go away for a time . . . to Cornwall, and no one is to know about it, least of all Captain Holland. You see,' she continued, waving away Charlotte's excited query, 'in the course of her . . . investigations, Mary uncovered a sort of . . . mystery having to do with her family, and she was obliged to go to Cornwall to . . . resolve it.'

'A *mystery*,' breathed Charlotte, her eyes shining. 'To do with White Ladies?'

'I haven't the least idea,' Miss Marchmont replied. 'It is a mystery, after all.'

'But why is Bobs not to know about it?'

'Those were Mary's instructions,' said Miss Marchmont sternly, 'and doubtless she had her reasons. Perhaps she was concerned that Captain Holland might . . . do something extravagant or be distracted from his work. Gentlemen often behave extravagantly when they are of a romantic temperament, and there is a war on, after all. One oughtn't to distract gentlemen in wartime.'

Charlotte questioned whether her cousin had a romantic temperament but acknowledged that his temper could be rather brisk, which might be much the same thing where extravagant behaviour was concerned. 'And Mary flying to Cornwall because of a family mystery would be just the thing to set him off. I wish that I had known about it,' she brooded. 'It sounds such fun – I should have liked to go with her.'

181

Rather than commenting upon that final remark, Miss Marchmont demanded from Charlotte a firm promise that she would not mention Mary's 'excursion' to Captain Holland – or to anyone else, for that matter. The readiness with which it was granted came as a pleasant surprise; Miss Marchmont had been anticipating a more difficult struggle. Having confirmed that Charlotte understood the meaning of 'anyone', she even began to feel hopeful that her little ruse would have no ill effects. Then Charlotte spoke again.

'I see that we mustn't encourage Bobs, but . . .' She frowned thoughtfully. 'What about Mary's London acquaintances? They are far more dangerous, you know, for they are here already, and their ears will be twitching for any sort of gossip. None of them must suspect that she is on the trail of a family mystery. Only imagine if they learned that her mother had died in an asylum or that her uncle had committed a murder.'

'Oh, Charlotte, what can you mean? Neither of those things has happened!'

'Well, someone is bound to suspect them – *I* would, and people always believe the most outrageous things if you do anything unusual.'

'What is unusual in coming up to London to review one's estate papers?' persisted Miss Marchmont.

'Day after day, with never a concert or party to make it bearable?' demanded Charlotte. 'It sounds *very* odd. The sort of thing you would do if you had lost your fortune and were trying to recover it through a desperate venture before cutting your throat in utter despair. And now that we have arrived, everyone will be told that Mary is in Town – or is *supposed* to be here. Mama is certain to meet people when she is not taking my uncle in hand, and I shan't be able to prevent her from mentioning Mary.'

'No, I see that,' Miss Marchmont acknowledged, gloomily. She cast an oblique glance in Charlotte's direction, as if Charlotte were indeed some elemental force, whose power might be harnessed for good, but which was far more likely to wreak devastation. Cautiously she asked, 'But what can be done about it?'

Charlotte was nothing if not positive. After a short interval, during which she consumed two slices of cake, she announced, 'I have thought of a perfect way round the difficulty. All we need do is to let people see that Mary *is* about, doing perfectly ordinary things like paying calls and going to the theatre. Then if we say that she is also quite busy with horrid estate matters, no one will give it a second thought.'

Her triumphant smile did little to reassure Miss Marchmont. 'But Mary is not here!' she complained. 'How on earth do you intend to produce her?'

'Oh, that is easily done.' Charlotte smiled archly.

'Do you mean—' Miss Marchmont gaped. 'Do you mean that you would pretend to *be* Mary?'

'Why not? I know that we are not quite alike in face and figure, but if I wore one of her hats I am certain that I could pass for her – at a distance, perhaps.'

'A very considerable distance.'

'Which is all we require – that people assume they have seen her from afar or have just missed her call. I should not try anything dangerous, you know, like holding a tea party here at Devonshire Square.'

'Good Heavens, no!' cried Miss Marchmont.

'No, we shall be terribly careful,' Charlotte agreed, but with an expression of delight that belied her serious tone. 'What could possibly go wrong?'

Some generals believe that untried soldiers should be prepared gradually for the shock of battle, while others argue that anticipation merely heightens the agony, and it is kinder simply to throw troops into the fray. Charlotte was of the second school, in that she was practically fearless and rarely saw the point of putting off until tomorrow what she wished to do that evening. No sooner had the notion occurred to her, therefore, than she acted upon it, descending upon Miss Marchmont to announce that their first sortie would be to the opera.

'The opera!' gasped Miss Marchmont.

'Yes, this evening,' said Charlotte, masterfully. 'It is all arranged.

We shall see *Ipermestra* at the King's Theatre. I have taken a box.' (It sounded so thrilling, 'a box at the opera' and quite did away with the fact that she did not particularly enjoy opera singing.)

Miss Marchmont raised a score of objections – it was too expensive, ladies ought not to attend the theatre unaccompanied, the night air was bad for one's throat, she felt a headache coming on, neither of them understood Italian – but Charlotte overcame them all. More than that, she convinced the flustered woman into consenting to Mary's wardrobe being ransacked for a suitable gown to complete their subterfuge.

'But you do not mean to pass yourself off as Mary *at the King's Theatre*?' Miss Marchmont cried, as if this would be the worst deception imaginable. Charlotte had outpaced her, and having puffed up the last of the stairs to Mary's bedchamber, Miss Marchmont found the doors to the clothes cupboard thrown wide, and Charlotte trying on a bonnet and a matching pair of gloves.

'I do not imagine that the king will be there,' said Charlotte, for whom Mary's sophisticated attire was a far more potent attraction. 'And we shall only attempt to deceive those persons who do not actually know Mary, of course. If we see any of our friends, we shall say that she has stepped out of the box for a moment.' She removed the gloves and began opening drawers. 'Now let me see . . .'

'Do be careful, Charlotte, you are wrinkling everything.'

'Is this the only pelisse? A beaded fringe would be much more fashionable.'

'I daresay Mary did not think it necessary to accommodate your exacting standards when she selected her wardrobe.'

'But this green silk will be perfect.' Charlotte drew the gown in question out of the cupboard and held it against herself.

The nicest of Mary's new gowns, it had remained behind only because green was considered a Royalist colour in France. Miss Marchmont uttered a despairing cry. 'It has not even been worn!'

'Oh, then it really *ought* to have an airing,' argued Charlotte practically. 'And it would not do for Mary to appear shabby at the opera. What do you think? Not with this bonnet, of course.'

'I think that it hardly matters what I think,' Miss Marchmont complained, collapsing in a chair.

She had recovered somewhat by the time they set off. Nazarian looked askance at Charlotte's gauzy headdress as he handed the two ladies into the hackney carriage, but Miss Marchmont was grateful for anything that would obscure Charlotte's features, and render more plausible what she was convinced was a hopeless charade. The headdress, moreover, was a vast improvement on Charlotte's earlier suggestion of a wig.

The drive to the theatre was uneventful, and under other circumstances Miss Marchmont would have enjoyed an evening in society. On this occasion, however, the opera passed for her like one of those awful dreams in which the dreamer is on the brink of a terrible revelation and cannot escape it. Throughout the first Act, she perched on the edge of her chair, unable to relax, and Ipermestra's horror when ordered by her father to slay her husband was as nothing to the torments that Miss Marchmont suffered when Charlotte nodded and waved to people from the front of the box.

'Come away from there!' she hissed. 'And do stop . . . gesturing like that! Mary would never behave so.'

'You do not think it elegant? I am sure I have seen the queen wave in exactly the same way. Perhaps it is not quite Mary's style, but we do want to be noticed. Shall I remove my scarf? It is rather warm.'

'No!'

The evening's trials were not yet over, however, for during the interval several visitors came to the box. Miss Marchmont would have barred the door – why did these silly creatures not keep to their own seats? Was the opera insufficient entertainment for them? But Charlotte overruled her with the confident assertion that Mary would certainly wish to see them. Indeed, who actually paid attention to the performance at the opera? 'I am sure I don't know what that man with the funny hat was singing about.'

The visitors came and went. Fortunately, those who knew Mary came together and departed after only a very few, heart-stopping minutes. The others lingered, but with no apparent ill effects. *And what does it matter*, Miss Marchmont asked herself, *if strangers come away with the idea that Mary is rather a silly young person? I doubt she ever meets them again – or rather, ever meets them at all*. She began to look forward to the opera ending, to returning safely to Devonshire Square and never leaving it again.

At last the assembled company of gods, goddesses, and triumphant mortals brought the opera to a close, and the curtain descended. Charlotte spoke of remaining for the ballet, but Miss Marchmont rejected this in no uncertain terms. 'No ballet! Nothing has happened *yet* – let us go home before it does!' Bundling her young friend into Mary's velvet cloak, she stormed through to the passageway.

They were not the only ones for whom *Ariadne and Bacchus* held insufficient appeal, but being a large woman as well as a determined one, Miss Marchmont was not easily swept aside; she could prod and elbow with the best of them. They reached the gallery, and then the foyer. Then came a dreadful moment when she and Charlotte were separated by people moving in the opposite direction, and Miss Marchmont feared that Charlotte might somehow be unmasked on this final lap of the course. *Too cruel!*

She trod upon a man's foot and hurriedly begged his pardon.

'Not at all, madam,' he replied, bowing as well as he could with someone pressed firmly against his back.

Another man, who seemed to be his associate, asked, 'Do you know, please, who is that young lady in the ivory cloak?'

'Oh yes,' Miss Marchmont replied distractedly. Her bonnet had been knocked askew, and she was endeavouring to straighten it. 'That is Miss Mary Finch – the Suffolk Heiress, you know.'

'The *Suffolk Heiress*?'

'Yes – Mary, dear!' She gestured, although Charlotte was now too far ahead to notice – she had nearly gained the longed-for door. 'Do go ahead, I am sure that our carriage is waiting!' Miss Marchmont cried. 'Please excuse me,' she added and surged forward.

At last she gained the door and then the pavement. The street was full of private vehicles and hackney carriages, and Charlotte had secured one of the latter. *The first sensible thing she has done all night*, Miss Marchmont complained to herself as she climbed aboard. Aloud, she directed the driver to 'Number Twelve Devonshire Square, please, as quick as you like,' which confirmed her disordered sensibilities, for she disliked fast driving and usually demanded to be told the route in advance, so that she could veto any questionable streets.

Now she merely leaned back in her seat and allowed Charlotte's breezy recollections to wash over her. '. . . And you would have been proud of me. That lady who came with her daughter – you know, they were both dressed in pink – pressed me most strongly to attend her musical evening next Thursday in Brook Street, but I said that I was so busy with "estate business" that I could not possibly promise.'

'Thank goodness for that,' Miss Marchmont agreed, reviving somewhat. 'We are certainly *not* going to Brook Street. Who was the older gentleman in grey silk? You spoke to him for rather a long time.'

'Oh yes, he was great fun. He is a French émigré.'

The word 'French' made Miss Marchmont's blood run cold, but she managed to restrict her fright to a small gasp, which Charlotte attributed to the unsteady motion of their vehicle. 'A Frenchman? What did he want?'

'Money, I believe,' said Charlotte with great complacency. 'Mama says that the émigrés are generally on the lookout for rich wives, but the only thing Lord Felix spoke about was raising funds for a *"grand rétablissement"*, which I believe has something to do with French politics.'

'*Lord Felix*? Really, Charlotte, you mustn't be so familiar! How do you know that he is a lord?'

'Well, he has a frightfully long title, but I know that *"seigneur"* means "lord", and when I asked whether I might call him

"Lord Felix", he said I might. He was ever so charming, and he hates Bonaparte even more than we do. I do hope we shall see him again.'

'Oh, Charlotte!'

After that fiery baptism, Charlotte's suggestions for promulgating what she described as 'Mary-o-the-wisp' assumed a less fearsome aspect. She and Miss Marchmont drove in the park and strolled through Doctors' Commons. Twice they called on ladies whom they knew were not at home and left Mary's name. 'Miss Mary Finch' purchased a morning gown at Doyley's warehouse in Covent Garden, and placed an order at T. & W. Breach for a fur pelisse that Charlotte particularly admired, specifying that it should be delivered to 12 Devonshire Square.

Then, just as quickly as it had begun, the scheme came to an end. Lady Armitage emerged from her duties in the sickroom to discover that Charlotte had been conducting herself with the same frivolous dedication to pleasure that had precipitated Mr Stephenson's collapse, and she forbade unsupervised excursions for the remainder of their stay in London.

Charlotte lamented the consequences of this new and terrible regime in a hurriedly penned note to Miss Marchmont, which arrived while she was eating breakfast.

I may only come to visit if you (and Mary – ha ha!) promise that we shall not do any shopping or amuse ourselves in any unseemly way. We would be allowed to attend church, only it must not be a pleasant, jolly service, such as we have at home with Mr Fortescue, but one of those gloomy places with hard pews and very long sermons.

Miss Marchmont smiled sympathetically. She had to admit (privately) that Charlotte's scheme had been surprisingly successful. Mary *had* received letters and invitations, but none of them pressing, and several had mentioned that 'I know you are very busy and scarcely able to venture out-of-doors'. Upon such statements, Miss Marchmont had naturally pounced when drafting her replies. *How easy it becomes to deceive people,* she had brooded, after dismissing an importunate young man, who had wished to leave the tribute of a small nosegay. *I suppose that it is all a question of practice. Hardened criminals must be terribly good at it.*

Nevertheless, she was relieved to know that Charlotte's reign was coming to an end. Not only had it been exhausting, but she had found it impossible to rid herself of the fear that something awful might result. A significant portion of her present sympathy resulted from the belief that she had had a fortunate escape from Charlotte's clutches.

'You sometimes attend the Nonconformist chapel on the square, do you not?' she asked Nazarian, who was hovering nearby, alert to any indication that he could begin to clear the table. 'Is the minister a good sort of person?'

'Mr Thomas? Yes, I know him. He is good man, but foolish. Can you believe, he try to convert me – *me!* – to his church. I tell him Armenians have been Christians since St Gregory's time, and if he don't know who St Gregory is, he should find out! But he is good man. I help them, sometimes, because these Baptists sing like mice squeaking. So I help them sometimes.' With a flourish he sang, or rather roared, *'O Lord, 'tis matter of high praise, Thy word on us doth shine, shine, But Happy they who feel its rays, And glorious power divine'* in a thundering bass.

'Indeed,' said Miss Marchmont, 'quite a musical foundation, then. And are the sermons, ahem, very long?'

'Long? Not long for me, but for the English, perhaps.'

Not knowing precisely how she ought to interpret that observation and conscious that she was not a very great sermon-listener and therefore unable to uphold the English side in any debate on the subject, Miss Marchmont retreated instead to Charlotte's note. 'Miss Armitage will shortly be returning to Norfolk, it seems.'

'She is leaving? Oh, that is very sad,' said Nazarian, his moustaches drooping in sympathy.

'Well, her uncle is unwell, you know, and they are taking him home to Norfolk – Miss Armitage and her mother.'

'After she go, no more visitors,' suggested Nazarian. 'I like to see Miss Armitage very much, but because of her we have people coming all the time – always knockering. That is not so good.'

Miss Marchmont replied confidently, 'There *has* been a bit of a disruption, but I expect that things will settle down again soon.'

'Good. Better for house to be peaceful. I will get dog, maybe.'

I hardly think that would render the house any more peaceful, thought Miss Marchmont. But she kept her opinion to herself, and he forgot all about it.

Nazarian remembered the dog when two men rapped sharply at the front door the following evening. The house was quiet, for Miss Marchmont had retired early to bed – not that her presence or absence made any difference to the old *varich*. Callers were *his* responsibility; whether they were admitted or their messages received depended on his determination of their integrity, or at least their harmlessness. A peek through the sitting-room curtains revealed that these petitioners were young men, well dressed, although not quite in the English style.

'Foreigners,' Nazarian muttered to himself, and unbolted the door. It never occurred to him that he could simply decline to answer a stranger's knock after dark. Dog or no dog, he was perfectly capable of dealing with any tramp or ruffian. He had proven as much over the past forty years.

'Yes?' he demanded. 'What do you want?'

They were, in fact, the two men whom Miss Marchmont had encountered as she hurried through the foyer of the King's Theatre, and they introduced themselves as such. Nazarian was sceptical both of this assertion and of their names – Mr Mortimer and Mr Oldcastle – and in any case he was not disposed to be hospitable. No, Miss Finch was not at home, nor was her friend, nor was it known when they would return. Every question, in fact, prompted a negative response.

'You are not very helpful, my friend,' complained Mortimer.

Nazarian agreed, with the caveat that he was not their friend. 'You go away now,' he said. 'Business all done here.'

The two strangers exchanged amused glances. There was something faintly ridiculous about being thwarted – nay, insulted – by this little old man with his bald head and embroidered waistcoat.

'Let us leave a message for Miss Finch,' Mortimer suggested.

'She don't want a message from you.'

Nazarian attempted to terminate the conversation in the usual way, but the second man, Mr Oldcastle, prevented him. He thrust his foot into the gap, and the pressure of his shoulder forced Nazarian back.

'Come now, grandfather,' urged Oldcastle, chuckling, 'give up the game and let us in.'

'And then you can tell us all about your mistress,' said Mortimer, '*and* her friends.'

Oldcastle stood astride the threshold, exchanging grins with his comrade and reaching into the darkened hallway as if he would grasp Nazarian. Suddenly his expression changed. The *varich* had been a powerful wrestler in his youth, and his hands were still terribly strong. The searching arm was seized and wrenched unnaturally. Oldcastle swore in a sick gasp; his knees buckled.

'What is it?' cried Mortimer, but even as he spoke Oldcastle was staggering backwards out of the doorway, the glowering Nazarian close behind.

He released his hold; a moment longer and the tendons in the younger man's arm would have snapped. 'Ha! You want more? *Grandfather* will give it to you.'

Mortimer retreated cautiously to the pavement. '*Merde,*' he whispered, then, more confidently, 'very well, we are going. But we will be back.'

'Back for what?' Nazarian jibed. 'More games? Next time I will set dog on you, and I don't think you will like him any better.'

Oldcastle stepped back, cradling his injured arm. Nazarian's contemptuous gaze shifted from one man to the other, but in that moment Oldcastle sprang forward again, and this time his blow struck home. Nazarian stumbled against the railing and collapsed.

'Arrêtez!' hissed Mortimer. *'Que faites-vous?'* Seizing his friend by the collar, he pulled him down the steps and onto the pavement.

'He nearly broke my arm.'

'So you strike an old man? Her servant? How does that help?'

Oldcastle tried to answer, but Mortimer cut him off. 'Come away, now, before someone sees us!'

Sally found him. She had been out with her young man, whom she was allowed to see one evening a week, on account of his being very respectable – a tailor's apprentice – and always brought her home by ten o'clock sharp. Nevertheless, she had been wondering, all the way along Bishopsgate, whether she would manage to get in again without waking Cook, who always made a fuss, notwithstanding that Sally had done nothing wrong and no one could say otherwise.

The huddled figure drove such thoughts from her mind. 'What on earth— Why, it's Mr Nazarene!' She let go of her young man's arm and ran up the steps. 'Sir! Sir! Oh, Bill, I think he's had a fit.'

'Poor old chap,' said Bill, kneeling beside her. 'Like my old dad, I reckon. Let's turn him over, careful now.'

Then they saw the blood – such a lot of it. The *varich's* face was chalky white.

'Lord!' cried Bill. 'Someone's killed him! Go for the Watch, Sal! No, a doctor! I think he's breathing still.'

Sally sprang to her feet. 'There's Dr Gordon at Number Five.' But even in this emergency her sense of propriety – of the 'honour of the house' – was not wholly forgotten. 'Do take him inside, Bill.' She thrust her latchkey into his hand. 'He mustn't lie there on our steps.' And then she was flying across the square.

Bill moved cautiously, but the effort of being lifted caused Nazarian to revive. Even weakened, his grip remained strong, and he clutched the young man's arm furiously, his eyes flashing. *'Fransatsi en!'* he cried. *'Tavajan!'*

192

'Ow!' gasped the would-be rescuer. 'It's me, sir, Bill Stokes.'

Nazarian relaxed his hold. 'Bill Stokes,' he repeated, and now he lightly tapped the other's arm. 'You are a good boy. You look after Sally, or I will make big trouble for you.'

'Yes, sir, I certainly shall,' Bill agreed. 'Sal's gone for the doctor and . . . can you say who did it, sir?'

But Nazarian did not speak again. Or rather, he repeated the words *'Fransatsi en'* in a fading voice, but as Bill did not understand Armenian, he could make nothing of them.

14

After the first interview with Samson Boyle, Holland's work progressed very well. He succeeded in befriending the old inventor and gaining a measure of his confidence. After a second, longer visit, during which they discussed Holland's ideas for an improved revolving pistol, Boyle even invited the visitor from America to take up residence in the convent, so that they might confer on matters scientific at their leisure. Most importantly, Boyle began to divulge information about the *Ammonite* – his undersea boat.

With progress came both hope and fear, as Holland grew to admire and to dread what Boyle was doing – and what he might yet achieve. Martel contacted Jens, therefore, and a conference took place in the latter's upstairs room on a bleak, blustery afternoon. The wind rattled the window as if eager to join the secret talks.

'I wouldn't say that the situation is desperate,' said Holland cautiously, glancing at Jens, Martel, and Mary in turn. 'It *may* never become so. But very soon we will lose the power to affect it one way or the other.'

His gaze rested on Mary. Although he had not mentioned her to Martel, Holland had very much hoped that she would attend. They had not met since their initial encounter almost a week ago, and he had been anxious to see her and know for certain that she was well. He disliked the idea of her rambling around Paris on her own – Paris, for God's sake! – but the sight of that dear, lovely, mischievous face lifted his heart. He smiled at her and missed the first part of Jens' question.

'You have actually seen the vessel?' asked Jens again, more pointedly. He had been less than pleased by the invasion of his premises by men whom he suspected of being little more than high-handed ruffians. The necessity of speaking English, that uncouth language, was a further source of irritation. The *Ammonite*, however, appealed to him as something approaching an artistic construction.

Holland nodded. 'The vessel that Boyle sailed off the Normandy coast is now in pieces. There were faults in the design, and he wanted to build smaller models in order to tackle them one by one. That's what he has been doing since coming to Paris. From what I've seen, he is making damned good progress.'

'When will he have a complete, working boat?'

'He won't – not if he carries on as he has. He would need a much larger workshop and more materials, and he won't get either unless the government approves the project. But against that is the fact that he can demonstrate almost every feature individually, now, to anyone with a good scientific understanding. It isn't possible actually to climb inside the *Ammonite* and sail it, and if that sort of proof is required, I don't see how Mr Boyle can produce it. But with a bit of imagination on the part of the French Navy—'

'The French executed their best Naval officers during the Terror,' complained Martel. He was seated casually, legs crossed and one arm leaning against the table. His position afforded him a partial view out of the window, and that seemed to interest him as much as the exchanges between Holland and Jens.

'Maybe they did,' Holland agreed, 'but everything changes when Bonaparte comes into the reckoning. Boyle is pinning his hopes for the *Ammonite* on Bonaparte.'

'But what could *he* know of such things?' asked Jens. 'Bonaparte is no sailor, surely. Do you speak of his political power? I admit that when he returns from Italy there may be changes in the government, but . . .' He frowned and shook his head, unwilling to hazard anything further on that score.

'I'll leave politics to you,' said Holland, 'but he *is* the most successful general in France, and I expect he'll have his way. It stands to reason that, with the Austrians out of the fight, he will be looking to invade England. The *Ammonite* wouldn't be of much use in a pitched battle, but it could be deadly against ships at anchor. Bonaparte doesn't need to understand the sea to appreciate that – God knows *I'm* no sailor. If Boyle explained the *Ammonite* to him, I expect he would tumble to its uses easily enough.'

Jens opened his mouth to reply, but before the words came, there was a rapping from somewhere below. Martel sprang to his feet. 'What is that?'

'Customers,' said Jens sourly. He had been obliged to close his shop an hour before his usual time, and this evidence of lost trade did not improve his temper. 'Customers who may never return. Vrillac's has a reputation to maintain, you know.'

Martel crept to the window; from behind the curtain he peered down into the dreary street. 'One man,' he reported, softly, 'and dressed like a beggar. I doubt he would have spent very much.'

Jens threw up his hands. 'So you say! He is probably a great artist.'

'Then I expect he'll come back,' said Holland. 'When does Bonaparte return from Italy?'

'Hmm? Oh, in days, weeks, perhaps. Already some members of his staff are in Paris – or so I have been told.'

'Well, Mr Boyle wants to meet him.'

'He shall have to wait his turn. General Bonaparte will be the most sought-after man in France. There will be parties, receptions, not to mention his official duties. Of course, it would be best if the hero of the Republic never became acquainted with Mr Boyle. How do you propose to keep them apart?'

Holland exhaled deeply. 'I would like to take Boyle back to England. I know it would be difficult,' he acknowledged, as

Jens leaned back in his chair, his arms folded uncompromis-ingly across his chest.

'*Extremely* difficult,' the other corrected. 'You hope to turn him against the French?'

'Against his ideas for the *Ammonite*, yes.'

Martel had returned to the table, but he remained standing. 'There is one sure way to achieve our goal that is also simple – we kill him.'

A chair squeaked, and Jens complained that men of blood inevitably favoured sanguinary solutions. 'Not that I would reject it out of hand if I were concerned in the matter,' he added thoughtfully, 'which I am not.'

'But you could not simply *murder* him,' cried Mary. 'An elderly clergyman . . .'

These were almost the first words she had spoken since the meeting had begun. She had been content to listen – it had seemed ages since she had heard Holland's voice – and now she glanced at him, fleetingly, although her question had been put to Martel.

It was Martel who replied. 'I tell you I could do it without the least hesitation. This machine threatens my men and my ship – naturally I will do what is necessary to destroy it. The circumstances of its inventor mean nothing to me, if he is an enemy. Besides' – he shrugged – 'I doubt if he is the first priest who has taken up arms.'

His tone was faintly surly, and Mary bristled. 'No, indeed. One need only think of Odo of Bayeux! And the bishop of Lichfield – I forget his name – once received a dispensation from the pope to hang people in Wales. They were criminals, of course. But if Mr Boyle could be made to see reason . . .'

'The British point of view, you mean?' quipped Jens.

Holland had begun coughing during her last contribution, and Mary was obliged to raise her voice. 'Well, yes, if you wish to put it that way. He does not seem to me so much a bad man as a misguided one. If he could be convinced to return to England – to his own side – that would be better for him and for us. Is that not right?' She turned to Holland.

'Yes, it would be better,' he replied. The tickle in his throat, if that is what it was, had settled, and his expression was sombre. 'If Boyle went to work for the Admiralty, we would gain the *Ammonite* and any other ideas he's got stored inside his head – and there are quite a few. It would be a damned shame to throw all of that away if we could save it.'

Martel shrugged grumpily, but said he supposed that was fair enough. 'The old fellow is a nuisance, however.'

'That is no reason for killing him,' Mary retorted.

Jens rapped on the table before Martel could continue. Although he was far from amicable himself, he disliked hearing other people's quarrels. 'Very well,' he said peremptorily. 'Thought must now be given to getting Mr Boyle and yourselves safely out of France. That will be my task, of course.'

'And mine,' said Martel.

Jens made a grudging gesture in Martel's direction, in recognition that his assistance might possibly be useful in a modest way. 'The real danger will commence when General Bonaparte arrives in Paris, and when he does, I think I know of a means by which we may learn something of his intentions.'

He produced a folded sheet of paper from his breast pocket and handed it to Mary. It contained three names. 'Who are they?' she asked.

'Those are eminent – or at least wealthy – individuals who wish to have their portraits painted by Citizen David. Unfortunately, he cannot oblige them. He has sent me their names, along with the suggestion that one of the young artists who have worked for me might possibly be granted the commissions.'

Mary scanned the list. 'I believe I see what you mean. And you think that Mr Vangenzen—'

'Precisely. The rest, of course, would be up to you, but,' – he shrugged – 'a connection in that place might prove valuable.'

The three visitors left Vrillac's together, but presently they parted, for Mary and Holland were going to the Maison des Chevrons, and Martel was returning to the convent. Mary wanted to say

198

something of the Boyle affair to the Vangenzens, but Holland judged it unwise to reveal anything about Martel unless it was absolutely necessary. (Whatever risk was involved did not apply to Holland himself, of course, because he was determined to see what sort of people had been looking after Mary.) If Martel had an opinion on the subject, he did not say so, merely remarking that he would 'listen for the bell' before disappearing into the early evening twilight.

'He and Jens do not agree very well,' said Mary, when they were alone.

'No,' said Holland. 'I don't think that Martel trusts anyone, apart from himself. What do you think about him? Jens, I mean.'

'Oh, I know that he is rather bad-tempered, but he means to be helpful. Only he must be treated delicately to stop him biting.'

'Mm.' Holland took her arm. The street was not crowded, but it was a polite gesture. 'And is that what you think I require? Delicate treatment to stop me biting?'

Mary did not answer straightaway. Thus far, her first real meeting with Holland had been remarkably easy, for the presence of Jens and Martel and the urgent matter of Mr Boyle's boat had prevented any mention of awkward, personal matters. Now, however . . . 'Oh no,' she replied, trying to sound confident. Presently she added, 'I thought you might be angry when you learned that I was in Paris.'

'I was,' he admitted, 'but fortunately I've had several days to recover my temper. I expect that by the time we have returned to England, I'll have forgotten all about it.'

Relying on his words rather than the tone in which he had uttered them, she murmured a sort of agreement – and immediately frowned at herself. What was the matter with her? She was certainly not frightened of him.

They passed a wine shop, several of whose customers had spilled good-naturedly into the street. Holland waited until they had been left behind before he spoke again. 'Dick Whittington saw you in Hare Court.'

This time she spoke up for herself. 'Ah, that was unlucky.

We were obliged to go through with the marriage ceremony for the sake of verisimilitude – in case we were ever questioned about it. Mr Shy said—'

'What marriage ceremony?' Holland demanded, stopping dead. Mary shushed him, and he whispered urgently, 'With whom?'

'Mr Vangenzen, of course. Did Jens not explain?'

'He told me that you were using that name, but he never . . . Do you mean to say that you've actually *married* this Vangenzen?' His voice was incredulous.

'No no, certainly not,' said Mary. 'What an odd idea.' She tugged his arm, and they resumed walking.

'Everything is odd where Shy's concerned. And if you went through with the ceremony, why *aren't* you married?'

'Principally because the licence was forged. To be married in the Temple Church, you must obtain a licence from the archbishop of Canterbury. Naturally we did not do this – one of Mr Shy's men forged Dr Moore's signature.'

'And what about this . . . Vangenzen – you're sure that *he* knows that the two of you aren't married?'

'He is not "this Vangenzen",' Mary corrected, 'he is Mr Samuel Vangenzen of New Jersey. And he could not help knowing that our wedding was unlawful – he is married already.'

The notion of a bigamous husband *and* a forged licence was too much for Holland, and Mary was obliged to explain the complex marital relations of the Vangenzens. At the end of which he professed a lack of surprise that the American should have agreed to participate in Shy's scheme.

'He's as mad as the rest of you.'

'We are not mad,' said Mary primly. 'Everything has worked out perfectly well. Indeed, the fact of Mr Vangenzen having a wife proved very reassuring when we were making our way to Paris. We were obliged to sleep in the same set of rooms, because everyone believed that we were married.'

'That detail had occurred to me. And this would mean . . . four nights?'

'Three, but the accommodation was only very . . . confined

on the first. Of course, I knew that Mr Vangenzen could be trusted to behave in a gentlemanlike manner, but learning that his feelings were firmly fixed upon another was a great comfort. Indeed—'

Just then they turned a corner, and Mary felt herself being forced into a dark entranceway. She stumbled against a step, mounted it and turned, but Holland was before her, blocking the view.

'What is it?' she whispered.

'Quiet.'

Then she heard footsteps and became aware that Holland was reaching for something in the pocket of his greatcoat – a weapon? Her heart began to pound. *Oh, have we been followed? What shall I do?*

The footsteps came closer, but Mary could see nothing. Then she heard voices – two men – what were they saying? She could not quite make it out. They drew closer.

'Le chat moucheté avec pieds blancs.'

'Dans notre ruelle? Non, je ne l'ai pas vu.'

Still closer, and then the sounds began to fade. The men had not stopped, and were moving away from them.

Holland's shoulders relaxed, but Mary did not attempt to move or speak until she saw him slowly return whatever he had been holding to his pocket. She descended the step and touched his arm. 'What was that? Who were those men?'

He turned towards her, shrugging. Her face was a pale oval in the gloomy portal, and a long curl had escaped and fallen onto her shoulder. 'I thought they had been behind us for rather a long time,' he said.

'And with *very* desperate intentions.' Her eyes twinkled as she explained about the tawny cat.

'Well, maybe I was mistaken, but let's give them another few minutes.' He tucked the curl behind her ear. 'Did you happen to bring your pistol with you to France?'

'Why yes, I did,' said Mary. 'It seemed unlikely, but I thought "there was no harm in being careful". You see how I am guided by your saws?'

'When they suit you,' Holland acknowledged. 'Tell me, what would you have said if I *was* still angry at finding you in Paris? You had reviewed your position, I expect.'

'Of course I had. My position is sound, and I had a great many excellent defences, which even you must have acknowledged.'

'Do you want to tell them to me?'

'Certainly not. It is not a game, you know, and besides . . .'

'Yes?' Holland was smiling.

Mary smiled too, but she tried to conceal it. 'They might yet prove useful.'

The arrival of Mary and Holland at the Maison des Chevrons inspired a combination of relief, confusion, and hurry. The relief was Minta's, for she had watched the evening shadows lengthen and been pricked by remorse – why had she allowed Mary to go out alone? Vangenzen supplied the confusion. Summoned from his studio and encouraged to reflect upon what *might* have happened even as he was presented with a perfectly safe and sound Mary, he merely agreed with all of Minta's exhortations and shook hands gravely with Holland. Almost immediately, however, a sense of hurry impressed itself on both husband and wife – a hurry to tidy, to make Holland comfortable, and to get supper on the table. Even Mary was drawn into the turmoil and did her share of rushing up and down stairs.

When at last they sat down to the somewhat eccentric meal, a combination of leftovers and Mary's expensive purchases, troubling thoughts crowded out more prosaic concerns about the sufficiency of the wine and whether the bread was stale. Who was this Captain Holland, and what new peril might he represent?

Mary explained what had brought him to Paris, thinking that it might not sound so daunting, coming from her. She emphasised that no one wished to impose further upon the Vangenzens, that Mr Boyle's affair had sprung up suddenly, and that it was very important.

'Yes, I see,' Vangenzen acknowledged. 'A vessel that sails underwater . . . an *armed* vessel, would be highly dangerous. The possibility that an unseen enemy might, at any moment, plant its deadly sting . . . Who would put to sea with such a lurking threat?'

'Well, sir, the Royal Navy would,' replied Holland matter-of-factly, 'but at very great risk. That's why Mr Boyle and the *Ammonite* must be got out of France.'

Minta had been slicing the bread – it *was* stale – but now she looked up from her task. 'We hear a great deal about the frustration of the Irish under English rule. Can Mr Boyle be persuaded to support Britain, when defeat might suit Ireland better?'

'Boyle is hardly more Irish than I am, ma'am,' said Holland. 'He had some fellowship or other at Oxford and would have happily remained there, but his family got him a living in County Wexford on the strength of a connection with the place in Queen Elizabeth's day. As for the other, I don't know – but getting hold of Mr Boyle would suit Britain better than killing him.'

'But that is not *your* only reason.'

'No,' Holland admitted, 'it isn't.' He shrugged helplessly, as if acknowledging a weakness. 'I like him, and I wouldn't like to see him harmed. He's a bit mad, of course . . .' He recounted Boyle's theory that the free passage of goods and ideas would bring about a natural harmony of mankind. The main obstacle to free trade was naval supremacy – the nation that controlled the seas could restrict access to foreign markets. 'Britain has naval superiority, so a way must be found to knock the Royal Navy on the head.'

'And Mr Boyle's way is the *Ammonite*,' said Mary.

'That's right. He thinks it will do away with naval warfare – and the threat of it – leaving the seas open to all. And if France in particular has the *Ammonite*, Bonaparte will defeat Britain and bring about a democratic revolution there, which will also contribute to the harmony of mankind.'

'Ah, I see,' said Vangenzen, cautiously. 'It sounds to me rather . . .'

'Fanciful?' suggested Holland. 'Of course, it's bl— it's nonsense. Underwater boats like the *Ammonite* won't end naval warfare. At best, they'll only check it until someone finds a way of defeating them.'

'And *could* they?'

The earnestness of Mary's question made Holland smile. 'Every weapon has its limitation.'

'Good. I mean, I would not want to encourage wars and fighting, but . . .' Her voice trailed off as she could not immediately think of a way of explaining herself that did not sound belligerent.

'Or, if I'm wrong and the *Ammonite* is invincible,' Holland continued, 'why should anyone suppose that the French would use it wisely and not to enforce their own domination of the seas? They're dominating Europe quite happily at the moment.'

'Democratic reform in England does not sound so bad to American ears,' Vangenzen observed.

'Well, sir,' said Holland, 'I am sworn to serve my king, but even if I were an advocate of democracy, I don't believe I'd fancy the French variety.'

'No, perhaps not. But would Mr Boyle?'

'God knows, but Mr Boyle tends to concentrate either on the boat itself or on these grand visions, and he forgets about all the awkward details in between. He's not one of those blood-thirsty priests who go about hanging Welshmen.'

'*What?*' demanded Vangenzen.

Holland flinched as Mary kicked him under the table. 'Ah— oh yes, they're not unknown, apparently. But Mr Boyle is not like that. He is a philosopher.'

'Indeed.' Vangenzen paused, frowning thoughtfully. 'I don't quite see how I'm to play a part in it – your getting him back to England, I mean. Or am I mistaken about that?'

'No,' said Mary, her glance shifting between Vangenzen and Minta, 'I mean, there *is* something, but it is not at all dangerous, and I hope you may even enjoy it. We are hoping that you might . . . paint the portrait of the minister of marine.'

Minta stared at her, and Vangenzen echoed, 'The minister of marine,' as though he could not believe his ears.

'Yes. The minister wants Citizen David to paint him, but David is too busy, so he asked Jens to recommend a young painter capable of executing the portrait.'

'And Jens believes that I could do it?'

'Certainly,' said Mary, smiling. 'Who better? His name is Admiral Le Pelley, and we thought, well, we would be interested in anything he or a member of his staff might happen to say regarding Mr Boyle's experiments.'

Vangenzen turned to Holland. 'You think that Admiral Le Pelley will decide either to approve or reject the boat? Does he have that authority?'

'He might have the authority, but I doubt whether he would have the nerve. It would take a bold man to make a decision on a new weapon before Bonaparte has had a chance to consider it.'

'But once General Bonaparte returns to Paris, he may discuss the matter with Admiral Le Pelley,' said Mary. 'Surely the admiral will be informed of his views. And if I were to accompany you to the Ministry, I might see or hear something useful.'

'Of course you have presumed in all this that he will grant me the commission,' said Vangenzen, still marvelling. 'He wanted *David*, after all.'

'And he will want you . . . if you are willing to visit him and show him your work.'

'Willing? Of course I am willing,' cried Vangenzen. 'The minister of marine! My dear, isn't this wonderful?'

'I suppose so,' said Minta softly. 'But I would have preferred the banker's wife.' She rose and began to clear the table, deftly gathering the plates and glasses, and removing the cloth. As she leaned to recover a cheese knife, she placed her hand upon Vangenzen's shoulder. He pressed it, interrupting her labours, and drew it briefly to his lips.

'There were two other names that David passed on to Jens,' Mary acknowledged, 'but we would be so grateful if you would try Admiral Le Pelley first.'

Vangenzen smiled. 'Unless the others are generals or *directeurs*,

I don't believe I could do better than the minister of marine – and I wouldn't have the chance of any of them if it weren't for you.'

'You are kind to say so,' said Mary, 'and it would be such a help to have this . . . way of discovering what General Bonaparte was thinking – if Captain Holland is not able to dissuade Mr Boyle beforehand.'

Observing their exchanges, Holland could not decide whether he was encouraged by the American's sympathy or irritated that he was so friendly with Mary. *Don't be a bloody fool*, he told himself.

Presently, he took his leave. Mary followed him onto the landing and closed the *appartement* door softly behind her. The passage was dark and chilly, and she shivered. Perhaps that was the reason why she did not resist when he placed the lighted candle in the niche beside the door, and then drew her into his arms.

'Well?' he asked in a low voice, inclining his head towards the door. 'Will they be all right?'

'Yes, I think so – and they had to know about Mr Boyle. Perhaps Mr Shy was wise to remain silent about *our* affairs, but it seemed unfair to keep this from them.' She frowned at Holland. 'You explained things marvellously, but I wish you had not mentioned the bishop of Lichfield.'

'Why not?'

'They must have thought it very odd' – now she was whispering – 'and besides, the story of Odo of Bayeux is much more interesting. He used a mace in battle because it did not draw blood, but that always seemed to me rather doubtful reasoning, because if he struck his opponent very hard—' She broke off. 'Why are you smiling? Have you heard this story before?'

'Well, I'd be a poor excuse for a British officer if I didn't know about the battle of Hastings.'

'Oh yes, of course. I had not thought of that.'

Holland enumerated the important details. 'The Normans pretending to flee, Odo and his mace, Harold killed by an arrow in the eye – and William lost his horse – or was that Richard III?'

'I believe they both had problems in that way,' said Mary, 'but you forgot William falling flat on his face when he landed and saying that he had taken England with both hands.' She gazed up at him triumphantly, and he kissed her. 'Oh my,' she murmured, when she was able. 'What was that for?'

'I wanted to kiss you at Vrillac's, and on the street, and even when you kicked me, but each time there were good reasons not to. But just now I couldn't think of any.'

Mary was blushing furiously and tried to look offended. Indeed, she knew that she ought to *be* offended; certainly she oughtn't to encourage him. 'Perhaps reasons might have occurred to *me*, if you had enquired,' she replied tartly.

'Have any?'

And yet, lying was also very wrong. She smiled and shook her head. 'No.'

'Good.' And he kissed her again.

In the sitting-room, a not dissimilar scene was being played out, albeit with fewer historical references. Minta stood before the ceramic stove, warming her hands and remembering how proud they had been when they had purchased it with the proceeds of Vangenzen's first significant sale. He came up behind her and slid his arms round her waist.

'Everything will be all right, you know,' he urged. 'You really mustn't worry about this portrait – I'm sure I shall be able to capture Le Pelley.'

'Oh, you,' she cried, turning into his arms. I have no fear of that! You are a wonderful artist!'

'And this other matter.' He shrugged. 'Very likely it will come to nothing. Captain Holland will convince Boyle to give up his scheme to reform the world, and I will have my commission. My dear, what a chance for us!'

'But what if Admiral Le Pelley *does* become involved with Mr Boyle?'

'Then . . . well, I don't know, but surely we needn't worry about a problem that we cannot identify and may not even happen.'

Minta turned away from him again, but not so strongly as to break the circle of his arms. 'It sounds silly I know, but . . . this *Ammonite* business is between the French and the British – it has nothing to do with us. Not even Shy has asked for your help this time.'

'No, but Mary is involved in it. You wouldn't want me to fail her, would you? And don't you feel that all of this is important? I do. Now that French forces are unmatched on land, General Bonaparte must not be allowed to have this new weapon to give him control of the sea as well.' He paused. 'We ought to care about these things.'

Minta sighed. 'For the *Ammonite*, and the war, and the harmony of mankind, I care nothing. Nothing at all. For Mary herself . . . I like her and would wish her well. But for our sakes, I would rather that Mary Finch were at the bottom of the sea than that she ever came with you to Paris.'

15

Vangenzen duly wrote to Admiral Le Pelley and received his reply. Both Citizen David and Citizen Jens had attested to the young man's artistic talents, as a result of which the admiral had decided to discuss a possible commission. Having been schooled by his profession never to waste a favourable wind, moreover, he had taken swift action. Would Citizen Vangenzen do him the honour of visiting him at the Hôtel de la Marine that afternoon?

He would indeed. Vangenzen left his breakfast uneaten in his eagerness to put together a suitable portfolio, while Minta hovered nearby, offering advice on what he ought to say and do. They agreed that Mary must accompany him, because a pretty woman's good opinion was generally worth giving, and she would also bolster Vangenzen's confidence. (Strictly speaking, only Minta had made these assertions, but Vangenzen had not denied them.) Mary said that she would be pleased to attend, although she was certain that the artist's talent would win the day. Privately she reminded herself that she was doing something that might tangibly help her friends and was unlikely to expose them to harm.

The offices of the Ministry of Marine were located in a large, elegant building on the north side of the Place de la Revolution. It had once been a storehouse for royal furnishings and furniture, and before the Revolution visitors had paid twelve francs to view treasures such as the crown jewels and a sword belonging to Henri IV. The treasures had since been removed to other quarters, but the building retained something of its former purpose. One class of government administrator had succeeded another, and odd pieces of luxurious furniture had made their way into offices and waiting-rooms, or had been stacked in corridors as though part of a very grand house move.

The first thing that Mary noticed, however, was the respectful attention with which she and Vangenzen were treated. As they followed a clerk across the courtyard and up a grand staircase, Mary felt not awe but excitement. The greater the sitter, after all, the more valuable the commission.

Le Pelley had a suite of rooms at the end of a passageway. His secretary conducted them to a large, gilded chamber, where they were introduced to the admiral, a tall, grey-haired man with a wooden leg. He greeted them cheerfully and at a pronounced volume. *He is used to making himself heard above the raging tempest, I believe*, thought Mary, nodding politely. It was without regret, however, that she withdrew to a chair by the window while Vangenzen presented his portfolio of sketches.

'Ah, very good!' called Le Pelley, as he examined the drawings. 'Excellent. I like this one particularly.' He turned in Mary's direction. 'What do you think, citizeness?'

'Well, admiral, I would hardly be a loyal wife if I did not praise my husband. But I believe you would be very happy with his portrait of you.'

'He has not suggested that I be made to look like one of those fellows in a gown and sandals, so that is a point in his favour. Citizen David is all for the Greeks and the ideal form, but I don't think it would suit me, as my form is not very ideal.'

'Surely you would wish to be painted in your uniform?' asked Mary. The sound of carriages clattering outside obliged her to raise her voice, and she thought, *Soon we shall all be shouting*. 'I think that would be much more splendid than . . .' The vision of the admiral dressed in a toga and crowned with a laurel wreath floated dangerously before her mind's eye and she added, '. . . than anything else!'

'Yes, indeed,' Vangenzen agreed. 'And for the background we might consider your office or the deck of your ship, with the symbols of your career. Your sword, naturally, but perhaps also a map, indicating the stations where you have served?'

'Perhaps.' Le Pelley frowned thoughtfully before soliciting Mary's opinion a second time. He particularly valued the feminine point of view. 'For you must know that this portrait is chiefly — no, entirely — for the delight of my dear wife. Who else would wish to see an old, battered figurehead such as mine memorialised? When I was in my prime, it was a different matter, but now?' He spread his arms.

Neither Mary nor Vangenzen had the temerity to answer these questions, although Vangenzen had certainly known far uglier persons eager to sit for their portraits. He kept this to himself, however, and Le Pelley continued. 'Therefore, I wish all to be done in the way that is most likely to gain my wife's approval. The artist may understand what accords with the principles of art, but if these do not find favour with my wife, we must cast them aside without regret. In the same way a captain ordered by his admiral to slip must not bemoan the loss of his cable and anchor, however valuable.'

'Certainly not,' said Vangenzen.

'One must have peace in the cabin,' said Le Pelley briskly, but then he smiled. 'How long have you been married, citizen?'

The words 'seven years' were almost on Vangenzen's lips when Mary interjected, 'Only one month, admiral, for we were married on the seventeenth of October. You must excuse me,' she added demurely, 'for I am not yet able to order the year according to the new French calendar.'

'Huh,' scoffed Le Pelley. 'I am not surprised, for it is the greatest foolishness — although one is not supposed to say so. "The month of flowering", "the time of meadows" — who can speak seriously of such things? Do you know that my secretary had to rely on a crib to keep the log correctly? He thought I did not know and I kept silent, for it would have been dangerous, in those days, to make a mistake in that way. "Contrary to the Revolution", people would have cried. Ridiculous! However, I mustn't be distracted. The point I want to make is about marriage. Do you know how long *I* have been married?'

They did not.

'Forty years. Therefore, my words on the subject have a proper ballast. I know that the support of one's wife is a gift that cannot be measured by ordinary standards. It is the true sheet anchor. You, Citizen Vangenzen, do not face the peril and the loneliness that we sailors know during a long commission, but every man has trials. Believe me – other supports may fail you, but a loving wife will not.'

The admiral completed his pronouncements by gesturing gravely towards Mary, which was just as well, because Vangenzen was not looking in her direction but at one of his sketches.

Oh dear, thought Mary, *it is very likely a picture of Minta!* In the hope that Le Pelley would not notice, and feeling rather disturbed by his praise, she returned to the matter of the painting. 'I think that this chamber would also make an excellent setting. It is certainly a great honour to be . . . "minister of marine". Is that the correct title?'

Le Pelley nodded, but he glanced about him with little apparent appreciation of ministerial glory. 'That is my wife's opinion, assuredly. Perhaps we should also examine the room next door, and we can decide which would be preferable. You must tell me what you think of the light. Light is of great importance for the artist, is it not?'

The inner room contained a proper desk and a case of well-thumbed books and journals. The admiral's greatcoat was draped over a chair, and a model of a ship called *Hirondelle* had pride of place on a side table, flanked by stacks of dog-eared files. The light was perhaps not as good as in the larger room, but the atmosphere was entirely more pleasing – more nautical, somehow, and less bureaucratic.

'Was the *Hirondelle* your first command, admiral?' asked Vangenzen.

212

'My first in the Navy. The others were fishing boats or privateers – not quite the thing, you know, although there were good fellows in all of them.' The admiral paused. 'You spoke of . . . symbols of my career. Perhaps we might consider a tribute I was fortunate enough to receive.' He explained how he had aided a British frigate that had run aground during a storm in the year '70, after which the Admiralty had presented him with a handsome silver urn.

'Oh yes, it must certainly be included in the portrait,' Mary enthused, 'as signifying both courage and magnanimity towards a foe.'

'England was not then our foe,' Le Pelley reminded her, 'but of course the demands of honour do not cease in wartime. I mention it, however, because my dear Marie Ursule has always admired that piece of silverware.'

'I think perhaps that the portrait would be best if set in this room, your true office,' Mary continued. 'The other is very grand, but it could be the room of any great man of state. This room reflects your character. That is what *I* would wish to see, if I were commissioning a portrait of my husband.'

Le Pelley threw up his hands. 'The wife's command – then it must be so! Are you content, Citizen Vangenzen?'

'Yes, admiral, very much so. And I thank you most sincerely for your faith in me.'

'It is well. Let us shake hands on the matter. For the next while I have appointments and matters that require my attention, but thereafter, I am at your service.'

When Rear Admiral Pléville Le Pelley, minister of marine, agreed to meet with Citizen Samson Boyle, inventor, on the morning of the third of Frimaire at the former convent of the Little Fathers, Mr Boyle was thrilled.

Holland was not. Indeed, he was becoming increasingly frustrated. Despite his efforts, Boyle's enthusiasm for the undersea vessel was unabated, although now he viewed it almost exclusively as a technical puzzle to be solved. Convincing the French that he had done so was part of that exercise, while the possibility that they might not actually use the *Ammonite* to bring about the freedom of the seas became a distant, ephemeral chance.

There was one advantage to this attitude; it did not precipitate a crisis of any kind with Holland. From Boyle's perspective, 'Mr Ogbourne worried a great deal' and perhaps did not concentrate on 'business' quite as much as one would like, but these were minor failings. Certainly Holland had been careful never to couch his words in any but a neutral frame. He spoke merely of the danger that the *Ammonite* would pose in the hands of a government bent on conquest, and the likelihood that rivals would soon strike back, either with defences that the *Ammonite* could not penetrate or with a superior underwater vessel. Boyle listened to these remarks, particularly those having to do with the *Ammonite*'s vulnerability, but they seemed rather to inspire than to chasten him.

'Yes, thicker hulls,' he would mutter, poring over his drawings, 'but my improved screw mechanism should deal with that. Is it likely that a tougher wood than oak might be commonly employed? I must make enquiries about exotic timber. And copper sheeting, of course . . . that would restrict the *Ammonite*'s use in tropical waters, where I believe coppering is more common.'

Boyle generally came round to the same conclusion, however, that all problems could be solved with time and effort – so long as the French approved the *Ammonite* in principle and authorised further research and expenditure. 'And even with her current specifications, my dear fellow, imagine the role that a fleet of *Ammonites* could play in the event of a landing in the south of England,' he would urge.

Holland could imagine it very well. He presented no very cheerful demeanour, therefore, when Admiral Le Pelley arrived, exact to his time and looking thoroughly competent. Elderly, and not likely to be one of those scientific sailors whom one sometimes encountered in the Royal Navy, but competent nevertheless. Accompanying him was a younger man, only five years or so older than Holland. Le Pelley introduced him as Captain Flynn.

'He is from your country, Mr Boyle,' Le Pelley explained,

'but he holds a commission in our Army, in case he is so unfortunate as to fall into British hands.'

Damn, an Irishman! thought Holland. The prospect of scrutiny by anyone more attentive than Mr Boyle made him distinctly uncomfortable, but he could hardly stand mute while the others conversed. 'Is such protection necessary, sir?' he asked. 'Surely the British are unlikely to venture onto the mainland of Europe in the near future?'

'Indeed, sir, I don't expect them to come calling anytime soon,' Flynn agreed, 'so I'm afraid we shall have to pay them a visit. That is why—'

Le Pelley interrupted him smoothly. 'Captain Flynn and I are in discussions about another matter,' he explained, 'which we shall resume later.'

'To be sure,' said Flynn, 'and I beg your pardon, sir. I only meant to say to the gentleman that the English have a way of letting others do their fighting for them, and this war is no different. But while their allies have been obliged to close up shop, I doubt if we shall see the shopkeepers themselves.'

The knowing look that accompanied that figure obliged Holland to ask, 'You have experience of military service yourself, sir?'

'I have too, in my youth, with His Majesty's forces in the 19th Regiment of Foot.'

Damn and blast, thought Holland.

'A very worthy regiment, I am certain,' pronounced Le Pelley, still genial, but clearly wishing to move things along. 'Mr Boyle, perhaps we might speak more particularly about your work?'

'With pleasure, sir.' Boyle clasped his hands eagerly, like a schoolboy who had been offered the chance to perform for one of his seniors. 'Would you care to begin with a general explanation, or proceed straightaway to the particular features of the device?'

Le Pelley said that he would leave the ordering of the discussion to Mr Boyle – but perhaps it might be conducted in a more private place?

The suggestion surprised Boyle, and he fumbled with his

215

eyepiece before replying, as if it might correct any defect in his hearing. 'Private? Why, it is just as you like, sir, but Mr Ogbourne has my complete confidence.'

'And I do not conceive you to be mistaken,' urged Le Pelley, nodding politely at Holland. 'However, when the affairs of my nation are concerned, I must exercise great care.'

Holland murmured that he quite understood, the gentlemen should not mind him, but made no move to withdraw. The plans of the *Ammonite*, he knew, were in that room, and he did not mean to let them be taken away without his knowledge. If the Frenchman required privacy, therefore, he and Mr Boyle could go elsewhere.

An awkward silence ensued, during which Holland resumed his seat. Feeling extremely boorish, he asked, 'Do you mean to show the admiral your models, sir?'

'Ah, yes,' said Boyle with a smile of relief, 'what an excellent suggestion. Much the best way to make the whole thing perfectly clear. Admiral Le Pelley, would you care to step this way?'

The admiral lowered the eyebrow he had raised in Holland's direction and bowed gravely. 'Certainly.'

The departure of Boyle and Le Pelley solved one problem for Holland but created another, for he was obliged to entertain the other inessential – Captain Flynn. It was certainly not a task that he relished. *An Irishman and a former British officer – my God, could anything be worse?*

Indeed it could, for Flynn had also been to America. Not to Connecticut, thankfully, but he spoke knowledgeably, or at least with great confidence, about South Carolina, where he had served as a lad during the last war, and Philadelphia, where he had lately resided. 'Their lordships in Dublin Castle and I did not see eye to eye in certain matters, and I was encouraged to emigrate.'

'I see,' said Holland glumly. He had no wish to discuss Irish politics, to which he was quite sure Flynn was referring, and was forced to cross the Atlantic, which he liked even less. 'And how did you find, er, Philadelphia?'

Flynn shook his head. 'Not at all to my taste, for the people

216

there are as grand as the English in their way, and great lovers of money. Meaning no disrespect to yourself, of course.'

'No no.'

'And the Quakers, though they don't hold with wealth, are a stiff-necked crew.' Flynn chuckled to himself. 'But I could never be at my ease with a man who won't take a drink with me. What are your own politics, if you don't mind my asking? Being an American, you must be either a Federalist or a Republican.'

Oh Christ, thought Holland, whose knowledge of American politics extended only to the fact that espousing either cause would be highly dangerous – especially in conversation with someone like Flynn. He replied, therefore, that he had no political affiliation.

'But what about your inclination?' Flynn persisted. 'For I cannot believe that you have no interest, sir, in how your country is governed.'

Holland could feel his face becoming hot. In desperation he said that he shunned all such worldly matters, on account of his religious convictions. He belonged to a small sect, based in England – in Kent – called the Fellowship of the Holy Conventicle. His parents had gone to Connecticut when he was a child.

Not surprisingly, Flynn professed himself ignorant of the Fellowship. (Holland was not even certain what a conventicle *was*, but he thought it had to do either with the promises or the premises of Dissenters.) 'But it explains your accent,' he affirmed, 'for you know, I thought you sounded more like an Englishman than any American I'd known.'

This was hardly an observation likely to inspire a greater conversational fluency, and Holland merely nodded. Then, as carefully as he dared, he added, 'The members of the Fellowship keep themselves to themselves.'

'Do they? Well, good luck to them, says I. If they keep quiet they can't do much harm.' Flynn explained that religion had been the curse of his own country, with Catholics and Protestants at each other's throats. 'Which is a terrible thing, when you consider that we were all of us taught "Love thy neighbour" in church of a Sunday morning.'

'Er, yes.'

'The French knew what they were about when they got rid of the lot of 'em – priests and ministers alike. Reason over superstition. But now I see that some of the old ways are creeping back again. The government doesn't want to follow Robespierre, I suppose, but no good can come of the other – you mark my words.'

Holland could do little more than mark them, for Organised Religion dashed what little hope he had of maintaining his end of the conversation. Fortunately, therefore, at that moment Martel entered and asked the gentlemen whether they would care for some refreshment.

'What sort of refreshment?' asked Flynn.

Martel shrugged in the way that often preceded a complaint against his employer, the gesture somehow indicating that the grievance had some remote or unidentifiable source, and he was merely its blameless messenger. 'With Americans it is always *le café*, but when one is in Paris, one should drink wine.'

Flynn affirmed that he was entirely of the valet's way of thinking. More importantly, when Martel returned with a bottle and glasses, Flynn urged him to stay. The offer was accepted, and straightaway the conversation became more buoyant, more convivial. In part this was because the bottle was shared only between two, for Holland did not judge that the Fellowship of the Holy Conventicle would countenance the drinking of wine. In part it was the result of Martel's interest in the American war. Flynn's role in that conflict had been decidedly minor, but Martel listened eagerly to every detail. The Irishman, in turn, was obliged to hear a lengthy account of the battle of the Chesapeake. 'My cousin was in the *Auguste*,' said Martel as he drew the opposing forces on the back of one of Boyle's notes, 'and has explained to me all of the manoeuvres.'

The manoeuvres of Sir Thomas Graves and the comte de Grasse kept them occupied until Boyle and Le Pelley returned – the first looking deflated, the second resolute. Holland felt his heart move in a far more pleasing fashion. Could it be that the admiral had rejected the *Ammonite*? Were he and Martel to be lucky and the French to fall at the first fence?

Without actually setting them out, Le Pelley had reservations. Moreover, he could not make an immediate decision even if he had so wished – the press of business must delay things. Mr Boyle's work was certainly very interesting, but . . . And he had misspoken when he used the word 'decision'. A recommendation would be the limit of his authority in this matter, and at present he would hesitate even to promise that. He was sorry to be so discouraging.

Boyle nodded gloomily; disappointment rendered him old and sad. Even Martel experienced a flicker of sympathy, and he shot Holland a tense look, as if he expected to detect a greater weakness in his colleague's expression. Holland remained stony, however, as he willed Le Pelley to take his leave.

And then suddenly Boyle revived. Rifling through the pile of documents on his desk, he pulled forth a flat leather wallet. At least, he urged, would the admiral be so good as to take the plans with him? Their careful scrutiny, after a period of reflection, might make all the difference.

'But I am leaving tomorrow for Le Havre,' Le Pelley protested. 'There can be no scrutiny until I return.'

'I understand, sir.' Boyle held out the wallet. 'But it would ease my mind considerably to know that the plans were in your keeping.'

'And so he practically forced Le Pelley to take the damned things,' Holland complained, scuffing the gravel. Only a few hours had passed since the interview at the convent, and his irritation was still fresh. 'He would have left without them – and probably never come back – but he has taken them out of politeness, and now anything might happen.'

'At least we have several days' grace before the admiral returns to Paris,' Mary remarked more temperately. 'And even then . . . We need do nothing straightaway.'

'We *can* do nothing straightaway.'

They were walking in the gardens of the Tuileries, a pleasant spot for a rendezvous if one were ignorant of its history. Men and women of all degrees strolled up and down the paths, or frequented the *cafés* and refreshment booths that filled the court-yard and lined the northern edge of the garden. Mary did not know that the king's Swiss Guards had been massacred on that very site, and thought merely that anonymity was often best maintained in a crowd.

'Did you learn anything more of the admiral's concerns?' she asked.

'Yes, Mr Boyle told me afterwards. Le Pelley considers an underwater boat immoral and contrary to the laws of war – which it may well be – and he thinks that *we* would consider it immoral, which might put French prisoners at risk of bad treatment. In retaliation, if you see what I mean.'

'Like King Henry after the battle of Agincourt. The French killed the boys who were minding the English tents and things, and Henry was in such a rage that he ordered all the French hostages to be executed. That was in the play, of course, but I expect Mr Shakespeare got it right.'

Holland did not offer an opinion on the bard's historical sensibilities, confining himself instead to more immediate concerns. If Admiral Le Pelley were to reject the boat – returning the plans with polite thanks and nothing more – Mr Boyle might conclude that the French did not deserve the *Ammonite*. It was a short step from disappointment to dislike, and if he no longer wished to help the French Navy, he might be persuaded to help the British instead.

'Yes, if he felt that he had been snubbed or unappreciated,' Mary agreed. They had stopped before one of the ponds, where children launched wooden boats under the watchful eye of their nurses. One little boy, whose brother refused to share launching duties, burst into tears and had to be taken away and consoled with a bon-bon. 'At least he might agree to leave France, and the French government would probably not object.'

'And you would leave too, wouldn't you?'

Mary did not immediately reply, and when she did, there was a frown in her voice. 'I do not know. There is still *my* work

220

to be considered. I ought to call upon Mr Marshall and renew my connection . . .' Her sentence trailed off, and then she asked, more urgently, 'But what if Admiral Le Pelley were to give a favourable recommendation?'

'Boyle would be cock-a-hoop.'

'*And* determined to carry on.' She remembered what Martel had said about the easiest way to halt Boyle's experiments. 'If that happened, could you really . . .?'

Holland took a deep breath and slowly exhaled. 'I wouldn't have much of a choice. God, what a racket.' He resumed walking, and Mary followed.

'And what of the actual plans of the *Ammonite*? If the French government were to approve the project, we must recover them as well as . . . stopping Mr Boyle.'

'Mm.'

They walked in silence, and then, '*We* could recover them,' said Mary firmly, 'Mr Vangenzen and I.'

Holland stopped abruptly. 'What? Oh no you couldn't – you and that . . . pottering about in Le Pelley's office? While Vangenzen was taking a break from his portrait, I suppose? Or he could ask Le Pelley to look this way and maintain a pose while you searched his coat for confidential papers?'

'I would *not* be "pottering about",' Mary retorted before urging him to lower his voice. 'And what is the alternative? No one else has an excuse to visit the Hôtel de la Marine. It would be far more dangerous for you or Captain Martel to attempt it.'

'Perhaps, but I don't . . . ' Holland struggled for a logical reply; his objections not being grounded in logic made this difficult. 'What about Jens?'

'*Jens* visit Admiral Le Pelley?' asked Mary incredulously.

'No, no, but he might have a better plan.' It was the first time that Holland had held up Jens as a figure of sagacity, but he did so now with conviction. 'I doubt whether *he* would support your going to the Ministry.'

Mary thought that he would, and perhaps for this reason she agreed to consult him. There was also something wonderful about Holland's desire to protect her, and she did not want to press him too far. *Not until we know whether Admiral Le Pelley is likely to approve the Ammonite.*

'Good. Promise you won't do anything until you've spoken with Jens.'

She gave the necessary pledge. '*If* we retrieved the plans, the Vangenzens and I would certainly leave France. I shall ask Jens about that, too. Mr Vangenzen has relations near Amsterdam, you see, and we might apply for travel documents to, er, *Holland.*'

While withholding support for Mary's wider proposal, Holland approved of her departing French soil, and agreed that she should take advantage of whatever privileges her neutral status afforded — even if it meant official scrutiny.

'My papers have passed every test thus far — but I am not strictly a neutral, you know.'

'You aren't?'

'Oh no. Even if I *had* married Mr Vangenzen — legally, I mean — I should not have become an American on the strength of it. Not according to English law. Sir Edward Coke is quite clear on the matter.'

'And who the devil is Sir Edward Coke? Some friend of Shy's?'

'No, he was a great jurist who lived in the last century,' said Mary with a smile. 'He caused a great deal of trouble to James I, but he understood the common law.'

Holland looked as if he did not care a great deal about James I or the common law, but he merely reiterated that Mary's papers stated that she was married to an American — a neutral. 'If anything happens, let's hope that the French haven't heard about Coke.'

Although certain of their colleagues kept more unusual hours, the regular staff at the Hôtel de la Police put down their pens at five o'clock each evening. Thereafter the doors were locked and most of the lights extinguished at the stately building opposite the Quai Voltaire. Those men who remained possessed their own keys and kept their own counsel as regards any out-of-hours activities.

As one of the senior clerks was locking the front door at three minutes past five, a hand closed suddenly upon his elbow. 'Oh!' he cried, flinching, and then he sighed, partly with relief and partly with irritation. 'Good evening, Captain Flynn. Shall I unlock?'

'Good evening to you. Yes, I'm afraid you must. I've highly important information that is sure to interest your chief.'

The clerk was rather less certain. Captain Flynn was a conscientious fellow. Conscientious and highly suspicious, with the result that he saw spies and informers hovering round him at all times and felt obliged to report these nefarious individuals regularly to the authorities. He lodged in the Rue de l'Ecole de Médécine, and the police of his section knew him very well. His visits to the Ministry were less frequent, but they had already resulted in the creation of a sizeable file. Most of what it contained was useless, but that was not the clerk's concern. He unlocked the door.

'Wait here and I will enquire,' he informed Flynn.

Sergeant Fondard had forgotten to make his usual supper arrangements at the usual time. The light tapping at his door, therefore, signifying the presence of someone who might be of service in this respect, cheered him considerably. 'Come in, come in!' he called. 'Ah, Clement — it is Clement, is it not? I thought so. Good evening. What can I do for you?'

The clerk's information did not wholly undermine this humour. One never knew when even Captain Flynn's information might prove useful. 'Have him come up,' Fondard affirmed, 'and wait for a little while yourself — I may have further instructions.'

Flynn duly appeared, and a short time later Fondard sat back in his chair, having absorbed a somewhat rambling account. 'So you believe that this fellow is not an American because of the way he pronounces a word?' He referred to the sheet of paper before him. 'Connect-i-cut,' he said, slowly. 'That is not correct? It looks correct.'

'No, sergeant, it ought to be pronounced "Connet-i-cut".'

'Ah.' Fondard struck a line through the offending letter. 'Well,

English is a strange language, but one word – it does not prove that the man is an impostor.'

'It might not,' said Flynn, 'but I have never heard it mistaken by anyone in America, and you know that I am well acquainted with the country. I was none too happy with the way he said "Philadelphia" either. But besides that, the fellow struck me as an Englishman. He had an explanation for that, but . . .'

'You did not credit it?'

'Well, I might have done, only . . . he had a way about him that called to mind military fellows I have known. You'll recall that I—'

'That you once served in the British Army? Yes, I recall it,' said Fondard. He thought for a few moments. He was far more intrigued by the fact that Admiral Le Pelley had held a confidential interview at the old convent than by the peculiarities of American diction. It had previously come to his attention that the Ministry of Marine was interested in the Little Fathers, but no further information had been forthcoming. On the contrary, his own chief had issued instructions that the affairs of the convent did not concern the police. If it could be established that something untoward was happening there, however, that instruction would surely change. 'What did the admiral discuss with this . . . Boyle?' he asked casually. 'Do you know?'

Flynn admitted that he did not. 'But it must have been important,' he reasoned, 'or why would he have been so close about it?'

'Perhaps he is a close fellow,' said Fondard. He added a further two sentences to his notes. When he raised his eyes again to the man sitting opposite him, he was smiling. 'And now I think that our business this evening is concluded, Captain Flynn. Please accept my thanks.' He rose and offered his hand.

'You'll consider what I have said?'

'Assuredly. I shall think of little else. A pleasant evening to you.'

Alone again, Fondard turned the matter over for the space of ten minutes and then raised his voice. 'Clement?'

The door opened, and the clerk appeared. 'Yes, citizen?'

'Do me a service, would you?' He held a slip of paper between

224

his fingers and gestured for Clement to take it. 'I am interested in this man – probably an American, although Captain Flynn has his doubts.'

'Captain Flynn . . .'

'Yes, I know. However, the name is faintly familiar to me. Which reports would I have seen in the last ten days or so?'

Clement glanced at the slip and then considered. 'Émigrés, postal receipts, and crimes committed on the river. Also prostitution.'

'I think we may omit the girls,' laughed Fondard. 'Perhaps you could check the others for me. You are alone tonight?'

'No, citizen. Escalle and Pilon are still here.'

'Excellent – divide the files between the three of you.'

'Very good, citizen.'

The clerk's shoulders sank at the prospect of a long, tedious search. He was thoroughly conscientious, however, and returned to his desk without further comment. Some time later he knocked again at Fondard's door.

'You have it?'

'I believe so, citizen, in a report from the Customs office. The person you identified is an artist, it seems.'

'An artist?' Fondard studied Clement's carefully written note. 'Hmm. So it appears. He is a man of many talents, this fellow, although he cannot say "Connecticut" in the accepted style. A consignment of prints to . . . Tobias Jens, at the Rue Geoffroy l'Asnier. Well, well.' He began to sing *La Carmagnole* under his breath. *'The Swiss have promised, the Swiss have promised / That they would shoot our friends, that they would shoot our friends.'*

'Will there be anything else, citizen?'

'But how they have jumped / How they have all danced! Yes, one thing more – will you join me for supper, my worthy Clement? I was going to send out, but I think that tonight we must treat ourselves. Shall we try the Restaurateurs? The duck is always good at the Restaurateurs, and they know me there.' He smiled broadly. *'Let's dance the Carmagnole, hooray for the sound, hooray for the sound / Let's dance the Carmagnole, hooray for the sound of the cannons!'*

225

16

Mary had intended to set off promptly the following morning for her consultation with Jens, in the hope that an early visit to Vrillac's would be less likely to provoke his ire. To the extent that his humphs, sighs, and other expressions of distress could be relied upon, he objected most strongly to matters 'outside his profession' when they interfered with his custom. Artists not being particularly early risers, Jens ought to prefer closing his shop in the morning than in the afternoon.

This sensible plan was dashed by a combination of minor misfortunes, starting with Mary's own failure to rise at her usual time. Then, in her hurry to set off, she broke a lace, thereby disqualifying her boots from immediate service. As she possessed no other footwear that could survive the Paris streets, she was obliged to borrow a pair of Minta's sabots. Minta herself had already departed for the market, so the pair that Mary borrowed were not only too big but also very smooth and somewhat broken down. They slowed her descent of the Rue Beauregard, and when she joined the crowd at the Porte Denis, she was at a considerable disadvantage in the struggle for cabriolets. Any but a slow, deliberate movement risked the loss of a shoe, and inevitably involved much slipping and flailing. More sprightly customers beat her to three different vehicles.

At last she was on her way, having tumbled into a forlorn cabriolet at the end of the queue (and losing her left sabot in

226

the process), whose driver was glad of any patronage. He took an unfamiliar route, which at least made the journey more interesting. *And not longer*, she hoped, wondering whether he had chosen it in order to increase the fare. She could hardly challenge him, however, and so contented herself with enquiring about any interesting buildings that they passed, in this way showing that she was sharp-eyed, if not very nimble, and would certainly know if they passed a landmark more than once.

They halted at the entrance to the Place de l'Indivisibilité, and Mary made her ponderous descent. A sense of caution had prompted her to choose that destination, for Vrillac's might remain in the driver's memory longer than one of the most well known squares in the city, if he were ever to be questioned on the subject. Not that he *was* likely to be questioned, of course, but . . .

She thought less well of her decision as she made her way gingerly along the Rue Antoine. One thing was clear – no amount of scrunching or gripping with one's foot inside a wooden shoe made the slightest difference either to one's speed or stability. *This is how I shall walk when I am an old woman*, she reflected, as the street seemed to extend interminably before her. *If Jens is particularly grumpy, I shall make a joke about these shoes – my Parisian disguise – and perhaps that will cheer him.*

It might have cheered him, had he been there to hear it, but when she finally reached Vrillac's, the door was locked and the window shuttered. Mary knocked, although it seemed a pointless exercise, and she was not surprised when it elicited no response. She retreated and gazed up at the first floor window; it too was dark.

Where was Jens? It was after ten o'clock – surely he ought to be somewhere about at this hour? He might have stepped out . . . for a cup of coffee, perhaps, but the shop looked as if it had not been opened at all that morning. *This is a nuisance*, thought Mary. *I particularly wished to speak with him.*

After a very few minutes it had become more than a nuisance, for having come this far, what ought she to do? She could not very well remain in front of the shop, waiting for Jens to return — it would look so very odd. Then too, she did not particularly like the Rue Geoffroy l'Asnier; it was so dark and morose-looking, as if only unhappy, disappointed people lived there.

She shivered at the prospect of encountering a gloomy resident loitering in a doorway. *And if I remain here much longer, I shall be just such a loiterer.* On the other hand, the idea of returning to the Maison des Chevrons without having spoken to Jens was extremely vexing, especially as he might turn up at any moment — very likely he would do. It would be a shame to miss him.

Little as she liked it, therefore, she decided to walk about the neighbourhood and try her luck again in a short while. *Oh dear, walking,* she silently complained. Rarely had the exercise been so unwelcome to her. But there were shops nearby. She could purchase something for supper . . . a pastry, perhaps, by which time Jens would undoubtedly have arrived and opened the shop.

Thus encouraged and armed with a purpose, she set off again, and discovered that if she thrust her feet forward and shuffled along, rather than attempting to lift them, she could move quite confidently, if inelegantly. This new form of locomotion also enabled her to fulfil the condition she had imposed upon herself — not to return to Vrillac's in less than half an hour. She mustn't haunt the street, after all.

She duly shuffled up and down the Rue des Droits-de-l'Homme, therefore, and returned to Vrillac's after an interval of thirty-three minutes, having purchased a pair of bootlaces and an apple tart. The artists' shop, however, remained closed.

Was there some reason why Jens would not have come to work that morning? Might he be ill, or might this be some sort of holiday? It was the fourth of Frimaire; she could not remember the real date. *November the something or other,* she told herself. But a holiday seemed very unlikely. After all, the boot maker had behaved as though it were a perfectly ordinary morning, and so had the woman in the pastry shop. If this were the anniversary of some notable French victory, or the day

228

when Brotherhood or Universal Justice were particularly celebrated, she felt sure that someone would have mentioned it.

While Mary was considering these matters, an elderly woman emerged from a courtyard on the opposite side of the street. She wore a kerchief tied over her straggly grey locks, and a shawl with frayed edges lay across her shoulders. Her face was wizened like an overripe apple, and her thin hands were red and cracked.

Her appearance, and at such a moment, was disturbing. *If ever I were to meet a witch*, Mary thought, *I expect she would look much the same*. She nodded a greeting, however, and observed, 'The shop is not open this morning.'

'No,' the woman agreed. She adjusted her shawl – or was she waiting to see what Mary would do?

I suppose I do not look like Jens' usual customers – I am a bit of a curiosity. Of course she could explain herself – she was the wife of an artist, after all – but she shrank from further conversation. And still the old woman did not move, but rather searched in the pockets of her voluminous skirt. Whatever had brought her into the street did not seem so very pressing.

Mary was deeply conscious that standing outside a dark, shuttered shop was strange. *And the longer I remain, the more strange it becomes*. Then she had a more unnerving thought – perhaps the old woman had observed Mary's first arrival and then her return. Perhaps she had come outside to investigate!

'Are you going to see Bithon?' asked the old woman suddenly in a creaking, high-pitched voice.

Mary could not hide her surprise. 'I beg your pardon?'

'Bithon,' repeated the other. At least, that was how Mary interpreted the word. The old woman had few teeth, and therefore spoke indistinctly. 'They have left already.' She made a vague gesture, exposing a thin, wasted arm. 'You had better hurry.'

'But I—' Mary hesitated long enough for the old woman to say 'Bithon' a third time. Then she answered, 'Yes, thank you,' and retreated a few steps.

'Quickly, or you will be too late,' urged the woman.

Mary assured her that she would follow this sound advice,

and turning, the speed of her shuffling steps increased. She had no idea to whom or what the old woman was referring and very little interest in finding out. Her own errand having proven unsuccessful, however, she decided to avail herself of this opportunity to withdraw. And Jens? *Perhaps he has gone to see Bithon, like everyone else.*

She turned right onto the Rue de la Mortellerie. This, she knew, would take her to the Place de Grève, where she was likely to find a cabriolet to take her home. *I am not going to walk all that way, whatever happens*, she resolved.

In addition to their other undesirable qualities, her sabots had contrived to rub against her feet most uncomfortably. It did not seem possible for such a large shoe to raise a blister, but her right sabot in particular had proven equal to the task. However she shifted her foot inside the commodious shoe, the point of irritation remained, and she began to limp.

As she approached the square, a very different sort of distraction presented itself. The street was becoming increasingly crowded, and presently she found herself part of a throng of people. A few of the men were well dressed, but most wore shabby work clothes or military uniforms. More surprising were the women. Many were hard faced, with dyed hair and dresses that managed to look both extravagant and tawdry. While the men were largely silent, these women laughed, and waved, and chattered among themselves, as if they were going to a party and part of the fun came in meeting friends along the route.

They halted at the edge of the square, or rather joined a larger crowd. Mary stood on tiptoes, trying to discover what was happening, and whether she should advance or retreat. In fact she could do neither easily, and even with the added inches of her sabots, she could see little beyond the people immediately in front of her. As they moved forward, however, Mary was obliged by those behind her to do likewise. Buffeted first on the right and then on the left, she clutched the package containing the apple tart and strove to keep her balance upon the slippery cobbles.

An unexpected surge forced her against a tawny-haired woman in a vulgar orange gown that exposed her bosom, or would have done had it not been covered with a great many cheap necklaces of spangles and glass beads.

'Oh! I beg your pardon,' cried Mary.

'Never you mind, my sister,' laughed the other, clapping her arm around Mary and hauling her upright. She had a rough, almost ferocious manner, although beneath her rouge and white paint she appeared very young. 'Have you come to see the fun?'

'Indeed, I hardly know—'

'Of course! But we must get a better view.' She turned to a companion on her other side, a thin, pale girl in a drab gown that was torn at the shoulder. 'Agathe – shall we try for the steps?'

'Oh, yes!' The thin girl's eyes shone hungrily. 'We shall see nothing behind these hulking men.'

'And you, sister?'

'Well, I . . . ' The wildness of the two girls frightened Mary, and she would have withdrawn if she could, but to move against the tide of people seemed impossible.

'Courage! What are men, after all? Nothing but babies, brutes, and braggarts,' affirmed the tawny-haired girl. 'Let us advance!' Clasping Mary's and the pale girl's hands, she strode forward, and Mary had to follow as best she could.

They forced their way through a close cordon of people with so little regard for toes or tempers that Mary thought there might be a fight, but in the event her tart was the only casualty, lost somehow in the mêlée. She and her new companions emerged unscathed, and now the crowd was not so dense, but had separated into distinct groups. In the open spaces ranged dogs, children, and men selling fruit and distributing handbills. From everywhere there rose an indistinct babble – cries, laughter, barking, and even singing.

Is it a holiday after all? Mary wondered. *Is there going to be a speech?*

They climbed the steps in front of the *hôtel de ville*, and at last she could see what had caused the excitement: a large

231

wooden scaffold, and standing upon it a guillotine. A guillotine! 'Is it an execution?' she gasped.

Agathe, the pale girl, gazed at her wonderingly. 'Yes, of course an execution. Do you not know Bisson?'

Mary shook her head.

'Who does not know Bisson?' demanded the tawny-haired girl, but Agathe explained, 'He killed a girl that we knew – a good girl! She lived on our street, not three doors from Celine and I. Poor Lucie. He was her lover, and he smothered her and took her money. Money that she had earned!'

'I warned her that he was no good, but she loved him,' said Celine. Two of her necklaces had become entangled, and she rearranged them absently. 'And see how her love was rewarded. Now he will have *his* reward, the filthy dog.' She spat expertly.

'And he killed her grandmother – Lucie's poor grandmother, who raised Lucie after her mother died and managed her affairs. It is too pitiful.'

'Pity for them, but not for him. I'll enjoy seeing his head in the basket! I'll dance and sing when I see it! Bring him out! Bring him out!' Celine shrieked, and Agathe piped, 'Bring out the murderer!'

Similar cries rang out across the square, and Mary perceived a great commotion taking place some distance away. A coach was advancing slowly through the press, accompanied by four mounted soldiers. 'Ah! He is coming!' 'Bisson, the murderer!' roared someone in the crowd. 'Bisson, your time has come!'

Despite having struggled so hard to win their places on the steps, Celine and Agathe immediately surrendered them and dashed towards the scaffold. They were soon lost in the heaving crowd as other people clambered up or down, eager for a good view or to be close to the great event.

An older woman, less spectacularly dressed, stood beside Mary. 'The girl who was killed was no better than she should have been, but in these days . . . ' She shrugged, and a large, heavy-set man demanded, 'And the old woman? What harm had she done that she should have her head dashed in by a scoundrel? Justice! We demand justice!' he roared.

232

Mary nodded, but her attention was focused on the drama before her. An execution! A man was about to be killed in her presence. A wicked man, no doubt, but . . . and before this baying crowd. She was horrified, yet fascinated by the scene.

A cart surrounded by more soldiers followed the carriage, and the howls and cries increased in volume. In the cart sat a man with his back to the horses; his hands were tied behind his back, and a red shirt or cloak hung across his shoulders. Another man – the executioner – hurried him out of the cart and onto the ground. There they were joined by a priest, dressed as a layman but bearing a crucifix, and he spoke to the prisoner for a short while, apparently oblivious to the shouts and furious gestures of those around him.

Not until he had mounted the scaffold did Mary see his face, and then only briefly. He was surprisingly ordinary looking; certainly there was no evidence of cruelty or malice in his features. He turned to hear the further injunctions of the priest, and then a board was drawn out of the guillotine and turned up perpendicularly on its hinge. Bisson was buckled onto it, face downwards, and the board was tilted back to a horizontal position.

Mary wanted to look away – she knew that she ought to – but she continued to stare. *I will close my eyes at the last moment*, she promised herself as Bisson's head was slipped under the blade and locked into place. The crowd fell silent; the blade hung suspended, and then the executioner withdrew the pin.

Whoosh! The blade fell and Mary shut her eyes. There was a horrible sound, like a cabbage being cloven in two, and then a dull thud. *Is he dead?* Mary asked herself. *Surely there should be some cry or*— Then the crowd's triumphant cheer confirmed that the sentence had been duly carried out.

When she opened her eyes again, the dead man's trunk was being tossed into a basket and his head after it. *Now he is nothing, and yet a moment ago he stood there, hearing the priest's words, able to speak and understand.* It was scarcely believable that life could be terminated so quickly and effortlessly. That knowledge,

together with the exultant cries of those around her, was sick-
ening. She caught a glimpse of Celine, dancing before the
scaffold as she had said she would, and even imagined that
she could detect the heavy odour of blood.

The executioner and his assistant slowly descended the steps
of the scaffold, the basket a heavy burden between them. The
image of what it contained swam before Mary's eyes – the
unnatural body, the dead eyes staring, the lips stretched in a
final grimace – and suddenly she felt herself grow cold and
sweaty. A roaring in her ears drowned out the sounds of celebration, and she sat down quickly.

Oh, I must not be sick! She closed her eyes and took several
slow, deep breaths.

'For God's sake! Mary!'

She opened her eyes and stared helplessly into Holland's
anxious face. Anxious and furious. 'What are you doing here?'

'I did not—'

'Are you hurt?' he demanded. 'Can you stand?'

'Yes, I . . .' She allowed him to help her to her feet. 'I did
not know what it was – that there was going to be an execution. And then . . .'

'All right, never mind. Let's get away from here.'

Holland scanned the square, few of whose occupants showed
signs of dispersing. The atmosphere had become celebratory,
with much singing and dancing, and two wine stalls had been
hastily erected. His arm protectively around Mary's shoulders,
he led her down the steps and then set a course for the north
side of the square that avoided most of the revellers.

He did not spare her his opinion of her conduct – venturing
alone into a crowded square, with God only knew how many
thieves and cutpurses, men *and women* of unsavoury occupation;
what the devil had she been thinking? – and Mary felt that she
must endure it. She had lost her apple tart and nearly fainted,
and it might have been far worse! She did correct him, however,
about the execution itself. 'I closed my eyes just in time.'

'Well, thank God for that,' Holland growled. 'Made you sick,
though, didn't it?'

'Yes,' Mary admitted. 'The sound was terrible. It made me imagine . . . *You* have seen a great many men die, I suppose, but—'

'That's different.'

Holland's profile was stony, but Mary thought that whatever distress he felt was probably more on her behalf than his own. He was a soldier, after all. 'Why were you here today?' she asked. 'I am very grateful that you were.'

'Boyle, of course. God knows *I* had no interest in it, but a guillotine is a machine, after all. There haven't been any executions since he came to Paris, and he wanted to see the damned thing in operation.'

'Then oughtn't you to—'

'Don't worry about that. Martel will look after him and make some excuse about me.' They reached the edge of the square, and now the press of traffic had eased. 'I doubt we're able to find a cabriolet straight off. Are you all right to walk for a bit?'

'Oh yes,' Mary assured him, instantly resolving to say nothing about her sabots. He would undoubtedly have a low opinion of them, and she was conscious that her stock with him was rather precarious at the moment.

Fortunately for her resolve and her feet, they secured a vehicle after only a short period of shuffling. Convincing Holland that he need not accompany her was less easily accomplished, but at last he agreed that he probably ought to go back for Mr Boyle if he could.

'You need not worry about me,' Mary assured him. 'I shall be home in half an hour and then I shall . . . read a book.' It was the most ordinary pastime she could imagine. 'A happy book with pleasant, cheerful characters.'

'Well . . . see that you do,' said Holland. 'And take off those damned shoes.'

No one seeing Mary that afternoon, eating bread and butter while Minta prepared an apple tart – the memory of the lost one had provided the inspiration – would have guessed the traumatic nature of her morning's adventure. Mary herself did not like to think about it. The tart and Jens' absence were the only details that she had revealed, along with the agonies of the sabots, which Minta found highly amusing.

'That is your punishment for having such small feet,' she laughed. 'You ought to have stuffed the shoes with straw. That is what we generally do here, if shoes do not fit.'

'Ah well, I shall try that the next time,' said Mary gravely, and she remembered Lagroix and the packets of straw that he had worn above his boots. French customs were decidedly odd, some of them. 'Brown bread,' she observed, 'is also common in France, and white almost never seen. Is that because white flour is scarce, or do the French prefer brown?'

'Some prefer it, or say that they do because they wish to call themselves good Republicans. White bread is very aristocratic, you know. But lately it has become the fashion to aspire to the wealth of kings and the corruption of kings, so I suppose that the bread of kings will not be far behind.'

'There is a nursery rhyme that has to do with kings and bread,' said Mary. 'I have never quite understood what it means. Do you know it?

The lion and the unicorn were fighting for the crown.
The lion beat the unicorn, all around the town.
Some gave them white bread, and some gave them brown,
And some gave them plum cake and drummed them out of town.'

Minta shook her head. 'Perhaps it has no particular meaning.'

'Oh, I think that all rhymes must mean *something*,' Mary protested. 'Something out of history or literature – or why would anyone have thought of them in the first place? Nursery rhymes would simply be nonsense about eggs and people going up and down hills, and the children would wonder—'

'*You* would wonder,' Minta laughed. 'What a trial you must have been to your mother.'

'Not at all,' said Mary, smiling. 'She always said that I was a great comfort. However, part of this rhyme is quite clear.

The lion and the unicorn are the emblems – I do not know the correct term in heraldry – of the English and Scottish kings. England and Scotland were often in dispute over one thing or another, until the two crowns were united in King James I, who was also King James the . . . VI in Scotland.'

'Is that the King James of the Bible?'

'Yes. But the rhyme clearly has to do with the situation before the union, when the two sides were still fighting, and the people of England and Scotland were supporting one or the other. Now, if people were giving different sorts of bread to the combatants, that must mean that they supported them more or less, but I cannot make out the last line at all.'

'Why not?'

'Well, plum cake is generally considered quite a good thing – *I* should certainly enjoy a slice – and so I would expect that if one king were given plum cake, that would mean that he was very popular. And yet . . . drumming someone out of town would not have been very nice. Military punishments are often inflicted to the accompaniment of drums to heighten the disgrace – or perhaps the solemnity of the occasion.'

· 'Indeed,' said Minta, absently. She was slicing the apples into the pastry shell. 'That does seem to be rather perplexing.'

'On the other hand,' Mary allowed, 'if an army surrenders and is awarded the honours of war – which might happen if the soldiers have fought very bravely, or if they have surrendered from a position of strength – then they are entitled to withdraw with "colours flying, drums beating, trumpets sounding, muskets loaded, and sabres drawn". So that if the rhyme means that the English or Scottish king was drummed out of town in that more honourable way, then it would not be such a bad thing. Certainly more in keeping with a gift of plum cake.'

Minta looked up from her work. 'How ever did you learn about military punishments and surrenders?'

'Oh, a . . . a military friend of mine – an acquaintance – informed me of these practices.' Mary answered lightly, but a wave of colour brightened her cheek.

'Captain Holland, perhaps?'

'Mm.' Mary smiled. 'Perhaps.'

Minta smiled back, but when she answered, the tone of her voice was arch. 'Well, *perhaps* the people simply wanted both kings to go away and leave them in peace, and they did not object to bribing them with plum cake.'

'They were Republicans, do you mean?' asked Mary. 'I have never thought of it that way.' *Traitors*, she added privately, for the rhyme came not from France nor America but England, where kings were still appreciated. *And were not the Americans also traitors, when one considers the matter squarely?*

'Well, I will tell you a story that has no meaning — or none that you will like,' said Minta. She had completed her task and was now seated on a stool before the oven, her hands still pale with flour. 'Shall we have a cup of coffee?'

Mary would have preferred tea or chocolate, but she agreed. As her contribution to the baking had been purely nominal, she ran upstairs for the coffee-making equipment, returning with the grinder, an elegant silver pot engraved with the initials A.V. d'R., two porcelain cups, and a small sack of roasted beans. Minta had placed a battered kettle on a trivet in the fireplace, and now she began to grind the beans, leaning into her work as her tale unfolded.

Although she had no memory of Africa, as a child she had listened to the stories and songs from that land, and now they formed a link for her with the beaches, lagoons, and tropical forests of her mother's country. Many of the stories concerned a creature called Anansi. Mary did not much care for these, partly because she disliked spiders and it was not clear to her whether Anansi was a spider or merely a man with spiderish features — both of which sounded dreadful. Worse than either, however, was the fact that Anansi seemed to be a very wicked, unpleasant individual, often playing tricks on the more virtuous animals and even deceiving his own family. Sometimes he suffered for his misconduct, but this was not always the case, and even when he was undone, it was doubtful whether his remorse would survive into the next tale.

As she sipped her coffee, Mary was pleased to hear that

Anansi would not be making an appearance; the hero of this tale, if such a term could be applied to her, was a tortoise. The tortoise fooled a gullible chief and his family, and was in turn badly treated by an inhospitable leopard. The tortoise had her revenge, tricking the leopard into surrendering his freedom, but he managed to escape thanks to a kind-hearted old monkey – whom he proceeded to eat. The story ended with the tortoise fleeing into the forest with the leopard in pursuit, having sworn eternal enmity between their kinds.

'And so,' Minta concluded, 'whenever one comes upon a leopard in the forest, he is sure to be hunting a tortoise.'

Mary did not like to criticise, but she thought that, really, the tale was as bitter as her drink, and how could a tortoise hope to outpace a leopard? Rather than mentioning either point, however, she asked whether crocodile eggs – which had been the tortoise's original object – were quite so delicious as had been described.

Minta did not know, but thought perhaps they were a great delicacy for tortoises. 'It is certainly difficult to imagine eating a boiled crocodile egg for one's breakfast or mixing it in a tart.' That was what the tortoise had done, and the incident recalled Minta to her object in telling the story, which had not been culinary. 'There is a great deal of wickedness in the world,' she observed. 'Often it is simply waiting to strike. In the end one either eats or is eaten.'

Mary, Minta, and Vangenzen were all happy to eat that evening, as first they enjoyed a splendid ragout and a mushroom omelette, and afterwards the apple tart. Everyone agreed that it surpassed any mere purchased confection. Mary was contemplating a second piece when a bold, triple knock sounded against the door.

'Oh, who can that be?' asked Minta, dropping her fork. 'We never have visitors at night.'

'Very likely Citizeness Grignard from downstairs, wanting to borrow something,' replied Vangenzen. 'What was it the last time?'

The recollection made Minta smile. 'Soap. And the time before that a bottle of Barsac.'

'Which she never replaced,' said Vangenzen. He glanced about, as if taking account of valuables likely to be at risk. 'Put the tart away until she leaves,' he advised, before slipping out of the room and into the passageway.

He returned without the acquisitive neighbour, and instead carrying an oblong wooden box, roughly the size of a large wine bottle.

Minta and Mary laughed when they saw it, thinking that, after all, Citizeness Grignard had been wrongly maligned, but Vangenzen's puzzled expression quickly stifled their mirth.

'What is it?' Minta demanded.

'A delivery from Vrillac's,' he said, and set the box down on the dining table. 'But I have no order outstanding. It seems odd that Jens should make a mistake.'

'There *is* something odd,' said Mary. 'This morning – I do not think that Jens had been at the shop at all.'

Both women had risen, and now the three of them stood round the table, staring at the box.

'Open it,' urged Mary.

'No! Do not,' Minta warned. 'It may be— I don't know.' She wrung her hands.

'Well, it cannot hurt us, whatever it is,' said Vangenzen, reasonably. He untied the string and lifted the lid. Inside were three jars packed in straw and sawdust. They bore the labels *'Sandarac Varnish'*, *'Dr Messier's Best Brown Varnish'*, and *'Amber Shellac'*, respectively.

'You are certain that you did not order these?' asked Mary.

'Oh yes. I would have remembered ordering Messier's – it is very expensive.'

'Perhaps it is not a mistake. May I?' Mary drew the box towards her and removed the jars. First she examined the box itself, and then sifted through the packing materials. Neither appeared in any way out of the ordinary. 'If Jens wished to send us a message,' she explained, 'how better than to place it among a box of painting supplies?'

'But why would he send a message?' asked Vangenzen. 'I mean, why—'

'Because he did not wish to communicate in the usual way,' said Mary. *Or could not*, she added, but not aloud.

She turned her attention to the jars themselves. While she had no knowledge of the products noted on the labels, it was clear that each jar contained some kind of liquid. None of them appeared unusual, until she noticed that the label on the middle jar had one raised corner. Sliding her thumbnail carefully under it, she managed to raise it a little bit more until it was large enough to grasp and peel back. It came away slowly but cleanly from the jar, and beneath it was a second, smaller piece of paper, folded in half. A message.

Mary scanned it quickly and then read it aloud. *'Questioned by police. Stay away. Connection TJ and AO, but not SV or MV.'* She paused and then added, *'Beware Fondard.'*

'Oh no,' murmured Minta. 'I *knew* that trouble would come of this! Questioned by the police! What shall we do?'

Mary waited for Vangenzen to speak, but he did not do so. Her own heart was pounding, and she took a deep breath before answering steadily, willing her voice to sound normal. 'It may not be as bad as you think.'

'Who is AO?' asked Minta.

'I . . . it must be Captain Holland as he is known here: Andrew Ogbourne.'

'We must warn him,' Vangenzen urged.

'No! We cannot!' Minta cried.

'Perhaps we ought to leave that to Jens,' said Mary slowly. 'We do not know what sort of connection the police have made. It may be a very casual one, and Jens may have explained it away.'

Even as she strove to reassure, however, an awful fear was growing within her. Fondard. Sergeant Fondard? The chubby sergeant who had helped them at the city gate? She had almost forgotten that there was such a person. Was he a . . . police agent? Had he known or suspected something about them – about *her* – all this time?

Her unspoken fear seemed to have communicated itself to Minta. 'And what if Jens has not satisfied the police?' she demanded. 'They are always watching. And their spies . . . Oh, why must he send us this package? Very likely the police are watching him, and now he has directed them here!'

Mary started to answer, but this time Vangenzen forestalled her. 'No, my dear, we should be grateful to Jens – firstly for shielding us, and secondly for this warning. And I doubt that a delivery would cause the police to suspect us any more than they would suspect any of his other customers – which would include every artist in Paris!'

'Who brought the box?' asked Minta. She stared at it distastefully.

'His regular boy from the shop. One of the neighbours downstairs let him in, and he said that he had several other deliveries to make.'

'That was sensible,' Mary offered. 'To conceal our package among several.'

'If only *we* had been sensible and never had anything to do with . . . spies and secret things.' Minta paused and then asked the question that Mary had been dreading. 'Who is Fondard?'

The others exchanged a sharp glance that contained a great many questions and one resolution: they would say nothing, at present, to Minta about their earlier meeting with Fondard.

'He . . . must have something to do with the police, I suppose,' said Vangenzen.

17

When Mary, Minta, and Vangenzen met for breakfast the following morning, it was evident that none had passed a restful night. Eyes were dull and expressions heavy; the women conversed in brief, muted exchanges, while Vangenzen yawned over his coffee. Their surroundings provided little vitality. Thin, pale light slipped in through the partially drawn curtains, and the sitting-room had a cluttered, unkempt appearance, as if some crisis had disrupted the household's careful routine. Minta reported that there was no milk and only a very little cheese, but Mary said that it did not matter.

And yet no crisis had occurred. Jens' message had warned, but it had also reassured, and with each passing hour that re-assurance became easier to believe. Whatever dangers lurked in the shadows, *they* were not suspected. *They* were not going to be taken away and questioned as Jens had been – and even he had been released.

Poor Jens. No one actually spoke of him, but he was present in all of their thoughts. Vangenzen's were the purest. He liked the fussy, ill-tempered, little fellow, and was distressed to know that Jens had attracted the attention of the authorities. Mary's sympathy was diluted by her fear for Robert Holland. What did the police know – or guess – about him? If he were taken to the Chatelet or some other dreadful place, would he manage to satisfy his questioners? Only Minta concentrated on the little world of the

Maison des Chevrons, and she privately cursed Jens for having disturbed it. Before setting off for the market, she paused on the threshold and studied Mary and Vangenzen as though she feared they might not be there when she returned.

In fact it was Minta who seemed to suffer most that morning, for she returned from her expedition in a very agitated state. Closing the *appartement* door firmly behind her, she reported that she had felt herself watched in the market. Then, as she had returned from the *lavoir*, a man had seemed to follow her across the Pont Neuf. She had almost dropped Vangenzen's clean shirts in her anxiety to get away from him.

From the perspective of a comfortable armchair and a cup of coffee, however, she admitted that there had probably been no untoward surveillance; her own fears had been the cause of her distress. 'I don't believe I was ever so unsettled,' she acknowledged, 'not even when we ran away to England. Every person I passed had the look of a police spy.'

Mary sympathised with Minta's distress. Although she had concealed it more successfully, her own fear was simmering. As the morning slipped away, she debated with herself – Holland's silence was prudent; no, it was the clearest indication of danger. He had been arrested; on the contrary, the fact that Jens had been questioned and released indicated that the police had no genuine interest in either man. Then why no message? Because there was nothing to tell. *Her* anxiety bore no necessary relation to *his*; indeed, he was often maddeningly cool. And yet, he might be longing to speak with her and unable to do so . . .

A walk in the fresh air might have done her good, but she could not bear the thought of missing his note – of Minta or Vangenzen receiving it rather than herself. So she haunted the *appartement*, her spirits sinking as she meditated on the possible part that Sergeant Fondard might yet play in her affairs. *If he is a sergeant – very likely he disguises himself to make people believe that he is not very important.* Forgotten dangers, or those that went unrecognised, were always the worst, for they sprang up unlooked for. That was not wholly true in this case, for Jens had done his best to put her on her guard. *'Beware Fondard'*, his message had said, but without more information, what was the use of such a warning?

It was as she stood at the sitting-room window, staring down at the anonymous passers-by, that a sudden commotion occurred behind her. Eager footsteps were clattering up the stairs. She turned – it was Vangenzen. He had gone out to buy milk, and now he was smiling, his breath coming fast, and looking rather absurd with his jug in one hand and a crumpled paper in the other.

Minta rose from her seat by the stove, clutching a half-darned stocking.

'What is it?' cried Mary.

'You cannot guess whom I met on the street – Mr Marshall! And thank goodness, for it put me in mind of the reception at Talon's.' Vangenzen chuckled, and then realising that his news had failed to impress his audience, he explained that Marshall had procured an invitation to an evening soirée given by Francois Talon, the former sieur de Bassac. 'It is Marshall's return for the visit to David's studio.'

'And this sieur de Bassac—'

'Citizen Talon, nowadays.'

Mary acknowledged the correction. 'He is an artist?'

'More of a society figure,' said Minta. 'His parties are much talked about.'

'And his salon is a very good place *for* artists' added Vangenzen. 'He knows a great many people – politicians, judges, contractors – the sort of people who buy works of art, even if they do not understand them.'

'Yes, I see,' said Mary. Her tone was wary. 'But how strange— surprising, I mean, that you should receive this invitation today. I do not suppose . . . but it is odd.'

'Oh, but I did not receive it today,' Vangenzen replied. 'It came – oh, I cannot remember when, precisely, but some time ago.' He handed her the paper. 'I meant to tell you, only something drove it from my mind. Then I saw Marshall, and . . . there it was in my pocket!'

Mary unfolded the paper and scanned its contents. It appeared genuine enough. *And why should it not be genuine?* she asked herself. It would be incredible if Mr Marshall were somehow in league with the French police. She glanced at the date – the twenty-ninth of Brumaire – six days ago. That too was evidence of an innocent purpose. Vangenzen happening to mention it today, when her head was full of Sergeant Fondard, was merely a coincidence. *And really, coincidences happen all the time, only we do not notice them except when they are very unusual.*

'It would be a marvellous opportunity,' Minta reluctantly acknowledged. 'They say that Barras and Thérésa Tallien attend his soirées – even Josephine Bonaparte. But how does Mr Marshall come to move in such circles? When you took him to David's, you said that he seemed starved of society.'

'And so he did. But now he has the benefit of Philibert Villette for a landlady.' Minta's expression indicated that the name Villette provided little in the way of illumination, and he added, 'She was formerly the marquise de Villette, and a great favourite of Voltaire. I believe he adopted her after the death of her husband. Naturally, she would know Talon and his friends.'

Another coincidence, thought Mary. She turned to Minta. 'Do you believe there would be a very great risk if we were to attend?'

The other woman did not answer straightaway. 'Greater, certainly, than remaining at home,' she said at last, her voice regretful. 'But . . . I would not wish to injure Samuel's chances for gaining new work.'

'No,' Mary agreed. Her own views were divided. She knew – she was fairly certain, anyway – that she ought to bide her time and wait upon events. *'Shun the fidgets', as Miss Marchmont would say.* But fidgeting, *doing things*, was in Mary's nature; she hated to sit by quietly when there was something to be achieved, or at least attempted. The soirée would be an excellent opportunity to renew her acquaintance with Mr Marshall. *Not so very long ago you would have rejoiced at this opportunity.* So she made a bargain with herself. *The soirée is in two days' time, if I hear nothing from Jens or Captain Holland by tomorrow*

246

afternoon, I shall go. Very likely it will suit my work as well as Mr Vangenzen's.

For a moment more than was comfortable, Mary considered Vangenzen himself. Was it possible that *he* might not be all that he seemed? He had 'remembered' Marshall's message very conveniently . . . was it possible that even Mr Shy had been deceived by the American's open, ingenuous manner? Then her common sense reasserted itself. *What sinister purpose could be served by my attending a fashionable soirée? And as for Mr Vangenzen . . . I cannot believe him capable of treachery, but if he had wished to betray me, he might have done so quite easily before now.*

A more prosaic thought occurred to her. 'Have you replied to Mr Marshall's invitation?'

'Oh yes,' said Vangenzen. He coloured, the flush deepening when Mary smiled at him. 'I did so straightaway so as not to, ahem, forget.'

Sergeant Fondard was not a happy man. Since his decision to arrest Jens, he had been obliged to work much harder, for fewer results, than contented him. And now, when he was tired and in need of a comforting supper, he must present a far from satisfactory report to Jean-Marie Sotin, the minister of police.

He did not fear the interview. At least he knew that his was the superior brain and that each of his actions had been justified. He had judged things to a nicety, going so far and no farther. On the other hand, he found it galling that puffed-up simpletons (and it was to this category that he consigned the minister) should sit in judgment on his efforts and that he – he, Fondard! – must submit to being scolded like a schoolboy.

It was with an air both confident and sullen, therefore, that he handed over a sheaf of documents. *Sotin will need a summary to understand what has been done*, he brooded. *Let him ask for it.*

Sotin's opinion of Fondard was not quite so damning. He recognised his subordinate's considerable talents, but he wished that the fellow were not so headstrong – so difficult to manage. The image of a temperamental racehorse occurred to him, but he rejected it. *Fondard, a racehorse? No, no. A . . . large animal of*

247

uncertain temperament, who needs a tight rein to run straight. Pleased with himself, he asked, 'Perhaps a summary, citizen?'

'Certainly,' replied Fondard. After a short pause, he stood up. 'As a consequence of my initial investigation, I ordered the art dealer, Tobias Jens, to be brought in for questioning. These questions led to a further scrutiny of his shop in the Rue Geoffroy l'Asnier.'

'After this scrutiny, he was released?'

'For the present, yes. However, I ordered one of my men to watch the old convent of the barefoot Augustinians, and—'

'No! My distinct orders – which even you, Citizen Fondard, must have known – were not to intrude there! The minister of marine has an interest in the affairs of that place.' Sotin knew that special arrangements had been made for an Irish scientist named Boyle to conduct experiments at the old convent. He would have liked to know more, but he did not care to run afoul of the Navy. He fingered a penknife and scowled at Fondard across the desk.

Neither held much menace for Fondard, however, who answered coolly enough. 'For that very reason, minister, the man had instructions merely to watch. To make certain that Admiral Le Pelley was not disobliged, I took it upon myself to visit him.'

'You made no accusations?' Sotin's tone was suspicious.

'None. The admiral is gone to Le Havre and does not return until tomorrow. In the meantime, that is to say, last night, I attended a lecture at the Académie des sciences, presented by the inventor, Boyle. Again, in fulfilment of your instructions, I observed only. The man who is of interest to us, Boyle's assistant, was also there.'

'What was the subject of the lecture?'

'Canals.'

'Very well, I will now read the report.'

Fondard resumed his seat. A series of thoughts, none of them very respectful, tripped through his brain as he waited for Sotin to finish reading – that great men were those who took risks when necessary; that a large desk could not obscure a small character; and that if he did not eat something soon, his stomach would begin to complain. He wanted to rise again and walk about the room, if only to mask the likely rumbling, but that would have exceeded the boundaries he set upon himself when dealing with his superior. A minister was a minister, after all.

At last Sotin sat back in his chair. Placing his hands on either side of the report, as if containing it, he said, 'Well, I find very little here of interest to this office.'

'No, minister?'

'No. Indeed, the interrogation of the art dealer, Jens, ought to have brought an end to the matter.' Sotin maintained his studied posture for a moment, and then leaned forward, a smile playing about his lips. 'Tell me, did he really compare you to a piece of chocolate?' With his finger on the place, he read aloud:

'F: You place great importance upon two letters, citizen.

J: As do you, citizen, I am certain, for it is but two letters that separate "Fondard" from "fondant".'

It was not often that Sotin had the opportunity to laugh at his agent, and he intended to make the most of it. 'Ho, ho!' he chuckled. 'Fondard and fondant. This Jens seems to be a very clever fellow.'

Fondard smiled thinly. 'He had his little joke.'

'But not only a joke,' pronounced Sotin, serious once more. 'You were alerted to a man called Ogbourne. The Customs records refer not to Ogbourne, but Og*burn*, while Jens received some drawings done by an artist named Osborne.'

'So he claims,' Fondard urged. 'The Customs officer might have made an error, and Jens' order book merely described the consignment as Dutch landscapes with no mention of the artist. And they were prints, not drawings.'

'You have seen them?'

'Yes. Unfortunately, the signature was not decipherable.'

'And so the accusation against Jens is unproven. That leaves Ogbourne, the American.'

'If he *is* an American.'

'Against whom there is no evidence other than the misgiving

249

of Captain Flynn, who sees a Royalist in every corner. Your own description of Ogbourne's conduct at the Académie is far more persuasive. *"Boyle did not express himself well in French, but his remarks were favourably received by the learned audience. Ogbourne assisted him and answered some of the questions in English or with diagrams. He seemed to understand Boyle's work, and Boyle relied upon him a great deal."'*

'Yes,' Fondard agreed. 'I am troubled by this seeming . . . expertise.'

'Bah,' scoffed Sotin. 'Of course he has expertise – he is Boyle's assistant. If he did not understand these . . . scientific matters, you would be suspicious of his presence in the convent. You cannot also be suspicious because he *does* understand them.'

Fondard started to protest but desisted when Sotin shook his head. 'No, I am not convinced. About your decision to watch the convent, I will say nothing other than that I expect the man to be withdrawn, and I expect *you* to free yourself for other important matters. You are aware, of course, that General Bonaparte will shortly be arriving in Paris.'

'Yes, minister.'

'Already he has won great victories. The future of France – of our Revolution – may depend upon him. Therefore, nothing untoward must occur while he is here, while his security is, in some degree, our responsibility. He has his own men, naturally, but I want you to communicate with one of them. I have requested that he meet with us tomorrow. Have you any questions?'

Fondard shook his head.

'Good. Now file this away' – he handed back the report – 'and good evening to you.'

Along with a great many other things, the word *'hôtel'* had been barred from private use at the time of the Revolution. However magnificent, therefore, the private residences of Paris had all become *'maisons'*. The older term was starting to creep back into use, but only by those who did not fear association with an aristocratic past. Francois-Xavier Talon had no such confidence, and although his hospitality was sought by the fashionable as well as the powerful, his residence in the Rue du Mont-Blanc bore the humble name, La Maison du Rossignol.

Nor was it so very long since the nightingales might have sung in the Rue du Mont-Blanc, for it was situated in one of the newer parts of the city, north of the old Porte Gaillon. Originally sought out by the rich because of its supposed healthy air, the area had not suffered unduly at the hands of the developers. Here were no narrow alleys, overhung by sagging eaves and polluted by noisome kennels, but broad thoroughfares along which stood mansions honouring Greek and Roman sensibilities. The naturalistic style of their gardens, moreover, recalled the homely efforts of the monks of St Mathurin, who had leased or sold much of the land only thirty years ago.

It was dark when Mary and Vangenzen set off for their evening's entertainment, but Mary could sense the grandeur of the quarter even before they reached it. From the Porte Denis their cabriolet proceeded westward along a wide, tree-lined boulevard. The traffic was steady, and consisted of well-appointed carriages, some accompanied by mounted servants. When they turned into the Rue du Mont-Blanc, Vangenzen mentioned some of the august personages who had lived behind the several imposing gates: aristocrats like the duc d'Antin, after whom the thoroughfare had once been named, but also Marie-Madeleine Guimard, the great opera dancer, and the dramatist Mirabeau. Mary issued herself a stern reminder that *she* need not make a favourable impression on anyone, but she could not wholly stifle a pang of regret that her nicest jewellery was in England.

The cabriolet set them down nearly at the junction with the Rue de Provence, and they entered the grounds of the Maison du Rossignol through a wide door. A cobbled passageway was flanked on both sides by stables and led to a small gatehouse. Beyond the gatehouse lay the courtyard, whose walls were softened by a ring of clipped bay trees in large earthenware pots. Above them at intervals hung lanterns of copper and glass, and by some trick of their design the light they produced seemed to twinkle.

'It is as one would imagine fairyland,' breathed Mary.

'Or Delphi,' said Vangenzen, and as she perceived the house itself, Mary amended her simile. Broad stone steps led to a semicircular porch fronted by four Ionic pillars. Footmen threw wide an elaborately carved door depicting the shield of Achilles, and Mary half-expected a sound of trumpets to announce their arrival.

I suppose they had trumpets in ancient Greece, she mused, smiling to herself. *And incense. One could not fully appreciate the words of the oracle without incense.*

There were neither trumpets nor incense, but only their host, rather plump and exquisitely dressed. Stationed in an armchair in the centre of the narrow entrance hall, he welcomed each of his guests – or rather, received their obeisance. The tableau was not quite as regal as it first appeared, for a cane and a footstool suggested that an injury, or perhaps the gout, kept Citizen Talon off his feet. Indeed, he said something of the kind to Vangenzen when the latter introduced himself.

'Old age, you know,' he explained with a shrug. 'It makes fools of us all. I much prefer it to the alternative, however.'

'Yes indeed, citizen,' Vangenzen agreed. 'May I present my wife?'

To curtsy or offer her hand? The debate occurred fleetingly to Mary as she stepped forward, but her knees were bending and her head inclining before she had determined which gesture would be most proper. 'Good evening,' she murmured.

'Ah, the old ways,' said Talon, nodding with approval. His eyes swept her up and down. 'Most charming, most delightful – an English rose among the nightingales. And now, my friends, you must please yourselves this evening – my house is at your disposal entirely, whether politics, or art, or dancing is your chief amusement. Even gossip, perhaps?'

Mary was smiling modestly as she rose, but the exchange had inspired an uncomfortable feeling of repugnance. From a distance, their host's illusion of fashionable middle age was possible, but not at close quarters. On the contrary, his sagging flesh and deep wrinkles were made more prominent by the attempts to disguise them with rouge and white lead, and the negligent curls that might have graced a younger head looked unnatural upon one of mature years.

His house, however, was lovely from every point of vantage. The drawing room had cream-coloured panelling picked out in gold, and a marble fireplace decorated with bronze floral garlands. Floor length curtains of gold damask alternated with fitted cases displaying books, sculptures, and fine porcelain. The carpet of rich blue and green was soft underfoot, and over all chandeliers of glass and gilded bronze cast a warm glow.

Citizen Talon's guests might have been chosen for their ability to enhance his décor. Here and there was evidence of too great a preference for fashion over physiognomy, but these were the exceptions. Most of the men and women who lounged upon low couches, or gathered about the pianoforte at one end of the room and a painting of Aeneas' farewell to Dido at the other, seemed to have a deep understanding of elegance and beauty, be it in a gown or a glance, a turn of the head or a tone of the voice.

It may not all be genuine, thought Mary, *but it is very beautiful.*

Presently she located Mr Marshall. His was not, it must be said, one of the more brilliant figures among the company, but all the more welcome for its sober, honest demeanour. Vangenzen followed her, and for a time the three of them engaged in friendly conversation. This was not Marshall's first visit to the Maison du Rossignol, and he detailed some of the house's principal artistic attractions. He also knew several of the other guests, and pointed out those who were particularly interested in painting.

Vangenzen did not require much persuasion to make himself known to these potential customers. Mary said that he must certainly do so. Why else had they come, that evening? Why else had Mr Marshall thought to gain them an invitation?

'Most young fellows need a bit of help in their careers,' affirmed Marshall.

'Well, if you would not mind,' Vangenzen replied, already edging away slightly. 'And only for a very little while, of course. I shall find you again directly.'

Mary smiled and added, 'Do not forget to mention your

most recent commission.' As he hurried away, she observed to Marshall, 'He is not always the best advocate for his talents. Perhaps I ought to go with him.'

Marshall considered this a bad idea, albeit well intentioned. 'A fellow likes to make his own way for himself – not trail along behind his wife's skirts. Besides, these people fancy themselves connoisseurs, and if they aren't given the chance to display their superior knowledge to the artist, why, they've missed half the fun.'

'You understand fashionable society very well, sir,' Mary observed.

'I have had more than ample opportunity for viewing it,' he replied with a grimace. 'But I mustn't complain, for Parisian society has much to recommend it. Come, let me show you the rest of the house. I believe there is to be dancing, and it would be a shame if none but your husband and I were to have the pleasure of seeing that gown tonight.'

Marshall's compliments were more to Mary's liking than Talon's, and she was also rather proud of her gown, a wisp of smoky silk that drew attention both to her figure and to the whiteness of her arms and neck. On Minta's advice she had gathered her hair into a chignon and dressed it with bandeaux of black velvet. It was not as daring an ensemble as many she observed that evening, but she was thankful that Miss Marchmont was not present, as that lady would undoubtedly have made many tiresome observations regarding draughts, chest colds, and the lack of propriety in the modern world.

She thought more highly of Miss Marchmont's opinions, at least in so far as the desirability of muffs and greatcoats, when Marshall led her down a passageway to the rear of the house and then through a pair of glass doors to the garden, at the bottom of which stood Talon's *cabinet de musique*. *Oh dear*, she shivered as the cold air struck her. *If only I had worn my velvet tippet. If only I had not minded whether French ladies wore tippets.* Marshall's anecdote on the sunken pool, whose mosaic floor was a copy of one discovered in the city of Herculaneum, received only a fraction of her attention as she made her way stoically along the path to the *cabinet*. It would not have done actually to run, she felt.

Inside it was warmer. Nevertheless, she urged Marshall not to linger by the door but to walk well into the body of the room, where they would obtain the best view of the dancing. Like the main part of the house, this was a very gracious space, with a polished parquet floor and hangings of *toile de Jouy* in a floral pattern on the walls. A small band of musicians played in one corner, and lighted sconces provided the proper balance of illumination – adding lustre to the dancers' forms and features but cloaking the odd misstep.

Not that a misstep was likely, judging by the technique on display. Everyone looked very graceful – languid and yet precise, as if they moved that way naturally, and not because they were performing. Initially Mary found this daunting, for she did not know the dances, and had to watch the steps carefully until she felt confident. But after a time she nodded to herself.

'Shall we have a go?' asked Marshall, who had apparently been watching her.

'I think so,' said Mary. 'Are you familiar with this one?'

'No, but I believe I can manage it. The last was something like a dance that we call "The Painted Chamber".'

'Why, so do we,' cried Mary. 'And that is what gave me courage – the first one was quite different from anything I have ever seen – perhaps it has something to do with the Revolution. But yes, let us try.'

The figure they joined was a slow, stately affair, hardly a country dance at all, and perhaps for that reason Mary and Marshall danced it creditably. They thoroughly enjoyed themselves, and returned to their places smiling and exchanging remarks about the *pas de bourée* and the *demi-coupé*. The musicians took a short break, and when they resumed, the rhythm of the music changed. Straightaway three couples stepped onto the floor.

'Oh my,' said Mary, watching them. 'Is the waltz danced in America?'

Marshall answered sternly. 'It is not. I have never seen it in polite society. Of course,' he added, 'one makes allowances – one

255

must recognise different customs – but I must say that I find it rather . . .' And there his eloquence failed him.

'Mm,' said Mary, nodding. She also found the dance 'rather . . .', but at the same time she longed to try it. There was something rather thrilling about the lilting, circular movement, and dancing only with a single partner. So long as one did not become dizzy, for the dancers moved very quickly, and rather close to each other. It was all *quite* unsuitable.

The image of Miss Marchmont fainting into the arms of Miss Trent, and the two of them overwhelming Mrs Tipton, appeared in her mind's eye. They would undoubtedly regard waltzing as the most reckless thing that Mary had done since coming to France – the very prospect would have hardened Miss Marchmont against the entire proposition. *You needn't worry*, Mary silently assured them. *I am hardly likely to waltz with Mr Marshall.*

More unscrupulous couples joined the dance, and Mary became aware of a lively conversation over her right shoulder. Perhaps she and Marshall ought to retire to a more secluded spot. They could talk, after all, if they did not mean to waltz. Suddenly she heard a voice.

'Can it be . . . is that *Miss Finch*?'

Those four English words had a curious effect on everything around her. The light faded, and the movements of the dancers blurred. Voices became inconsequential murmurings; Marshall was a featureless shadow; even the floor beneath her feet seemed less solid.

She gazed up at him. Surprise had softened his features, which were more stern than she remembered, but no less handsome. He was in military dress, but his blue coat with white facings and snowy breeches were nothing like the ragged, mismatched uniforms she had seen on her journey to Paris. Without apprehending the gesture, she extended her hand. 'Mr Déprez!'

He clasped it lightly and bore it to his lips. 'I thought I recognised you, but did not— What are you doing in France?'

This second question caused the world to resume its proper

focus. Mary heard the music and was conscious of her surroundings. Her own equilibrium, however, was not so easily restored. She felt dazed, as if she were suffering from a fever, or had drunk more than two glasses of wine. *Mr Déprez! He ought to be dead — dead or in Guiana. How ever did he . . .?* 'I am . . . I have come to France to live. Forgive me,' she added, for her heart was pounding, and it was strangely difficult to breathe. She turned to Marshall. 'May I present Mr . . . I am afraid I do not know your Army rank.'

'I have the honour to serve as a *chef de brigade* in the *chasseurs à pied*. What you would call a colonel in the light infantry,' Déprez explained.

Mary nodded. 'Of course. Colonel Déprez. And this is Mr Marshall, an envoy of the American government.'

The two men shook hands, and each reported briefly on his present career. Déprez, it seemed, had recently returned from the Italian campaign. 'I congratulate you on your triumphs, sir,' said Marshall.

Déprez acknowledged the compliment with a slight bow. 'We were fortunate in our commander — the greatest soldier of the age. But perhaps French victories are not so pleasant to the ears of an Englishwoman?'

'Hmm?' asked Mary, dismayed to find herself returning to the conversation so quickly. 'I beg your pardon?'

Marshall cleared his throat. 'Indeed, sir, whatever the lady's former allegiances, I trust she has put them aside since her marriage to my countryman.'

'Marriage?' cried Déprez, his gaze swooping immediately to Mary's hand and his smile losing some of its vivacity. 'Well, well. I mean . . . *Pardon*. May I offer my sincere felicitations?'

Mary murmured her thanks, but the words sounded unnatural in her ears. Even as she explained about Vangenzen's profession, the astonishing fact of Déprez's appearance was turning her orderly thoughts upside down. *That he should be here, that we should be speaking together like old friends — can anything be ordinary after this?*

Her sentence trailed off, and she became aware that he was observing her quizzically. Suddenly he turned, as if only perceiving at that moment that music was playing. 'Come,' he said, taking her hand again. 'You will do me the honour of dancing with me?'

'Oh, but—' She resisted. 'I have never—'

'Then you must take the chance,' teased Déprez, drawing her towards him.

Heavens, thought Mary frantically, *this is my punishment for making light of waltzing.*

Marshall uttered a protest, but somehow Mary found herself following Déprez. Then they were in the middle of the floor, surrounded by sweeping, swirling couples, and it was hard to keep still. Her left hand crept to his shoulder and her right clasped his hand as they began to move, while his right arm came to rest upon her waist. *Oh my.*

'You dance very well,' he remarked, 'and it has brought the colour to your cheeks again. Ah!' He stepped backwards. 'Although I believe it is usual for the lady to permit her partner to lead her steps.'

'I beg your pardon,' said Mary. They stopped, waited for the next phrase of the music, and began again. 'Our housekeeper taught me the steps, and we took turns being the man.'

'There, that is better,' Déprez agreed. 'And is he here tonight – your husband?'

Mary nodded. 'He is . . .' She glanced about, wondering if Vangenzen were nearby and what he might think if he were to see her. The blush so admired by Déprez had nothing to do with the exertions of the dance, and she thought she would feel better if she kept talking. 'We are hoping that he will meet someone here who will buy one of his paintings.'

Déprez thought there was a fair chance of a commission. 'There are many lovers of art here tonight, even if—'

'Even if they do not understand it?'

'Exactly.' He smiled. 'And so you are no longer English but American?'

'My husband is an American,' Mary acknowledged. 'I . . . do not know the precise legal position as regards myself.'

'You do not know what is the position under English law?'

258

asked Déprez with mock seriousness. They turned gracefully, her left hand and his right meeting overhead between their bodies. 'That does not sound like the Mary Finch that I knew. She would have consulted the legal experts and made a full enquiry into the matter.'

'Well, perhaps,' Mary allowed, and she could not help smiling in her turn, 'but we do not plan to return to England. My . . . inheritance was sadly encumbered, you see. I do know what the American Congress has determined in their Naturalization Act. If I wish to become a citizen, I must renounce any foreign allegiance, reside in America for a period of five years, and forsake any hereditary title. The last would not be applicable in my case, however, for I have no title to renounce.'

Déprez nodded. 'You reassure me. You have not lost your old skills.'

The pattern of the dance called for Mary to clasp her hands behind her back while both of Déprez's rested upon her waist. The more daring couples drew quite close to each other at this point, and Déprez might have had similar designs. Mary, however, anticipated the next position by placing her hands upon his forearms – which limited, if it did not wholly defeat, his longer reach. Her manoeuvre seemed to amuse him, and he asked whether they were fencing or dancing.

'Dancing,' Mary replied, raising innocent eyes. 'Have I made another mistake?'

He did not answer, and when she had turned beneath his upraised arm, she asked what had brought him to the Maison du Rossignol that evening.

'When one is in Paris and not in prison, one comes to Talon's,' he explained with a shrug.

'But . . . have you been in prison?' echoed Mary. She could feel her heart beating again as the conversation became dangerous, as though they were dancing towards a precipice, and the ground was beginning to crumble beneath her.

'Briefly,' said Déprez, 'for failing to capture Captain Holland. My efforts in that matter were judged insufficient by the government of the day. They did not want my head, fortunately, but they sentenced me to a term in Guiana, which was considered much the same thing by a slower process. Fortunately, I managed to profit from the stay of execution.'

'You escaped!'

'Exactly. Even more to my advantage was making the acquaintance of General Bonaparte, for he thought that a man who could evade the "dry guillotine" might be worth a trial. And so I return to Paris a victorious soldier of the Republic and a member of the general's staff.'

'That was very clever of you,' said Mary. 'Escaping, I mean.' She shrugged and considered a gambit. 'And also becoming an officer, for I suppose you held no actual commission when you were in England?'

'No, not quite,' Déprez admitted. He guided her silently around the floor and then observed, 'Perhaps my work is more honourable now, and for that I have you to thank.'

'Me?' she queried. It was not quite the reply she had expected.

'Certainly. If you had not defeated me, I shudder to think in what mischief I might have engaged myself.'

Mary protested that 'defeated' was putting it too strongly, although she recognised the false modesty of her claim. She *had* defeated him, and that fact buoyed her confidence. Her chin rose.

He noticed and smiled. 'Which word would you prefer? "Routed"? "Vanquished"? But do not worry – I forgive you. And tell me, what do you hear of Captain Holland these days?' He nodded slightly, managing to convey in that gesture more than a hint of self-mocking. 'Naturally I am interested in *his* welfare.'

'I believe he— I beg your pardon, but did you not have a connection of some kind with Montreuil?' Mary frowned perplexedly. 'We passed through it on our way to Paris, and the name seemed familiar to me.'

Déprez inclined his head. 'My grandfather came from Montreuil. I am honoured that you remembered it.'

'Of course, and your grandmother was from . . . Hampshire.' The frown became a smile of triumph as she resolved the mystery. 'I remember talking about it with you at Mr Somerville's

260

dinner party. They are both in good health, by the way, Mr and Mrs Somerville.'

'I am pleased to hear it. And Captain Holland?'

'Hmm? Oh, I believe that he is at Gibraltar. At least, that is what I understood two years ago. Gibraltar or Spain. However, I do not suppose that there are any British officers in Spain nowadays.'

'None who present themselves as such,' Déprez agreed. 'Gibraltar is a good place for him – a true British stronghold. He will be safe there.'

'Safe from your mischief?' She gazed up at him. 'But, as you say, there is little chance of that since you have joined General Bonaparte's staff. Unless you capture Gibraltar.'

Déprez agreed that mischief and the capture of Gibraltar were both unlikely – although the latter was not impossible. 'I did not like to lose Captain Holland, of course, but those are the fortunes of war.'

'Well, I hope that in America we shall leave all such fortunes, good or bad, behind us,' said Mary.

The music stopped and Déprez bowed. He started to return her to where Marshall was standing, looking thunderous, but she pointed instead to a tall, fair-haired man on the other side of the room. She was never so relieved to see him as in that moment. 'There is my husband.'

'Permit me to congratulate you,' said Déprez after Mary had named Vangenzen. 'You have a remarkable wife.'

'Thank you,' replied the other man, smiling fondly at Mary. 'I believe I must agree with you.'

'My dear, this is Colonel Déprez, whom I once knew in England.' She raised her chin a second time. 'Pray, colonel, I meant to ask about a watch you borrowed from me – do you have it still?'

Déprez burst out laughing. 'Oh ho,' he chuckled, 'the watch! Thank God for it. Until this moment I was wondering if perhaps this evening was a dream. But now I am convinced that you are truly Miss Mary Finch. I beg your pardon – Mrs Vangenzen.'

18

Tap, tap.

Martel stood before the long wooden table in the convent kitchen, assembling the ingredients for a morning pot of tea. Dressed in a nightshirt, rumpled dressing-gown, and boots, his hair hanging limply about his shoulders, there was little about him or his errand to recall the Little Fathers.

'Tea, always there must be tea,' he muttered to himself. 'That is why your stomach is disordered, sir, because of the quantities that you drink of this foul beverage. Only the English—'

Tap, tap, tap.

A teaspoon clattered to the floor as he spun quickly on his heel. A cloaked figure stared back at him through the window. 'My God.'

The heavy bolt resisted Martel's efforts, but when the door moved, protesting against its hinges, Mary slipped through the narrow opening. He closed it again behind her and growled, 'It is most dangerous for you to come here.'

'Yes, I know that,' said Mary, drawing back her hood, 'but I do not think that anyone can have seen me. I came through the garden behind the Maison des Etrangers.'

'In the Rue Vivienne? That was good thinking,' Martel acknowledged. 'You must go back the same way.' He paused, frowning. 'You never climbed over the wall?'

Mary admitted that she had. 'But it has fallen down in places, you know. I was scrambling more than climbing.' Her hands, nevertheless, were stained where she had gripped moss-covered stone, and her boots were scuffed and muddy.

Martel noticed these things and forgave her for startling him. 'Well, what is it? Do you have news? A message?'

'Yes.' The journey from the Vangenzen lodgings to the convent had not proved as difficult as she had feared, but now she felt giddy, as if she had been running in circles and had lost her balance. She took a deep breath and steadied herself against a chair back; a broken leg made it wobble. 'It is very urgent. I have seen—'

'Wait.' Martel had experience of over-excited young officers babbling their news. 'I will fetch him.' He tightened the belt of his dressing-gown and nodded in the direction of the charcoal burner, upon which a kettle perched, a faint wisp of steam rising from its spout.

'What? Oh, of course,' she affirmed.

'And do not forget to warm the pot,' he warned. 'That is the most grievous sin among the drinkers of tea, I have found.'

Before the water had boiled, light footsteps were audible in the passageway, and the door opened. Holland was less in a state of undress than Martel, but he was unshaven, and his shirt and breeches looked to have been hastily donned.

He smiled at her and she clutched his arm, needing further evidence that the danger was not yet upon them – or if it was, that they could defeat it.

'You are all right?' she asked. 'You have not been arrested?'

His hand closed over hers. 'No, although I thought it very likely at one point.'

'You know about Jens?'

Holland knew, but not through any warning. Shortly after Mary's failure, Martel had also paid a visit to Vrillac's, only to discover the police in possession and apparently searching the premises.

'Thank goodness they found nothing,' cried Mary. 'At least, I hope they have not. But why did they suspect Jens? What do they know?'

'Something about us, that is clear,' said Martel. 'For two days and nights the police have had a man outside, keeping watch on us. Then, last night, instead of the guard changing at midnight, he departed altogether.'

The colour drained from Mary's face. 'Was he watching the garden?'

'No, the front entrance. He was not a very enterprising fellow. Still, I am glad that you did not visit us yesterday.' As he spoke Martel removed the kettle from the burner and prepared the tea according to his particular method. After a slight pause, he filled a mug and slid it across the table towards Mary. In Holland's place he would certainly have embraced her. *These English.* 'I advise the sugar,' he murmured.

'Hmm? Oh, yes, thank you.' Politeness obliged her to smile, and she touched the mug. 'Not yesterday, but I did think about coming last night,' she admitted, turning to Holland. 'I wanted to let you know straightaway – Mr Déprez is in Paris.'

'Déprez?!' echoed Holland. 'Did he see you? Of all the damned— I thought he was in Guiana.'

'No, he escaped from prison and has been in France all along – or with the French Army. And now he is an officer on Bonaparte's staff.' She recounted, in so far as she could remember it, the conversation of the night before. The waltzing did not figure in her report – it seemed such an odd thing to have done – but she was conscious of the omission and concluded lamely, 'He was very surprised to find me in Paris, of course.'

Neither of the men appeared to notice. Holland briefly informed Martel of Paul Déprez's efforts as a double agent and how they had nearly resulted in Holland visiting Paris as an unwilling guest of the French government.

Martel cursed under his breath. 'He will recognise you, of course.'

'I'm afraid so – if our paths were to cross.'

'And already he has asked about you,' Martel complained. 'Naturally he would connect Captain Holland and Miss Finch in his mind.'

'Perhaps not now that she's married,' said Holland wryly. As quickly as it had faded, Mary's colour bloomed again, and he continued, 'It sounds as if that fact interested him more than whether I was at Gibraltar.'

'I hope that it did,' said Martel.

'Of course, he has no reason to connect me or Captain Holland with Andrew Ogbourne,' said Mary, 'but there is something else. In his message, Jens warned me of someone – Sergeant Fondard. Mr Vangenzen and I met him on the road to Paris. He is plump, dark-haired, and he often sings – not at all dangerous-seeming – but I have a very bad feeling about him.'

Holland and Martel exchanged glances. 'I think he attended the lecture,' said Holland, and to Mary he added, 'Mr Boyle gave a lecture at the Académie des Sciences on his plan for small-gauge canals.'

'Yes, I marked him, the fat fellow,' said Martel. 'I knew that he was no scientist – he could only just keep his eyes open. Mark you, between the subject matter and Mr Boyle's French, he had my sympathies. Still, I think you passed inspection as a *savant*, my friend, or at least as his assistant.'

'Thank goodness for that,' said Mary, 'but what ought we to do now? The withdrawal by the police might be a trick. I do not trust Sergeant Fondard, and now that Mr Déprez is here as well . . .'

'I think the time has come for us to withdraw,' Holland agreed.

'Withdraw from France?' demanded Martel. 'Good. These dogs of spies and police are too close. Let us put several miles of blue water between them and ourselves.'

Holland waited for Mary's fervent nod and then continued. 'Right, then we're agreed. I think we have a little time yet, so let's take advantage of it. If possible, I would still like to have Jens' advice on how we should go.'

'I will speak with Jens,' countered Martel, 'if it is possible. My presence in that neighbourhood will provoke far less attention, and he and I will confer with the most advantage to our cause. You, Mr Ogbourne, should rather concentrate your energies upon convincing Mr Boyle to accompany us, if that is still your aim.'

'It is,' said Holland, 'but I'm afraid that his triumph at the

Académie with those damned canals may have turned his head.' His expression was grim. 'Very well. You try Jens, and I'll sort out Boyle, one way or the other.'

'And *I* will go to the Hôtel de la Marine and recover the plans of the *Ammonite*,' said Mary firmly.

Her words halted the conversation like a sudden blow, although to Holland at least, they were not unexpected. He knew Mary's resolve and the logic that she would employ in support, and in that moment he hated both.

'Neither they nor Mr Boyle must remain in Paris,' she continued, before he could do more than look his displeasure.

'No,' acknowledged Martel, and Holland shook his head.

Mary could feel a wall of objections rising between herself and the two men. Nothing daunted, she took aim against Holland's section. 'There are three jobs to be done and three of us. Captain Martel and Jens know France, and only you can convince Mr Boyle – but neither of you can enter the Hôtel de la Marine without suspicion, while I can.' She paused. 'We agreed that I would do this if it became necessary.'

'No, we didn't, and it's a hell of a risk.'

'But someone must take it, and it is less for me than for anyone else.'

Martel shrugged. 'She got in here all right.'

'When no one was watching.'

'Nor will anyone be watching at the Ministry,' said Mary. 'At least, they will not be watching *me*, and I have already thought of how to manage it.' This last point was not strictly true, but she knew that she must give no quarter. 'I can go this afternoon and then return here with the plans.'

'I will go to Vrillac's straightaway,' agreed Martel. 'Mr Boyle will not object to preparing his own breakfast, I think.'

Holland nodded slowly. 'All right, but . . . for God's sake, be careful. And ask Vangenzen to go with you. He's the artist, after all – he has the best reason of anyone for visiting Le Pelley's office.'

Minta sat by the cherished ceramic stove, listening for the sound of Mary's return. The sun brightened a patch of carpet near her

266

chair and the stove did its duty, but she could not warm herself, somehow. The heat surrounded but failed to touch her; instead, cold fingers seemed to play across her shoulders and down her spine as she imagined what might be happening to her friend at the convent of the Little Fathers. For Mary *was* her friend, despite all that Minta had told herself to the contrary. Even now she wished it were not so. It made everything so difficult.

The door to the *appartement* opened and she sprang to her feet. Mary was still in the passageway, hanging her cloak upon the peg, when Minta gripped her arm, and the garment slipped to the floor. 'What happened?'

Mary answered in a low voice. 'We are leaving Paris – Captain Holland and I, Captain Martel, and – I hope – Mr Boyle.'

'Thank God,' breathed Minta, her hold loosening. 'I mean—'

'You needn't explain,' said Mary, stooping to retrieve the cloak. 'I think that you and Mr Vangenzen should also return to England.'

From relief Minta's expression shifted to one of alarm as Mary related their plans, such as they were. 'Return to England? But Samuel is not here, and—'

'Not here? When will he return?'

'I don't know, he did not say where he was going – but please do not ask him to go to the Hôtel de la Marine,' Minta begged. 'He is— Of course he would wish to help, but he might so easily say the wrong thing. He often does when he is flustered. I'm sure he would make a mistake if someone questioned him.'

'He need only sketch while I search for the plans,' Mary reminded her. 'What other excuse have we for visiting the minister's office?'

Minta bit her lip. 'Couldn't *you* make the sketches? I have seen your drawings – they are very good!'

Retrieve the plans alone? Mary's heart trembled at the prospect. Since parting from Holland she had assumed that she would have a partner in the venture. *But that does not matter, I can do it alone, and besides, I mustn't wait.* 'Would anyone believe that *I* had been sent to make sketches for the admiral's portrait?'

'Why not? There are women artists in Paris. If you said that you were Samuel's assistant, anyone would believe you ... And he has done so much for you already.'

That was certainly true; Vangenzen had been a loyal comrade. It would be a cruel fate if he were caught in a scheme that had nothing to do with Mr Shy's original request – not that Mary had any intention of being caught. 'Very well,' she agreed, and then she smiled wanly. 'And afterwards – we will *all* leave for England?'

Minta hesitated. 'Yes. And I will come with you now, to keep watch, or search, or help in some other way. It might look odd, a woman on her own at the Ministry.'

'I do not know that two will look any better.'

'Less suspicious,' Minta urged. 'What sort of burglar takes along her housekeeper?'

Paul Déprez was not thinking about Mary. This may have been because he had spent much of the previous night doing so and had become tired of the exercise. More probable, however, was the fact that he had an appointment at the Foreign Ministry, and when one paid a call on Citizen Talleyrand-Périgord it was wise to give that matter one's full attention.

The appointment was the result of a note, apparently dashed off by the foreign minister and delivered to Déprez's lodgings. It had, in fact, interrupted his breakfast, which he had consumed after returning from a morning ride. Was it important? That was hard to say.

Maison Gallifet
Rue du Bac

8th Frimaire Year VI

Maison du Lierre
Rue de Surene

Colonel Déprez,
Permit me to congratulate you on your successful return to Paris, and your part in the triumph of our forces in the field. May I also

268

*beg a favour? Reports have just arrived from our London agents,
and if I could have the benefit of your opinion on their contents, I
would be most grateful. I know that you are a busy man, but if
you could spare some portion of your time, you would infinitely
oblige*

    Talleyrand-Périgord

The subject of the message appeared innocuous, and its tone
was friendly, even flattering; but Déprez was on his guard. He
knew that the foreign minister did few frivolous or unconsid-
ered things, and that this request was unlikely to be one of
them.

Déprez was right to be cautious. His knowledge of the English
situation was stale and of little interest to the minister. What
Talleyrand wanted was influence with General Bonaparte, such
as might be gained through a timely piece of information or
a friendly word in the great man's ear. A member of Bonaparte's
staff would be very useful in that regard, particularly if he had
a weakness. Déprez's weakness was his failure in England and
the sentence of exile that had never been overturned. Plainly
stated, therefore, the message from Talleyrand might have said,
*'I know that you were once an agent, and that your last assignment
was unsuccessful. At present you are secure, but a man who has failed
once may do so again. Indeed, there is no one so easy to blame as he
whom the State has already condemned. Others also know this. I can
help you, if you make it worth my while.'* Plain speaking, however,
was not the foreign minister's way.

Déprez presented himself at the Maison Gallifet and was
ushered into the minister's private rooms. Talleyrand was seated
at a large, ornate desk before the window. A rather short, sleek
man, with a dull complexion and pale blue eyes, his countenance was at once mild and faintly mocking.

'Ah, good morning, Colonel Déprez,' he cried, rising from
his chair. 'So good of you to answer my little call for aid.'

The minister was slightly lame in his right foot and walked
with a limp. It was said that this waxed or waned according to
whether he wished to elicit sympathy. Déprez was dubious of

this – and anyway, sympathy was a very dangerous sentiment. 'Not at all, minister,' he replied. 'Naturally it is my privilege to serve you if I can.'

'You are most kind.'

Déprez spread his hands in a gesture that accepted the compliment while questioning its justice. His expression, too, was modest. 'You will not say so, perhaps, when I tell you that my time today is indeed limited – not more than one hour. I have promised to attend the minister of police at three o'clock in order to discuss the security arrangements for General Bonaparte during his stay in Paris.'

'Ah, indeed, a task of the greatest importance,' Talleyrand agreed. He observed the clock on his mantelpiece; the hands showed half past one. 'It is unfortunate that my message did not reach you earlier, but' – he shrugged – 'I would not wish to jeopardise the general's safety, and twenty minutes should be sufficient to review the London files. My secretary will show them to you. Afterwards, perhaps, we could exchange ideas?'

Déprez bowed. 'I would be honoured, minister.'

Twenty minutes – but in making his prediction, Talleyrand had failed to reckon with Déprez's zeal. Not content merely with the most recent reports, he insisted upon being given those of the past two years. Only by reviewing what had taken place since his withdrawal (he did not like to use the word 'flight'), could he understand the current situation, and of what use was an assessment based upon incomplete information?

In fact, Déprez cared little about London, but he had rightly perceived that a lengthy exchange of ideas with the minister might be perilous. On the other hand, Talleyrand was a dangerous man to disoblige. The best way of avoiding the former without risking the latter was to pursue the ostensible task with such vigour that it consumed all of the available time. Talleyrand could hardly complain if his guest merely did what had been asked of him.

He read diligently, therefore, referring back and forth between reports and questioning the reliability of this or that agent. Twice he asked for the original encoded messages so that he could compare them with their transcriptions, and he impressed (and dismayed) the clerks when he discovered several small errors. Covent Garden was not a garden but a market, and the Haymarket was not a market but a theatre.

'A matter of slight importance,' he acknowledged, when correcting the spelling of 'Piccadilly'. 'But it is well to be accurate.'

'Assuredly, colonel,' agreed the secretary, who was not the one who would have to prepare the new, clean copies.

Déprez glanced at his watch – Mary's watch, as it happened – and noted the time. Ten more minutes, and then he would make his regretful apologies and depart. The task had become tedious in the extreme, but he congratulated himself that his perseverance would soon be rewarded. One last report, and he would have played as neat a trick—

The sentence hovered, incomplete, as quite different words leaped from the page in front of him. He read the passage a second time. It concerned the surveillance of one Felix August Saint-Hilaire, the former vicomte de Toul, who had fled to England in 1792. He was known to be in communication with the Royalist factions in France, and was suspected of raising funds on their behalf. The report was provided by an agent calling himself John Mortimer.

14th November. Weather fair, S-H drove in the park, where exchanged polite greetings with many people, including Mr Jenkinson. Later, dined alone and attended the theatre with Mrs Cuthbertson. Visited the box of Miss Finch, a noted heiress. Returned to Conduit Street after the ballet with Mrs Cuthbertson.

18th November. Morning rain, S-H received callers, a delivery of books. Afternoon, weather cleared, S-H called upon Richard Halpern, conveyancer, regarding lease of property in Mount Street. Evening, Miss Finch suspicious of JM and WO, led to hostile interview with servant at 12 Devonshire Square.

19th November. Morning clear, S-H attended service at St George's Church with Mrs Cuthbertson. JM and WO unable to pursue inquiries at Devonshire Square. (Finch country residence is in county of Suffolk.) Evening, clear and cold, S-H attended supper given by Mr Rose.

As a confidential dossier it was rather amateurish, but Déprez found himself full of admiration for Mr Mortimer's powers. Who could not esteem an agent who had managed to place Mary Finch in London, possessed of both her fortune and her maidenhood, at a time when she had surely been living frugally in Paris, the wife of an American artist?

There was little to encourage Mary and Minta as they set off for the Hôtel de la Marine. The morning sunshine had faded, and low, grey clouds were drifting across the sky. The driver of their cabriolet complained that his horse was lame, and they must pay extra for such a long journey. When asked why he accepted passengers if his horse was unfit, his response was to suck his teeth and demand whether they preferred to walk.

'I hope you will drive him gently, at least,' said Mary.

'It is because we must go slow that the fare is higher,' he replied in an aggrieved tone. 'I will have fewer customers today, with him in this woeful condition.'

'And when he is *not* in this condition, will you charge less?' snapped Minta, vexation overcoming the enforced diffidence of her station. 'Or will you say, "I have carried you so efficiently, you must pay more"?'

'The fare is the fare,' grumbled the driver, and motioned with his whip. 'But there is your way if you prefer it, citizens, on your own feet. The road is free to all.'

'No, no,' replied Mary, 'we will pay,' and Minta retreated, scowling, into the folds of her cloak.

The journey was indeed a slow one, and a light rain had begun to fall before they reached the Ministry. *What sort of burglar is driven to the scene of her crime by a lame horse?* thought Mary as they rolled unhurriedly over the cobbles. She could feel the tension building inside her, and this seemed to heighten her awareness of external sensations. Every bump was a mighty jolt, and the drops of rain became a drum roll. A worse thought occurred to her – what if the plans were not in the admiral's office? What if he had taken them with him to Le Havre?

They disembarked at last and huddled beneath the umbrella that Minta had brought along, less because she had suspected the weather than because she wished to carry something. Mary, they had decided, would not entrust a servant with her precious artist's materials. These were contained in a small valise, along with a set of Mr Boyle's plans for an improved carriage-braking mechanism. Mary meant to exchange these for the *Ammonite*'s, in the hope that, when he came to study them, the admiral would believe that he had received the wrong plans from Mr Boyle in the first place, thus reducing his sense of alarm.

Confidence, Mary reminded herself as they climbed the ministry steps and approached the porter. *'A great deal may be achieved through an amiable countenance and a confident manner.'* This was another of Miss Marchmont's sayings from her days as a teacher of deportment, and it stood Mary in good stead on this occasion. The porter let them in, and if the two women attracted admiring glances from the men they passed on the way to Admiral Le Pelley's office, they ignored them both amiably and confidently.

This combination also succeeded with the admiral's secretary, who greeted Mary when she reminded him of her previous visit. Nor did he appear particularly surprised by her request to sketch the portion of the admiral's office that would comprise the background of his portrait. 'Ah, yes – the admiral has spoken of you.'

'Spoken of me? Indeed,' said Mary, managing to transform the start of surprise into a nod.

'Of the portrait. He is greatly looking forward to it. He means it as a present to his wife, you know.'

'So he informed me.'

Mary suffered a second, more severe shock on being shown into the small, private chamber. Folded over the back of a chair was a greatcoat, and a fire burned cheerfully in the grate. 'Oh, I— I understood— Has the admiral returned to Paris?' she cried.

'Yes, he returned last night,' replied the secretary. He frowned at the coat and hung it on the back of the door. 'But do not be dismayed. He is in a meeting at present with some men from the Académie, and when he is finished I am certain he will wish to greet you.'

Which prospect was worse – that Admiral Le Pelley might descend upon her at any moment, or that he was, even then, handing round the *Ammonite* plans to a group of eager French scientists? Mary's gaze was drawn to his desk, as if there might be an empty file labelled 'Confidential Naval Plans' on display.

'Mm,' she murmured, trying to sound confident as her stomach tensed with anxiety. 'It would be my pleasure to see the admiral again.' *Oh dear, oh dear!* Admiral Le Pelley might not be an artist, but he had a sharp eye. At the very least he might be displeased that Vangenzen was not doing all of the work on the portrait himself. At worst . . .

With a conscious effort, she reined in those dangerous thoughts, which served no purpose other than to frighten her. *You do not know that anything terrible has happened – or shall.* The first thing to do, clearly, was to make the sketches – one at least. This would delay her search for the *Ammonite* plans, but she must have something tangible to show the admiral if he made an appearance. *He is like a sort of . . . sword of Damocles. Oh, stop that!*

Having removed her cloak and gloves, she took a seat in the armchair opposite the admiral's desk and arranged her materials: drawing board, paper, drawing pins, and three lead pencils of different grades. Then she looked about for something to sketch. The model ship? Too difficult; she would leave that until last. The desk itself? No, that would be very dull – from where she was sitting it was a simple rectangle with turned legs, hardly requiring a preliminary sketch. She settled on an oil lamp. It was interesting enough, and likely to figure in any portrait of the admiral that was eventually produced.

Minta had dragged a second armchair from the corner of the office and manoeuvred it into the doorway. There she sat primly, with her bonnet balanced upon her knee. The move meant that Mary could see her out of the corner of her eye, which was rather distracting. More importantly, however, it screened Mary from view by anyone else. The secretary had left ajar the door between the admiral's office and his own, but now he would have to rise and actually peer round the corner to see anything apart from Minta and her hat.

Mary drew quickly, and in less than half an hour she had completed several sketches of the lamp, an inkwell and pen, and the top half of the bookcase that stood behind the admiral's desk. *A reasonable start*, she decided, squinting at the last critically and refining a shadow. Then she lowered the board to her lap and glanced at Minta, who turned slowly and gazed through the open door. Resuming her original pose, she made a slight gesture with her hand, indicating that it was safe to rise.

Straightaway Mary laid down her drawing things and went to the desk. There were no helpfully labelled files, but two stacks of documents and a large leather wallet were available for inspection. She studied them quickly, although the latter was fastened with a knotted string, which had to be worried and unpicked. Nothing. *If I wished to know about the Toulon fleet*, she brooded, *I should be well away*. For an instant, the idea of carrying off the most recent of those papers occurred to her – Captain Martel would probably say that they were extremely valuable – but she quickly rejected it. *Only let me find the plans*, she pleaded irreverently to the god of clandestine theft, *and I will be content. And let me also take them safely away*, she added.

She tried the desk drawers – were they locked? No, but the first was empty and the topmost document in the second was dated seven months ago. The bottom drawer resisted her efforts and, when opened, would not close. *Oh Heavens, I have broken it!* She jogged the drawer, hoping to coax it back into place, and then pushed hard. It closed with a thud, and Minta coughed loudly into her handkerchief.

Mary peered at her across the desk – there was relief and anxiety in her eyes – and shook her head. On her feet again, she crept past the open door towards the side table, all the time thinking that the desk had seemed so much more likely. On the table stood the model of the *Hirondelle*, looking rakish and fragile, and another stack of papers. The Naval dispositions at Brest were their main subject, together with reports of several courts martial. All of those accused seemed to have been convicted, she noted grimly.

Where are the plans? Where can they be? Against Mary's will, an image of learned members of the Académie appeared in her mind's eye. *'Oh, this man Boyle is a genius,'* they seemed to be saying. *'First the small-gauge canals and now this marvellous invention to defeat the British!'*

Then she noticed a second wallet on the floor, leaning against the table leg; it was fastened with a buckle and strap. She opened it . . . and there it was: *The entire plan, explanation, and justification of THE AMMONITE, an underwater ship of war, designed and constructed by THE REVEREND SAMSON BOYLE, according to scientific principles developed by MR PAPIN and MR BUSHNELL, among others, but with important improvements of his own discovery.*

A surge of triumph sent shivers down her spine, and she wanted to brandish the papers – six sheets of foolscap secured with red ties – for Minta's benefit. She had them!

But she did nothing so reckless. Instead, she quickly substituted the plans that Holland had given her, fastened up the wallet, and laid it carefully down again. Suddenly she heard a noise – voices! Minta gasped and Mary raced back to her chair. The plans of the *Ammonite* were on the seat, and she sat down, concealing them. Somehow she retrieved her drawing board and was bending to select a pencil from her valise when Admiral Le Pelley stumped into view.

'Ah, Citizeness Vangenzen!' he cried. 'What a delightful surprise!'

'Delightful,' Mary stammered in reply. 'Good afternoon, admiral.'

Whatever etiquette demanded, Mary had no intention of rising, but instead nodded demurely at him. A slight wave of the arm almost transformed it into a passable curtsy – if that manoeuvre could be accomplished sitting down. Minta hauled her chair out of the way and performed a more traditional obeisance as he passed, her anguish concealed by a bowed head and lowered eyes.

Admiral Le Pelley thought it was charming that Mary should assist her husband – he only hoped the job was not too tedious.

'Oh no, not at all tedious.'

'And what of Citizen Vangenzen   is he well?'

'Yes, quite well.'

'And busy, no doubt – a young man of his skill. I shall be seeing him soon, I hope?'

Mary indicated that this hope would undoubtedly be gratified. With each exchange, however, booming on his side and temperate on hers, she was dreading a crisis. What if the admiral required the use of his office? What if he opened the wallet? What if she were obliged to stand up?

'Your pardon, admiral,' piped Minta, 'but might I . . . would you care for a cup of coffee? I could fetch coffee for you and my mistress.' She was clutching the back of her chair, and her voice wavered.

'Hmm? Coffee, did you say?' asked the admiral, cocking his head in Minta's direction, 'I didn't quite hear.'

Minta repeated her suggestion, adding that she could easily obtain coffee or some other beverage from one of the *cafés* nearby – the admiral need only say what he would prefer.

It was a brief distraction, but sufficient for Mary to extract the plans and slide them into the only hiding-place available, among her sketches on the floor.

'Ah, very thoughtful of you, my good girl, but I never drink coffee at this time of the day. I used to do so, when I was younger, but when you are my age, you must choose between such pleasures and a good night's sleep.' He turned to Mary. 'But for you, citizeness? Will you take some refreshment?'

Mary frantically debated her reply. Of all things, she wanted to escape from that room, but immediate flight was impossible. It would seem so strange, and she was afraid to risk exposing the plans for a second time. Even folded they were large and unwieldy, and their present concealment uncertain. If only the admiral would go away again! Without looking down, she moved her foot surreptitiously, in an effort to neaten the pile.

Le Pelley's eye caught the motion. 'Ho ho!' he cried. 'Now

I perceive the reason for your shyness. The artist's labours have been interrupted! You must allow me to see what you have achieved.'

'My— Oh, no,' gasped Mary, clutching her drawing-board in a panic. 'They are only . . . I would rather not.'

'Come, come,' urged Le Pelley, holding out his hand. His smile was encouraging. 'I am not too severe a critic, I think.'

'No, but . . .' She forced herself to assume a more natural expression, and to think – think! Beyond the admiral she could see Minta standing motionless, frozen with dread, but somehow the sight helped her. *All is lost unless you do something.*

She rose then with a desperate idea, clutching the papers in both hands. The *Ammonite* plans were somewhere near the bottom of the pile. 'I will show you the best ones,' she offered.

'You are too modest to judge which are the best,' said Le Pelley. He moved to the desk and sat down; from the other side she handed him the topmost sheet. 'Ah, this is very good indeed,' he said. 'And this too,' as he received the second. 'You have captured the lamp to a nicety.'

'It is not so bad,' she acknowledged, placing another in front of him, 'but here, you see, the perspective is wrong, and I ought to have taken more care with that one to capture the shine of the brass.'

'Hmm. If they were finished drawings, perhaps. But as sketches they are more than sufficient.'

Only a few drawings remained. He held out his hand for them, but she pretended not to notice.

'And here is the last.' She retreated a step, and then another. 'We agreed, remember, only the best?'

'I made no such agreement,' Le Pelley protested. 'Oh!' His exclamation corresponded to the sight of the last papers being tossed onto the fire. 'What a pity!'

'No, no,' Mary assured him gravely. 'It was better that they were not seen.'

19

Déprez's meeting with the minister of police and his chief agent, Fondard, was largely a ceremonial one, with mutual expressions of goodwill and promises of unreserved support during General Bonaparte's stay in the capital. Usually Déprez found such protocol tiresome, but on this occasion he welcomed it, for his mind was elsewhere, and he could return the minister's platitudes without taxing himself unduly.

Of far greater moment was the question: what ought he to do about Mary Finch? (Always in his thoughts she retained her maiden name.) How far should he take his suspicions, and to whom would it be safe to acknowledge them?

That the entire business might be a test of some kind, concocted by Citizen Talleyrand, had not escaped him. Indeed, it would exactly suit the minister: *for if I recognise the danger and keep silent, I am damned. If I do not recognise it, I am a fool, and if I inform Talleyrand, I am drawn into his net. True, there would be an obligation on his side, but that might prove more costly to me than to him.*

More tantalising to Déprez was the possibility that he had discovered an actual secret, known only to himself. If that secret could be exploited, it might prove very valuable indeed. It could, for example, erase the stain of his failure in the Holland affair, and far more effectively than by invoking some legal hocus-pocus to overturn his conviction. *What had they called it? 'Failing to pursue the objects of the Republic with sufficient courage and resourcefulness.' Damn them.* Exploiting the secret, however, was not so simple, and might require assistance. But could he find an assistant or (less appealing) a partner upon whom he could rely?

Certainly not the minister of police, whom Déprez dismissed as a true *rond-de-cuir*, a bureaucrat characterised by diligence, obedience, and caution. At no stage during their conversation was Déprez tempted to reveal anything more profound than that he expected General Bonaparte to reside at his wife's house in the Rue Chantereine. Sergeant Fondard, on the other hand, he found intriguing. Fondard's assessment of the political situation in Paris demonstrated a fine understanding of the various streams and rivulets – some clear-running, others murky and subterranean.

Déprez was nothing if not decisive. Upon being left alone with Fondard to 'discuss the finer details' of the general's stay, he did not hesitate more than a few minutes before raising another matter.

Fondard listened warily. His initial view of Déprez, that he might cut a figure in battle but would shrink from slitting a throat in the dark, had changed slightly over the course of the minister's presentation. He still considered Déprez 'a fine gentleman', but he also perceived both calculation and strength of purpose beneath the showy façade. *At least,* he reflected, *the colonel believes himself a man of great talents, and what mythology is more powerful than the one we construct for ourselves?*

'You understand the British arrangements for security and intelligence?' he asked. They had moved to Fondard's drab office, an anonymous space broken only by a bare desk with a sloping top such as a schoolmaster might have, an oak armoire, and two chairs. The walls were blank apart from maps of France and Paris, which had been affixed to unvarnished boards and now hung, precariously, from single nails thrust deep into the plaster.

In deference to his host's bulk, Déprez had chosen the smaller, less accommodating chair, and now he rather regretted it. 'I know something of their systems,' he said, 'such as they were.

I have not been personally concerned in such matters for almost two years.'

'Mm, yes,' Fondard agreed. 'That was an unfortunate affair.' His tone was neutral, comfortable. He did not wish to discourage Déprez, but only to establish the proper foundations for their relationship. The seating arrangement was a good start. After a slight pause, he continued, 'It would not be a bad idea to recruit a woman, if she had a strong character. Most women suffer from nerves. But the best – or the worst – can be formidable.'

'This one has a strong character.'

Which means that she bested you in some way, thought Fondard, *or perhaps you are merely in love with her.* 'You know her well?'

'Well enough.'

'And the husband also? What do you think of him?'

'Amiable, good-hearted . . . Not her equal.'

Naturally, you would not think so. 'And what do you suppose to be this intrepid lady's purpose in coming to France?'

'To Paris,' Déprez corrected, 'with an American husband, at the very moment when the Americans have sent envoys to conduct negotiations with the French government. Does that not suggest a purpose? What is more, there is a friendship between her and one of these men: John Marshall. She introduced me to him at Talon's. I do not suggest that it is an improper friendship,' he added.

'Of course not,' said Fondard with a smirk. 'But you think she is working for the British?'

Déprez could feel himself blushing, and it irritated him. He replied less calmly than he would have liked. 'Yes, but perhaps for the Americans as well. There may be an understanding of some kind. The Federal Party in America favours reconciliation with Britain, just as their Republicans look to maintain the alliance with France. The British may be trying to drive a wedge between ourselves and the Americans, or perhaps the American government has already made its decision. The Jay treaty was not the act of an ally.'

Fondard acknowledged the truth, or at least the plausibility, of all that Déprez had said. 'You did not choose to raise your suspicions at the Maison Gallifet?' It was a question to which he already knew the answer. Clearly, if the matter had already attracted the attention of Talleyrand, it would not now be coming to the police. But why had Déprez eschewed the most obvious route?

'I would prefer to bring *facts* to the foreign minister,' said Déprez. 'Evidence, rather than suspicions. At present, I can suggest that an attempt is being made to hide the departure of Mary Finch from England. By whom, if not the British government? For what reason, other than to protect some secret business in France? What business could she perform? Only one involving the American negotiations. But my evidence is slight and easy to discount. The report from London may have been mistaken . . . I cannot prove a connection between Mary Finch and any of the British intelligence services.'

'And there are only two letters between Fondard and a piece of chocolate. No, go on,' he urged, in answer to Déprez's curious look.

'There is no more,' said Déprez, 'other than that I do not choose to play the fool before Talleyrand, or to be told not to cause trouble for him with my suspicions.'

'Always, when one is doing one's duty, there is a warning not to cause trouble!' sighed Fondard, more to himself than to the man opposite. He frowned thoughtfully. 'But sometimes trouble is a good thing. And sometimes it is deserved.'

'Nevertheless,' warned Déprez.

Fondard nodded. 'As you say. Not until we know more.'

He rose to his feet and adjusted his waistcoat, which had crumpled across his belly, and fished out a ring of keys from his breeches pocket. One unlocked the door to the armoire. It had been fitted with shelves, on which were neat stacks of files and bundles of paper. 'One moment,' he muttered, peering unsuccessfully into the depths. Then another thought struck him and he moved to his desk. 'Ah.'

The desk was duly opened, and this time he found what he wanted. 'Perhaps the Vangenzen family is not quite as it appears. We received a letter two days ago.'

282

Déprez read the proffered document – half a dozen lines on a single sheet of paper. 'But this—'

'Says very little,' completed Fondard in a dampening tone, 'and is not at all unusual.' He resumed his seat with a grunt. 'Most denunciations are not of enemies, you know, but of friends – the lover, the colleague, the neighbour – done in a moment of spitefulness or jealousy. It is very sad, really, this weakness of character. The priests would say it is evidence of Original Sin. Perhaps they are right.'

'A message like this would not ordinarily have aroused your suspicions?'

Fondard shook his head. 'An enquiry would have been made, of course. Indeed, I would have done so before now, only' – he spread his hands – 'I have not so many men as I would like, and I have been distracted by another matter. However, my chief has closed that investigation – for the present – and now your information about Citizeness Vangenzen makes me wonder whether there might be something in this warning after all.'

'Then you will help me?' asked Déprez.

'Yes, colonel, I will help you, for today at least.' Déprez had already risen; Fondard did so now more slowly. 'Let us pay a call. The address is the Rue Beauregard, I believe?'

Déprez nodded. 'Yes.'

Fondard slipped a cloak over his shoulders, muttering something about the rain. 'Did I tell you that I have met Citizeness Vangenzen?' He shrugged in reply to Déprez's surprised stare. 'On the road to Paris from Chantilly.'

'And what did you think of her?'

'Oh, I agree that she is an interesting woman. Very charming. I look forward to renewing our acquaintance.'

Minta staggered down the grand stairs of the Hôtel de la Marine, her knees shaking. Mary was beside her, ramrod straight, clutching her valise in one hand and the umbrella in the other. They negotiated the passageway and colonnade, but on reaching the street, they hesitated. Neither was willing to speak or even release the breath that each was holding, as if the slightest exhalation would expose their guilt. A gust of cold, damp air made them shiver, but this helped to break the spell.

'Oh my word,' breathed Mary, 'that was a near miss. I thought . . .' She shook her head to dispel the memory.

'I don't know how you managed it,' Minta admitted in a similarly hushed tone, 'but thank Heaven you did!'

Mary smiled at her. 'I would be upstairs now, unable to move, if *you* had not managed to distract Admiral Le Pelley.'

'Well . . .' Minta reclaimed the umbrella and unfurled it tentatively, but the rain had stopped. 'Shall I hail a cabriolet?' she asked, nodding at the row of vehicles on the opposite side of the square.

'No, let us walk for a while,' said Mary. 'I cannot possibly sit still. If it were possible to run all the way to the Maison des Chevrons, I believe I would do so.'

She did not attempt this feat, but set off at a strong pace. Minta followed, hoisting her skirt as well as she could with her free hand. 'What will you do, now that the plans have been lost?'

'*We* are not lost, that is the main thing,' said Mary firmly. 'And the next step must be . . . I think I must go to the convent.'

'The *convent*?' Minta echoed, aghast. 'Now?'

'I must explain what has happened. It might make a difference – although I trust that I have not burned the only copy . . .' The thought that she had done exactly that caused her to shiver again. *I hope not, and besides, there is still Mr Boyle.* Mary uttered these last words to herself, but then seemed to remember her companion. 'Oh, but you need not come with me. Do please go home if you would rather.'

'I *would* rather, but you cannot wander the streets alone,' Minta complained. 'It is growing dark, and you don't know the way to the Little Fathers from here, do you?'

Mary said that she did, but her vague gesture towards the north was not convincing.

'Yes, and Flanders also lies in that direction,' Minta agreed pettishly. 'Now wait a moment and let me think.' She paused and then led the way back towards the Tuileries gardens, down a narrow passage whose looks Mary did not like, and finally onto a broad street, the Rue Honoré. 'This is our best route,' Minta pronounced, pointing with the umbrella in a way that suddenly brought Mrs Tipton to mind.

Mary smiled to herself. She did not feel that all was well, exactly, but she slipped her arm companionably through Minta's as they set off again.

Ahead of them stood the former convent of the Feuillants, which had become the headquarters of a political club suppressed, in its turn, during the Terror. Minta stopped short, as though the ghostly members might assail them, and turned instead into the Place des Piques.

Here was a far more pleasing prospect, of pale stonework, arcades, and columns. The dormer windows that pierced the high-pitched roofs looked like the edging of an elegant pie-crust. In the dim twilight, it was easy to imagine oneself in Paris before the Revolution. Only a knot of idle men, lounging about a raised statue in the centre of the square, spoiled the scene. Roughly dressed, they were throwing dice upon a wooden board, and their raucous calls inspired both repugnance and disquiet among respectable passers-by. Mary and Minta gave them a wide berth.

At the far end of the square they turned right again, and now Mary admitted that she was hopelessly confused. 'I thought that the Rue des Petits Champs ran north and south *between* the Rue Honoré and the Place des Victoires.'

'It does,' Minta explained. 'This is the Rue *Neuve* des Petits Champs. We are approaching the Place des Victoires, but from the west.'

Mary replied cautiously. 'Ah yes, I see. I am glad to know that I have not lost *all* sense of direction.'

They crossed the Rue de la Loi, and suddenly Mary knew where she was. This sense of the familiar was comforting, although it really had no stronger foundation than Minta's asser-tion that they were heading in the right direction. *I would rather rely on myself, I suppose*, she mused, *which is rather vain when one stops to think about it.*

285

She resisted the temptation to affirm, 'Here we are,' for, of course, Minta had been aware of the 'here' all along. A close observer, however, would have discerned a marked confidence in Mary's step that had been lacking when she ceded control of the expedition.

As she had that morning, Mary turned into the Rue Vivienne, intending to approach the convent by way of the garden of an inn and eating-house on that street – the Maison des Etrangers. *I wonder*, she thought, *whether we ought to go inside and order something to eat or drink? If anyone sees us in the garden, they will think it so odd*. Weighing up whether it would appear more or less odd to creep along a muddy patch of tilled ground after supper or a cup of coffee occupied her thoughts for almost fifteen yards. A conclusion, however, eluded her.

The inn was a highly respectable establishment, but on this afternoon some tumult or other had occurred. A crowd of people had gathered in the street, and as she drew near Mary heard snatches of garbled conversations. 'Did you see the engine?' 'Ah, it was nothing to the blaze last year in the Rue des Amandiers. Three floors collapsed, just like that!' 'I saw two engines.' 'Everyone knows they were storing royal treasures there.' 'Property of the state, you mean, of the people of France, and now some damned Royalist spy has destroyed it.' 'Here is Georges with his spies again! You are just angry because they will suspend the stock exchange, and you will lose your money!' 'Was the stock exchange destroyed?' 'I saw at least three engines.' 'At the Rue des Amandiers there were four.'

'What is it?' Mary demanded, pushing forward. 'Has there been a fire at the inn?'

Her questions interrupted an argument about the Rue des Amandiers and whether it could have accommodated four engines. A burly, middle-aged man turned to her. 'No, not here, at the old convent. It is still burning.'

'The Little Fathers?' As she spoke Mary became aware that an unnatural darkness had fallen; the air smelled of smoke.

'And the office of the stock exchange,' piped someone.

'What do you know of it, Pierre?' argued the burly man.

'I tell you, the fire was at the other end — it never reached the church.'

'Not yet!' cried another, with indecent relish. 'I say burn the speculators *and* their damned exchange!'

Mary tried to ask how the fire had started and whether anyone had been injured, but her moment had passed, and now she would have to compete for her place in the debate. 'But can you tell—'

'Usurers and speculators are an abomination,' urged a gaunt, balding man in a dark coat. 'This is a sign from God that His houses ought not to be used for profane purposes.'

The burly man threw up his hands. 'Ah, don't talk to me about God and priests!'

After being buffeted by a man attempting to intercede on behalf of God, Mary withdrew. She would learn nothing from these quarrellers — at least not without a louder voice and more time than she could spare. The notion of Royalist spies was ridiculous, but had there been treachery? Were Captain Holland and the others safe? Where *was* Captain Holland?

That question provoked a greater urgency — as if she had arrived at precisely the moment when he might be plucked from danger. There was a passageway between the inn and its neighbour, and Mary sped towards this, pulling Minta along. 'Come,' she cried, 'this way,' with as little heed to Minta's queries as the quarrelling patrons of the Maison des Etrangers had paid hers.

The ground was muddy underfoot, and the darkness deepened as they left the street behind. Then the way opened before them; they were in a courtyard, and ahead lay a small building like a shed or a workshop. Mary plunged on, tripping over something in her haste, for beyond and to the left she could see a red glow — the fire rising over the convent wall. 'Hurry!' she urged.

They ran across the garden of the Maison des Etrangers, trampling cabbages and floundering in the soft earth where onions had been lifted. Minta yelped as the rough branch of a dwarfish plum tree scraped her face and clung to her shoulder. She batted another aside with the umbrella. 'Wait!' she cried, as ahead of her Mary was clambering over part of the broken wall.

Then they were both in the convent grounds. A wooden building to their left was burning; others had collapsed in smoky ruins. Leather buckets lay strewn between the well and the burning buildings; their puny efforts had been insufficient against the blaze. The convent itself looked to have suffered some damage, although it was difficult to gauge in the uncertain light. The door through which Mary had passed that morning was ajar, and smoke issued from one of the shuttered first-floor windows.

Mary started towards the main building, but Minta stopped her. 'Are you mad?' she demanded. 'You cannot go in there!'

'No,' Mary agreed, 'but . . .' She glanced about urgently; to the right, beyond a bushy hedge, was the outline of a church steeple. *The stock exchange.* 'We may reach the street if we go that way.'

'Yes, all right,' said Minta, 'but be careful!'

They ducked through the hedge and hurried along the remains of a flagstone path. On either side loomed the former convent and church, both dark and inhospitable. A rusted iron gate caused a slight delay. It clanged shut behind them, and they were in the street.

At which point their progress stopped. The street was jammed with onlookers, fire-fighting equipment, and the uniformed members of the *corps des gardes-pompes*. A man on a ladder smashed open a shuttered window, and foul-smelling smoke billowed forth. There were shouts for a hose, for more water, even as the *pompiers* sent streams into the building. On the other side of the street a man attempted to lead a frightened horse past the mayhem, but it reared and slipped on the wet cobbles. Dogs barked and ran among the hoses, offering battle to these strange, snake-like creatures. The crowd parted as another machine, drawn by a team of uniformed men, entered from the north.

That makes four machines, thought Mary distractedly, *as many as in the Rue des Amandiers.*

288

It required only a few minutes' observation of the seething tumult for her to conclude that they could advance no farther towards the front of the convent. Minta had not even entertained the possibility of doing so, and she bawled in Mary's ear, 'Come away! We can do nothing here!'

'No,' Mary agreed a second time, but with little inclination to follow her friend's advice. Standing on tiptoes, she tried to see into the crowd and spot a familiar face. 'Martel!' she shouted hopefully. She could not see him, but his was the only name that would not seem out of place. 'Martel!'

A woman turned to her. 'Who are you looking for, citizen?'

'Have you seen— Was anyone inside?' Mary asked.

'Oh no, it was a storehouse only. No one has lived there since the Little Fathers were sent away.' The woman gazed at Mary curiously, noting her handsome cloak and incongruous valise, which had somehow survived the dash through the gardens. 'Who are you looking for?' she repeated.

'Her brother,' said Minta hurriedly. 'A clerk – he works nearby.'

'Ah, at the exchange,' said the woman, nodding.

'Yes, at the exchange,' Minta agreed. She turned to Mary. 'But we have seen that the exchange is safe, and doubtless . . . your brother also. We should go home now and wait there for him.'

Mary knew that Minta was right, but leaving before she knew what had happened – before she had seen Holland – felt very much more like flight than a sensible retreat. *He would not abandon me if our places were reversed, hoping that I would turn up safely. And yet, what good can I do here? I may be wasting time – there may be a message at the Maison des Chevrons, or even . . .*

The curious woman had moved to one side, and now she was speaking furtively to a man in a short coat and round hat and pointing in Mary's direction.

Something about the fellow's bearing sent a shiver of trepidation down Mary's spine; she knew immediately that he was an official of some kind. 'You are right,' she said, surrendering to Minta's plea. 'We will wait for him at home.'

★   ★   ★

There was no reason why the act of slipping into the lobby of the Maison des Chevrons should have caused any uneasiness. They had reached the end of a difficult journey, after all, and were safe. The door creaked no more loudly than usual, and the darkness was no more profound. Nor had either Mary or Minta noticed the anonymous figure standing in the doorway opposite, who had tossed away his cigar and walked quickly down the street shortly after they arrived. They *were* uneasy, however. As they climbed the stairs, an unaccountable breeze blew, causing their shadows to shrink and expand. The wick of their candle sizzled when its flame touched the edge of softened wax.

Suddenly a voice whispered hoarsely, 'Minta? You mustn't go up.'

Mary started, but Minta turned in recognition. 'Is that you, Citizeness Grignard? What is the matter?'

The borrower of soap and sweet wine crept onto the landing beneath them, a dim, dumpy figure wrapped in a shawl. 'The police have been.'

'Police?' cried Mary. 'Are they upstairs now?'

'Hush! Hush!' urged the old woman. 'No, they went away again, but—' and now she moved forward into the light, 'they have taken Citizen Vangenzen.'

'Oh!' gasped Minta, her hand over her mouth, and Mary demanded, 'He has been arrested?'

'Why else would he go with them? The poor fellow – he will be thrown into prison or made to fight in the Army.'

Mary tried to restrain the doleful predictions and at the same time drag Minta away from them. 'Please, Citizeness! You mustn't say those things! Come – perhaps there is a message or some explanation upstairs,' she urged.

'Ha!' scoffed the voice from below. 'The same thing happened to my sister in Bourges. Her husband was taken away in the dead of night, and now she is a widow.'

The door to the *appartement* was locked, and Mary fumbled for her key.

'I should have come straight back,' groaned Minta. 'I ought never to have left him alone!'

'What good would that have done? If they *have* arrested him, you could not have prevented it.'

'I might have explained. I might—' All at once Minta stiffened, and her voice became harsh. 'What do you mean, "*if* they have arrested him"? You do not think that he has betrayed you? That he went voluntarily?'

'Shh,' Mary hissed. The door swung open, and she pushed Minta into the darkness. 'Of course not,' she continued, once they were both safe inside. 'I only meant . . .' She hesitated, not knowing quite what she had meant. 'We do not know what has happened. There may have been a mistake or . . . something quite unconnected to . . .'

'To this terrible business of yours!' Minta cried. 'Oh, why did you have to come to Paris? And why drag Samuel into your schemes? You and your friend Shy — you have ruined us!'

The urge to defend herself was immediate and almost overpowering, but Mary made no return. *She will not listen*, a warning voice informed her, *and besides that, she is right. It will be your fault if Vangenzen comes to harm.*

Mary repeated the final condition to herself. Taking the candle from Minta, she moved cautiously into the sitting-room. 'He may have left something.'

'Oh yes, very likely,' Minta snapped.

She followed the feeble glow, however, and as the sitting-room was gradually illuminated by additional candles, a strange sight emerged. Three places had been set at the dining table, and the traces of a light repast remained: plates, forks, cups and saucers, and a last slice of the apple tart. Mary touched the silver coffee pot; it was cold.

She tried to offer encouragement, but her own thoughts were confused. Why would the police consume coffee and sweets with a man whom they meant to arrest? 'Everything was done peacefully,' she observed. 'They must have questioned him and . . .'

'This is where he sat,' said Minta, indicating the cup whose handle was turned to the left. 'He is left-handed.' Her anger had collapsed as quickly as it had peaked. Dully, in a lifeless imitation of housewifely zeal, she stacked the plates and saucers. 'Only one of them ate anything.'

'We mustn't forget that Jens was also arrested – and then let go.'

'Jens is another plotter,' Minta replied, her voice despondent. 'I daresay he knows very well how to talk his way out of a tight place.'

Mary did not answer, and presently Minta became aware of this. 'What are you thinking?' she asked at last.

What she was thinking was that the police had learned of the plan to return Mr Boyle to England, and the convent fire had been the consequence. Either Holland and Martel had attempted to destroy all evidence of the *Ammonite*, or the police had tried to smoke them out like badgers from a set. But how had they acquired their knowledge in the first place? From Vangenzen? Was he in truth a traitor? Had he shared a friendly meal with the police and then calmly led them to the convent of the Little Fathers?

Instinctively she recoiled from such a cold-blooded accusation, at least from expressing it aloud, and instead said, 'Mr Vangenzen would not *volunteer* information about Captain Holland and the *Ammonite*, and why should the police have thought to ask him?'

'What do you mean?' Minta demanded. 'You *do* think that he has betrayed you!'

'Not intentionally – of course not – but it is too extraordinary that the convent should burn on the very day that he is arrested, and there should be no connection.'

Just then they heard a sound in the passageway, as if someone were knocking gently against the outer door.

'Have they heard us?' Minta whispered.

Mary raised her hands helplessly. If the police had returned, what did it matter if they had heard or not? They would do as they liked – they would break down the door! And if they knew about Vangenzen, what else did they know?

They heard it again – a light, regular tapping – and inspired by a sense of friendship, or at least unwillingness to let the other face the danger alone, they moved together towards the door. Mary opened it.

Holland entered and closed the door behind him. He frowned at the two women, white-faced and dressed to go out. 'What's happened? Are you all right?' Then he looked past them. 'Where is Vangenzen?'

They began in a confused, relieved jumble, but Mary's voice soon took charge, and in this way at least chronological order was imposed. She explained about the ministry, the sight of the convent, and the dreadful news about Vangenzen. As she spoke, she looked Holland up and down for injuries. His coat was torn, singed perhaps, and his face was streaked with sweat and smoke. *Not burned – thank God! – but he has suffered a hurt of some kind.* 'Where is Captain Martel?'

'Dead,' he replied curtly, '*and* Boyle,' but he shook his head at her look of horror and said that he would tell her later. 'Now I want a pen and paper, if there is any to hand.'

'Yes, I think so,' said Mary, 'but why?'

'So I can make another copy of the *Ammonite* plans. Not all of them, but I remember enough to help the Admiralty if we can get them back to England. Quick!' he ordered, as she stared at him.

'But have we time for that?'

'Yes, I think so. If Jens is still at his post he can wait another ten minutes.'

'Jens?' Mary demanded as she searched the drawers of the sideboard. 'Is he— Have arrangements been made for us to leave Paris?'

She produced the writing equipment, and he sat down at the dining table amid the crockery.

'Yes. We're meeting him in the Rue Hurepoix. We should have been there an hour ago.' He thought for a moment, eyeing the tart, and then began to write. Slowly a trail of words and formulae appeared on the sheet of paper. He paused again and then produced a diagram.

'But what of . . . *Mr Vangenzen*?' Minta had left them together, but Mary could not help lowering her voice. 'Did he not . . .

have the police not learned of you and Captain Martel *from him*?'

'The fire, you mean?' asked Holland. 'No, it was nothing to do with him or the police – at least, not in the way you mean.'

'Thank Heaven for that,' breathed Mary. She watched him write; he had moved on to a second sheet, which was soon covered by drawings and mathematical calculations. *He seems to be concentrating very deeply, but I wish he would hurry!*

Holland *was* concentrating, otherwise he would have told her not to interrupt, and for God's sake to stop looming over him like that. 'Almost finished,' he muttered as he filled a third sheet.

'If we leave Paris, what will happen to Mr Vangenzen and Minta? She could— But she will never go without him.'

Holland admitted that he did not know. 'I can't think why they arrested him. They may just be nosing about, and if he keeps his nerve, they will release him as they did Jens. But if *we* don't go now, we may not get another chance. And now that you've exchanged the plans at the Ministry of Marine—'

'But you said that would raise no suspicion,' she cried. 'Admiral Le Pelley would think that Mr Boyle had given him the wrong plans by mistake.'

'I hope he will,' Holland agreed. 'But I'd rather he thought about it after you were out of his reach, especially with that damned fire destroying everything else to do with the *Ammonite*.'

'Yes, I see,' she replied, 'but it would still be strange if he were to suspect *me* of anything untoward.' Her eyes entreated him. 'Do you not think it would be strange?'

Holland responded to the plea in her voice, whatever he thought of the substance of her argument. 'Probably.'

She experienced a momentary relief on behalf of those who would remain behind. If she and Holland could only get away before any real suspicion was directed at Minta and Vangenzen . . . but suddenly a different, terrible thought sent a great wave of coldness through her body. 'Do you suppose that Sergeant Fondard came here tonight?' Holland glanced at her questioningly, and she continued, 'He *knows* us, remember – Mr Vangenzen and myself. What if the name "Vangenzen" were to come to his attention again? He might remember, and then . . .'

Abruptly she left the sitting-room and opened the door to her bed chamber. When she returned, her face was grave and she spoke with a forced calmness, both of which brought Holland to his feet. 'They have searched my room. There is nothing to connect me with the *Ammonite*, but—'

'But if they have also seen Vangenzen's room – which I presume he shares with Minta – they will guess that you are not his wife.'

Holland heard the sound of a pistol being cocked behind him. He spun round and faced Minta.

'They will guess more than that,' she said.

20

Mary found her voice first. 'Minta!' she gasped. 'What are you doing?'

She tried to advance, but Holland restrained her. 'She means to give us up,' he said calmly. 'Trade us for Vangenzen.'

Minta nodded. Both panic and resolve were etched across her features, but she held the weapon steadily.

'Or maybe Vangenzen has also betrayed us.' Even as he spoke, Holland was gauging that steadiness and triangulating the distance between the three of them. The pistol he recognised as Mary's. Had Minta loaded it properly? Would she really fire?

'Never!' snapped Minta. 'He was always faithful – and see what it has earned him! I told them that it was she who—'

'*You* have been to the police?' Mary demanded, her voice choking with disbelief. 'When?'

Minta *had* left a message at the Hôtel de Police, and she was not ashamed of having done so, but the tone stung her, somehow, and she turned to Mary in frustration. 'I had to do something! When they arrested Jens, I *knew* they would trace everything to us – and then where would we be? In prison! Andrew Ogbourne and the Little Fathers . . . *That* was never part of the arrangement with Shy. Keep back!' she warned, as Holland moved towards her. 'If only I had been here today – but now I will make things right for us.'

'Not if you think you're going to save Vangenzen,' Holland

countered. 'He has known about everything from the start. If you give us up, we'll do the same for him.'

'But I will explain—'

'That he was playing a double game?' Holland was scornful. 'They will never believe it.'

'Then I— Then I will kill you!' Minta cried, pointing the pistol first at Holland and then at Mary. 'And you will tell no tales!'

'You can't kill us both – you've only one shot. Whichever of us is left will make damned sure that Vangenzen goes to the guillotine.' Holland moved again, a calculated step to one side.

'Please!' cried Mary, 'don't let's speak of killing and betraying each other! We are all friends – I know we are – and there must be a way to resolve this without anyone being harmed. Minta, what have you said to the police?'

'Only that you were a bad wife, and' – she lowered her voice – 'I suspected you of . . . treachery.'

'Very likely *that* is what brought the police here in the first place,' Holland observed. 'That's all the good you've managed to do Vangenzen – you've had him arrested.'

Minta was stunned by this condemnation; she turned impulsively to Mary. 'But I never—'

Holland seized Minta's wrist in a crushing grip, and the pistol slipped from her fingers. Both women cried out, and Mary found herself holding Minta's other arm in a mixture of support and restraint. Holland stepped back again and checked the pistol before motioning Minta to the nearest chair.

'Don't be a damned fool,' he cautioned, as she hesitated. When she had sat down, he nodded to Mary. 'What were you going to say?'

She stared back at him for a moment and then rallied her thoughts. 'I was . . . I was going to say that things may not be so different from what we thought a moment ago. Mr Vangenzen will do his best to convince the police that their suspicions are mistaken, and very likely he will succeed. The police will have seen that our domestic arrangements are . . . odd, but I expect such things are not so very unusual, especially in France.' She turned to Minta. 'So he will probably be released, and if *you* say nothing further, you will both be safe.'

'But what if the police are not convinced?' asked Minta. 'They may want to speak to you, and if you are not here . . .' She eyed Mary pleadingly. 'If you were to remain in Paris – just for a little while – to reassure them, and then . . .'

Mary hesitated. 'I—'

'Absolutely not,' barked Holland. 'You've placed Mary in enough danger. She cannot possibly stay in Paris a minute longer.' To Mary he demanded, 'Is there a room that can be made secure?'

'No, I . . . I do not know.'

'Get some rope then. Something to tie her up.'

When Mary returned with a length of cord, he handed her the pistol and bound Minta in place, explaining, 'If Vangenzen is released, he'll untie her, and there's no harm done. But if the police return, she can say – truthfully – that she tried to stop us, and she'll look the part.' Glancing up at Minta as he bound her ankles he added, 'It's the best we can do.'

Mary watched, frowning, as the process was carried out, but she nodded in acceptance of Holland's decision. 'Yes, I am afraid we must.' She checked the knots to make certain that they were not too tight, and murmured, 'I am sorry,' as she touched the other woman's hand.

Minta flinched at the contact, but she did not speak.

'All right,' said Holland brusquely, 'let's go. Put on your boots and your warmest clothes, and if you've any money, bring it. Quick march, now.'

Mary made her preparations, and her thoughts moved as quickly as her fingers, if not with the same dexterity. She felt as though she were navigating a steep path littered with boulders, and it was necessary to keep moving from one insecure place to another, or she would lose her balance entirely. *He is right*, she told herself as she did up the buttons of a steel coloured wool gown. It was not quite her warmest, but the cut and colour were suited to what might be headlong travel arrangements. *There is nothing more that we can do here – and we must find Jens!*

Suitably dressed and shod, and with a reticule weighed down by pistol balls and a powder flask, she opened the door of her bedchamber. Holland was standing on the threshold. 'What if—' she began, but before she could finish he was bustling her through the *appartement*, pausing only to hand over her cloak and shrug into his greatcoat. He shut the outer door behind him, and she locked it with her key.

They crept quietly down the darkened staircase, not wishing to advertise their presence even with a lighted candle. In her agitation, Mary lost count of the steps, and instead let the banister under her hand guide her descent. When they reached the lobby, she turned to Holland. 'Did you . . . gag her?'

Holland nodded. 'It probably won't stop her shouting to the neighbours, but . . .'

'If the police return, she may tell them everything.'

'Mm. It would have been safer to kill her.'

'*Kill* her?' Mary hissed. 'You could never have done such a thing!'

'Well, I didn't, anyway.'

Mary started to defend Minta, but then changed her mind. 'I am certain that Mr Vangenzen can be trusted.'

'Maybe, but I don't know how convincing he's likely to be.' Holland opened the door and motioned her forward. 'Come on. The sooner we're away from here, the better.'

They made their way to the Rue Hurepoix by cabriolet – Holland driving and Mary beside him, giving directions. When they arrived, Holland handed the reins to the attendant and instructed Mary to wait in the vehicle until it was clear that descent was both safe and worthwhile. If Jens had abandoned the rendezvous, they would have to make their own way to the city gates alone. 'If there's any trouble,' Holland whispered, 'don't take any chances, but get away from here as fast as you can.'

Whatever his other foibles, however, Jens was faithful, or at least very stubborn. He emerged from a deeply shadowed doorway, exercised less by concerns for his own safety than by his colleagues' timekeeping. What was the meaning of this tardiness? It was hardly the conduct that a person in his situation expected.

A second shower of rain had provoked him further, but it had also improved conditions for the meeting. There were few passers-by that evening, and even fewer interested in any but their own affairs. It was possible, therefore, to conduct a huddled conversation, in English, with little fear of attracting attention.

Jens was not the sort of person to display the more tender sentiments, even when he had not been rained upon, but he nodded sombrely when informed that Boyle and Martel had perished at the convent. 'And this will make matters more difficult for you,' he murmured. 'I had expected that Martel would guide you to the coast. He certainly had a great deal of confidence in his ability to do so. Did he mention my proposal?'

'Yes, a little,' said Holland.

'And you are content, I presume? Good. At least I needn't begin again – which would be awkward at this time of night. Fortunately Mrs Vangenzen knows the Calais road.' He nodded in Mary's direction.

'We are going to Calais?' gasped Mary as the members of the Committee of Public Safety appeared, scowling, in her mind's eye.

'No, Dunkerque,' said Jens. 'A further thirty miles or so along the coast. It is quite as amenable as Calais for maritime purposes, and it has the particular advantage of being the home port – in France – of ships all belonging to Mr Cornelius Vangenzen of Dan Helder.'

'Ah, I see,' breathed Mary. She noticed then that the building opposite housed the offices of a shipping agent and insurer.

'I hope that you do,' said Jens. 'There may be trouble with your passports – you should expect that there will be – and if anyone is willing to chance his ship for you, it will probably be your, ahem, husband's cousin. If you had managed to keep this appointment, we might have arranged things properly with Cornelius Vangenzen's agent – letters of introduction, time-tables. Unfortunately the office is closed, and you will have to take your chances in Dunkerque. Hopefully, one of Vangenzen's ships will be there when you arrive.'

'But would a Dutch ship be allowed to sail to England?'

300

asked Mary. The reference to her husband was disconcerting, and she spoke hurriedly. 'By our Navy, I mean.'

'Certainly not, but that too is a problem for another day. Before you can land in England, you must succeed in leaving France.'

Mary had a sudden vision of a ship sailing up and down the Channel, unable either to complete the voyage or return to port, but Holland's matter-of-fact reply dissolved it. He was certain that they would get across somehow. There were always fishermen or smugglers who would land them for a price.

'Oh yes,' Mary agreed, but she frowned as Holland thanked Jens, and the two men shook hands. 'But do you not mean to come with us?' she asked. 'You cannot remain in Paris, surely, after what has happened?'

'No, I fear that cursed woman will have the police banging on my door again,' Jens growled, 'and they may not behave so moderately a second time. To think that a man in my profession should be subjected to such indignities!'

'Then come with us,' Mary urged.

He shook his head. 'No, I do not think that would be wise, for our paths do not naturally coincide. You will not be safe until you are back in England, but I prefer to remain in France if I can, and perhaps creep back into Paris when things have quieted down. There is Vrillac's to consider, after all.'

'Well, don't consider it too much,' advised Holland.

'Material possessions lose their lustre in such times as these,' Jens agreed. '"Of what value is a golden gallows, if they are going to hang you?" That is a saying of my country, you know. And now I think that we ought to part. Several of the north-bound coaches leave from the Compas d'Or in the Rue Montorgueil – if you can secure places, that would be the safest way to leave Paris.'

'I don't like the idea of a coach full of people being able to describe us,' said Holland.

'No, but their curiosity is unlikely to be lethal. You can always change to a more private form of transport once you are out of the city.'

Jens' other offering was of a more tangible form – a small purse of coins. When one was travelling, he said, a good supply of ready money was always advisable.

'Oh, thank you,' said Mary, 'but are you certain you can spare it?' The purse felt quite heavy. 'You will also have travelling expenses.'

She attempted to return it, but Jens held up his hands, fending her off. 'No, no,' he protested fussily. 'It is purely a matter of business. London will receive a full account of my expenses, you may be certain of that.'

As Jens was protesting against any suggestion of chivalry, a messenger arrived at the Hôtel de Police with urgent information for Sergeant Fondard. Urgency was a matter of degree, however. The sergeant was known to be pursuing an inquiry with a suspected person, and no one liked to disturb him when he was thus engaged. So a brief note was composed and sent up to him by a clerk with a particular facility for neither hearing nor seeing what oughtn't to concern him.

In fact, its arrival was opportune. The sergeant's 'inquiries' could comprise several forms of interrogation, but this one had not advanced beyond the stage of simple question and answer, with the result that very little of interest had been learned. Vangenzen might not be a very clever strategist, but he understood that professions of goodwill coupled with a consistent lack of substance would serve him best.

'Ah,' said Fondard as he read the note. 'Some good news at last.' To Vangenzen he explained, 'The women of your household have returned from their little expedition. Shopping, I believe you said, and yes, the shops must all be shut at this hour. I hope they have not been too extravagant in their purchases,' he teased, wagging a reproving finger.

Déprez had already risen, and he said, 'Yes, certainly,' when Fondard asked whether he would care to accompany him to the Maison des Chevrons.

'But they can tell you nothing!' Vangenzen protested.

'You don't think so?' asked Fondard. 'Well, we shall see. At the

302

very least we can assure them that no mischief has befallen you, for they might grow nervous in your absence. Women often suffer in that way and require comforting.'

Vangenzen bit his lip. 'Thank you,' he said, forcing himself to speak normally. 'I would be grateful if you would tell them that I am well.'

'Of course! And remind me, which of the two produced the delicious apple tart? Your housekeeper, I think?'

'Yes, Minta.'

'I thought it would be that way,' said Fondard. 'Citizeness Vangenzen has not been in France so long that she could have learned how to make a proper apple tart, and the English have no natural understanding of pastry. I shall certainly pay Citizeness Minta my sincere compliments.'

From the Rue Hurepoix one could reach the Compas d'Or in a quarter of an hour, Jens had said. After the same space of time, however, Mary and Holland were instead knocking at the door of a somewhat dilapidated mansion on the Rue Vaugirard. It had taken most of the journey to convince Holland that this was not a pointless detour. Indeed, he still thought as much, but he had stopped saying so.

'We can't spare more than five minutes,' he warned.

'Yes, yes, I know,' Mary agreed. 'I am certain he will understand.'

A servant ushered them into a small study; the gentleman was dressing for an evening engagement, and would be with them shortly.

Five minutes, said Holland to himself, and stood, arms folded, beside the marble fireplace. Mary, who had thanked the servant, perched on the edge of an upholstered armchair. They both watched as he lit candles and stirred the fire before leaving them in silence.

The door opened and a tall man entered; he was wearing a dressing-gown over his evening clothes.

'Mr Marshall!' cried Mary, springing to her feet. 'I am sorry to intrude upon you in this way, but, well, this gentleman and

I—' She turned to Holland, and he named himself. 'We must leave Paris straightaway, and we would be terribly grateful if you could help us.'

Marshall's gaze moved from Mary to Holland and back again, and he frowned. Closing the door softly behind him, he murmured, 'Indeed, ma'am, I hope that I can. Although I am surprised not to see your husband here.'

In the space of two sentences, Mary's expression changed from relief to mortification, and her face flamed more brightly than the fire. 'Oh, it is not *that* kind of help,' she urged. 'You may still find it all rather . . . but please let me explain.'

She managed a neat balance between illumination and concision. Mr Shy was not mentioned and Holland's actions remained somewhat shadowy, but her essential plea was clear: Mr Vangenzen had been arrested and might find himself in serious trouble. If he did, would Mr Marshall please render any assistance that he could?

Marshall had seated himself at his desk during Mary's recital – it had not been *that* succinct – and when it ended he considered her thoughtfully. 'Am I to understand that your own . . . connection with Great Britain is not quite ended?'

'Yes sir, that is correct.'

'Despite which, both you and this gentleman have held yourselves out to be American citizens or closely connected to my nation.' Marshall's voice grew stern. 'As an American, I am offended by that deceit, and if you had employed it to harm American interests, I could not countenance it. No, ma'am, not in the slightest degree.' He paused, frowning and fingering the edge of the blotter. 'However . . . I don't believe that you managed to do us any harm, and who knows but we may find ourselves allied with Britain in the future – even the near future.'

'I hope so, sir,' said Mary.

'Well, perhaps we had better leave our hopes to one side, but there is also a practical point to be made. Knowing the true state of affairs, I would find myself in a difficult position if you were apprehended by the French authorities and attempted to trade upon your American credentials.'

'We would not do so,' Mary promised.

'If the French come after us, they will know that we're English,' said Holland, 'whatever we might say.'

'Hm, very likely,' Marshall agreed. 'You have given me another problem, however. Having availed myself of the legal protection of the French government, I am obliged to render what Mr Blackstone calls "local allegiance" while I remain in this country. I am duty bound, therefore, neither to behave in a treacherous manner towards France, nor to give aid or counsel to anyone who would do the same, and it seems to me that whatever you have been up to comes perilously close to treachery.'

Holland blew out his breath; time was passing, and if Marshall did not mean to help, why couldn't he say so plainly? *Blackstone, for God's sake.* Trying hard not to sound impatient, he said, 'I'm no lawyer, sir, but as I see it, if it hadn't been for a kind of treachery against Britain, the . . . information that I'm concerned with would never have come to France in the first place. I am simply trying to retrieve it.'

His effort was not wholly successful; certainly Mary heard the note of irritation, and somewhat more smoothly she added, 'The situation is rather like the pursuit of a criminal when the hue and cry is raised. Of course, there was no actual hue and cry in this case, but surely Captain Holland was performing his lawful duty in recovering *British* information, and not committing a crime.'

'That is an interesting way of putting it,' said Marshall. 'We certainly know of the hue and cry in America, but how the doctrine squares with that of local allegiance, I could not say. There may be no firm precedent, in which case I must be guided by my conscience and general legal principles.'

Oh God, Holland groaned to himself; he was half-expecting another lecture on general legal principles.

In fact, Marshall was almost finished. 'I am grateful for the warning about Mr Vangenzen,' he said. 'My position here is not very certain, but I will do what I can for him, although I wish he had not involved himself in this business.'

'Oh, thank you,' breathed Mary. 'Thank you so much. I cannot tell you how— And you will try to help Minta too?'

'She is his lawful wife?'

'Yes. Aminata Vangenzen.'

'Very well. And what about the two of you?'

'You don't owe us anything, sir,' said Holland.

'No, but . . .' Marshall smiled. 'I would like to assist a gallant lady, especially one who can equate the clandestine actions of a British officer to the hue and cry.'

'Well, I—' Mary turned to Holland.

'If you had a map of France, sir, that would be the greatest help.'

'Yes, I believe I do.' Marshall consulted his bookcase and produced a volume of highly detailed plates. 'It's the old Cassini, I am afraid, and rather out of date.'

'That's fine, sir,' said Holland. He surveyed the pages quickly. 'Even the Revolution won't have changed the geography.'

'Take what you like. I have been meaning to buy a copy of the *Atlas National*, and this will give me a good excuse.'

Holland tore out several pages. 'It might be an idea, sir, to destroy this book, in case the police trace us to you.'

'I shall do so,' said Marshall, 'and I shall take care to forget the very fact of this meeting. I must thank you for it, however. I doubt very much whether anything at the Théâtre des Arts will interest me quite so much.'

The candles were still burning in the sitting-room when Sergeant Fondard turned Vangenzen's key in the lock and opened the door to the *appartement*. Several men under his command waited below in a darkened carriage; only Déprez had followed him up the three flights of stairs and now stepped over the threshold and into the silent passageway.

A muffled cry alerted them to someone's presence in the room beyond. Fondard had drawn his pistol, and the two men advanced cautiously. They relaxed when they saw Minta, and Fondard returned his weapon to his coat pocket. Having removed her gag, he assumed a meditative pose, arms folded, while she caught her breath. After a moment's hesitation, Déprez untied the cords that bound her to the chair, as his colleague seemed little inclined to perform that service.

'Citizeness Minta, I believe?' Fondard's chin all but disappeared in the thick folds of his neck as he stared down at her. 'I am Fondard, and this is Colonel Déprez of the Army. What, pray, is the meaning of this?'

'My— What have you done with Citizen Vangenzen?' she demanded, scowling at him in return. 'Where is he? He has done nothing wrong!'

'Oh ho!' cried Fondard. 'You must answer our questions first, I think, for we find you in a situation that demands an explanation.'

She shrugged as if dismissing this man as well as the Ministry of Police, and in truth despair had made her fearless. 'Beware Fondard', Jens's note had said, but what choice did she have, even if he were a devil? 'Well?' Her tone was brusque.

'Where is your mistress?' Déprez asked. 'Where is Mad— Citizeness Vangenzen?'

'Ha! You are very proper, colonel, but I am his wife, not her. She is a bad woman – a spy and a traitor, just as I said in my letter.'

'A spy?' Fondard demanded. 'For the British?'

Minta nodded. 'And now she has run away with the secret plans that she stole from the Ministry of Marine. She and that man. I tried to stop them, but—'

'What man?'

'He calls himself Ogbourne, but his real name is Holland.'

'Ogbourne!' 'Holland!' Fondard and Déprez repeated the names in tones of amazement.

'Captain Robert Holland?' Déprez persisted. 'Are you certain? My God,' he murmured, 'I cannot believe it – he is in Paris and almost under my hand,' and then, more urgently, 'we must find this man, sergeant!'

'We must find them both, for they are two great prizes, I think. But first we must gather our forces.' He turned to Minta, and now the tone of command was clear. 'So, woman, tell me immediately what you know of these two. Firstly, when did they leave this place, and where were they going?'

'What is the time?'

Déprez consulted his watch. 'It is now a quarter to eight.'

'They have been gone almost an hour,' said Minta. 'They meant to leave Paris straightaway, but first they were going to the Rue Hurepoix to meet Jens.'

'Jens the art dealer? Damn him!'

Minta nodded. 'He is one of their confederates. There was another, but he is dead – as is Boyle, the inventor, whom they wished to spirit out of France.'

'Ah,' cried Fondard, his eyes sparkling, 'this becomes more intriguing by the moment! You will tell the rest, but first—' He strode to the window and flung it open. 'You there!'

A voice came floating up from the street. 'Yes, Sergeant Fondard?'

'Go, all of you, and pass the word at each of the city gates. A close watch is to be kept tonight for two men and a woman – the woman English, and one of the men also, but they may claim to be American. The names on their papers are Vangenzen and Ogbourne. The other man is a Swiss called Jens. They are to be held under guard, and I am to be informed immediately.' He considered. 'No English or Americans are permitted to leave Paris – whatever their names. Do you understand?'

'Yes, sergeant.'

'Good. Then go quickly.'

Fondard left the open window and turned back into the room. A gust of cold air whirled the curtains behind him, and caused the candles to smoke and gutter. 'And now, if you please,' he ordered, 'I will hear the rest of your tale.'

In so far as she was able, Minta told it. She had considered what she would say if the police appeared, so her account was largely credible. It also had the advantage of being true, in so far as it went.

And that was the problem. Having decided, miserably, that she must sell Mary to save Vangenzen, she felt obliged to show herself a substantial informer. Yet the more she revealed, the harder it was to present Vangenzen as an innocent victim of the schemes and stratagems being woven around him. She was vaguely conscious of not having quite managed it, and attempted to disguise her failure by a confident conclusion. 'They were all in league together. They have used my poor husband, who trusted them, and also Citizen Boyle, both of whom wished only to serve France.'

'I see, yes,' said Fondard, nodding, 'a most fascinating and remarkable account. One thing puzzles me. How did Citizen Vangenzen ever come to marry this Englishwoman?'

'Well, I suppose . . . she is very beautiful, and charming.' Without thinking Minta turned to Déprez. He was more sympathetic somehow. 'Many men have been fooled by pretty women.'

Déprez found her scrutiny uncomfortable. 'Indeed,' he began, 'but—'

'But was he not married to you at the time?' finished Fondard, apparently bewildered. 'It is strange indeed that he should have forgotten that fact when he went to England – for paint, I think you said?'

'Yes,' said Minta nervously, 'I mean, no, he did not forget, only . . . he was confused. He thought, perhaps, that our marriage was not quite legal – and she encouraged him. She said . . . I don't remember, but it was something about the law.'

That detail, plucked in desperation, touched a chord with Déprez, and he nodded. 'Miss Finch has a considerable interest in English law. If you were also married in England—'

'We were.'

'Then she might have known of some impediment.' Déprez did not express his belief that Mary Finch would never have employed such a device to entrap a man, for, in truth, what did he really know of her character? *You like to hold her up as some kind of ideal, but that is nonsense.* He frowned in self-condemnation.

'Well, perhaps,' Fondard acknowledged, 'it is possible. But really, it is a matter for curiosity, which we may resolve later. The important task is to recover the plans and bring these spies to justice. I hope we will receive word of them soon.'

'And if they have already left Paris?' asked Déprez.

'Then we shall pursue them. At least, I shall do so. Perhaps you have other duties, colonel?'

'None that take precedence over this,' said Déprez. 'The

capture of these spies will bring me the greatest pleasure. I have a particular interest in this fellow, Holland.'

'I thought you might. Well, I believe our work here is finished. I propose that we withdraw to the Café de Chartres and await developments.'

'The Café de Chartres?' queried Déprez. 'Why?'

'Why not? It would be a shame to miss our dinner, and later we may not have the chance.'

The two men started to withdraw, but the sound of Minta's voice stopped them, as it had previously drawn them into the *appartement*. 'You are leaving?'

'It is as I have said, citizeness.'

She hesitated. 'I am not to be arrested?'

Fondard shook his head. 'On the contrary, you have been most helpful.'

'What of Citizen Vangenzen?'

'He has suffered no harm. He has been taken to the Hôtel de Police for questioning.'

'And now?' A tightness in her throat made the words difficult to utter.

Fondard paused, but not like one who is uncertain of his reply. On the contrary, his words came easily. 'And now he will go to the Châtelet. There is little point in sending him to the Temple, as he will assuredly be condemned to death in a day or so.'

'Death?' gasped Minta. 'But I have told you—'

Fondard spread his hands. 'The man is a traitor, my dear.'

'No!'

The next things happened very quickly. Minta sprang at Fondard like a tigress, and calmly as a hunter he drew his pistol and shot her down.

'My God!' cried Déprez, recoiling. Then he knelt at her side. She was quite dead. 'Was that necessary?'

Fondard returned the spent pistol to his pocket. 'A pity,' he agreed. 'I liked her spirit. But I must return to Paris when this is over, and believe me, colonel, there is nothing so dangerous as a vengeful woman at your back.'

21

That compliment was almost all that Fondard had to say on the subject of Minta Vangenzen, and he descended the stairs of the Maison des Chevrons without the slightest evidence of discomfiture. After instructing one of his remaining subordinates to 'make the appropriate arrangements in the lodgings on the third floor,' he climbed into the carriage and gave directions to his favourite restaurant. Déprez, still somewhat shaken, joined him in the vehicle, and they set off.

Only a few words were exchanged during the drive to the Café de Chartres. Another shower of rain drummed lightly on the roof, and this provided a counterpoint to the horse's clipping tread even when conversation lagged.

'They will make for one of the Channel ports,' observed Fondard.

'Yes,' Déprez agreed, 'unless they have made some particular arrangements. Some rendezvous or other.'

'What rendezvous? Their actions tonight were not planned.'

'No, they are seeking safety only.'

The restaurant was crowded when they arrived, but it was clear that the democracy of the dinner queue did not apply to Sergeant Fondard. No sooner had he made his presence known to the *maitre d'hôtel* than he and Déprez were unobtrusively conducted to a secluded table at the back of the room, away from the noise and bustle.

'Not too near the kitchen, Pierre,' murmured Fondard.

'No, citizen. Certainly not.'

The proprietor, who knew Fondard very well, paid a special visit to their table. The two of them conducted a lengthy disquisition on the evening's menu, during which several dishes were dismissed as ample for the ordinary customer but beneath the good sergeant's standard. The *cassoulet* was perhaps a trifle salty tonight, and the *gigot à la cuillère* . . .

'Not tonight. I could not recommend it in all candour.' (This was said gravely, with a hand to the heart.)

'Hmm, and much as I admire your goose *confit*, Benoit, I believe I would prefer something light. Light but tasty.'

In the end they agreed upon a veal *consommé*, partridges with onion sauce, a salad with hazelnuts and truffles, and a sweet omelette.

Déprez suffered this performance with scarcely concealed impatience. Were they awaiting vital intelligence that would set them instantly on the chase, or were they kicking their heels, at leisure for the evening? It was infuriating. But even he could not wholly resist the proprietor's earnest attention. When a look of horror greeted Déprez's request for a simple cup of coffee, he grudgingly amended this to a bowl of soup.

'If the colonel does not object to rustic fare, I would suggest the *sobronade* and perhaps some *pâté*?' The proprietor posed his suggestion hopefully. 'A beautiful duck *foie gras*?'

'Yes, yes, very well,' muttered Déprez.

'And the coffee to follow,' added Fondard. 'We are complete? Good.' When they were alone again he explained, 'You see, my friend, coffee *after* the meal. That is correct, but without food, at this time of the day?' He shuddered.

'I thought we were in a hurry.'

'Of course we are, but I fear we must make haste slowly, as our grandfathers taught. It may take some time before we receive word of our quarry, and until we do, it would be madness to upset the digestion.'

Déprez lapsed into a discontented silence. When the bread arrived, he said, 'I am curious about the encounter with Jens.

Why do you suppose they arranged to meet in the Rue Hurepoix?'

'Who can say?' replied Fondard with a shrug. 'It was judged to be convenient. And I doubt very much that any of them are there now.'

'Convenient in what way?' Déprez persisted. 'Did you not say that Jens' shop is in the Rue Geoffroy l'Asnier? Why not meet there?'

'He feared it was being watched?'

'Perhaps, but why choose the Rue Hurepoix in particular?' Déprez frowned and then pushed back his chair. 'I will go there now and have a look.'

'As you wish,' said Fondard largely. 'If one cannot eat in peace, it is better not to make the attempt. This little . . . investigation may bring you some tranquillity. I shall ask Benoit to keep the soup warm for you.'

Déprez wished to be active, to be up and doing, but he disliked Fondard's tone – as if a child's whim were being indulged. With an effort he replied evenly. 'Please not trouble yourself. I am not hungry.'

Fondard toyed absently with the stem of his wineglass. Next to actually being undismayed by his professional responsibilities, he valued the appearance of tranquillity. In this, it was fair to say that he was largely successful. Few people observing him that evening would have imagined that he had any cares beyond the culinary. In truth, however, he had given but half his attention to the ordering of his meal. With the other, he had been considering the problem of the two English spies, and the exercise had not left him in a good humour. In all likelihood they had already left the city. From Paris they would undoubtedly proceed west or northwest towards England. Dieppe was the closest port, but Calais and Le Havre were also possible, and neutral vessels sailed from all three. *Three roads and three ports – how to choose between them?*

In the present circumstances, he could think of no satisfactory answer. *Unless one of the guards has been keeping a closer watch than usual tonight and has marked their passage at the gates.* It was

313

not impossible. Two Americans, or two English, or one of each. *No, not impossible, but not as likely as one would hope.* 'Ah, excellent,' he murmured as the steaming bowl of soup was placed before him. 'And the bread? You have not forgotten the extra bread, I am sure?'

'No, sergeant,' said the waiter, bowing, and he motioned imperatively to one of his assistants.

Fondard was partway through his salad when a messenger arrived, the most reliable of his subordinates. Hovering deferentially over his chief's shoulder, he relayed his information in a toneless murmur. 'Twice they have been seen, sergeant, or maybe not at all. The guard at the Barrière Nationale says he remembers a man and a woman with American papers – he *thinks* he remembers them – and there is a second report of an American at the Barrière de Passy. No woman was mentioned at the Barrière de Passy, however.'

'Hmm. No woman.' Fondard popped the last of the hazelnuts into his mouth. The first report sounded promising: a man and a woman, and the Barrière Nationale was convenient for the Calais road. *However, the other is just as convenient for Dieppe, and the woman's papers were predominantly English, as I recall, which might account for the omission.*

'Very well,' he replied, wiping his lips. 'Let us see what they can tell us at the gates.' He hoisted himself to his feet and told the constable to ready the carriage. 'And leave word for Colonel Déprez. I expect he will join us, when he has exhausted his passion for the Rue Hurepoix.'

It was raining again when Fondard arrived at the Barrière de Passy, and the information he received did not justify a descent into the wet. The American who had passed through turned out to be one of a group of artists visiting Versailles to make sketches. Fondard made a wry face at the mention of that profession, but the artists in question appeared to have set off before noon. It was highly unlikely, therefore, that their sojourn was of interest to the police.

The same could not be said for the man and woman who had passed through the Barrière Nationale, at least not immediately.

314

They had left Paris at approximately eight o'clock, on board the coach for Peronne.

'Peronne,' repeated Fondard thoughtfully, and climbed down from his carriage.

The guard could remember nothing more about either traveller, but he was conscious that they were important in some way, and that trouble might be visited upon whoever was found to be at fault for their escape. *He* could not justly be blamed for it, but when blame was being tossed about, it stuck to the poor fellow doing his duty more easily than the important ones who turned up afterwards asking questions.

In an effort to establish his diligence, therefore, he volunteered several details of his encounter with the two fugitives (as he now considered them). The man had appeared shifty; there had been an odd cast to his eye, such as one noted in the old days of superstition.

'The Evil Eye?' asked Fondard doubtfully.

'Exactly.' The guard tapped his own cheekbone to emphasise the difference. 'And the woman . . . I am convinced she was also a bad one.'

'On what do you base that conviction?'

'Oh, she had a way about her, citizen, and also jewels.'

'Jewels?'

'Yes, citizen. I noticed them particularly when she handed out her papers. Far too many rubies and diamonds for a good Republican. Perhaps she is an émigré, making use of false papers to spy on us?'

'Perhaps,' Fondard allowed with a slow nod. He nodded a second time as he caught sight of Déprez about to be interviewed by another of the guards. 'Let him pass,' he called, and then continued, 'Well, my friend, you seem to have been most careful and most attentive. I congratulate you.'

The guard permitted himself a modest bow. 'Thank you, citizen. Naturally, having received no warning, I took no formal notice of these persons, but it is my duty at all times to—'

'Would you say that they were travelling *together* on the Peronne coach, this man and woman?'

315

Being interrupted by an unexpected question resulted in a gaping, piscine expression that rather undermined the guard's show of confidence. 'I . . . the coach was dark, citizen, and full of people.'

'Ah, the coach was dark, of course!' agreed Fondard in the tone of one for whom many dark corners had suddenly been illuminated. He touched his finger to his lips and continued, 'Perhaps it contained other dangerous passengers? An entire coach load, perhaps?'

'Perhaps,' muttered the guard.

The admission seemed to gratify Fondard, and his tone was pleasant as he turned aside to greet Déprez. 'You missed a good dinner,' he chided, 'but naturally you fellows of the general's staff are above such concerns.'

Déprez replied curtly. 'But we are not above following a trail – however unlikely. Miss Finch and Captain Holland are making for Dunkerque.' With some satisfaction he explained what he had discovered in the Rue Hurepoix – the office of the shipping agent, the list of vessels belonging to his principals, and the French ports that they frequented. He had even seen a timetable, although he could not vouch for its accuracy.

It was a coup, a damned clever coup, and Fondard had a deep suspicion of cleverness in other people. 'How did you manage to obtain the lists at this time of night?' he demanded.

'One of the clerks lives above the office, and he was willing to be helpful.'

'Ah, that was fortunate – you had good luck. Ships sailing out of Dunkerque are owned by Vangenzen, you say? Well, well. Everyone is full of mystery tonight. I thought the fellow was an artist.'

'The ship-owner is a cousin – a relation of some kind. A Dutchman. Indeed, Miss Finch said something to me about the family having shipping interests in the old world and the new.'

'And you remembered it,' said Fondard. 'Well, well.' He smiled thinly, but paused only a moment before clapping Déprez on the shoulder and calling him a clever fellow to have put the pieces together so neatly. 'What do you say – perhaps this fanciful story of a sorcerer and an adventuress travelling to Peronne is another trail worth following?'

The question was a ludicrous one – of course even a fanciful report must be pursued, especially when it put two Americans on a northbound coach! There was enough of an edge to Fondard's voice, however, to warn Déprez not to overstep the mark; not to presume on having put on a good show. Command of the chase, such as it was, rested with the police agent.

'I think it would be advisable to pursue the Peronne coach with all haste,' Déprez replied soberly.

Fondard seemed to consider this, and then answered thoughtfully. 'Pursue it, yes, but not with all haste.'

'No?'

There was genuine surprise in Déprez's voice, and Fondard smiled. *We are not quite so brilliant as we think.* 'I shall – if you permit – first send word to Lille,' he purred, 'to block the road to Dunkerque.'

'Yes, of course,' Déprez agreed. He was also a proud man, and the words did not come easily to him. 'I had forgotten.'

'An easy mistake,' said Fondard largely. 'We will pay a short visit to the Montmartre station and then be on our way. I hope you will not be discommoded if we travel through the night? No? Excellent. But of course you are familiar with the hardships of the campaign.' He smiled. 'And your mention of the Dutchman reminds me of another matter that one oughtn't to forget. It may be some few days before our attention can be turned again to Citizen Vangenzen. I will have him sent to the Temple after all.'

There was one flaw in the planned pursuit, which was that Mary and Holland were no longer on the Peronne coach. They had passed through the Barrière Nationale at a little past eight o'clock, but on arriving in the village of Franciade, a fortunate disturbance had taken place. The posting-house courtyard had been congested, with several coaches changing their teams, and the postilions from rival services to Beauvais loudly disputing the right to a pair of horses. A sudden, brisk fall of

317

rain had sent grooms and travellers scurrying, and in the resulting confusion Holland had bundled Mary out of their vehicle and into one bound for Amiens.

After that tumult, the night's journey had been largely uneventful. The changes had been straightforward, and the condition of the road itself had not occasioned any delays. The only real difficulties had fallen upon Holland. Their coach was a heavy, ponderous vehicle, with dubious springs and plenty of room for passengers. The motion, a regular if uneven sway, sway, sway, dip, had produced Holland's usual internal distress. An open window might have alleviated this, but unfortunately an old woman had objected to such madness, lest she and her granddaughter expire from the draught and the falling damps. For almost fifteen miles, therefore, deep breathing and concentration had provided his only relief. Holland had not been sorry to part from these two valetudinarians at Creil, and before their places could be filled, he had moved to the empty place beside Mary and also disabled the window fastening. And thus the night's adventure had ended well. The three men who boarded the coach had merely turned up their collars, and Mary had fallen asleep with her head against Holland's shoulder.

The following morning they arrived at Breteuil, where their postilion announced a longer stop in order that the passengers might refresh themselves. Mary ordered breakfast for herself and Holland, and she was also charged with finding out — by casual conversation — what sort of onward travel arrangements might be possible when they reached Amiens. Holland, who could never have too much fresh air when travelling, walked up and down in the courtyard.

While not large, the posting-house boasted a comfortable public room. Having given her order, Mary stood by the fire, warming her hands and thinking about the journey to come. When they reached Amiens they would be nearly halfway to Dunkerque. Halfway home? *No*, she reminded herself, for there was still the crossing to be arranged. *But halfway to the coast of France, and so far, all is well*. She crossed her fingers in a fold of her gown. *Perhaps Mr Vangenzen has been released, and he and Minta are laughing about our precautions. Well, not laughing, perhaps, but . . .* She crossed the fingers of her other hand.

The heat of the fire had nearly penetrated her boots when the coffee arrived, so she returned to her table. The innkeeper presented the beverage with a flourish and pronounced it a speciality of the house, but it was particularly bitter and required most of the milk to render it drinkable. Mary said that it was delightful in the hope that this would inspire further conversation. It did, but before she was able to learn anything useful about Amiens, the arrival of a second coach and a flurry of orders for food, drink, and hot water for a lady who had slipped in the yard and spoiled her dress, drew her host away.

A young woman brought breakfast: two portions of eggs, a generous basket of rolls, a pot of jam, and a large knob of sweet butter. It looked delicious, and Mary wondered how long she ought to wait for Holland. Travelling generally did away with his appetite, she knew, and it would be a nuisance to let her food grow cold if he were only going to pick at his.

Suddenly it occurred to her that, at least as regards this meal, she was in charge and Holland her dependant. *How funny to think that I have both the funds and the authority to manage them.* Of course, she had grown used to spending money – sometimes the ease with which she dispersed large sums quite surprised her – but she had never had the opportunity of displaying her skill in Captain Holland's company. *I daresay he will dislike my having the run of things,* she thought, *but that is what comes of not learning French.*

Presently the young woman returned and asked whether she should take away the second plate. It would be no trouble; she could easily keep everything warm until the gentleman – 'citizen', she meant – returned.

The girl's question was surprising; her apparent concern was hardly in keeping with Mary's experience of French servants, and how had she known that the second breakfast was for a man? A polite, perfunctory answer was on the tip of Mary's tongue, but she paused and studied her interrogator. She was quite pretty, 'with a good deal more dash than was good for her', as Mrs Tipton would say.

Mary found herself stiffening. She disliked silly girls, and she began to suspect that she was conversing with one. 'I do not think the citizen cares very much about breakfast,' she remarked loftily.

The girl giggled and stroked the rim of the plate. 'No,' she agreed, 'neither do I.' Her glance flashed in the direction of Mary's half-consumed meal – or perhaps merely at her left hand and its forkful of egg. 'He is your husband?'

'Oh no, we . . . met on the coach.' She and Holland had decided to admit no familiarity other than what had resulted from their shared knowledge of English. At that moment, however, Mary was tempted to break their agreement. It was difficult to say, 'He is an American,' with an air of propriety, but she made the attempt.

The girl did not notice. 'He is very handsome,' she confided. 'You do not see it, of course, being married.' Her tone was sympathetic, as if the wedded state had dulled Mary's senses.

Mary gaped, stammered, and was abandoned. From her position the girl could view the courtyard, and after standing first on tiptoes and then leaning forward, she snatched up the coffee pot and hurried towards the kitchen. 'I do not believe that he speaks French!' Mary advised the retreating figure. *Ridiculous creature . . . hussy*, she stormed to herself. *And not pretty at all, really. I doubt he pays her the slightest attention.*

With considerable self-possession, she buttered and ate half a roll. Then she surveyed the other tables and their occupants. No, none of the men could be described as handsome. The window to the courtyard was behind her. She was certainly not going to turn round, but her cloak had slipped from the back of her chair, and in retrieving it, she caught a glimpse – by chance – through the window. There they were, side by side on a bench, chattering away like old friends. At least, *she* was speaking, and laughing; his role seemed to be that of attentive listener.

Mary ate her eggs slowly, but she was finished by the time

320

Holland slid onto the empty chair opposite her. 'That was a bit of luck,' he observed in a low voice.

'I expect that Breteuil sees very few handsome visitors,' Mary agreed.

Confusion followed by wry humour flashed across Holland's face. 'If we weren't in a damned fix, I'd laugh at you,' he warned. 'You're jealous of a girl who spoke to me for five minutes.'

'I am not jealous,' Mary protested, adding privately, *it was more than five minutes.*

'Well then, put your chin back where it belongs and listen. That girl's young man – whom I admit she doesn't deserve – works at the telegraph station in Belloy.'

The note of warning was clear, and Mary leaned towards him across the table. 'What is that?' she whispered.

'A telegraph,' he repeated, and now his words were barely audible, 'like the one we have between London and Portsmouth.' This comparison failed to enlighten her, so with his fork Holland divided his eggs into a line of small mounds. 'Each of these is a station,' he explained, 'five or six miles apart. They're built on hills, usually, or on the top of church steeples. A message is sent from the first station to the second, which then repeats it to the third, and so on.'

'A message,' Mary repeated. 'Any sort of message? I mean, how is it sent?'

'By code. Our machines use shutters, and the different combinations of open and closed shutters correspond to different letters. I expect the French use something similar.'

A tense, anxious feeling began to flip-flop in the pit of Mary's stomach. 'The first station . . .' She took a deep breath. 'Is in Paris?'

Holland nodded. 'Yes, and the line runs north. To Lille, Marie said.'

That name pierced her anxiety, but no sooner had it done so than she told herself not to be ridiculous. 'And you think— But *would* the police send a message about us?'

'The police or the Army. We're spies, remember. And if Minta has told them about . . . they will want to make damned sure *it* doesn't get back to England.'

Holland had set down his fork, but now he was fiddling with it, his finger running up and down the narrow handle. 'This is my fault. I should have known about . . . Now that I think of it, I'm certain that I heard something about the French having a telegraph – maybe even that it ran from Paris to Lille. It certainly sounds damned familiar now. But I must have forgotten about it.'

The apologetic tone in his voice made Mary frown. For what had he to apologise? Not remembering that the French had a telegraph, when he had had the *Ammonite*, and Mr Boyle, and Mary herself to consider? The fact that he had heard about it in the first place seemed extraordinary. *I wonder if the French know all about our telegraph – perhaps they do. I suppose it would be of great interest to their agents.*

French agents. The image of Paul Déprez appeared in her mind's eye. *Thank goodness he is not part of our troubles.* 'Well, it does not matter,' she urged. 'And we know about it *now*, which is something. I suppose a telegraph is a very reliable means of communicating?'

'I think so. It isn't any use at night, of course, but in daylight, if the weather is clear . . . The real problem is the speed – a message sent this morning from Paris would outrun us in half an hour.'

'Good Heavens!' gasped Mary. 'Then we may be arrested at any moment.' She quickly scanned the room, with little thought now to the attractiveness of their fellow patrons.

'Well, don't forget that we set out last night for Peronne. Perhaps they won't have traced us at all, or they'll think that we're somewhere on the Flanders road. Lille is the biggest danger, though, because it must have a sizeable garrison.'

Mary's fear ebbed and flowed with each sentence – yet surely the last was good news? 'But we have no intention of going to Lille,' she urged.

'No, but anyone chasing us will guess that we're heading for the Channel. If a troop of cavalry is sent west from Lille, they will cut us off before we can reach the coast.'

Then if we are not captured today, we shall be trapped tomorrow.

Mary remembered being stopped by soldiers on her way to Paris – her dread of being questioned, of making a mistake – and her heart began to pound. Yes, she had managed it then, but the danger had been slight, negligible, whereas now . . . Now there would be armed men searching for them; a cordon of soldiers with their backs to the sea.

The image wavered, and she pushed it aside. Then she smiled at Holland – a thin smile. 'What should we do?'

Holland had watched the play of emotions across her face. Was there another girl in the world who would respond to danger as she did? Even as he wished that she were a hundred miles away, that she had never left England, he experienced a strange delight that she was there with him. 'Carry on to Dunkerque as quick as we can,' he said. 'We can't exactly lose ourselves among the locals, and if we hang about we're bound to attract the attention of someone who has heard about us.'

'Yes, I agree,' said Mary. 'But ought we to remain on the coach? There may be soldiers in Amiens.'

'We'll have to risk that. And the coach is our only choice – unless there are horses.'

There were no horses. At least, those at the inn were needed for the coach traffic, and the innkeeper knew of no farmers who would hire out their animals to strangers. Not even old Jacques, who loved money more than anything. It was impossible.

'Impossible,' he repeated, and folded his arms across his chest in pointed illustration of that fact.

'I see. Well, thank you,' said Mary.

It had not, perhaps, been the ideal moment to seek the innkeeper's aid. He had not liked to see Marie – his daughter, and a great trial to him – flirting with the American, and now this Englishwoman was also behaving strangely. Whoever heard of riding for pleasure when there was a perfectly good coach practically waiting at the door? Why did his customers insist on making things difficult when they were really very simple? (The woman who had slipped in the courtyard had also made a nuisance of herself. Was it his fault that the yard was slippery? When they were wet, stones were slippery; another simple matter.) Having banished Marie to the kitchen, he wanted nothing more from the morning's visitors than that they should settle themselves into their vehicles and leave him in peace. Customers! They would be the death of him.

Mary knew nothing of Marie nor of the innkeeper's particular travails, but her suggestion that it was fine weather for the time of year – that one often rode for pleasure in England, right through till Christmas – was received with such incredulity that she soon gave way.

'The Amiens coach leaves in ten minutes exactly – do you care to board, citizeness?'

Mary nodded.

'And the citizen also?' A curt jerk of the head indicated Holland, who was standing in the doorway.

'Yes.'

Mary and the innkeeper wished each other good day, with very little enthusiasm on either side. She followed Holland into the courtyard, and the innkeeper began to clear their table – another task that fell to him until Marie had learned to behave herself.

One of the breakfasts had barely been touched. 'English,' he muttered to himself, and then, with almost the same note of weary condemnation, 'Americans.'

22

Mary and Holland set off again, together with the three phlegmatic men and a woman whose luggage consisted of two sacks of vegetables and a basket containing a live chicken. Mary had little direct experience of farm animals, and the bird's beady gaze made her feel vaguely uneasy. *You will be someone's dinner,* was her firm but silent pronouncement, and she tried to remember which king of France had said that all of his subjects ought to have a chicken in the pot every Sunday.

Presently, however, her opinion moderated. The fowl was well behaved, and the presence of onions and turnips brought a reassuring domesticity to their coach. The bird's owner also looked placid, hardworking, and unlikely to be associated in anyone's mind with espionage. She was like the farmer's wife who went marketing in the village on Tuesdays, or visited her daughter, perhaps bringing a jar of preserves as a gift for the rector. *Of course, that is how it would be in England. In France, I daresay the farmers' wives declared the market an unjust prerogative of the nobility and drowned the priest in the river.*

The woman and her luggage left the coach at Hebecourt, and two of the men exchanged remarks on not very interesting subjects such as the likelihood of rain, and whether a recent interruption of the postal service would be over soon. One took a generally positive view of things – rain was natural at this time of year; indeed, it was necessary for the crops – while the other was unreservedly gloomy – an invoice from his business associate had not come through; very likely it had been stolen; thefts were common nowadays; the order would be cancelled, and his business would fail. Their differing outlooks were illustrated through the windows of the coach. On one side, the sun shone, while on the other dark, brooding clouds gathered. *A storm*, thought Mary, *but is it coming or going?*

They reached Amiens shortly before noon and had no difficulty entering the city. A soldier and a vaguely uniformed member of the National Guard obliged them to halt at the city gate, but their interrogation was perfunctory and conducted largely with the postilion. By the time Mary's stomach muscles had unclenched and her heart had resumed its normal rate of beating, they had passed the market and the stately *hôtel de ville*, and were approaching their destination, a comfortable posting-house in the shadow of the cathedral.

The landlady of the Lion d'Or was a stout, red-faced woman who looked as if she rarely descended from her perch behind the bar. She revived amazingly, however, with the appearance of visitors, and initiated a remarkable flow of questions and commentary.

Holland found shelter at a corner table beyond her line of sight, but politeness drew Mary forward. In a very short time she had revealed her name and a history of her journey from Paris (both fictitious), and had learned some surprising facts about her hostess. Madame Pollet – '"Citizeness Pollet", I suppose I ought to say, but I was married for nearly forty years, and no decent revolution would suggest otherwise' – had not always lived in Amiens – 'no, nor always had this figure, although you mightn't think it, looking at me now'. She had spent her girlhood in Paris, and had worked as a chambermaid in one of the most exclusive townhouses in the Place Royale. 'And how is the dear old Place? I suppose I oughtn't to call it the "Place Royale", but old habits are hard to break.'

'Oh, it is quite well, I believe,' said Mary cautiously. 'I mean, quite as it has always been.'

Madame Pollet recognised that Mary's accent was not Parisian, although she could not place it. She frowned thoughtfully, attempting to do so.

'Oh no,' Mary admitted, 'I am from . . . Toulouse.' It was the most distant French city that she could think of, and she hoped that sounded sufficiently exotic to Madame Pollet.

'Ah, you are quite the traveller! I was a great one for travelling when I was a girl, although I daresay those days are behind me now, on account of my bad leg. And what brings you to Amiens?'

Madame having been a great traveller brought Mary's heart to her mouth, but the actual question posed was not quite so formidable. Mary had resolved to broach the subject of her onward travel and transport by a series of general enquiries that would gradually include Dunkerque, and she began to put that plan into operation. But before she could utter more than the first syllable of 'Abbeville', there was a clatter of booted feet on the stairs, and a uniformed man – an officer – strode into the room. His right sleeve was folded across his chest, and he was clumsily fastening his sword belt with his left hand.

An officer! Mary gasped and turned away from him. Holland leaned forward, his hand thrust into the pocket of his greatcoat.

'Captain Fabre!' cried Madame Pollet. 'Come and meet our visitor!'

'Not now, grandmother, I am busy!' He completed his task, advanced a pace, and adjusted the scabbard.

'You, busy? Have the Austrians begun fighting again? The Holy Roman Emperor, perhaps?' She winked at Mary.

'Not him, the scoundrel, but important work nevertheless! I must rouse my men immediately – there is not a moment to lose.'

With a curt gesture not unlike a salute, he strode past the two women and through the door to the courtyard, his cocked hat under his good arm.

For two in the room the surprise and relief were palpable. Holland sat back in his chair, and Mary exhaled deeply. 'Oh

327

my,' she murmured, in what she hoped was an exclamation of innocent surprise.

'*His men,*' scoffed Madame Pollet, although not unkindly. 'Most men are children, longing to dress up, and the ones who actually do so – these soldiers – are the worst. You would think this was the battle of Fleurus, from the way he talks. That was where he lost his arm, you know, but the battle was a great triumph for France. He often speaks of it.'

'Wh-what do you suppose is the matter?' asked Mary, although she could make a very good guess. The telegraphed warning had come through – and now they would be trapped in Amiens!

'Some nonsense or other. A messenger arrived for him a short while ago, very full of himself and giving *me* orders! I could have boxed his ears! Still, I hope it *is* important, for poor Captain Fabre's sake. He has been dreadfully unhappy since coming to Amiens. He considers it a punishment, for nothing exciting ever happens here.'

Mary could feel herself growing hot; her blushes would surely betray her. *You must answer calmly. Whatever may happen, it has not done so yet.* 'But surely it is better if the town remains quiet.'

'Of course it is, for anyone who is not a soldier. But men think nothing of such things. They are so impractical – like children! Before the war we had six coaches a day – to Calais, Lille, Rouen, and all the Paris machines, of course. We kept fifty horses, and this parlour was crowded at all hours. But who can afford to travel, nowadays?'

'I—'

'Who can afford to buy things, even our lovely Amiens velvet?'

Mary shook her head sympathetically.

'Soldiers do not wear velvet, you know.'

'No, I—' Mary started to answer, but this time her sentence was truncated by something more formidable than Madame Pollet's imperious tongue. From the corner of her eye she could see Holland rise and move stealthily towards the stairway. *Heavens! What is he doing?*

His path would take him partway behind the bar, but so

long as she did not turn, Madame Pollet would not see him. *Oh please, let her not turn!* Mary forced herself to look away so as not to stare over her hostess's shoulder, and hurriedly affirmed that soldiers most certainly did not wear velvet, and that it was the same in Toulouse.

'You also weave velvet in Toulouse?' asked Madame Pollet. 'I had not heard that.'

Mary's mouth had gone dry, and she swallowed painfully before uttering a non-committal 'Mm.' Holland had reached the stairs, but if he made a sound, a squeak . . . 'Not velvet, silk!' she boomed, as if in celebration of that glorious fabric. 'From silkworms, you know.'

But no sooner had the words been uttered than she felt a prickle of doubt. Was it in Toulouse or Toulon that the French silk industry was based? Or perhaps Lyon? Her entire knowledge of the subject came from a disquisition by Vartan Nazarian on the Levant trade, and she could not quite remember what he had said. Where was Toulouse anyway? Unable to conjure even the slightest impression of Mr Marshall's maps of France, she assumed a confident smile.

'Oh yes, of course,' said Madame Pollet. 'Silk.'

'The silkworms eat the leaves of mulberry trees,' croaked Mary, one of the facts that she had retained with certainty. 'A great deal of European silk is made in Italy.' Pausing with his hand on the banister, Holland stared at her meaningfully and began to ascend. Up, up, up, and then he disappeared through the door at the top of the stairs.

Perhaps not surprisingly, Madame Pollet was not so very interested in either silkworms or their diet, nor did she have much to say – at least not very much that was good – about Italians. ('General Bonaparte has made them hop, from what Captain Fabre tells me.') She *was* happy to discuss silk dresses and the latest Paris fashions – 'I always made a particular point of my appearance when I was a girl, although you might not think so, seeing me now.'

Mary offered a few comments, but the silk incident had made her timid, and now she hesitated to put herself forward on the subject of Morocco leather, whitework embroidery, or French knots. Did one even call them 'French knots' in France? After a pause, therefore, during which Mary was certain she could hear someone moving in the room above their heads, Madame Pollet remarked, 'You are going to Abbeville, I think you said?'

This topic too necessitated a certain degree of creativity on Mary's part, but she had rehearsed it beforehand, and besides, its wholly fictitious nature was something of a defence. Quite confidently, therefore, she explained that she was paying a visit to a sickly relation – her husband's great aunt. Of course, the lady in question was not really ill, but she was lonely and liked attention. And there was an inheritance for those of her relatives who did not displease her.

'Ah, an inheritance,' said Madame Pollet knowingly. 'It is well to remember such things. I do not say to ignore charity and family feeling, but one must also be practical.'

'Yes, indeed,' Mary agreed.

If Captain Holland's disappearance had been surprising – and alarming – what happened next was worse. The door at the top of the stairs closed and down he came, firm of step and confidently dressed in the uniform of a French officer. He looked remarkably like Captain Fabre, in fact, apart from having two arms. With scarcely a glance to right or left, he crossed the parlour and moved towards the front door.

'I always think— Oh! Was that Lieutenant Vidal?' asked Madame Pollet. 'I did not see him come in. Lieutenant! Lieutenant!' she called, waving her handkerchief, but he was gone.

And in a moment, so was Mary. Crying distractedly that she had left her hat in the coach, she turned and hurried outside, deaf to Madame Pollet's calls.

Holland had just secured his own headgear, and now he slid Mary's arm through his. 'Quick march,' he ordered curtly.

Of necessity she fell into step beside him. 'What are we doing?' she hissed.

He glanced at the stables – empty, apart from the team that

330

had drawn their coach. A boy in a leather apron looked up from polishing a saddle and gazed at them disinterestedly. 'Getting out of Amiens, of course,' said Holland.

They crossed the courtyard and entered the street. The cathedral was on their right. 'Do you know the city at all?' he asked, keeping his voice low.

'No, I . . . that way is north, however.'

He turned immediately in the direction she had indicated, into a wider street that was bustling with shops and stalls. The sky had grown dull and overcast, and a cold wind was blowing, but it was midday and many people were abroad. Women walked arm-in-arm, or carrying a basket between them; a man trundled a barrow over the cobbles, and another led a horse, unsaddled and swishing its tail.

'That's what we want,' said Holland under his breath.

Mary's heart was pounding, but she felt strangely excited. Of course! When there were soldiers about, the best way to pass among them was in military dress. *Thank goodness Captain Holland thought to take this chance, and thank goodness he looks like an officer! He has exactly the walk and bearing, and now that he is in uniform* . . . It was still a terribly bold manoeuvre, but if they were quick, why should they not march right away? No one could possibly suspect them. 'What shall we do if we meet another soldier?' she whispered.

'Nothing, so long as I outrank him.' They paused at a junction and then hurried across. 'We're all right unless we meet the one-armed captain.'

'Captain Fabre? Why?'

'This is his dress uniform. I think he'll recognise it.'

On their left, they passed a substantial house whose wooden gates were ajar. Holland stopped short; inside, a groom was walking a beautiful grey horse up and down – saddled and apparently ready to be ridden. One horse, and they needed two. *Damn.* One was better than none, however. *If the groom goes inside, even if he doesn't, it might be worth—*

Before he could weigh up the risks of a confrontation against the prize of the grey, the exercise became moot. A second man, well dressed, appeared at the front door and began conversing with the groom. That made the odds too great, and Holland and Mary resumed their walk.

They crossed a bridge. Beneath them lay a canal or sluggish river, upon which men punted slowly in narrow boats with high, ungainly sterns. Several of the craft were moored beside the bridge, but even in their present need, Holland had no intention of attempting an escape by water. He hated boats, and a foreign boat on a strange river would be the worst possible combination.

They crossed another bridge. Now to their right the streets were narrower; small cottages leaned towards each other like old friends, with only a cobbled passage between them. Ought they to turn? It would be more secluded than their present route, but would it take them out of the city or only into a maze of courts and alleys?

Holland chose to carry on and almost immediately regretted his decision. Approaching them at a brisk pace were four soldiers and an officer. A junior officer? That seemed likely for such a small detail of men, but Holland was unfamiliar with the French insignias and could not be sure. Well, he would have to bluff it out. He could feel Mary's grip tighten on his arm, and he patted it. 'Eyes on me,' he whispered as the men advanced, 'and smile.'

Mary's knees were trembling, and the colour had drained from her face, but she did as she was bid, even smoothing Holland's collar, as if it had become disarranged. *Ignore them!* she commanded herself. She and Holland must seem to have not the slightest interest in anything but their own conversation. *We are making a promenade.*

Pitching her voice to suit the occasion, she began chatting to him casually. *'J'ai demandé au capitaine Fabre de bien vouloir m'éclairer sur la bataille dans laquelle nous avons vaincu les Autrichiens.'*

Holland nodded. 'Mm.'

'Le cher capitaine était très instructif, et il a fourni une explication d'une clarté exceptionelle.'

Closer, closer. Mary did not look, but she could sense the

soldiers' furtive glances, their studiously blank expressions. *'Quelle histoire passionnante,'* she chirped, *'et que vous êtes des héros, les soldats!'*

Fortunately the Frenchmen saluted first, and Holland was able to give the proper reply. *'Mais j'étais desolée quand il nous a renseigné au sujet de sa blessure,'* said Mary, and they were past.

Holland did not speak, but he patted her hand a second time. Mary continued to smile, but she breathed a silent prayer. *Thank God, thank God. Now please let us get out of the city.*

For some reason the precise nature of their onward flight had not occurred to her. While she knew, logically, that they could not very well walk to Dunkerque, her immediate attention was so focused on their current march that she had not thought beyond it. She was momentarily confused, therefore, when Holland turned sharply into a tavern courtyard – she bumped into him – and then led her into the establishment's modest stable. There were two stalls, and both were occupied.

Without a word, Holland saddled the first animal, quickly adjusting bridle, blanket, saddle girths, and stirrups. Then he turned to Mary. 'We'll go much faster on two horses,' he said, as though the matter had long been under discussion. 'Could you ride him?'

Ride, of course we must ride; and quickly too, or they will close the gates. But the horses looked enormous, and she had only ridden astride once in her life. Could she possibly make a French horse understand her? What if the commands were different? She bit her lip. 'Yes, of course.'

In what seemed like an instant, she was leading her horse, a black creature with three white stockings, through to the rear of the stable. *At least he follows readily enough.* Holland unbolted the doors, which opened onto another street, and lifted her into the saddle. He had shortened her stirrups, but a further adjustment was required before she felt even moderately secure.

Holland smiled up at her. 'All right?'

It seemed to Mary that she was sitting astride the roof of a house – a roof that moved. She answered in a small voice. 'Yes.'

Holland mounted his horse, turned him expertly, and walked

333

forward. Would Mary's do likewise? No. She applied a tentative heel to the animal's flank, and this produced an awkward sideways movement. She tried again, with no greater result than a lowering and then a shaking of the enormous head. Holland's horse was now almost ten yards ahead of her, and in a panic she kicked hard with both heels and her horse jumped, nearly unseating her.

Oh bother, you horrid thing! Behave! At least they were moving, however, and when she drew up beside Holland and the end of the street, she did not feel quite so terrified.

'All right?' he asked again.

This time her reply was slightly more confident. Then, peering left, she suddenly recognised a familiar scene. That was the way she and Vangenzen had entered Amiens! She turned to Holland, but he was looking straight ahead, and he spoke before she could enlighten him.

'Damn, I think . . . up ahead, that's the citadel.'

Mary had no idea what a citadel was, but the large, angled wall or earthworks looked very imposing. Then she noticed a flag – was it some kind of castle? 'This is the way to Abbeville,' she cried, pointing.

They wanted to go north, not west, and Holland hesitated. But to go north they must run a gauntlet of soldiers, and if the north gate was already closed, they would be trapped. 'Let's go,' he agreed.

They moved off, first walking and then trotting. Both Mary and Holland were listening tensely for an order to halt, and they rode in silence, willing their horses to hurry, but not daring to canter or exhibit any sort of alarm.

Holland thought that he heard a commotion behind them, but he did not turn. 'Whatever happens, don't stop unless I say so,' he said. 'If the gate is open when we get there, go straight on.'

Whatever happens; whatever happens. The words repeated uncomfortably in Mary's ears, a fitting accompaniment to her physical unease. She felt more like a sack than a rider, bumping along with little faith that she could manage her horse if required.

334

But with every stride they were drawing closer to the gate. She could see it, an opening in the old city walls. Yes, there were soldiers, and worse, a coach! The occupants were being questioned, and the vehicle blocked the way. Or did it? No, there was a gap between it and the wall! A gap – but it looked terribly small.

Holland had increased his speed, and Mary fell in behind him. *Whatever happens!* Now the gate was before them; she could see the road beyond. Someone called out, and her horse shied. *Oh God!* She caught a glimpse of a startled face through the window of the coach as her horse skipped forward. A soldier made a grab for her bridle, missed, and they were through, Mary ducking her head, as if she might not clear the arch.

They were through! A soldier ran after them, shaking his fist. Were they mad? Were they drunk? 'You are required to show me your papers!' he shouted.

Holland turned and waved his hat, smiling and acknowledging the apparent joke. Turning to Mary, he said, 'All right, let's go before they figure it out.'

And then the race began in earnest, more than a mile of furious galloping that sent them north and east in a sweep around the city. Mary had never ridden so quickly or so recklessly, but she could not help herself. Her horse was out of control – at least *she* could not stop his mad flight – and as he sped over the ground her one thought was to hang on. *Whatever happens!*

Fear and the intense awareness of sound, speed, and motion actually gave her a much better seat than she had ever displayed. She suddenly understood her horse's rhythm and adjusted to it. Her hold on the reins was titanic, but her hands settled naturally along his neck; she managed both to grip with her knees and to press her heels down into the stirrups, and she leaned forward like a jockey.

A jockey who lacked the elation of victory. She was white-faced and shaking when Holland indicated that they might slacken speed. Afterwards, she was not certain which of them had actually orchestrated the manoeuvre – she or her horse – but they had managed it somehow and with a minimum of fuss. As they walked and trotted a few steps, and then walked again, she was breathing as freely as if she had run the distance from Amiens herself.

'Well done,' said Holland, who had been dividing his attention between Mary, the way ahead, and the road behind them.

'Are they— Is anyone chasing us?' Mary gasped. She unpried her fingers from the reins and tried to smooth a sweaty tendril of hair away from her face.

'Not yet,' said Holland, 'but we're still too close to the city for my liking. We'll let them walk for a bit – to that tree with the broken branch – and then we must push on as swiftly as we can.'

The specified landmark appeared all too quickly, but the horses seemed reasonably fit, and the respite had revived them. At the word of command, they set out again at a brisk trot, and presently they joined the road to Doullens.

Perhaps the horses know this road, thought Mary. *Perhaps they regularly make this journey with their masters, and do not realise that today they are helping enemies to escape.*

'How are you feeling?' asked Holland. 'A bit more sure of yourself now?'

'Yes,' said Mary, 'although this horse does have an odd way of *bouncing*, sometimes, which makes me lose my place.'

'Lose your place?'

'You know, in the up-down-up-down. When I am *posting*.'

'Ah.'

'And I am certain that there is something wrong with this saddle – I am forever slipping and sliding about on it.'

'There is nothing wrong with the saddle,' said Holland, glancing first at it and then at the part of Mary with which it came into contact, 'only it's too big for you – which is no bad thing.'

Mary frowned at him, and when she realised what he meant, frowned more decidedly. She *was* feeling more comfortable riding, however, and could achieve the repeated changes of pace with a growing sense that her horse was responding to her orders and not merely walking or trotting as he saw fit. Walk, trot, the occasional canter, and back to the trot. It reminded her of riding lessons at White Ladies, under the censorious eye of Forrest, her groom.

White Ladies! She suffered a momentary pang that almost produced a sentimental observation about home and England. *Do you remember* . . . Further reflection, however, stifled the words before they could reach her lips. How ridiculous to speak as if White Ladies were nothing but a memory, and they would never see Mrs Tipton or any of their friends – well, *her* friends, at least – again. Besides, it might bring bad luck.

Mary resolutely turned her attention to the country passing on either side of them; gently rolling hills with a patchwork of fields, meadows, and woods. Now it wore a particularly sombre aspect, for the sky was grey and darker clouds wheeled overhead, but in the spring this would be a very pretty land. *When the trees are not so bare, and there is more than stubble in the fields. Even in England the countryside often looks dead in winter.* She tried to calculate how many weeks had passed since she had come to France, and then another thought occurred to her. She had meant to raise it before, only they had had so few opportunities for private speech since leaving Paris.

'I was wondering . . . what happened at the convent of the Little Fathers?' She glanced across at Holland as she spoke, and it seemed to her that his profile hardened. His unshaven cheek contrasted with the glory of his uniform, as if he were part of and estranged from military authority. 'You needn't tell me if you would rather not.'

'No,' he said, 'I don't mind.' But he did not answer straight-away, and when he did begin his account, his voice was remote, diffident. 'You've guessed that they were killed in the fire, of course.'

'Yes. What a terrible accident.'

'Mm, an accident,' Holland agreed, 'but we made a damned mess of it all, between the three of us. I made things clear to Mr Boyle at last, not just about myself, but about leaving France.

337

It came as a shock to him, but not as much as I thought it would. He didn't seem to mind returning to England.'

'I expect he was homesick,' said Mary.

'Maybe, but it meant knocking his idea about freedom of the seas on its head, and he had been dead keen— I mean, I had never managed to shake his belief in it before.'

'You might have done so, only he did not like to admit it. That is often the way with inventors and philosophers, I believe.'

'Well, whatever he thought about it all, he seemed willing to leave Paris, and so I . . . I sort of, put him to one side. I don't mean that I forgot about him, but I thought I could leave him to pack up his things, you know, and potter about, while Martel and I took care of everything else. Martel was going to see Jens, and I thought, depending on what he advised, I might . . .' He looked at her.

'I thought we had agreed that *I* would deal with the Ministry of Marine,' Mary complained.

'Yes, but it was such a mad thing to do – going back there – and especially on your own.'

'I was *not* on my own – Minta was with me.'

'And of course *that* ought to have reassured me.'

'But—'

'All right, I know, she stayed true at the Ministry. And I didn't go after you, but I wasn't thinking about things in the convent as clearly as I should have been. If I were, I wouldn't have let Martel anywhere near the *Ammonite*.'

'The *Ammonite*,' Mary repeated confusedly. 'But did it actually exist? I thought—'

'No, but Mr Boyle had made various models, and he still had a few sections of the boat he had sailed off the coast of Normandy. There was also the device that actually allowed the *Ammonite* to attack its target – the stinger, he called it. Naturally, we couldn't allow any of these things to fall into French hands.'

'Oh no,' Mary agreed. 'That would have been like leaving them the plans.'

'Exactly. Well, I ought to have seen to their destruction myself,' said Holland. 'I would have been more careful about it, if only to spare Mr Boyle's feelings. The *Ammonite* had been his work – his great triumph, after all.'

'It would have been difficult to see it destroyed, even if he knew it to be necessary.'

'I don't think that he *did* know it,' said Holland. 'I don't think he had actually thought through what was going to happen. He was quite old, you know, and not always strictly sensible. And then Martel finished with Jens more quickly than I'd expected, and he decided he might as well sort out the *Ammonite*. He didn't have a great deal of faith in anyone besides himself, you know, and he didn't like to hang about.'

Mary stared at him. 'Captain Martel set fire to the monastery?'

'He didn't mean to. The idea was only to burn the models and things, which were kept in one of the sheds. Unfortunately, he wasn't as clever with fire as he thought he was, and there must have been other things – flammable things – nearby. The fire took hold very fast, and then it spread to the main building. There were all sorts of treasures – furniture and things – stored in the upper rooms, and when they caught fire it was too much for us.'

'Goodness!' cried Mary. 'I saw the buckets scattered about in the garden.'

'Yes, the buckets,' said Holland. 'I had the devil of a time making Martel see that it was no good. It was his fire, and he was going to put it out. I did manage, at last, but then Mr Boyle . . .'

His voice died away, and they rode for a time in silence. Holland eased his horse into a canter, and Mary followed after only a short pause. She had not met the Reverend Samson Boyle, and consequently he had never seemed quite real to her. He had existed more as a problem than a person. She knew that Holland had liked him, however, and that knowledge informed her view. And whatever he had intended by bringing the *Ammonite* to France, he had not deserved such a terrible fate. Her stomach tightened at the thought of burning. *Like Joan of Arc.*

When they resumed the trot, Holland continued, 'Mr Boyle

went back inside the convent. Before I could stop him. I never thought he would do such a thing, and . . . he got away from me.'

'Of course you never thought it,' Mary assured him. 'He must have been mad to return to a burning building.'

'The smoke was worse. The passageway was like a black pit – like the entrance to hell. Nothing could have lived in there.' Holland paused and adjusted his reins. 'And then Martel went in after him.'

Captain Martel. Mary had a fleeting, but perfectly clear image of Martel in his dressing-gown, gravely passing her the sugar from a small, chipped pot.

Holland shrugged. 'He had never felt much sympathy for Mr Boyle. He thought it was ridiculous that I should try to argue with him.'

Mary nodded. 'I remember.'

'And he said Mr Boyle was a damned fool. But he went in after him. It was his fire, I suppose. And neither of them came out.'

23

Sergeant Fondard and Colonel Déprez set out from Paris in a light, sturdy carriage, attended by a postilion and two outriders. A galloper was immediately sent on ahead to organise swift changes, for, despite what he had said about the Lille telegraph, Fondard did not intend to cede the glory of capture to the Army if he could avoid it. Having once begun, therefore, he conducted the chase with an efficiency that seemed so at odds with his appearance but was entirely in keeping with his character.

The Peronne coach was overtaken at Conchy-les-Pots, and after a thorough and bad-tempered review of the situation, Fondard decided to turn west towards Clermont. As a precaution, he ordered the galloper to continue with all speed on the Peronne road for a further hour. A second rider was despatched when they reached Clermont. From the vague recollections of the sleepy innkeeper, Fondard was nearly positive that Mary and Holland had proceeded north, but it was possible that they had gone west instead. He left nothing to chance, therefore, but ordered his man to ride to Beauvais. If he found the trail there cold, he should make his way to Amiens as quickly as possible.

A mile outside Wavigny, they suffered bad luck in the form of a broken wheel, and Fondard raged at the resulting delay, for even he could not command the immediate services of a wheelwright in the early hours of the morning. When the fellow *was* found and set to work, so forcefully did the postilion and the third rider impress upon him the importance of his task that he lost all confidence in himself. Instead of performing a quick, basic repair that would almost certainly have sufficed until a replacement coach was obtained at the next stop, he employed all his expertise to rebuild the wheel, with the result that they rolled into Breteuil in perfect condition and after a delay of several hours.

There, however, the news was good. The innkeeper of the Hôtel de l'Ange required neither hints nor descriptions to charge his memory; he remembered the two travellers very well. 'An American and an Englishwoman – yes, they were on the Amiens coach this morning. No, they gave no particular trouble, but I did not like the look of them.' (He repeated this assertion after summoning Marie from the kitchen to testify before the awe-inspiring men from Paris, at which point she agreed that *she* had not liked the look of them either, particularly the woman.)

The hunters reached Amiens, therefore, full of confidence; they had caught their quarry's scent and would soon have them in view. This confidence suffered only a slight check when they entered the city and discovered that Captain Fabre and a party of dragoons had set off west towards Abbeville and a second had ridden north. Which road should the following party choose?

The evidence of Madame Pollet (stated effusively and at great length) and of the soldiers at the western gate suggested Abbeville, but Déprez was sceptical. North, and not west from Amiens was the quickest road to Dunkerque, and he trusted that Captain Holland and Miss Finch would know this. They were not fools, after all – far from it. Abbeville was a ruse, a feint, as Peronne had been.

Fondard did not like to be seen taking another's advice – indeed, he regretted failing to make his own view known before Déprez could speak. But he liked even less the prospect of making the wrong decision – of being fooled – and by a couple of English spies! Spies whom he might have arrested in Paris and spared himself all this trouble. He took what comfort he could in sending his third horseman to Abbeville and saying that Déprez's assessment agreed with his own. They would go north.

Since leaving Amiens, Holland had looked periodically over his shoulder, so it was hardly surprising that he saw them first – three spots on the horizon. And when they topped a rise, a fourth. By his calculation, the pursuit was at least an hour behind them.

'If they *are* pursuers,' said Mary hopefully. 'They might be simple travellers. They might have nothing to do with us.'

'They might,' Holland agreed, his tone indicating that he was willing to entertain all manner of unlikely hypotheses, but they would not affect his present conduct.

'I thought . . . I hoped that they would believe we were going to Abbeville. That is what I told Madame Pollet, and we left Amiens by the Abbeville gate.'

'Maybe they did believe it. If there are cavalry in Amiens and Captain Fabre has any sense, he will have sent some west and some north.'

'Cavalry,' Mary echoed. Somehow that word imparted a new fearsomeness to their opponents, for a cavalryman's very purpose was to ride the enemy down, was it not? She envisioned a mad chase, like a foxhunt. *Only we are the fox, and there is no covert.* 'Can we outrun them? Or hide, perhaps?'

Holland said that they might have to do both. They would also have to stop quite soon to give the horses a rest and a feed; they were definitely tiring. Already the pale afternoon light had gone, and he wanted to carry on as far as they could before stopping for the night. In order to have the strength for that, however, they must rest now.

They skirted the town of Doullens and turned off onto a smaller road, finally stopping at a village east of Frévent. It was not a very remarkable place, merely a cluster of farmhouses and cottages at the intersection of two narrow tracks, but it boasted an inn, or public house of sorts, which called itself the Chapeau Rouge.

A good Republican name, thought Mary grimly.

They halted, and Holland thundered on the door with the toe of his boot. The host appeared at an upstairs window and opened the casement partway. The visage he displayed was scrawny and his greeting cautious, like that of an ill-fed mouse who suspected that the cat had come to call.

'Yes?' he quavered. 'Who is that? We are closed. My wife has the toothache.'

Mary had taught Holland how to express their wants: food and drink for themselves, and fodder for their horses; they must be on their way again in half an hour. Her French included none of the warmer expressions with which an officer might have expressed himself, but Holland's tone was brusque, and his impatient gestures brooked no argument – toothache or not. The host descended and opened the door, and the two riders dismounted.

After Holland's curt *'Non, non,'* disqualified the parlour, they were conducted into the establishment's version of a private chamber. There the timid host served them soup, bread, cheese, and a drink resembling English cider. Was it sufficient? Holland grunted and dismissed the fellow with a wave.

Mary had doubted the wisdom of stopping – she imagined their pursuers riding on and on with never a break – but once they had stopped she realised that she was very tired indeed. Tired, hungry, and sore. When she moved, every muscle complained, and when she was seated on an unforgiving bench in the bare, mean little room that smelled of damp, she felt heavy and stupid. The danger behind them grew remote, a response to it difficult to contemplate.

The food and drink refreshed her, however, and when Holland spread out the map on the table between them, she was able to take an interest in his calculation of where they were and how many miles they might still travel that night.

Although they were alone, Holland spoke in a low voice. 'Another ten miles at least,' he murmured, tracing likely routes, 'fifteen would be better. Then, with luck and hard riding, we can reach Dunkerque tomorrow night.'

Mary moved the candle closer and squinted at the area he had indicated. 'Tonight I think we should make for . . . St Pol,' she said.

'Why?'

'Well . . .' She hesitated. 'It has a friendly sound, somehow. I . . . I believe that the Count of St Pol was something important in one of the Crusades – I am quite certain of it.'

Holland smiled at her. 'St Pol it is.'

They set off slowly, easing the horses into their work, which soon settled into a sturdy trot. After returning briefly to the main road, they left it again in favour of a byway that appeared to run roughly northwest. The weather had changed while they were in the Chapeau Rouge, for the air felt heavier, and the cold no longer trifled with cuffs and collars, but rather seeped through one's boots and cloak.

Mary shivered, partly from the chill and partly from a growing sense of unease. The darkness ought to have been a comfort, for it helped to conceal them, but it also hid their pursuers. What if the soldiers had managed to catch them up and set a trap? When she and Holland passed a cottage or a thicket of trees, it was easy to imagine that someone was watching, and the broken hedgerows emitted ominous sounds – creaking branches and the rustlings of small animals – which one did not notice when the sun was high. From somewhere close by she could hear a stream, and it seemed to be whispering.

There is nothing to be gained by imagining horrors, Mary told herself sternly, and not for the first time. *Of course there are animals about, and the wind, and they all make noises, but they are nothing to be frightened about.*

To prove this point, something small hopped onto the road in front of them, froze, and then sped into the gorse and dead grass. *Oh!* It was a rabbit, she concluded, or perhaps a hare. Her horse snorted in derision, and Mary thought that she might at least display the same level of courage as her mount. Captain Holland, she knew, was not concerned in the least.

345

He would certainly laugh at her if she admitted that the knocking of two branches against each other had sounded distinctly like a coded communication. *'What sort of code would that be?'* he would ask. *'Between an oak and a hazel?'* Of course it was all very well to—

It happened in an instant. Her horse stumbled, lowered his shoulder, and she was off – thrown forward into space. She fell awkwardly, with no chance to prepare for the thump of solid ground. A bush – something spiky – seemed to rush towards her; she stretched out her arms and closed her eyes.

Then she was on the ground, on hands and knees, almost before she realised that she had fallen. *Am I hurt?* she asked herself, and could make no answer. Next Holland was beside her, his voice strangely urgent. Could it be that he *was* afraid?

'Mary! Don't move,' he ordered, and she could feel his hands on her shoulders. His touch was gentle, comforting, but at the same time a distraction from whatever had happened to her. 'Are you hurt? That was a nasty one.'

'I think . . . I think I am all right,' said Mary vaguely, as if she were assessing another's injuries. There was still no shooting pain, but her wrists hurt, and her right knee where she had landed on something hard and pointed. With Holland's arm about her, she rose cautiously to her feet.

'Slowly,' he warned. 'Can you walk?'

A wave of dizziness washed over her, but it soon passed. She took a deep breath and allowed him to lead her forward a few steps.

'Better?' he asked.

She nodded. 'Yes. It was the surprise, I think.'

Holland agreed that that was often the worst part of a tumble, and guided her to a fallen tree trunk. 'Sit here a moment.'

'I am sorry,' she murmured. 'I have never fallen from a horse before.'

'Sorry? For a fall? Don't be daft. I've landed on my head – or my backside – more times than I care to mention.'

He left her, but that did not seem at all strange. She was not yet thinking very clearly, and had little attention for anything beyond her immediate situation. The log was rough in places and too low; she was obliged to sit awkwardly, either with her legs bent to one side, which hurt her back, or stretched out in front of her, which was almost equally uncomfortable. As she retied her boot she noticed that the bottom of her cloak was torn. *But I am not badly injured, thank goodness. I suppose there is a proper way of falling, so that one is unlikely to be hurt, but learning it must be very unpleasant. And one would have to know when a fall was coming. Mine simply—*

The crack of a pistol made her start, and she sprang to her feet in alarm. *Soldiers! The cavalry! Oh God, they have found us!*

Holland loomed up beside her. 'That was me,' he explained. 'Your horse had broken his left foreleg, I'm afraid.'

'And you *shot him*?' Mary was aghast. 'But—'

'It seems cruel, but it's the kindest thing to do. Horses can't survive on three legs while the bad one's mending.' He took her arm. 'Come on, we've got to move.'

'Have you seen them? The cavalry?'

'No, but they're somewhere about, and if any of them heard that shot . . .'

She halted. 'They will know it was our doing?'

'They'll be suspicious.'

He helped her to mount his horse and swung up behind her. On they rode, and more urgently than before. To Mary's ears the hooves sounded like thunder on the hard-packed ground, but she strained to pick out other sounds – men's voices or hurrying feet. At the same time she tried to catch a glimpse of a friendly refuge. She was the lookout while Holland drove them forward. But where might they safely stop, if soldiers were close at hand?

On and on, still at the same pitch of anxiety, but now – now they were slowing! Their horse's trot was becoming laboured. Holland let him walk, and he breathed more easily, but when called upon to resume his earlier gait he answered half-heartedly and then not at all.

'What is the matter?' Mary cried, and she patted his neck. It was slick with sweat. 'Is he hurt?' It was terrible, standing

347

there in the middle of the road while their horse gasped and shivered.

A word and a kick got them moving again, but at a sluggard's pace. 'Can we not help him?' asked Mary. 'He has done so well.'

'No, he's spent,' said Holland.

They drew up to a substantial farmhouse; there were lights within. A granary or a dairy stood beside it, and beyond that a stable. Briefly, Holland explained his proposal: they would continue on foot, across country. It would be slower than the road, but far less dangerous, especially in the dark. 'If we're quiet, I doubt they'll be able to follow us.'

'And our horse?'

'We must leave him − at least for tonight − and the best place to do that is where he won't be found straightaway.' Holland studied her. 'Are you all right to walk?'

The fall had wrenched all those muscles not already strained from a long ride, but she nodded firmly. 'Yes, I think so.'

Mary spent several nervous minutes crouching under a hedgerow by the side of the road while Holland stabled the horse, and then he was beside her, taking her hand. Together they hurried across a field, stumbling over the rough clods of earth. Beyond the field lay a stretch of woodland, but before entering it, Holland paused, checking Mary with a light touch. He stood motionless, listening.

'What is it?' she whispered.

'Shssh,' he replied in a like tone, and then, 'Horses. Maybe a coach.'

Horses! Oh God! And only a field between us! But surely a forest must baffle even cavalry mounts, and she plunged gratefully into the shelter of the trees with Holland close behind.

A shelter, but one that was difficult to navigate. Saplings and broad trunks sprang out of the darkness to block their way. Some trees had fallen or been uprooted in last year's storms; others were disguised by blankets of ivy. Mary and Holland scrambled over and around these obstacles, tripping over roots and ducking their heads to avoid low branches. Mary's knee began to ache, and brambles clawed at the tattered hem of her cloak.

Their footfalls were quiet, at least, muffled by dead leaves, but there seemed to be no path, no certain way through. Whatever moonlight might have aided them was swallowed by the deep, black shadows of the trees. Mary began to grow uneasy, but what was the good in saying so? And stopping would be worse – an acknowledgment that they were lost. Lost in a wood, and with soldiers prowling about. *Prowling.* The word made her think of wild animals . . . and robbers. *Say nothing,* she commanded herself, *and keep walking.*

At last they came to the edge of the woods and halted under the open sky, Mary catching her breath, and Holland, apparently, deciding upon their next course.

'This way,' he said, pointing.

Up and down a hill and across a meadow, and then into another wood. Mary steeled herself, but after an initial uneasiness, she felt strangely calm. The trees seemed less forbidding, somehow, less wild. *But that is ridiculous – how could a forest be other than wild?* Almost immediately the answer came to her. *When it has been planted, of course, or at least managed. When it is a park.*

A park that knew no present owner, perhaps, but even a path of broken flagstones did not occur naturally, and someone had planted the yew hedge that now stood twice as tall as Holland. A row of holly trees, some stunted and others enormous, led to what had once been a considerable structure of some kind, but which was now a ruin. To one side, however, a smaller building remained: a chapel.

Might this be the looked for covert? A place to hide themselves, at least for a few hours, until the pursuit turned elsewhere? Mary posed the idea to Holland and he agreed, but when they tried the door they found it locked. And not merely locked; the door appeared sound, and the shuttered windows on either side had not been tampered with. Whatever assaults had been suffered by other religious buildings across France, nothing violent had happened here.

She remembered the fairytale feeling that she had experienced outside the Maison du Rossignol. This was not quite the same, but similar – a sense of being in a place of enchantment. Perhaps it was not a very strong sensation, however, for she did not mention it to Holland. His scepticism, moreover, would have been quite out of place. As she was reflecting on the matter, a new danger suddenly displaced all other thoughts. Someone was coming!

For an instant she stood petrified, like the rabbit in the road, and then Holland dragged her into a thick growth of ivy that clung to the side of the chapel. A poor refuge, but better than none. Hearts pounding, they listened as the sounds drew closer. Now it was possible to distinguish several sounds – men's voices, horses' hooves, and rolling wheels.

Mary closed her eyes. *Let them pass, oh God – let them pass!*

'. . . et le tout sans un seul mensonge.'

Je vous en félicite. Cependant, vous étiez très fier de vos moutons. "Rouge de l'Ouest, citoyen, et les miens sont les plus beaux en France". La fierté est un péché, vous savez.'

'*Assurément. Mais c'était également nécessaire à la ruse. Et certains de mes paroissiens ont des visages roses.'*

'*Ah, je pensais que vous alliez dire qu'il leur fallait également eu berger prudent.'*

'*C'est également vrai!'*

Mary opened her eyes. A deception? Parishioners? Pink-faced sheep? Surely this was a strange conversation for cavalrymen? Holland understood only a few of the words, but the elderly, querulous voices that uttered them made him relax and – for he had kept his eyes open – he doubted that the French Army generally travelled by donkey-cart.

The cart halted and the men descended. After a brief conference they determined to strike a light – it would be necessary inside and, thanks to the deception, there was very little risk that it would be seen by unfriendly eyes.

'*Il n'y a aucun risque, à moins que vous ne craigniez les fantômes.'*

'*Non, en effet. Et le vieux chevalier est un bon fantôme – très pieux.'*

The determination was more easily arrived at than its execution, but finally a lantern was lit and the shade adjusted. In the meantime, something bulky had been lifted from the back of the cart. With their respective burdens the two men moved towards the door of the chapel. One of the donkeys stamped his feet and the other shook his head, but otherwise they appeared content to remain where they were.

Holland's curiosity was greater, and after he heard a key turn in the lock and the door open, he crept round the corner of the chapel and then up the three shallow steps. As he did so he argued with himself. *The cart is an unlooked-for chance — we ought to take it and go . . . but that would leave these two old fellows to raise the alarm.*

Mary followed at a prudent distance, for Holland would certainly tell her to wait, to go back, and to leave anything dangerous (and interesting) to him. For that reason she hesitated to join him inside. When she finally did so, concealing herself partly behind the ancient font, she could see that an astonishing scene was taking place in the body of the chapel. A small, white-haired man held the lantern aloft, while his grizzled companion knelt and plucked a jewelled cross and a large gold plate from a bundle of straw.

The door creaked and the little man spun round. In the moment before it fell to the floor, Holland was revealed in the lantern's flash.

'*Sainte Mère de Dieu! Les soldats!*'

Holland walked slowly forward. '*Non,*' he said slowly, '*je ne suis pas un soldat français.*'

Silence, and then another voice answered, 'You'll be English, I'm thinking?'

'Yes,' said Holland.

Mary flinched, for the questioning voice had spoken in flawless, if oddly accentuated, English. She crept forward, but it was too dark to make out anything beyond two vague, grey shapes. 'I— I beg your pardon,' she stammered in the same language, 'but who are you?'

'Dear me, and an English lady besides. What a night for it. I am Father Andries, and this is Father Théodore.'

'You're priests?' demanded Holland.

'Just so.'

Well I'm damned, thought Holland. He re-lit the lantern and set it on a pew. 'Yes, sir, we're from England. But you're not a Frenchman, I think.'

'Certainly not. I am a Hainaulter, from Mons.'

'I thought you were Irish,' Mary admitted. 'I mean—'

'Ah, that will be Father Michael's doing – Father Michael Kelly from County Mayo. We were at the seminary together.'

'In Ireland?' asked Mary dubiously.

'No, no, at the university in Douai, many a year ago and more. It was a great place for Irishmen in those days – even for a few right-thinking Englishmen – but it was Father Michael who taught me the language. The university is closed now, of course, thanks to these French rapparees – saving your presence, Father Théodore.'

The French priest spread his hands. *'C'est une tragédie.'*

'But we are very pleased to meet the pair of you,' said Father Andries. 'More pleased than I can say, considering the alternative. You gave us quite a turn with that coat of yours, sir. Lent by a friend of yours, perhaps?'

'Perhaps,' Holland agreed. He glanced from one grey head to the other. Neither came higher than his shoulder. 'And perhaps you might tell me what you're doing? Are you highwaymen as well as priests?'

Father Andries chuckled at this, as did Father Théodore when 'highwayman' was translated into French. He could follow most conversations in English, up to a point, but he was not so confident speaking in that language. And he was not so sure of these mysterious strangers. It was a strange matter entirely.

Father Andries described himself as one of the faithful, by which he meant those priests in the former Austrian territories to the north who opposed the French religious policies, particularly the dissolution of the monasteries and the ban on public administration of the mass. 'We continue to perform our duties in secret, of course.'

'But I thought that church services were generally permitted again in France,' said Mary. 'I have certainly heard of services resuming in some Parisian churches.'

'They don't extend the same privileges to enemy territory,' replied Father Andries, 'although I understand we have now been handed over completely by the Austrians, the rogues. We are the spoils of war, my dear, and we are being made to feel it. The French think to break our spirit with their decrees and their resolutions, which they never shall, but it's a sore trial for our people.'

One of the trials was the loss of Church property – the buildings ravaged and sold for scrap, and the treasures seized. 'To think that the treasures of the Holy Church should be used to fund this godless war, or to line the pocket of some Republican pirate!'

The thought had not only enraged Father Andries, it had stirred him to action. He had taken it upon himself to locate valuable items and transport them secretly to places of safety. A surprising number had been saved from the first assault, but they were vulnerable so long as they remained in Flanders. Fortunately he had good friends in France, such as Father Théodore, who were willing to help.

'You mean to hide those things here?' asked Holland, nodding at the cross and plate.

'Yes, and it's a grand place for it, what with one thing and another. The chapel has not been used for more than a generation – not since the last chevalier de Saint-Simon died and the château fell to bits. It is quite a secret place.'

'For the present, perhaps,' said Holland. 'Tell me, did you happen to meet anyone on your way here tonight?'

'We did,' said Father Andries, 'mounted soldiers on the main road. A weary and miserable pair they were, too. We did not want them to imagine that we had any but worldly business, so Father Théodore threw dust in their eyes with an account of his pink-faced sheep. We are frequently obliged to employ such deceptions in order to protect our holy treasures, and so far – with the blessing – we have been successful. I doubt we see more of them tonight.'

'*En plus, il y a le fantôme,*' piped Father Théodore.

'Indeed, the ghost,' said Father Andries. 'Not that *we* believe such foolishness, but he is well known hereabouts, and much feared. If the old fellow discourages any quick-fingered rascals from disturbing our work, then I shall be very much beholden to him.'

The priest spoke lightly, but his glance was keen, and he had been appraising Holland from the moment he saw him. Was he to be trusted? The English might hate the French, but most of them were not of the Faith. *And what in God's name is an Englishman doing in France, dressed as he is and with a young woman in tow? A young woman!* The possibility of an escapade – a scandalous escapade – took shape in his mind, and he frowned sternly. 'So there you have it, sir, Father Théodore and myself doing God's work as we are able. Could you tell me something of yourself, at all?'

Holland was aware of Father Andries' speculations, if not of their precise nature. He was also conscious of what honour demanded in the present circumstances. Honour demanded that he deal fairly with the two priests. They had spoken frankly, and they deserved the same in return. *Not that they could help themselves, with all that gold on display.* Gold . . . and jewels that might make the difference between passage back to England and a French prison. Prison and execution. And outside was transportation just waiting to be taken. Father Andries and Father Théodore could hardly stop him from doing exactly as he liked. If they went to the authorities, they would still lose their treasures and very likely suffer imprisonment themselves – if not worse.

All of these things had occurred to Holland by the time Father Andries finished with the ghost. *A ghost to protect your treasure, by God. As if we're in a bloody fairy tale.* 'We are not robbers,' he said slowly, 'nor murderers, and we mean you no harm. I'm an English officer.'

Father Théodore gasped and crossed himself, but the expression of the other priest was difficult to read, and he answered in a curious tone. 'An English officer in a French coat. Spies, is it?' he asked. 'You're an agent working against the French?'

'That's right, sir.'

'And this young woman?'

Holland nodded and looked hard at each of the priests. 'It's my duty to make sure she gets safely back to England. And I'll do what I must to gain that end.'

'We must *both* return, if we can,' said Mary.

The priests exchanged glances. Father Théodore looked anxious.

'Well, sir, you are a man of violence – which I deplore – but in other ways we are alike,' said Father Andries. 'No soft words, no sophistry. It is clear that this young lady needs our protection – she has it. And if your returning to England will confound these devilish Frenchmen – your pardon, my friend—'

'*Bien sûr,*' breathed Father Théodore.

'Then you have our help in that as well.'

24

Nightfall having frustrated their efforts, the troopers from Amiens made their way resignedly to St Pol. There they found the garrison in a higher than usual state of alertness but with no particular information about the English spies. No travellers, apart from local men, had entered St Pol since the warning had come through from Lille. It was scant consolation, therefore, to conclude that their quarry was no longer in front of them, when they themselves were subjected to a rigorous and even patronising examination before being allowed to pass.

They proceeded at last to an inn that they all knew from more festive occasions, with no further thoughts than to stable their horses and take a well-deserved rest. Whether they must resume the chase in the morning would depend on their superiors or a renewal of the mysterious instructions that had set them on the road in the first place. Instructions from Paris, it was rumoured; some reckoned from the *directeurs* themselves – the chief ministers of the government. But surely such matters could wait until tomorrow.

That is certainly what the corporal, a grey, faded, competent man had imagined. He was surprised and rather discouraged, therefore, to be roused from a very comfortable chair before the fire, obliged to resume his boots and present himself in a private room to which soldiers were not generally admitted. There he encountered, not members of the Directory, but important men nevertheless – Sergeant Fondard and Colonel Déprez, whose coach had just arrived.

The corporal eyed the two men cautiously. He thought he knew where he was with a colonel of infantry, but the sergeant's uniform gave him pause. Quite clearly the man's ostensible rank had little to do with his authority. *But then, he has come from Paris, and they do things differently there.* 'We set out after the spies,' he explained, 'and I believe we had them in our sights for most of the afternoon. But when it grew dark . . . they eluded us.'

'Out-paced you, you mean,' Fondard complained. 'They are on their way to Dunkerque while we . . .' He surveyed the corporal's open tunic. 'Take our ease.'

The corporal flushed crimson. 'I do not think so, sergeant. At least, they have not come so far as St Pol. I believe that they are somewhere about, but it was not possible to conduct a search in the darkness.' He hesitated and then asked, 'It is known that they are bound for Dunkerque?'

'Yes.'

'It makes sense that they would have left the road at some point,' said Déprez.

'What do you mean, "left the road"?' Fondard demanded. 'Left all roads? Why should they do such a thing?'

'Because they believed that we would not,' said Déprez. 'They know that they cannot win a straightforward chase, for they cannot rely upon fresh mounts, as we can. So they have hidden themselves in some secret place, trusting that we will run on ahead, never noticing that our prey is behind us.'

'But their object is to escape, which would be more difficult on foot. Nor can they easily lead horses across fields and through the woods.' Fondard looked to the corporal for confirmation of the last point.

The look caught the corporal in the middle of a ferocious yawn, which he attempted to conceal by coughing hurriedly. 'Ahem— Your pardon. It would be very difficult to travel for long across the country,' he admitted.

'Well, I am glad to hear that much,' Fondard snapped. He was also tired, despite having spent the day in a moderately comfortable coach and not in the saddle. He had not slept much during the previous night. At that stage their passage had been eager, and the likelihood of an early capture had kept him awake. Today there had been intermittent bouts of excitement, but without a final reward. It was difficult now to avoid feeling jaded and discouraged.

A map lay open on the table, and Déprez consulted it. 'It appears to me that there are two courses before us. We can resume the hunt, in this vicinity, tomorrow. So long as the spies avoid the main roads their progress must be slow. On the other hand, we must also move slowly, and if they go to ground we will have a difficult task locating them.'

'And your other course is . . . to continue to Dunkerque?' asked Fondard.

'Exactly. By now the Lille garrison should have alerted all the towns between here and the coast. The cordon is in place, and where we cannot keep watch ourselves, we have men to do so for us. If Captain Holland and Miss Finch are not so clever, they will be caught somewhere in this region.' He traced the relevant area with his finger.

'And if they are clever, we shall greet them in Dunkerque. Perhaps in the company of the merchant, Cornelius Vangenzen.' Fondard smiled; the notion appealed to him. 'What does he carry, usually, on board his ships? Herring, I suppose, as he is a Dutchman . . . and cheese.'

'Very likely it is something of that kind,' Déprez agreed sullenly. He was weary, and he disliked the way that Fondard gloated over the prospect of success . . . as soon as the chase seemed to favour them again. *The man is a bully — equally unpleasant whether he succeeds or fails.*

'Well, we shall make certain that he does not leave Dunkerque with any other cargo,' said Fondard with a grin. He was feeling rather better, suddenly, and the mention of cheese reminded him that he was hungry. 'We shall remain here tonight,' he decreed, 'and carry on to Dunkerque in the morning.'

*　　*　　*

For the most part, the trend of Holland's thinking was the same as that of his pursuers. He guessed that the nearby garrisons had been alerted by means of the Lille telegraph, and that there would now be no easy passage to the coast. The main roads would be watched, and if he and Mary were seen, they were unlikely to evade a determined chase.

Their own circumstances did little to lighten this gloomy assessment. True, they had acquired a mode of transport other than their feet, but it was of limited usefulness. ('You would do precious little dashing with this cart,' said Father Andries. 'David and Jonathan are grand little fellows, but they've no heart for running – nor legs for it.') The ruse that had proved valuable in Amiens, moreover, now created a further problem. Holland's uniform must attract attention, particularly as its wearer could not speak French. Mary might pass a casual interview, and the priests' company would help, but Holland needed a thorough disguise. If at all possible, in fact, he must be neither seen nor heard.

At first they despaired of a solution. After some consideration, however, Father Andries proposed one that gained general support. Rather than by road, Mary and Holland should travel by water. There were canals in this part of France, and one of them linked St Omer to the sea. To be sure, the barges were slow, but that was also an advantage. Because escape by canal was so unlikely the Army might reject it out of hand. Certainly the soldiers would not scrutinise freight barges as carefully as they would coaches and horsemen.

'I suppose that a barge would be reasonably steady?' asked Holland, with an attempted casualness. 'I mean, there are no waves or currents in a canal.'

'Oh no, nothing to speak of in that way,' said Father Andries. 'And as for steadiness, your canal is far superior to your roadway, with never a rut or awkward turning. I expect you would sleep for most of the journey.'

'Mm,' said Holland. 'I expect so.'

There remained the question of how to travel to St Omer, a distance Father Théodore reckoned to be nearly ten miles. The donkey-cart was the only practical means, and Holland thought that they should set out immediately, so long as the priests were fit for the journey.

'Don't you worry about us, young fellow,' cried Father Andries. 'We're used to short commons and long watches in our line of work, you know.'

But how was Holland to be concealed? The darkness would cover him initially, but in the morning he must be on show to anyone whom they encountered – and soldiers, it was feared, rose very early. This was said with a critical nod in Holland's direction, as if to say that he and men of his profession were doubly bothersome.

'I do not suppose you could *borrow* a coat or cloak from someone nearby?' asked Mary. 'Or we could pay for it.' In the present company it was impossible to suggest anything in the nature of an involuntary surrender of property, and she was thankful that the account of their escape from Amiens on stolen horses had not been discussed in any detail.

Father Théodore thought that involving anyone beyond themselves in the affair would be unwise. Firstly, his parish lay in the opposite direction – they would waste valuable time seeking help. And secondly – he spread his hands – it was not fair, perhaps, to place temptation in the way of poor people. The inhabitants of Haumont were good, honest souls for the most part, but the best of them were curious, and the prospect of a reward might get the better of others. And they were good Frenchmen, after all. They might question whether it was right to help the English at such a time. Father Théodore's tone suggested that he had some sympathy with that point of view.

Mary asked whether everything in the chapel belonged to the Catholic Church. She was studying the bare walls and dust-covered pews, as much as this was possible by lantern-light.

'*Ah oui, bien sûr,*' said Father Théodore.

'It's too bad that neither of us is a match for yourself in height, Captain Holland,' mused Father Andries. 'But were you to change clothes with either Father Théodore or myself, I don't think it would answer – not if we're hoping for concealment.'

'No, sir,' Holland agreed, 'I don't think it would answer.'

360

It was also faintly ludicrous to imagine either of the priests attempting to pass himself off as an officer. Ludicrous and dangerous – far more dangerous than anything Holland intended to allow them to undertake. Driving the cart to St Omer was risk enough for two old men who ought to have been home in bed at that hour. He said nothing of this, however.

'*Si seulement nous avions encore une botte de paille,*' sighed Father Théodore, and with another critical glance at Holland, '*une plus grande.*'

'I have an idea,' said Mary slowly, 'but it would—'

'No!' cried Father Andries, '*not* another bale of straw, but you've got the right idea.' He conferred hurriedly with his colleague. '*La couverture peut servir de linçeul. La couverture dans la charrette.*'

'*C'est une bonne idée,*' acknowledged Father Théodore, '*mais la couverture, est-elle assez grande?*' His tone was dubious.

Father Andries had no such qualms. '*Oui, bien sûr,*' he urged. '*Qui examinerait de manière rigoureuse une telle cargaison?*' His eyes twinkled as he asked Holland, 'Would you object at all to being a corpse, sir, so long as it wasn't a permanent condition?'

Before departing the chapel, Father Andries and Father Théodore explained that the Flemish treasures must be concealed in a small compartment beneath the altar. This involved shifting a heavy stone slab, and Holland was encouraged to make himself useful. 'Lend your back to God's work,' as Father Andries said. There was a trick to 'unlocking' the compartment, but the task still required considerable strength; how the priests would have managed it alone was not made clear. *Perhaps they expected the ghost to help them*, thought Holland, as he heaved the stone back into place with the aid of a metal bar.

It was agreed that both priests would make the journey to St Omer. There was a chance that Father Théodore would know some of the men at the canal, and his authority might prove helpful. Once on board, responsibility for 'the body' would pass to Father Andries until they reached Dunkerque. Nor was it possible to shift him from his determination to see Mary and

Holland safely on board a ship for England. He must see the matter through, he said. His eagerness for the adventure did not escape notice, however, nor his very unclerical delight at the prospect of confounding the French authorities, of giving them one in the eye, the devils.

'Always saving your presence, of course, Father Théodore.'

'*Naturellement.*'

They set off promptly, and although their pace was modest, they made steady progress along back roads that Father Théodore knew. He drove the cart and Father Andries sat beside him, while Mary and Holland rode in the back. Sometimes, when the track was rough or he thought it advisable to spare David and Jonathan, Holland would descend. He did not mind walking, and he would have ample opportunity for resting when they reached St Omer.

'I hope you will not mind it,' said Mary. 'It seems rather awful, but . . .'

Holland assured her that masquerading as a corpse in a makeshift shroud would not cause him the slightest uneasiness. Indeed, Father Andries' prediction about sleeping on the barge appeared likely to come true.

'Well, see that you do not snore,' Mary advised. 'That would be most inappropriate.'

'I *don't* snore,' Holland protested. Privately he wondered about the smooth motion of the barge, however, and requested that he be stowed facing forward if possible.

'I do not suppose that there is an etiquette for the arrangement of bodies,' said Mary thoughtfully. 'Or if there is, I doubt that the barge keepers will be familiar with it.'

Only she would think of such a thing. Holland's smile faded at an uncomfortable association of ideas. *How Mr Boyle would have enjoyed travelling to the coast by barge. It would have been the perfect opportunity to refine his ideas on small-gauge canals . . . and to explain them to anyone who could understand his appalling French.*

He walked in silence for a while, and Mary dozed. Holland liked to plan ahead, in so far as that was possible, and the steady tramp, the darkness, even the cold facilitated the orderly arrangement of thoughts. There would be soldiers in Dunkerque, but

362

it might be possible to avoid them, having arrived by barge. The canal, most likely, would terminate close to the harbour. At least Mary ought to get through, especially with Father Andries' help.

Everything depended, of course, on their reaching St Omer and convincing a barge captain to carry them. Holland felt reasonably confident about the first, but the second would take a bit of luck. He considered that elusive quality – its importance in desperate ventures and its finite nature. Some men were naturally unlucky, and even those who had enjoyed good fortune – and he counted himself among the latter – could not depend upon it. He and Mary had been lucky so far. Meeting Father Théodore and Father Andries had been damned— *very* lucky. Their scheme to avoid capture was more than a bit mad, but that did not mean that it would fail. And if it did, well . . .

Then another thought occurred to him. Mary had awakened, and he asked, 'What was your idea about how we might avoid the soldiers? You started to say, but never finished.'

'Hmm? Oh, I daresay it was terribly impractical,' said Mary hurriedly. 'And you would not have liked it.'

Holland could well believe the first of these remarks, but he only said, 'I doubt if I'd have liked it any less than being dead in an old horse blanket.'

'*Donkey* blanket,' Mary corrected, 'and I think it is quite a nice one. Not smelly, I mean, and I am certain that neither David nor Jonathan has fleas, so you are unlikely to be bitten. And it will be airy too, not like—' She paused. 'Not like being in a coffin.'

She completed the sentence with the same offhandedness that had characterised Holland's query about the steadiness of the barge, and for that reason its falsity was immediately apparent to him. 'A *coffin*?' he demanded. 'How on earth— Where did you suppose we were going to find a coffin?'

'Well, I presumed that the chapel had a crypt, since it had belonged to a family, and it would contain quite a few coffins. Of course, moving one might have been a problem, but I think

363

we could have managed it, between four of us. I do not mean the outer casket, which would have been of lead, or perhaps even stone.'

'Oh no, not the *outer* casket,' Holland agreed. '*That* would have been difficult. But opening the damn thing and tipping out whoever was inside it—'

'Would have been horrible,' finished Mary. 'You needn't laugh at me, for I quite see your objections – I saw them straightaway, only I could not think of any other way of disguising you.'

The practicalities of Mary's plan, even at this remove, were extremely unpleasant, and Holland missed her observation that he really ought to have learned French – it would have made matters so much easier. 'A body in a coffin might be like one of those mummies, I suppose,' he said.

'Yes, exactly,' said Mary, and the keenness of her tone made him wonder whether she was not a little disappointed. 'I thought that if the person had died a long time ago . . . but of course no one buried in that chapel could have been of a truly mummyish age, for *they* must be very old indeed if you think of the pharaohs in the Bible. Even Cleopatra was *quite* old.'

'Ah.'

'And there would have been other difficulties. It would have meant extra work for David and Jonathan, and I do not know how you would have breathed. We should have had to drill holes, I suppose. I thought it all out, you see.' She sighed. 'But of course the shroud *is* much easier.'

They reached St Omer before dawn, having completed Holland's transformation into the last earthly remains of Jean Lefebvre, lately of the village of Fleury. The soldiers at the makeshift barrier were conscientious but sleepy, and they conducted their examination of Father Théodore as though by rote.

'Where are you taking this body, citizen?'

'To Mardyck. My colleague, who is the priest of that parish, accompanies the body of poor Jean and also his widow Citizeness Lefebvre.'

'And why to Mardyck? Why do you not bury him in Fleury?'

'He came but recently to our village, and his family live in Mardyck still. This arrangement will be a great comfort to his mother, who has been devastated by his death.'

'How did he die?'

'An accident on the road – a most tragic accident. He was a mender of roads.'

'He had no disease?'

'Oh no, his health was perfect until the accident. A great calamity to have happened to one in the prime of life. Our time on this earth may be long or short, however. We would be advised to take note of this example.'

'Very well, you may pass.'

Securing a passage on one of the freight barges proved somewhat more difficult. Xavier Guillot, the owner and captain of the leading vessel, had no official concerns, but he did not like the idea of transporting a corpse, however tragic had been its demise. A dead body was unlucky; its presence would frighten the horse; why did not the holy Fathers ask Claude Moreau to take it? Claude Moreau did not mind what he carried, and today he had a load of empty fish crates, which a corpse could not possibly injure.

Fortunately, however, Father Andries and Father Théodore managed to overcome these objections. Father Théodore in particular fastened onto Guillot's reference to 'holy Fathers' and hinted that things might not go so well with anyone who considered himself a Catholic and yet turned the widow from his door – his vessel – in her hour of need. Father Andries poured scorn on the notion that the barge horse would be disturbed by the presence of poor Jean Lefebvre, who had always loved horses in life. Had the priests' donkeys been disturbed? Certainly not, and neither would any other beast, for God had given them good sense as well as strong backs. It was a pity that the same could not always be said for their human masters.

Guillot relented in the face of these arguments and grudgingly permitted the body to be brought on board. It was stowed facing forward, according to Father Andries' instructions, but below deck. (There was certainly no need to advertise the

365

presence of such an unusual cargo, after all.) Mary bade farewell to Father Théodore and received his anxious benediction, and then they were off. The barge captain signalled to his son, a chubby lad who stood at the horse's head, and the animal stepped forward. The towrope slid along the ground, grew taut, and slowly pulled the barge along the bank.

What followed was a long, slow, almost timeless day. A grey day too, which made the passing hours more difficult to calculate. Such scenery as could be observed from the deck was pleasant, if rather monotonous; flat fields, a low horizon, and a line of trees on either side of the canal. In the summer these would provide shade for the horses, patiently trudging up and down the towpath, but at present they were leafless and stark.

Birds flew overhead – ducks whose wings beat the air with a rhythmic whir, whir, whir – and nondescript brown birds that hopped from branch to branch, twittering. Waterfowl paddled in the canal, indifferent to the immense creature that surged past them; they slipped over the rippling wake as nonchalantly as a horseman clearing a fence. Sometimes there were cows in the fields, and they champed impassively and swished their tails. People, however, were few, and when she ventured on deck for a breath of air, Mary found the emptiness, and the sense that they were moving silently through a silent land, unsettling.

Guillot and his son exchanged brief remarks that seemed to be mostly to do with their course – slight adjustments of speed or the angle of the rope that were necessary to keep the barge straight. Perhaps there was more to their calls of 'mind her', 'steady', and 'straighten up, now', but Mary found their accents strange, and some of their words unintelligible. Once, Guillot noticed her and nodded, but he did not speak, which was just as well. She was supposed to be a grief-stricken widow, after all, and mustn't appear eager for casual conversation.

Below deck, the atmosphere was only slightly more convivial. The three passengers occupied a small, dim space that had been formed by shifting the regular cargo of crates and bales. It was warmer, but also rather stuffy, and Guillot's pipe smoke was far more noticeable. Mary did not mind the odour particularly, but its prevalence, together with the occasional sound of footsteps overhead made her feel as if someone close at hand was keeping them under observation – perhaps peering at them from a hidden vantage.

For this reason she hesitated to converse with Father Andries on any but the most casual of subjects, and of course it would have been madness for Holland to speak at all. Father Andries did loosen some of the fastenings that bound the makeshift shroud in place, so that Holland was able to drink some water and eat the heel of bread he had saved from their previous day's meal at the Chapeau Rouge, but he was far from an energetic travelling companion.

He does snore too, Mary noted, prodding him with a certain satisfaction before her own eyelids began to feel heavy. She sat down beside Father Andries and made herself as comfortable as she could, leaning against a large, straw-covered bundle. And finally she fell asleep.

Mary opened her eyes. The light had faded, and Holland's face was dimly visible in the lower-deck gloom. He was bending over her, his hand on her arm. Behind him on the improvised shelf of boxes, the donkey-blanket cum shroud lay in a dark, disordered heap. In the few moments of confused half-sleep, she thought they were in the cellar at White Ladies – *no, a tomb, the Empty Tomb; 'Quem quaeritis in sepulchro?'; imagine thinking that Jesus was the gardener . . .*

'What is it?' she whispered. 'Why have we stopped?'

'We're here,' Holland replied. 'In Dunkerque.'

'Dunkerque – we have done it! Where is Father Andries?'

'He's gone up top to have a look about and try to get directions to Vangenzen's – and we haven't *done* anything until we're safely aboard a ship and away from France.'

'Yes, of course,' Mary agreed. 'Are we going there straightaway? To Mr Vangenzen's house?'

'There, or wherever he conducts his business on shore. I expect he has an office somewhere near the harbour.' Holland sat down beside Mary, and his hand slid into hers. 'This is the plan. You and

Father Andries will go ahead and fix things up with Vangenzen.'
Mary started to protest, and Holland urged, 'You may find it
hard enough to convince him as things stand. Having me there
would only complicate matters.' He smiled. 'I doubt if even you
could tell a convincing tale to explain why Mr Andrew Ogbourne
of America had donned a French captain's uniform.'

'Well, perhaps, but . . . what about you?'

'I'll stay here, and join you when everything's settled. Once
we've got Vangenzen's approval, it won't be so hard to bluff our
way on board.'

'But what if someone comes here, in the meantime?'

'I doubt very much that they will. And if the barge captain
gets curious, I'll move and give him the fright of his life.'

That made Mary smile, but only briefly. 'We ought to stay
together.'

Before Holland could reply, there was a sound on the stairs.
He lowered his pistol as Father Andries made his way to join
them. The priest's stature was an advantage below deck; he did
not have to stoop.

'We shall be together soon enough,' Holland promised. 'All
well, sir?'

'Yes, all is well,' murmured Father Andries, his voice quietly
confident. 'Nothing out of the ordinary, as far as I can tell.'

'What about Vangenzen's?'

Father Andries explained that Vangenzen & De Groot had a
warehouse close to the harbour. The partners were considerable men in Dunkerque, it seemed, and between them owned
three ships: the *Pijl*, the *Haarlem*, and the *Knappe Dame*. Guillot
thought it very likely that at least one was in port at the
moment, although of course he could not say for certain.

'In port and ready to sail,' Holland agreed. He paused for a
few moments, frowning thoughtfully, and then said that – his
three ships aside – it would have been better if Citizen Vangenzen
were not so eminent a fellow.

'Why would that be?' asked Father Andries. 'You're thinking
he won't have the time for us? Or the interest in taking a risk?'

'No,' said Holland, 'but that might be true as well. I was

368

thinking that, if our two names have been sent through by the telegraph – our assumed names, I mean – then it won't take a very brilliant commander here in Dunkerque to recognise the name "Vangenzen".'

'No one in Paris *knew* that we were coming to Dunkerque,' said Mary slowly, 'and if we do *not* ask for help from Vangenzen & De Groot . . .'

'I'm not suggesting that we change course now,' Holland replied. 'The name is still a long shot – we might have obtained false papers, after all, and there are a score of other likely places on the coast we might have tried. I'm only saying—'

'That we should keep our wits about us when we visit Mr Vangenzen,' said Father Andries. 'And indeed we shall.'

Holland nodded. 'All right, you had better go. Sir, I shall hope to hear from you shortly.'

He extended his hand to the priest, who clasped it in both of his and then whispered a short prayer. 'With the blessing I shall come straight back,' he promised, 'and with news of a ship for the pair of you.'

Holland nodded. Turning to Mary, he drew a folded square of papers out of his pocket and handed it to her. 'I'm giving you the plans of the *Ammonite*,' he said.

She did not take them immediately. However sensible, the prospect of parting from him had felt wrong and this was much worse. It presumed that he would not manage to escape. 'But I—'

'I'll have them back again when we've sailed. This is just a precaution. So look after them, but remember – you're more important than they are.' His look managed to be tender and commanding at the same time. 'I'll be as quick as I can, but don't wait for me or do anything daft. And promise me that your first aim will be to get yourself on board that ship.'

'But—' She meant to say more, but his look prevented her. 'I promise.'

'Word of honour, mind.'

'Word of honour,' she repeated.

25

Dunkerque had been somewhat knocked about in 1793 when it was besieged by British forces led by the Duke of York. The siege had failed, however, and the town was much the same as it had been at the end of the Seven Years War. Roughly circular in shape, it stood just above the high water mark, and was protected on both its landward and seaward sides by fortifications designed by the great French military engineer, Gaspard Vauban. A wide stretch of beach provided further protection at low tide, and even when the tide was in, vessels could not enter the town's harbour promiscuously, but only by means of a guarded tidal gateway, approximately half a mile in length.

The town had a garrison and ample resources with which to defend itself, but balanced against this was a keen interest in profit. Merchant ships and privateers used it as a base, and no fewer than five canals linked Dunkerque with its neighbours to the north, east, and south. Barges from St Omer typically docked in the basin of the Bourbourg canal before transporting their cargoes either to the market or the warehouses in the central part of the town. A few vessels were engaged in this latter activity when Mary and Father Andries disembarked, and they might have negotiated a ride in one of the punts or rowing boats that plied between the barges like busy water bugs. They were not eager to expose themselves to strangers, however, and preferred to approach the

Vangenzen & De Groot warehouse as discreetly as possible and under their own power.

It was a decision that might easily have proved disastrous, for Mary could only guess that the harbour was somewhere in front of them, and Father Andries' knowledge depended entirely on the vague directions provided by Guillot's son. But luck, as Holland had observed, was with them. Firstly, they were already reasonably close to their destination, and had neither to pass through the lower town nor risk the main military installations. Secondly, their instructions to 'cross the bridge, follow the water right round, cross again and then straight on' proved wholly sufficient to bring them to the harbour.

The harbour was tranquil at that hour. A sluice operated to keep vessels afloat whatever the exigencies of the tide, but in fact there were only a few small craft tied up at the quay, together with a two-masted sloop or schooner. Mary knew very little about ships of any kind, but the sloop's elegant, even rakish lines appealed to her. The prospect of such a vessel – which anyone could see was eminently suited for dashing across the Channel – so close at hand, raised her spirits tremendously. Dismay at parting from Holland and the fear that had gripped her during the anxious walk from the barge gave way to relief, excitement, and zeal. Was *this* their rescuer? This the very means to carry them home?

This bundle of emotions, coming hard upon the release of tension, was almost overpowering. She had to stop herself from ordering Father Andries to return to the barge immediately and alert Captain Holland. As it was, her grip on the priest's hand was a painful one, and she seriously considered going aboard the sloop. Why need they trouble Cornelius Vangenzen at all? If someone in authority was aboard, they could fix things up straightaway!

Good sense, or at least caution, prevailed, however, and after a final glance at the sloop, she turned her attention towards the buildings that lined the harbour.

The headquarters of Vangenzen & De Groot was obvious when they found it; a neat brass plaque adjacent to the door made all clear. It was not the largest establishment – the brick building on the other side of the harbour was much more imposing – but it had a tidy, well-kept air. Such was Mary's judgement, at least. It arose from the fact that a lantern illuminated the front steps, and inside, the clerk perched behind a high desk greeted them immediately rather than carrying on until he had reached the end of his column of figures.

Mindful of Holland's warning, Father Andries asked for Citizen Vangenzen in Dutch and with a studied casualness. Citizen Vangenzen or Citizen De Groot – either would do just as well. Was one or other of them at leisure to discuss a small matter of business, please?

The clerk answered in the same language. 'I shall enquire. What name shall I say?'

'Father Andries de Brouckere – if you would be so kind.'

The clerk recorded the name on a scrap of paper and handed it to a small boy who, unnoticed until that moment, had been sitting cross-legged on the floor beside his desk. The child sped down the corridor that ran parallel with the front of the building, returning after a short interval at a comparable pace. His announcement, 'They are to step inside, Papa,' was delivered as an audible whisper into the parental ear.

'You are to step into the master's office,' affirmed the clerk. 'Joos will show you the way.'

'Ah, thank you,' beamed Father Andries, and to the boy, 'please to lead the way, my child.'

The perception of tidy competence continued when they reached their destination, a smallish room furnished with a desk, glass-fronted cupboards containing ledgers and papers, and two armchairs. Beyond partially drawn curtains, tall sash windows afforded a view of the harbour.

The room's occupant accorded well with his surroundings, and Mary thought she saw a resemblance with *her* Mr Vangenzen. This one was older, however, and his manner less friendly. *He is Samuel Vangenzen after twenty years at a desk instead of an easel,* she decided.

She had expected to conduct the negotiations – at least to

present the documents proving that she was Samuel Vangenzen's wife – but this did not happen. Instead, she listened attentively, albeit ignorantly, as the merchant and Father Andries spoke together in Dutch. It was difficult to judge a person's character in a foreign language, but she was also aware that the priest's tone was distinctly more encouraging.

Cornelius Vangenzen sat back in his chair and observed Mary from behind lowered eyelids. Then he addressed her in English. 'So,' he remarked, 'you are Mrs Vangenzen . . . and also Miss Finch, from England.'

Mary glanced at Father Andries, who shrugged helplessly. 'He has heard all about you, it seems.'

'Even to a description of sorts,' affirmed Vangenzen. 'The woman young and attractive, the man tall and dark-haired. I presume that the latter did not refer to Father Andries.'

'No,' said Mary. 'Father Andries has helped us – myself and . . . You were warned that we might come to Dunkerque?'

'Not warned, *informed* that it was your intention to obtain passage to England on board one of my ships. I was assured, of course, that you would not manage it – that you and your friend – Ogbourne? – would be captured long before you reached this place. That confidence appears to have been misjudged.'

Mary stared at him. 'But how did—'

'I do not know how your plans were discovered. What I can say is that no ship in Dunkerque will dare to carry you to England, now that the authorities have involved themselves. *I* do not dare do so, and apart from my captains the others are Frenchmen.'

It was a disaster – not only were their plans known, but their only source of aid had failed them! What could she possibly say to recover the situation? A wave of fear, of panic, forced Mary to speak, but before she could form more than a word or so, Father Andries interrupted indignantly.

'You cannot betray this young woman,' cried the priest. His tone was one of astonishment, and he pointed at Mary as if seeking clarification. Surely not *this* young woman?

'I am not betraying her,' Vangenzen replied sulkily. 'I am merely standing to one side.'

'A Jesuitical distinction,' scorned Father Andries. 'You are a Calvinist, I suppose?'

'Yes.' A truculent shrug of the shoulders accompanied the word.

'Then it is worse than Jesuitical. A Jesuit would scorn such reasoning. Think of the harm that the Revolutionaries have done – in France and elsewhere. This terrible war . . . your own people killed . . . Do you approve of such things?'

'No, nor did I approve when the English attacked the Dutch fleet at Kamperduin.'

The merchant had recovered something of his confidence with that remark, but Father Andries brushed it aside. 'Such things happen in war,' he remarked. 'And at sea the English are seldom bested – your comrades ought not to have risked their ships in an encounter.'

'Perhaps. But what can I do? You forget, I am no . . . fire-brand. I am a man of business.'

'So was the Good Samaritan – a practical man of business – but *he* did not stand to one side.'

A tense silence greeted that riposte. Then Vangenzen rose from his chair and began to stride up and down the room, his hands clasped behind his back. Mary and Father Andries exchanged glances – on her side, questioning; on his, critical, hopeful, stern. At the fourth turn, Vangenzen stopped in front of Mary. 'My cousin – he knows about your activities?'

'Yes, sir, he does.'

'And he wishes to assist the British?'

'Yes.'

Vangenzen resumed his pacing, and now he spoke under his breath, scraps of a conversation with himself. Mary was again reduced to an observer, and even Father Andries strained to hear what was being said. *'Samuel is een kunstenaar en heeft, zoals alle kunstenaars, nog wel eens wat fantastische ideeen . . . Volgens zijn vader is hij verkeerd gegaan. De vader zelf ook . . . het is een rare familie – vreemdelingen eigenlijk nadat zij naar Amerika gingen. Maar natuurlijk*

wil men hulp aanbieden, als dat nochtans mogelijk is. War er maar een
ander schip, of een andere kapitein . . . Mischien dan . . .'

Turning again to Mary he explained slowly that there *was* a
ship, an American vessel called the *Tiger*. He knew nothing of
it – he could promise nothing – but as Mary and her associate
had American papers, the captain of the *Tiger* might possibly
be willing to help them. 'She is in the *grande rade*, however.
You would have to go to her.'

'What is the *grande rade*?'

'It is the harbour – the natural harbour – between the low-
water mark and the sandbanks.' He opened a map and spread
it across his desk, so that Mary was at last able to appreciate
the true composition of the town and its relationship to the
sea. 'We are here,' he explained, 'and now, with the tide receding
and the strand unsafe for any but small craft, all of the ships
are either here, in the *petite rade*, or here, in the *grande rade*. The
Tiger did not come into the strand when she arrived last night,
but went straight to the *grande rade*. Perhaps she is a pirate of
some kind and wishes to keep to herself. But you would not
object to that, I suppose.'

'No, indeed,' said Mary. The possibility occurred to her that
the *Tiger* might prey on English merchants, but she ignored it.
'To reach this . . . anchorage, we would leave Dunkerque and
cross this beach – the strand.' She drew a line with her finger.
'Is it very far?'

'Less than a mile.' Vangenzen stared at her across the map.
'You would like to try it?'

'Oh yes.'

'*Zeer goed*. I promise nothing, mind, but I will send someone
now in a boat to the *Tiger* and try to make the arrangements.'

At the end of a day's work, it was Guillot's habit to come
ashore, prepare a small supper, drink a cup of wine, and relax
by the fire before turning in. His friend Claude Moreau often
joined him on these occasions, usually contributing a sausage
to the repast. They were so employed when a pair of horsemen
came trotting along the towpath – soldiers of some kind,

375

although their uniforms were hard to identify in the twilight. Guillot told his son to go on board – to wait in the cabin. The boy was well below the age of conscription, but who could tell what the government might decree? And there had been rumours . . .

The soldiers, however, appeared not to be interested in recruits. Dismounting, they approached each barge in turn and spoke briefly with their operators. At last they came to Guillot and Moreau, and asked whether they were carrying any passengers. The light of the fire revealed the speaker to be a grey-haired corporal of dragoons.

Guillot spat a fragment of tobacco into the flames. 'Is it a crime to take passengers?'

'No, but . . . They paid you to take them to Dunkerque?'

'Naturally they paid. I am not a rich man who can afford to take passengers for free.'

After a few more exchanges of a similar type, it was revealed that two passengers had joined Guillot's barge in St Omer: a woman and a priest.

'He has disguised himself,' said the corporal. 'Why do you say he was a priest?'

'Why do I say it? Because he was a priest, of course! Do you suppose that I cannot distinguish a priest from one who is not a priest? I, who served beside Father Henri every day for five years when I was a boy? Is such a thing possible?'

Moreau shook his head sympathetically. Nevertheless, the rhetorical force of Guillot's query was lessened somewhat by his admission that the fellow *had* appeared to be a foreigner.

The corporal repeated, 'A foreigner,' in a highly significant tone and looked at his colleague.

'From the north,' affirmed Guillot, gesturing vaguely in that direction. 'A Fleming, perhaps, or a Dutchman.'

'Where are they now?' The other soldier's voice was curt, like an officer's, but as he stood outside the circle of firelight, his rank was unclear.

Guillot explained that the woman and the priest (he emphasised that word) had gone into the town; they had some business

376

to arrange. Not being a curious man, and having better things to do than to ask foolish questions, he had not enquired further into the matter.

The corporal rubbed his chin. 'You do not know where they were going in the town, I suppose? They did not happen to mention it to you?'

Guillot deliberated, puffing slowly on his pipe. 'They did mention it,' he said at last. 'At least, the priest spoke of Vangenzen's — Vangenzen & De Groot is the proper name of the establishment, but the priest mentioned only Vangenzen. He asked for directions.'

'Did you give them?'

'Certainly.'

'Certainly he did,' said Moreau. 'Who could doubt it?'

'And besides, it would be a simple matter to find Vangenzen & De Groot in Dunkerque. Everyone knows their warehouse – outside, by the red doors and inside, by De Groot's belly.'

This observation seemed to satisfy the two soldiers; they remounted their horses and rode quickly away.

'That is the Army for you,' said Guillot, nodding in the direction of the fading hoof beats. 'Always in a hurry.'

'Yes, they seem very fervent,' Moreau agreed. He swallowed the last of his wine, and when the night was quiet again, he added, 'You did not mention the dead body that you took on board in St Omer.'

'No,' Guillot admitted, 'because they asked only about passengers, and a dead body is not a passenger. Would you call a dead cow a passenger?'

'Assuredly not.' *Nor a live one*, thought Moreau.

'And neither is a dead man. Both are freight. If they had asked about freight, then I would have told them. I have nothing to hide.'

At that moment, a quavering voice called from the waterside, followed by the sound of someone scrambling – or jumping. 'Papa?'

'What is it?' called Guillot. 'You can come out now – they are gone. You were not afraid of those soldiers, surely?'

The boy hurried across the grass and stood between his father and Moreau; he glanced fearfully over his shoulder. 'No, but . . .'

'Well, what is it? Is the port side leaking again? Damn those caulkers! If they have ruined another cargo of linen with their shoddy repairs they will pay for it! I will have them before the judge and—'

'No, no, there is no leak,' cried the boy. 'At least, I did not notice. But I went below just now, and the *body* . . . the one they called Lefebvre . . .'

'Well?'

'It is gone!'

Twenty minutes, said Mary to herself. *He has been gone at least twenty minutes.*

She resisted the temptation to consult her watch in case it had only been five, and instead rose from her chair. Father Andries had a considerable facility for patience, but Mary found it difficult to sit and wait – to do nothing. She went to the window and twitched the curtain aside, but the view held no appeal. From the nautical perspective, her interest was focused solely on the *Tiger*, and it lay beyond the harbour and the beach. She turned away with a sigh. Charts of the Channel and the North Sea had been tacked to the wall behind Mr Vangenzen's desk, and she surveyed these in turn, plotting voyages to England that took little account of wind or tide.

If the ship agrees to take us, she mused, *we shall be back in Dover tonight! And then up to London by the mail, or we may hire a coach, perhaps. Captain Holland will want to go straight to the Admiralty and—*

She turned to Father Andries, who was sitting quietly in a chair before the smouldering fire. 'Oughtn't we to fetch Captain Holland? It would save time if we were ready to set out as soon as Mr Vangenzen returned.'

'It would,' he agreed, 'if we were certain of his success with the captain of the American ship. If he has not managed to organise a passage—'

'Then we must endeavour to do so ourselves. We can go down to the strand as easily as Mr Vangenzen, and it is dangerous hanging about here.'

The priest acknowledged this fact and rose creakily to his feet. In accordance with their agreement, *he* would fetch Captain Holland. He said this with a particular emphasis, for Mary's nervous excitement had not eluded him. 'And do sit down, I beg, and compose yourself while—'

He did not complete the sentence, for at that moment foot-steps and raised voices sounded in the corridor. The clerk's outraged cry rose above a series of curt demands. Then the door opened, and a uniformed figure strode into the room.

Mary stared. 'Mr Déprez!' she cried, forgetting, in her confusion, even to speak in French.

'Good evening,' replied Déprez, bowing slightly. 'I am happy to see you again, Miss Finch. I am afraid I never cared for "Citizeness Vangenzen". It did not suit you.' He glanced about the room. 'Well, where is he?'

That question helped to steady her – Mr Déprez, Sergeant Fondard, what did it matter? She would defy them all. 'As you see, Captain Holland is not here,' she said with as much bravado as she could manage. 'He . . . did not come to Dunkerque. We left Paris together, but then we parted – in order to confuse the soldiers.'

Déprez regarded her suspiciously. He had caught the note of fear in her voice – and the hesitation. *And yet the bargeman said she was travelling only with a priest.* 'Where did you separate?'

'Amiens. Captain Holland went to Abbeville, and I came here.'

'And who is this?'

Mary named Father Andries. 'He *has* helped me, but only because I could not speak Dutch. He has nothing to do with . . . anything else.'

'Perhaps,' Déprez allowed, his glance moving between them before settling again on Mary. 'And I suppose that Captain Holland has the plans to the *Ammonite*?'

'Yes.' Mary followed no clear plan in answering Déprez, other than to defend every position until it was lost. 'I really know

379

nothing about that. It was always Captain Holland's concern – not mine. That is not why I came to France.'

She thought she detected a slight softening in Déprez's eyes, and a wild hope sprang up – only to be dashed. 'You are lying,' he said, 'but it does not matter. The truth is that you are in very grave danger. There are soldiers guarding the door, and very soon Sergeant Fondard will be here. Once that happens, you will be in his hands.'

'But I can tell him nothing,' Mary insisted. 'Not about the *Ammonite*,' she started to say, but he cut her off.

'Enough! You do not understand. I will help you if I can, but . . . this is his affair.' He finished in a rush and then regarded her angrily or perhaps in frustration.

She did *not* understand. Was it some kind of trick? 'Why should you wish to help me?'

'Because I do not wish to see you – *any woman* – guillotined,' he snapped, 'or shot before my eyes. And if you try to thwart Fondard, that is what will happen!' She stared at him, and he bit his lip. 'Think, now. Is there something that would protect you? Some . . . I don't know – some reason why you must be kept safe, even until we reach Paris?'

Mary still found his words baffling, but a plan of sorts began to take shape. Anything that she could say to delay matters, to keep the conversation away from Holland, must strengthen his chances of escape. If only it were possible to warn him, and to tell him about the American ship . . .

She made up her mind. 'I do know something, a secret about Citizen Talleyrand and the American envoys.' Déprez frowned and said that any information about Talleyrand would be more likely to kill than to preserve, but she saw the look of surprise that the name provoked and determined to press whatever advantage she had. 'And it is important. I will tell you after you have let Father Andries go.'

'What?' He was dumbfounded. 'You would bargain with me?'

Father Andries tried to intervene. He understood the conversation least of all, but whatever sort of agreement was being suggested sounded wrong to him. 'No, please,' he urged, but no one paid him any heed.

'Let him go,' said Mary.

Déprez smiled thinly. 'Very well.'

Just then the door opened behind him. 'Ah, colonel,' said Fondard in a smiling, pleasant voice. 'Have you begun the inquisition without me?' He stepped into the room. 'And Citizeness Vangenzen, how charming to see you again. And the good Father . . . Andries, I think? Good evening, Father. Well, well, we have only to add Captain Holland and our party will be complete.'

Mary gasped and retreated a step — she was certain that Holland was about to be dragged forward — and Déprez stiffened as if he had been shot. How long had that devil been listening at the door? What had he heard?

'But where *is* Captain Holland?' Fondard continued, apparently to the room at large. 'There were but two passengers on the barge from St Omer, we have been told. Is it possible that he has abandoned the young lady?' He turned to Déprez. 'Colleague, what have you learned of this strange affair?'

'She claims that Holland has gone to Abbeville,' muttered Déprez. 'But . . . perhaps he is somewhere close by.'

'You give voice to my thoughts,' purred Fondard. 'He may indeed be close by, and if we were content to wait, no doubt he would make himself known to us.' Then his expression hardened. 'But I am not a patient man. Citizeness, do you still say that Holland is not in Dunkerque?'

'Yes.'

'You are certain?' he warned and smiled again. 'Remember our old friendship. You would like to help Fondard, yes?'

'I do not know where he is.' Mary's voice was strained, her face pale.

'You are courageous for one who is absent,' he acknowledged, 'let us see how far it extends towards one who is present.' In a single, expert motion he drew a pistol from his pocket, cocked it, and pointed it at Father Andries. Mary watched with horror as he advanced until the end of the barrel was touching the priest's temple. Father Andries closed his eyes; his lips moved silently.

'He will do it,' whispered Déprez.

'Indeed I will,' said Fondard. 'I have a short way with spies and traitors, as your friend Minta Vangenzen discovered.'

Mary heard the last words as through a closed door, muffled and indistinct. Minta was dead? *Dead?* She felt suddenly cold. 'You . . . killed her?' she stammered.

'Certainly. And now?'

'I do not know where he is,' she repeated. 'But . . . Here.' The folded papers emerged from the pocket of her gown and fell onto the desk, slightly beyond the reach of his hand.

Fondard's lips curled into a smile. 'Oh ho!' he cried. 'Here is something of interest, I think!' Then he lowered and uncocked the weapon, placing it first on the top of the cupboard and then, having clucked at his lack of care, restoring it to his pocket.

He examined the papers gloatingly. 'The minister of marine will be glad to have these restored. He ought to be relieved that his stupidity has not proven more costly to France. Here is a precious gift, courtesy of Fondard of the Paris police. And I will not forget you, dear colleague.'

'No, I thought not,' said Déprez grimly.

Fondard turned over the final page and then lowered the plans to stare frowningly at the window. The curtains were worn in places and not fully closed; a flickering light pierced the opening and turned the worn fabric to gold. 'What is that light?' he asked. 'It seems to be coming from the harbour. One might almost imagine the morning sun—'

Suddenly a soldier thrust open the door. 'Fire! Emergency! The harbour is on fire!'

'What?' demanded Fondard. 'Impossible.'

But Déprez had suddenly revived. 'It is Holland, of course!' he cried. 'He *is* somewhere about. Damn him!'

He pushed past the soldier, ordering, 'Come with me,' and raced along the corridor to the front door. Flinging it open, he paused on the steps. Yes, there was a fire, not in the harbour but in the long, brick building that stood between the harbour and the basin. It was a ropewalk, and filled with stores of hemp, tar, and other flammable materials. Now its interior was a red, glowing maw, visible through the row of windows, and where these were open or broken, the flames rushed outwards, climbing the walls and mingling with the darkness to create an eerie, unnatural radiance.

Already the scene was chaotic. Black, noxious smoke filled the air, together with shouts, cries, and the low roar of the fire. Partially illuminated figures rushed along the quay – some in flight and others with half-formed notions of combating the blaze. A similar turmoil was occurring on the water as men made frantic attempts to unmoor boats and move them out of danger. The sloop that Mary had admired could only be freed at the bow end – the stern was chained to a bollard – and it slewed out sideways, impeding the traffic behind. A sudden blast hurled burning fragments skyward, and some fell, sizzling, into the harbour.

A knot of soldiers gathered round Déprez, together with men from the warehouse. Many of the latter did not wish to leave their masters' property undefended. They had an obligation to Vangenzen & de Groot.

'If you do not stop the fire now, you will have nothing to defend,' snapped Déprez. He ordered some to assist with the sloop – to shoot away the chain if necessary – and the rest to come with him. With a clatter of boots and wooden shoes on the cobbled way they plunged into the fray.

Fondard drew back the curtains in Vangenzen's office, and even he was transfixed by the scene of hungry destruction. Then he cursed and fumbled with the window. Heaving it open, he thrust his head through the gap and shouted to the soldiers who had followed Déprez towards the fire. 'Wait! Not all of you, you fools! Come back here immediately! I have not released you!'

He cursed in frustration and withdrew his head, but no sooner had he cleared the glass than a furious assailant knocked

383

him sideways. It was Father Andries, who now clung to him with despairing strength and shouted to Mary to run, to escape!

Surprise contributed to the actual force of the priest's attack, and Fondard stumbled and gave ground. Together they struck the side of the desk, and its legs screeched as it shot across the floor. One gnarled hand grasped Fondard's wrist, and a thin, wiry arm was flung about his neck. 'Fly! Fly!' cried a voice in his ear.

For a moment Fondard was vulnerable, but only a moment. Father Andries could not press his advantage against a younger, more powerful opponent, nor even hold his own. He must be beaten down. But he was not. First because he held on, regardless of the powerful surge that restored Fondard to his feet and freed his right hand, and then because he was seized in his opponent's mighty grip – held upright as his own grasp failed.

'Ha! Ha!' crowed Fondard as his hands knotted around the priest's neck. Something tugged at his coat, but it was a mere trifle, easily ignored. Indeed, exaltation at his triumph drove out all other thoughts. He shook the little rag of a man who had dared to challenge him, delighting in the red, gasping face, the fluttering eyes.

The sound and the blow struck him instantaneously: a roaring blast and a searing pain that pierced his side at point blank range. He staggered, and for a moment his brain resumed its normal function. What had happened? Why had the room gone out of focus? He could not seem to grip properly, or even to stand . . .

Mary ducked awkwardly and watched Fondard sway and fall. The kick of the recoil had sent the pistol spinning out of her hand and over her shoulder, and now she retrieved it cautiously. Her breath was coming in great gasps, and her heartbeat seemed to echo all through her body, but she held the pistol steadily now, and in both hands. She did not remember that most pistols had to be reloaded between shots, but simply stared along the barrel, breathing, breathing, and willing him not to move.

Father Andries raised himself slowly, first to his knees, then to one knee, and finally to a painful stoop, achieved with the help of a chair back. He hobbled to Mary's side and gently removed the pistol from her grasp. A pool of dark blood had almost reached her feet. 'You have saved me, my child,' he murmured.

'Is he . . .?' she whispered.

'Come,' he urged, turning her away from the terrible sight. 'Let us away to the sea.'

The words revived her. 'Yes, yes – of course.' She looked at the pistol – horrible thing – and immediately knew that it was no longer dangerous, nor of any immediate use. What had she been thinking of? But Fondard was dead. Dead, and she had killed him.

Not now, she commanded herself, *do not think about that now,* and to Father Andries she asked, 'Do you . . . think that Captain Holland set the fire?'

'He may have too,' said the priest, 'as a diversion for our sake. But the Dear knows where he is now, poor fellow.'

An urgent tattoo on the window made Mary start. She turned, but it was Holland, grimy and coatless; his white shirt was stained with tar and soot. He flung up the sash. 'Are you all right?' he demanded. 'Come on!'

They hurried outside to meet him. 'Thank God!' cried Mary, when she saw that he was unharmed. 'How did you—'

'Never mind that now. Is there a ship?'

She said there was, but they must run for it. 'Well, lead the way,' urged Holland, 'and quick as you can. I'll help Father Andries.'

'Don't mind me!' piped the priest, but he accepted Holland's arm around his thin shoulders.

Mary had only a vague idea of where to go, and none about negotiating the fortifications on the seaward side of the town. They must keep the harbour on their left, and this course – she hoped – would bring them to the tidal channel that linked Dunkerque to the sea. At present there would be dry land on either side, beyond which lay the two natural harbours: the *petite rade* to the left and the *grande rade* to the right. 'We must find a way down to the strand on *this* side of the channel,' she urged.

They made their way by a series of short darts and slow, cautious advances past houses and shuttered buildings. A noisy tavern proved that news of the fire had not spread to all quarters. Not yet. Meanwhile, awful, unanswerable questions were distracting Mary. *What if there are guards ahead? A locked gate or no way down?* If they could only gain the strand, she felt certain they would be safe – an unreasonable certainty, but something to cling to. But where was the strand?

Two men ran past; then another, who regarded them curiously but did not stop; then a party of soldiers and a young officer. *Damn*, thought Holland. He had shed his coat, at least, but the rest of his 'disguise' would not bear close inspection.

'Is he hurt?' asked the officer, checking his stride. Mary explained that the poor priest had been overcome by the smoke – he needed fresh air. Father Andries coughed weakly, and the officer nodded. 'Very well.'

They set off again, and seemed finally to be coming to the last of the buildings. The harbour had narrowed and curved sharply to the left – which surely had to be the way to the sea. Mary felt a surge of excitement – *we must be nearly there* – when Holland suddenly whispered, 'Barracks ahead – keep going . . . steady.' Barracks, and they looked vast. Two wings, fronting a wide parade. Uniformed men were milling about. *Oh dear, what are they waiting for? Orders? For the fire – yes, to fight the fire – nothing to do with us.*

Steady, steady. She wanted to run, but now the barracks and the forming squads of soldiers were behind them. Ahead was a bridge – they crossed it – and then a guardhouse. *Oh God!* Mary's heart was hammering in her chest as she walked. She expected a challenge – an order to stop; what would she say? But no order came. They were past, and now . . . now they were coming to a set of stairs. Fifteen stairs built into a sloping wall of stone. An open space, more stairs, and then sand beneath their feet. They had reached the strand.

A clean, brisk wind blew in from the sea, and the stars gleamed and winked behind a thin curtain of cloud. The firm sand felt wonderful beneath her boots. Every step now was taking them towards something hopeful and not merely away from something terrible. The strand, the sea, the ship, and home.

'The name of the ship is the *Tiger*,' she explained as they hurried. 'From America.'

'Not one of Vangenzen's, then?' asked Holland.

'No, but he was going to speak with the captain on our behalf. He hoped the captain would agree to help us, because of our American papers. You may have to be Andrew Ogbourne a little longer.'

'I'll be anyone you like, so long as it gets us to England,' Holland affirmed. 'And you too, sir – I mean, you must come with us.'

Father Andries, however, was not so sure. 'There is my work to do on this side, you know. I mustn't shirk it.'

'I fear you will have to . . . interrupt it for a time,' said Mary. 'It would not be safe for you to remain in France – certainly not *here*. And besides . . .' She was now propping him up on the other side.

'Well, I'm not so young as I once was,' admitted Father Andries. 'But I am feeling much better now.' He breathed deeply. 'It must be the air. Fresh and free, as the Lord intended.'

They came at last to the shore – a faint line of white and the sound of small waves rushing and tumbling onto the sand. The water was still receding, or it gave that impression; each thrust forward was slightly less than the one before. *As if the ocean itself is shy and unwilling to know us*, thought Mary.

The thought made her anxious, and she looked along the shore and across the water for a boat, for lights, for *something*. They must find a way off that beach! It was Father Andries, however, who spotted it first: a dark shape that proved to be a small boat, pulled up onto the sand.

'Can it be meant for us?' he asked as they drew near.

Mary scarcely cared, but she answered yes, she thought so.

'Ah, look,' said the priest, 'it says *Haarlem* here on the side, so it must belong to Mr Vangenzen's ship. Thank God for His mercies.'

Holland ordered them to jump in. Mary clambered on board

387

and gave her hand to Father Andries. Did Holland think that they would manage to find the *Tiger*?

It belonged to that category of damned silly questions that Holland, in his wisdom, considered particularly feminine. He merely smiled to himself, set his shoulder to the gunwale, and pushed. 'If we don't, I'll row this damned thing to Dover.'

The thud of horses' hooves and Mary's cry came in the same instant. Then a shouted command in English: 'Halt or we fire!'

Holland heaved the boat more strongly and followed it into the surf. A bullet whizzed past him; another struck the side of the boat.

'Hurry!' begged Mary. 'Get in!'

Holland gave another push; the water was nearly up to his waist; now it was chest high. 'Grab the oars,' he ordered and prepared to heave himself aboard.

Up he rose as the boat dipped under his weight; his white shirt made a clear target for the men on shore. He felt the blow like a sharp, hot stab, and tumbled into the boat. Somehow the oars came into his hands as he climbed onto the thwart. 'Get down, right down!' he shouted, and took a powerful stroke.

Another stroke, and another — *God, what an awkward tub!* — but they were moving, surely they were moving away from the shore. Some of the horses had entered the water, but they could not go far. A chip of wood flew into the air as a bullet hit the gunwale. Another stroke, and the ebbing tide was helping. Another stroke. *Come on, damn you!*

'I see something!' said Mary, as she peered over the bow.

'I told you to keep down.' The pain was spreading across his back.

'Yes, but I think it is a light — perhaps a ship's lantern.'

'I see it,' affirmed Father Andries. 'And can this be a rudder of some kind?' He waggled it tentatively. 'You know, I think it must be.'

'All right,' said Holland. 'Sir, ship the tiller if you can. Mary, sing out when you see them, and let's hope it's not a French ship.'

From the shore, the sound of the voices was fading. The

patch of white was still visible, but Déprez's horse disliked the water and would go no farther. And what was the point? The men behind him had given up – and they were right.

But failure was hard. He reloaded and took a final shot, knowing that his target was out of range. Still he waited, until all that he could see was a golden light somewhere in the offing, and the night was silent except for the waves breaking on the sand behind him.

26

Joseph Davey, captain of the *Tiger*, considered the two visitors perched on makeshift chairs in his day-cabin. *Passengers*, he supposed he ought to call them, for he had agreed not merely to their coming aboard, but also that they should be carried to England. *'To England or wherever we may set them down conveniently in those waters'* – those had been the terms he had made with old Vangenzen, and damned good terms too, when no fare was to be charged for involving himself and his ship in what seemed to be a very peculiar venture.

Davey was no stranger to peculiarities at sea, and he doubted whether he ought to pry too deeply into this one. Least said was soonest mended, after all. But the evening's events had certainly piqued his curiosity. Cornelius Vangenzen's request, shots fired on the strand, what looked like a serious fire in the town, and finally these two passengers – three, counting the fellow who had been shot – ranging up alongside and calmly asking was this the *Tiger*, please? – as though it might have been the coach to Duxbury. Now, as he listened to the woman's vague account, he doubted very much whether his curiosity would be satisfied. She was very pretty, however, and when she smiled and thanked him for taking so much trouble for them, he was largely content.

'Oh, it wasn't a great deal of trouble,' he assured her, smiling in his turn. 'Although it might have been, if we hadn't been ready to sail just as soon as you came aboard. We were also lucky not to come across either of the French gunboats.'

'*Gunboats?*' cried Mary, with rather more anxiety than she would have wished to convey. 'I had not understood Dunkerque to be a Navy port.'

'It isn't, but there are gunboats all the same. They patrol the *rade*, sometimes. But I expect the fire got their attention tonight.'

'Ah, yes, the fire,' Mary agreed. 'That was . . .' She consciously lightened her tone. 'The gunboats could have had no interest in *us*, of course, but it would have been tiresome, having to submit to their enquiries.'

'Yes, ma'am, it certainly would. I don't hold with warships, especially when they make it their business to interrupt mine. And we'll have the same trouble on the other side, I expect.'

'Ah yes, from the British, you mean.' The prospect of trouble from the Royal Navy came as a welcome relief to Mary. Since boarding the *Tiger* she had struggled to compose her thoughts. Relief at having escaped Dunkerque warred with anxiety over their present situation. What did Captain Davey know or suspect? Could he be trusted? They *were* safe now, weren't they?

Glancing at him as he frowned across the table, she felt reasonably certain of his good faith, particularly if she could keep the conversation away from herself. Whatever explanation Mr Cornelius Vangenzen had given, she mustn't say anything to undermine it until they were safely in England, or under the watchful eye of the Navy. 'When shall we . . . When do you suppose we shall arrive?' she asked.

Davey consulted his watch. 'If the breeze holds and we don't fall in with the North Sea fleet, we may reach Dover by midnight. And then we shall wait upon the tide, of course. In the meantime, would either of you care for some refreshment? We don't go in for luxury on board the *Tiger*, but I believe we can promise you a private corner and a bite of supper.'

Mary glanced at Father Andries and nodded. 'Thank you, Captain – that would be most kind. But might I perhaps see Mr Ogbourne now?'

Certainly she could see Mr Ogbourne; Davey would have

someone show her to the cockpit immediately. He moved towards the door, preparing to issue the order, and paused. 'You won't mind the sight of blood, I trust?'

Mary had also risen, and the ship's motion made her stagger. *Cockpit? Blood?* A terrible new fear welled up suddenly. 'You do not think he is badly hurt?' she demanded.

'Oh no,' said Davey. 'There is certain to be blood, however, and it can turn your stomach if you come upon it sudden. Perhaps you had better wait here. One of the boys could make you a cup of tea.'

Mary assured him that she did not require any sort of restorative, and, in fact, she was spared both the cockpit and the blood. Holland was no longer in the small, damp space that passed on the *Tiger* for a sickbay, but had gone on deck. She found him looking pale and tired in a borrowed boat cloak, leaning against the rail.

'How are you feeling?' she asked. 'Ought you to be inside— below, I mean? The night air . . .'

Holland smiled, but the look of weariness remained. 'I'm all right,' he assured her, explaining that the ball that had struck him had been nearly spent, and that superficial wounds always bled like the devil. 'No, I was thinking about Martel and Boyle – wondering whether we could all have got out of France. I like to think that, between us, we could have managed it, somehow, but that only makes me feel worse about the fire.'

Mary reminded him that the fire had not been his fault, but paused midway through her defence. 'Minta is dead,' she murmured.

'*Dead?* How in God's name— What happened?'

'I do not know,' said Mary. A lump had arisen suddenly in her throat, and she swallowed awkwardly. 'It was Fondard, of course. He boasted of it! He said . . .' She shivered against the memory.

Holland swore under his breath. 'A woman, on her own . . . Damn him! Why didn't he just arrest her?'

'Minta must have . . . thwarted him somehow.' She raised anxious eyes to his. 'Perhaps, in the end, she refused to help him – refused to give us up.'

'Perhaps,' Holland allowed.

'Why else would he have killed her? And if that is why she died' – Mary's voice grew tense – 'then really, it is my fault. It is my fault regardless, for if I had not come to Paris, she and Mr Vangenzen would have been safe!'

'It *is* your fault, if you put it that way,' Holland agreed, 'and mine, and Shy's, and Vangenzen's. He agreed to help Shy of his own free will.'

'But he never really understood—'

'Nevertheless, he agreed. And so did Minta.'

'Only because she wanted to support Mr Vangenzen . . . and protect him.'

'But in the end, she couldn't do both,' said Holland. He took Mary's hand. 'And if you hadn't come to Paris, you would not have found out about the Americans or been able to help me with the *Ammonite*. You must include those things in the reckoning.'

'Yes, but . . . I suppose . . .' Mary struggled to resolve the conflict between guilt and duty. *Principles are difficult, as Mr Vangenzen said, but one has to take responsibility for what one believes in.* 'No, of course, you are right. What I did *was* worth doing, especially as regards the *Ammonite* . . .' She glanced down at her side and frowned perplexedly. 'I must have left my reticule in Captain Davey's— No! I never . . . Oh, you fool!'

The sudden change surprised Holland. 'What is it?'

'The plans for the *Ammonite*!' she blurted, clutching his hand. 'I left them in Dunkerque!'

He did not answer, but now her words came quickly as she revealed what had taken place in Cornelius Vangenzen's office. 'And then, when I realised that Sergeant Fondard was dead, I forgot . . . I forgot to take the plans back again! He must have dropped them when he was fighting with Father Andries, but I never thought to look.'

'*You shot Fondard?*'

'I had to! It was dreadful, but . . . I was not thinking properly afterwards, because the plans *must* have been close by.'

She shivered again, and Holland drew her into his arms.

'My dear,' he murmured, and then, 'no wonder Father Andries needed a hand getting down to the ship.'

'Yes, he was terribly brave.'

'I think that you both were.'

'Well . . . but then I made such a mess of it! After all we had done to keep the *Ammonite* out of French hands – we might just as well have stayed in Paris!'

'I wouldn't say that,' said Holland dryly.

Mary shook her head. How *could* she have been so foolish as to forget the very thing for which they had been striving?

'Don't be daft,' Holland urged. 'I told you' – emphasising his words with a kiss to her forehead – 'that you were more important than any bit of paper.'

'Yes, but I thought—' She stared up at him. Did he really not care about the plans? Surely that was impossible. *He means to comfort me – to make me believe that I am not the worst blockhead . . .*

Before she could complete that damning assessment, a quite different one began to take shape – not about herself, but the man beside her. Holland was not romantic – not in a thoughtless, indulgent sort of way – and if he meant to offer reassurance, there must be a reason for it. *And as we cannot go back to Dunkerque for the plans . . .*

'The copy that you made . . . it was not genuine, was it?' she asked slowly.

'Oh, it was genuine all right, but—'

'But?'

'But of course I included a few important errors. It was a help to write down most of Boyle's ideas and equations rather than trying to remember them, but I wasn't such a damned fool as to make up a perfect set of plans. Not when I thought the French police might be chasing us all the way to the coast!'

Relief overwhelmed her even before he had finished his sentence. Relief that could not be measured – only surrendered to. Relief that— *Wait, you had better make quite certain.* Her eyes had closed; now she opened them. 'Do you mean that *if* Mr Déprez recovers the plans, the French will *not* be able to build a boat like the *Ammonite* from them?' Her voice held a mixture of hope and disbelief. 'You are convinced of that?'

His conveyed no such dichotomy. 'They couldn't build one that floated, or that sank as Boyle intended. Not without a great deal of work to find the errors and correct them.'

'Oh my,' she murmured, and now the feeling of reprieve and liberation spread like a warm drink, like a potent, soothing medicine. A tonic. Was Holland laughing at her? She did not mind.

'In fact,' mused Holland, 'it would be a damned good thing if they *did* find the plans.'

'Indeed?'

'Yes. Déprez would be bound to consider them authentic and believe that he had won the prize after all. Damn it, I would like to see his face! And the Ministry of Marine might spend time and money . . . I hope they do, by God.' He grinned at her. 'Better the *Ammonite* than invasion barges, my dear.' It was, perhaps, a surprising prelude to a kiss, but not an objectionable one.

Paul Déprez did find the plans of the *Ammonite*, bloodstained and crumpled beneath Sergeant Fondard's body. 'This is the first occasion on which I find myself grateful to you, sergeant,' he informed the corpse. 'The first and the last, I expect.'

The memory of that event, a strange culmination to what had been a strange partnership, remained with him all the way back to Paris. He thought about it again on the evening of his return, as he sat outside General Bonaparte's office. Having delivered his report to a dour young clerk, Déprez was waiting for his interview. It would not be a pleasant meeting, of that he had no doubt. The general would not look kindly on a man who had failed a second time, and the fact that the situation might have been worse – Fondard might have survived to tell tales – was scant consolation when Déprez's current prospects seemed so precarious. Could he justify his conduct? *No, and better not to try.* What about defences? He felt the stiff, folded sheets of paper in his coat pocket. *Well, we shall soon see.*

He knocked at the appointed hour and entered. At least, he

opened the door and crossed the threshold, but there he halted. 'Minister,' he croaked. 'I did not expect—'

'No, it is quite a surprise,' acknowledged Talleyrand blandly. 'But not a bad one, I trust. Do come and sit by the fire – there is a nasty draught in that corridor, as I am sure you noticed.'

The foreign minister limped towards the hearth, where a comfortable fire was crackling, and Déprez followed dazedly. His thoughts whirled as he tried to assess what Talleyrand's presence might portend. *Does he mean to get his knife into me first? But where would be the profit in that if I am already damned?* Two things seemed certain – Talleyrand did nothing impetuously, and he was no fool. It could not bode well for Déprez, therefore, that the minister had judged it safe to show himself as General Bonaparte's delegate.

Yet, when he began to speak, it was to assure Déprez of his friendship and his concern. Having recited the several failures that had characterised 'this most unfortunate enterprise', he went on to suggest, delicately, that the colonel might be in need of a protector. To offer himself in that role, moreover, had been Talleyrand's object in seeking this conversation. 'For you know, the escape of those two English spies has deeply disturbed the general.'

No offer of assistance from Talleyrand came without conditions, but how to refuse it? And *could* it be refused? Uncertain of his ground, Déprez fell back upon his only defence. The enterprise had not wholly failed – there was still the *Ammonite*. Might not this marvellous invention, so coveted by the English, be used against them? Might not a French *Ammonite* assist in the expected invasion of England? What were two spies when weighed against that?

The foreign minister listened politely, and when Déprez produced the plans he examined them, but with little obvious interest. The *Ammonite,* he remarked, was a purely theoretical weapon.

'It could easily become a real one,' urged Déprez. 'With the support of the Navy . . . with *your* support.'

'Oh, you flatter me, but you know the minister of marine has reservations. He suggests that this boat would be dishonourable.

396

You would not wish France to conduct herself dishonourably, would you, colonel? Even against the British?'

'Certainly not.'

And the invasion of England – that is a theoretical campaign. It may come to pass, and it may not.'

'But General Bonaparte—'

'Thinks as I do on this matter,' said Talleyrand. 'He wonders whether our Naval forces are as yet sufficient to undertake a successful landing in England. In fact, I think you will find his attention is tending in an easterly direction . . . towards Egypt. I hardly think that an undersea boat would be of much use in Egypt, do you? It is a desert, after all.'

'No, minister, it would not be very useful in Egypt.'

'Unless, of course, the general were minded to take a cruise along the Nile. Which leaves you, I am afraid, in a rather awkward situation – or it would do, if I did not have a liking for you.' Talleyrand smiled. 'Somehow I always think of you as belonging to the Foreign Ministry, whatever your present appointment. A legacy of your former services, I suppose.'

Déprez sat quietly, weighing the minister's words. Then he said that perhaps it might be possible – for one who stood well with the Ministry of Marine *and* General Bonaparte – to assure them of the *Ammonite*'s eventual usefulness, and to remind them that recovery of the plans had been a valuable service to the Republic.

Talleyrand agreed that such assurances might be possible, in exchange for future services. What services? Time would tell.

'Time will tell indeed,' Déprez muttered as he departed shortly afterwards. Rain had fallen, and he shivered as he stood in the damp, ill-lit courtyard, drawing on his gloves and fastening his cloak as he waited for his horse to be produced. The thought of becoming the foreign minister's creature sickened him. One did what one must to survive, of course, but it left a bad taste in the mouth, and pragmatism was hard to bear on a cold, wet evening.

Then he smiled to himself. From somewhere in the back of his mind came the memory of Mary Finch – not her escape, nor her defiance of Fondard, nor even the time that they had waltzed together and she had blushed in his arms. *'A secret about Talleyrand and the American envoys,'* she said. *'An important secret.' That fellow Marshall was her particular friend, I remember, and one of the envoys. Perhaps I will pay him a visit. Yes, I think that would be in order. And then we shall see which of us holds the trump card, minister.*

An interview of a somewhat less equivocal nature occurred when Mary and Holland returned to England. As Mary had predicted, they went immediately to London, where Holland reported on the mixed fortunes of the Boyle affair. He also reproduced, in so far as he was able, the plans of the *Ammonite*. Mr Nepean congratulated Holland on his safe return, but Martel's death sensibly dampened his good humour.

'And I regret that I was not able to recover Mr Boyle himself, sir,' said Holland. 'That is what we set out to do, after all.'

'Yes, that would have been the prize of prizes,' Nepean agreed, 'but I would have been sorrier still if the attempt to gain it had landed all of you in a French prison. You would never have come out, you know. We might possibly have done something for Miss Finch, but not you.' He gazed at Holland speculatively.

'No, sir, I know that.'

'Well, you are a damned fool, Captain Holland, but I am glad to have you back, if only' – Neapean consulted a paper on his desk – 'to return you to your regiment with the Admiralty's compliments. This is the second letter I have had from Colonel Congreve, wondering when you might return to your proper job. I believe he imagines you have been on holiday.'

Holland smiled. 'Yes, sir. I'll go down to Woolwich straight-away and sort things out.'

As for the *Ammonite* itself, Nepean doubted whether anything would ever come of such a strange vessel, but he promised that the plans would be filed, for prompt use if circumstances demanded and sufficient money could be found. Unfortunately, their lord-ships were notoriously cautious when it came to spending money on speculative, one might even say *theoretical* projects.

* * *

After this meeting Holland did return to Woolwich, where he submitted a tactful report to his commanding officer and let slip just enough information to content Drake. He did not consider the matter closed, however, not by a long chalk. As soon as he could decently manage it, he must return to London, specifically to 12 Devonshire Square.

Mary, of course, had taken up residence again at that address. She was delighted to see Miss Marchmont again, but dismayed to learn of the vicious assault upon Nazarian. By random miscreants, Miss Marchmont said, although Mary was less certain. The redoubtable *varich* had survived, but was still confined to his bed, and it was in his bedchamber at the top of the house that the two women met to discuss his case.

'I hope you are being a good patient?' asked Mary, having received an account of pills, poultices, strengthening potions, and hot water bottles.

'Very good,' Nazarian confirmed, but he darted a wary glance at Miss Marchmont.

'A good patient?' scoffed that lady. 'Wilful, fractious . . . convinced he knows better than the doctor—'

'I *do* know better,' Nazarian protested. 'Doctor said I would die! I don't follow *his* advice, I think.' He spread his hands. 'A little cut kill me? Pooh! I am all better now, almost.'

'He is forever trying to get round Sally and Mrs Jakes. I found him trying to creep down the stairs only yesterday with some foolish idea of issuing orders regarding our store of coal.'

'Oh dear,' said Mary, trying to look severe. 'That does not sound wise.'

'It certainly was not. Nor shall it be repeated. Until he is quite well, the rest of us are perfectly capable of managing the house.' Miss Marchmont folded her arms beneath her ample bosom and stared down at the patient. 'I believe we understand each other now, however, do we not?'

Nazarian attempted a mutinous look, but quailed under the other's merciless gaze. 'Yes, lady,' he growled.

★   ★   ★

Nazarian's eventual liberation from his bedchamber (although not from Miss Marchmont's supervision) coincided with Holland's visit to Devonshire Square. Indeed, Holland was pressed into service to assist the first, perilous descent to the ground floor parlour, where Nazarian was immediately settled in a comfortable chair, swathed in blankets, and made to drink a strong cup of proper English tea. (Neither Miss Marchmont nor Mrs Jakes had much faith in the restorative properties of 'foreign concoctions', despite Nazarian's protest that all Armenians lived to one hundred – at least – and they all drank Armenian tea.)

Mary and Holland retreated to the dining room, remote and undistinguished at that time of day, but affording privacy. Word had come from Cuthbert Shy at last, in the form of a memorandum, together with a bundle of legal documents relating to the early history of White Ladies. *Probably forged by one of Mr Shy's agents*, Mary thought as she leafed through them.

The memorandum, at least, provided authentic information. Tobias Jens had returned to Paris, although he had not yet felt it wise to re-open Vrillac's. (He grieved for his customers.) He also reported that Samuel Vangenzen had been freed from the Temple prison, where he had been held without charge since his arrest by Sergeant Fondard. And not only freed, but permitted – even encouraged – to return to America.

'Marshall kept his word, it seems,' said Holland. They were standing on opposite sides of the table, and he glanced across, first at the spread of legal papers and then at the memorandum which she consulted.

'I never doubted he would use his best efforts,' said Mary, 'but Jens says that Citizen Talleyrand had as much to do with the actual success of the venture as Mr Marshall – perhaps more so.'

'Talleyrand? Why would he have involved himself?'

'That is not clear, but Jens suggests that it may be part of the foreign minister's wider campaign regarding Mr Marshall and his colleagues. The negotiations have yet to begin, and Talleyrand is as subtle as a *Vipera berus*, according to Jens.'

Holland started to reply and then paused as he observed

Mary. She continued to read the memorandum, and chuckled as she did so. 'What is it? Has Jens submitted his bill?'

She smiled across at him. 'Apparently I have achieved a certain eminence among the agents who work for Mr Shy. *He* offers no opinion, of course, but says that, in consequence of my recent activities – *our* activities, he should say, yours and mine – I have become one of the most notable of "Shy's Men". What do you think of that?'

'I'm quite happy to be left out of it, thank you very much.'

'But it is quite an honour – I daresay Mr Shy's agents have done dozens of marvellous things, and for them to say . . . And you know, it *was* rather astonishing, our getting away from France as we did.'

'Astonishing is a good word for it – a one in a hundred chance – which I hope you'll remember the next time Shy comes to you with another damn fool scheme.'

'This was not— And what makes you imagine that there will *be* a next time?'

It was not a challenge that Holland could resist. Rounding the table, he closed the distance between them. Mary handed him the memorandum, but he dropped it onto the table. 'Because he sent you that message, of course. That's meant to keep you on the lead, so that you'll answer when he tugs it. I'm not saying that he doesn't need you, only that this is his cock-eyed way of showing it.'

Mary's forehead creased in a frown, but then her expression softened. 'What a fortunate thing for me that you are not romantic.'

'I beg your pardon?'

'I mean, well, you do not say things merely to be polite. One can rely on you – and I am afraid that one cannot always rely on Mr Shy. In that way, I mean.'

'I'm glad you think I have some advantage over Shy,' said Holland, smiling in turn. Then he raised her chin, which had fallen during her last remark, and placed both her hands upon his shoulders. 'How should you like to marry me, then? You have already named my good points, such as they are, so I won't bore you by repeating them. I've no money, but you know that too, and I don't care much for Mrs Tipton, or Slipper—'

She stared up at him. 'But I thought we had already decided that — to be married, I mean.'

'We had,' Holland agreed, 'but as you've married someone else in the meantime, I thought I had better re-establish my position, before you hared off to America on the strength of some mad plot or other.'

'I do not think *that* is very likely,' said Mary primly.

'Don't you?'

'No — at least, not without telling you. But with regard to your first question, *yes*, I should like to very much.'

'Good. Now what about this house?'

She had been smiling and blushing very prettily, but now she was startled again. 'This house?'

'Wasn't there a house in Devonshire Square that you thought we ought to buy? If we're to marry we must have a place in Town.'

'Yes, but that was Number Three. I do not know whether Number Twelve is for sale.'

'Well, you would rather have this place, wouldn't you? Especially if Nazarian came along with it? Shall we find out whether there's a chance?' He paused and then continued evenly, 'You would have to pay for it.'

'Oh yes, do let's try,' cried Mary. 'Only, you must do the bargaining, and then we shall decide. We ought to be a partnership, after all, and do things together.'

'All right.' He captured one of her hands and kissed it, then drew her closer.

From somewhere in the back of her mind, Mr Shy's voice came to her. *'Secrets'* he seemed to whisper. *'What fond couple does not keep secrets?'* She rebuffed the whispers, but even as she did so, she was back in Paris, in the music room of the Maison du Rossignol, and she could feel her colour rise again. Raising her eyes to Holland, she asked, 'My dear, what do you think of waltzing?'

402

Author's Note

The adventures told in *The Mistaken Wife* are fictitious, but are based upon actual historical events. In the autumn of 1797, American envoys were sent to Paris to attempt to resolve differences arising out of American neutrality and the depredations of French privateers. The negotiations were thwarted, however, in part by agents allegedly acting on behalf of the French foreign minister, Talleyrand-Périgord. Their assertions that significant loans and bribes were a prerequisite to any negotiations were revealed to President John Adams in the spring of 1798. His presentation to Congress of the 'WXYZ despatches' – so named in reference to the letters designating the four principal agents – led ultimately to the 'Quasi-War' of 1798–1800. The WXYZ affair is also the basis for the dramatic retort, sometimes ascribed to Colonel Pinckney when the bribe was proposed to the envoys: 'Millions for defence, sir, but not one cent for tribute!' Mary's own assignment has a parallel in that ascribed to Madame de Villette, with whom two of the envoys lodged in Paris. Some scholars have suggested that she was Talleyrand's agent, although no firm evidence for this has been uncovered.

Mr Boyle's experiments and views on free trade resemble those of the American inventor and populariser Robert Fulton, who came to Paris in 1797 hoping to sell his submarine, the *Nautilus*, to the French government. (He was also interested in small-gauge canals.) The *Nautilus* bore similarities to the *Turtle*, built by David Bushnell during the American Revolution, and it has been suggested that Bushnell and Fulton had met in Paris in 1790. Admiral Le Pelley approved the *Nautilus*, pending further analysis, in 1798, at about the time that General Bonaparte decided to postpone the invasion of England on the grounds that the French Navy was not yet sufficient to undertake the venture. (He launched his Egyptian campaign instead.) The *Nautilus* was successfully tested in 1800 and 1801. In September of 1801 Bonaparte expressed interest in seeing the vessel, but by that time it had been dismantled and several of its important components destroyed by Fulton, who had lost enthusiasm – either for the project or for French support. In 1804 he went to England, where he failed to convince the British government to take the *Nautilus* project forward. Two years later he returned to America and concentrated instead on his plan for a commercial steamboat, which he had also begun while in France. The vessel that became known as the *Clermont* finally brought him success.